"Kelly Irvin's *The Beekeeper's Son* is a beautiful story of faith, hope, and second chances. Her characters are so real that they feel like old friends. Once you open the book, you won't put it down until you've reached the last page."

—AMY CLIPSTON, BESTSELLING
AUTHOR OF *A GIFT OF GRACE*

"*The Beekeeper's Son* is a perfect depiction of how God makes all things beautiful in His way. Rich with vivid descriptions and characters you can immediately relate to, Kelly Irvin's book is a must-read for Amish fans."

—RUTH REID, BESTSELLING
AUTHOR OF *A MIRACLE OF HOPE*

"Kelly Irvin writes a moving tale that is sure to delight all fans of Amish fiction. Highly recommended."

—KATHLEEN FULLER, AUTHOR OF
THE HEARTS OF MIDDLEFIELD AND
MIDDLEFIELD FAMILY NOVELS

The BISHOP'S son

OTHER BOOKS BY KELLY IRVIN

The
BISHOP'S
son

KELLY IRVIN

ZONDERVAN®

ZONDERVAN

The Bishop's Son

Copyright © 2015 by Kelly Irvin

This title is also available as a Zondervan e-book. Visit www.zondervan.com.

Requests for information should be addressed to:

Zondervan, *Grand Rapids, Michigan 49546*

Irvin, Kelly.
The bishop's son / Kelly Irvin.
pages ; cm. -- (The Amish of Bee County)
ISBN 978-0-310-33954-0 (softcover)
1. Young women--Fiction. 2. Mate selection--Fiction. 3. Amish--Fiction. I.
Title.
PS3609.R82B57 2015
813'.6--dc23
2015013803

Interior design: Mallory Perkins

Printed in the United States of America

15 16 17 18 19 20 / RRD / 20 19 18 17 16 15 14 13 12 11 10 9 8 7 6 5 4 3 2 1

To my family, love always.

You, then, why do you judge your brother or sister? Or why do you treat them with contempt? For we will all stand before God's judgment seat. It is written:

> "'As surely as I live,' says the Lord,
> 'every knee will bow before me;
> every tongue will acknowledge God.'"

So then, each of us will give an account of ourselves to God.
Therefore let us stop passing judgment on one another. Instead, make up your mind not to put any stumbling block or obstacle in the way of a brother or sister.

ROMANS 14:10–13 NIV

For there is one body and one Spirit, just as you have been called to one glorious hope for the future. There is one Lord, one faith, one baptism, and one God and Father of all, who is over all, in all, and living through all.

EPHESIANS 4:4–6 NLT

— *DEUTSCH* VOCABULARY* —

aenti: aunt

bopli: baby

bruder: brother

daed: father

danki: thank you

dawdy haus: grandparents' house

dochder: daughter

doplisch: clumsy

eck: "corner table" where bridal party, including groom and
     bride, sits during wedding celebrations

Englischer: English or non-Amish

fraa: wife

gmay: church district meeting

Gott: God

groossdaadi: grandpa

groossmammi: grandma

guder mariye: good morning

gut: good

hund: dog

jah: yes
kaffi: coffee
kapp: prayer cap
kinner: children
lieb: love
mann: husband
meidnung: shunning
mudder: mother
nee: no
onkel: uncle
Ordnung: written and unwritten rules in an Amish district
rumspringa: period of running around
schtinkich: stink, stinky
schweschder: sister
wunderbarr: wonderful

*The German dialect spoken by the Amish is not a written language and varies depending on the location and origin of the settlement. These spellings are approximations. Most Amish children learn English after they start school. They also learn high German, which is used in their Sunday services.

— FEATURED BEE COUNTY — AMISH FAMILIES

Mordecai and Abigail (Lantz) King
Leila
Rebekah
Caleb
Hazel
Esther
Samuel
Jacob
Susan King (Mordecai's sister)

Abram and Theresa King

Deborah and Phineas King

Stephen and Ruth Anne Stetler

Leroy (bishop) and Naomi Glick
Adam
Jesse
Joseph
Simon
Sally
Mary
Elizabeth
Solomon Glick (grandfather)

Andrew and Sadie Glick
Will
Patty
Henry
Catherine
Nehemiah

ONE

Goose bumps prickled up Leila Lantz's arms. Her mother, wearing a blue cotton dress she'd finished sewing earlier in the week and black tights, marched with a determined air past their entire community of family and friends. The pink blush on her cheeks told the story of a woman who didn't welcome being the center of attention from so many folks, some who'd traveled from as far away as Missouri and Tennessee to share in this wedding. The rubber soles of her black shoes squeaked on the linoleum of her future son-in-law's front room, loud in a silence replete with anticipation. Her witnesses scampered after her, their cheeks equally pink, smiles irrepressible.

It seemed like a dream, watching *Mudder* marry another man. This man, Mordecai King, who stood tall, a broad smile on his craggy face, his witnesses at his side.

A man not Leila's father, now dead for more than three years.

Leila inhaled the scent of fresh-baked bread, rolls, cakes, and cookies that wafted from the kitchen. The aroma of shared happiness and celebration floated around them, reminding them that today two hearts would join as one in a sacred ritual that could not, should not, be torn asunder.

Mudder should marry again. Leila, her sisters, and her brother needed a father. Back aching, Leila wiggled on the hard pine bench. Still, how strange to think of Mordecai sitting at the head of the supper table each evening, from now on, in that place that had once been reserved for *Daed*.

A new daed. *Nee*. Mordecai could never fill those work boots.

Nor would he try. Mordecai had proven himself to be a wise man in the year and a half since Leila's mother had moved her family from Tennessee to south Texas. Kind and funny, he'd tried to be helpful in the year since he began to court Mudder in that strange way older folks did who were too grown up to shine flashlights in windows late at night and go for rides, laughing and whispering secrets in the pitch-black countryside.

At least that's what Leila supposed happened on those buggy rides. She'd not experienced one—yet. Her glance slid across the room to the men's side. Jesse sat between his older brother, Adam, and his cousin Will. They seemed as entranced as everyone else by the spectacle of this widow and widower, each on the north side of forty, becoming *mann* and *fraa*.

Jesse coughed, a harsh, grating sound in the still quiet of this time-honored tradition, and slapped a hand to his mouth. His gaze shifted for a second and landed on her. The tanned skin on his smooth face reddened. He ducked his head covered with dark brown, thick curls usually hidden by his straw hat.

Her own face burning, Leila whipped her head toward the front. He should look embarrassed. The man talked a good talk, but not once had he followed through with a flashlight shining in her window. No buggy rides, much as his gaze seemed to promise something. Nothing had materialized.

What did she lack that made him hesitate? Leila asked herself that question over and over.

She rubbed her sweaty hands together, then forced them to lie still in her lap. The bench creaked and skirts rustled. She hazarded a glance at her sisters. Deborah, Rebekah, Hazel, and her soon-to-be stepsister, Esther, sat in a row in their gray dresses, their expressions serene for this most solemn yet joyous occasion. If they felt any of this welter of warring emotions, it didn't show.

Leila forced her gaze back to the front of the room. Leroy Glick posed each of the questions in that no-nonsense tone he employed during the nearly three-hour sermon that had preceded the vows. Would they remain together until death? Would they be loyal and care for each other during adversity, affliction, sickness, and weakness? Each time, Mudder's soft *jah* followed Mordecai's gruff, firm response. Each jah brought them closer to that moment in which the act of marriage would become irrevocable. Every muscle in Leila's body tensed. Her bones ached. Her jaw pulsed with the pressure of her gritted teeth.

Gott, Thy will be done. Thy will be done.

A sharp elbow jabbed her ribs.

"Ouch." She covered her mouth with her hand and glared at Deborah.

Her sister leaned so close her warm breath brushed Leila's ear. "Sit still. You're rocking."

"I wasn't—"

Deborah, hands now resting on a swollen belly no apron could hide, shook her head so hard the strings of her white *kapp* flopped and wisps of her blonde hair escaped. Her frown turned her into a replica of their mother when the cornmeal mush burned or the clothesline fell down under the weight of the men's wet pants. "Not now."

Not now indeed. Mudder's moment should not be marred. Leila swallowed back hot tears of joy for her mudder's happiness. For Mudder's happiness, but also for Daed. He would've wanted this. He would've said that his days on earth had numbered less. They were complete. Mudder's were not. Nor were Mordecai's. Gott's plan, however unfathomable to Leila, was His plan.

Leroy took Mudder's hand and placed it in Mordecai's. His own calloused hands, big as catcher's mitts, covered theirs.

"So then I may say with Raguel the Gott of Abraham, the Gott of Isaac, and the Gott of Jacob be with you and help you together and fulfill His blessing abundantly upon you, through Jesus Christ. Go forward as mann and fraa."

The now-married couple turned and faced their friends and family, Mordecai's tall, muscle-bound frame dwarfing Mudder's smaller, slighter figure. Her wide, tremulous smile made her cheeks dimple. She glowed. No other word could describe the transformation. She looked no less radiant than any first-time bride Leila had ever seen. Years fell away. Time and heartache disappeared in that rare moment of happiness that stood between what had been and what would come in her new life as Mordecai King's fraa. Whatever new obstacles, whatever new tragedy or pain, whatever came, she would share it with her new husband.

Praise God. Leila rose on trembling legs and heaved a breath. God willing, one day soon she, too, would look like that. *Please, Gott.*

Deborah dabbed at her face with a handkerchief. Hazel whooped. Rebekah grinned and hoisted the younger girl to her hip. "Hallelujah."

Hallelujah indeed.

"What is wrong with you?" Deborah whispered in her ear as she pinched Leila's arm. "You look like you just ate a slice of armadillo. This is Mudder's day. Don't be spoiling it for her."

Leila rubbed her arm. "I'm not. I just . . . I'm . . . I'll go help with the serving."

Deborah's expression softened. "We're all thinking of him too. He'd be happy for Mudder."

"Jah." Leila swallowed against the tears yet again. "He *would* be happy for her."

"Because that is the kind of man he was."

"Jah."

Deborah patted a comforting, circular pattern on Leila's back, her hand warm and soft. "Get a breath of fresh air. You're white as a sheet. Go for a little walk."

"I don't need air."

"The others will understand. Phineas understands. He's thinking of his mudder today too. It's not like Mordecai isn't thinking of his first fraa. Or Mudder of Daed. It's only natural."

The knot in Leila's throat threatened to explode. Why couldn't she be more like her older sister? Somehow marriage to Phineas had changed Deborah. Impending motherhood had changed her. Each day, she sprouted new wisdom like a baby bird growing its first feathers. Leila managed a quick jerk of a nod. "Just a few minutes. I'll be back to help."

Deborah gave her shoulder a last, quick squeeze and moved away, enveloped in the flow of folks surging forward to congratulate the newlyweds. Leila pressed herself along the wall, edging her way toward the door, out onto the porch and into the muggy air of late September in south Texas. Butch, Mordecai's dog—or maybe he was Deborah's, Leila couldn't tell anymore—raised his head, stood, and stretched. The black patches on the *hund's* white face made him look like a pirate, an old, mangy pirate. "Stay, hund." Leila didn't need a companion, not even the four-legged kind. She longed for solitude. Fat chance in this place. "I'll be back soon."

Butch yawned and flopped back on the cement porch. He surely looked as if he were smiling at her with that grizzled snout of his.

Shaking her head at her own flight of fancy, Leila skirted the dozens of buggies and vans parked across the yard and made a beeline for the barn. Beyond it stood a thicket of mesquite, live oak, and hackberry trees interspersed with clusters of nopales, pale green against the faded blue sky. She could walk a few minutes out of sight of the house and all the visitors crammed into Phineas's home, spilling out into the backyard where picnic tables had been set up to serve the overflow.

Her head down against a dank southeasterly wind, she rounded the corner of the barn, intent on finding peace in the stark landscape she'd grown to love in the last year. No one would call it pretty, but she found it easy to turn to Gott for direction in such a barren place.

"You said you wouldn't tell." A barely contained river of anger coursed through the low, hoarse statement.

"Tell what?" Leila stepped into the shadows of an old live oak just in time to realize the words hadn't been directed at her. The acrid *schtinkich* of burning tobacco filled her nostrils. As she rubbed her hand across the rough bark of the broad trunk and peeked beyond it, she realized her words had been lost in the wind and the rustling of the leaves.

Will Glick stood in the shadows cast by the barn in the

late-afternoon sun, a glowing cigarette raised to his lips, the smoke curling and wafting over the wide brim of his Sunday-service black hat. Jesse Glick had his back to her. Will took a puff on the cigarette and let his hand drop, his fingers cupping it. "I didn't tell." He coughed and sneezed. "Do you think *Onkel* Leroy needs this on top of everything else? The drought. The Planks leaving? Even my daed is talking about whether we should stay or go. The district is fading away, and you're thinking of making it worse."

Leila slapped a hand to her mouth to muffle her soft cry of denial. Mudder had uprooted her family and moved them here from Tennessee less than two years earlier. She hadn't said a word. Did she know of this? If she did, she'd done well at keeping such a big secret.

"Onkel Andrew moved here when he was a boy." Jesse's scoffing tone grated on Leila's ears. "Your daed grew up here. He'll never leave."

"Daed says we have to go where Gott leads us."

"If he goes, will you go?" Jesse's tone softened. He sounded like a kid missing his friend already. "You're old enough to stay here on your own."

"Without my family?" Will's tone matched his cousin's. "I don't know. Would you miss me?"

They were so different in every way—Will, tall and wiry and blond, Jesse, shorter and sturdy and built like a barrel, with dark, almost black hair—yet they sounded like brothers when they talked, brothers knit together by time and circumstance.

"Jah, I would miss all of you—"

"All I know is worry is a sin. Gott has a plan." Will took another pull on the cigarette, the fiery red end throbbing in the shadows. "Do you think carrying on the way you are is part of His plan?"

Jesse whirled and stomped toward the tree without answering. Pain etched his chiseled features. Why? What was he thinking of doing? Whatever the topic, it wasn't intended for Leila's ears. She shouldn't be acting like a small child playing a game of hide-and-seek. She stepped from behind the tree.

Jesse slammed to a halt. "What are you doing here?"

"I'm stretching my legs." To her chagrin, her voice quavered. She couldn't tell them how bittersweet the day had been, seeing Mudder marry Mordecai. "I needed a breath of fresh air before the celebration begins."

Stop rambling. She picked her way through the weeds, intent on resuming her walk before she embarrassed herself more.

"It's not what you think." Jesse stepped into her path, forcing her to stop again. "We were just talking."

"You can argue all you want. You can smoke if you want. It doesn't make me no never-mind." Leila pretended to misunderstand. They needn't worry. She wouldn't repeat their conversation about the district's future. It would only sow seeds of worry and division with the others. "You can smoke if you want. It's your *rumspringa.*"

"Like Will said, we were just talking . . . about stuff."

Will flicked the lit cigarette to the ground with his thumb and forefinger, then dug the heel of his boot into it until it disappeared into the muddy soil underfoot. "Yeah, we're just talking."

"About what?" Leila couldn't help herself. They looked as guilty as the coyote caught eating cantaloupe in the garden over the summer. That they shouldn't have been talking about the future of the district was a given. Or smoking. "How to burn up hard-earned cash with a match?"

"Nee. We were talking about getting jobs in town."

Jobs in town. To earn money. To help their families make it

through another winter in Bee County so they could stay, so they could keep their community together. Leroy hadn't allowed but a few of the young men to take jobs with *Englischers*. The men had met to talk about it after the drought had decimated crops this year and orders for buggies had dropped off at the same time. "Have you asked Leroy—your father?"

Jesse shrugged. "Not yet. I'm thinking I'll ride into town and see what I can find first. If I have something to offer, it will be harder to say no. Bird in the hand and all."

A man like Leroy would not make his decision based on anything other than the dictates of his conscience and the *Ordnung*. "How can you spend money on cigarettes when we can hardly put food on the table?"

"We didn't." The cellophane of the package crackled between Will's fingers. "One of the guys in town asked me to hold them when we were playing pool last week. He left before I could give them back, that's all." He handed the cigarettes to Jesse. "Here, you keep them or do whatever you want with them."

Jesse accepted his offering. "I'm throwing them away."

"They cost like seven dollars a package."

"What's going on here?"

Leila closed her eyes, hoping the gruff voice that rumbled behind her didn't belong to the last person who should see her standing behind the barn in broad daylight with two men and a package of cigarettes.

"Well, someone answer me."

She opened her eyes.

Leroy cupped one mammoth hand to his forehead to shelter his eyes from the sun. "Are you deaf? I said what's going on here?"

TWO

Simply at the wrong place at the wrong time. That's how Leila wanted to answer Leroy's question. But she didn't. It wasn't her place. She waited for Jesse or Will to answer him. Jesse was his son, Will, his nephew. They should do the explaining, not her. She had no idea what they were doing out behind the barn. Other than smoking. And arguing.

A dog barked. Crickets sang. A mourning dove cooed.

"I don't like to repeat myself." Leroy's voice boomed. His silver beard bobbed and swayed as he shook his head, his eyes sharp behind wire-rimmed glasses perched low on his long nose. "Has the hearing gone bad on all three of you? What's going on here?"

"Nothing, Daed." The fingers of one hand wrapped around his suspenders, Jesse back-stepped until he stood next to Leila. "We were talking."

Something about Jesse's tone suggested the conversation had been between Leila and him. She opened her mouth, then shut it.

"I reckon Leila should be up at the house helping her sisters with the wedding meal." Leroy's gruff voice boomed again. "You boys can water the horses."

Jesse's boots made squelching sounds in the mud and scraggly grass. Leila didn't move, thinking Will would tell the bishop the cigarettes didn't belong to his son, but instead to his nephew. Will stood as if frozen. "I'm sorry, Onkel, I—"

"Your cousins came all the way from Missouri and Tennessee. You should be visiting with them." The edge in Leroy's voice could've cut stone. "I hope all three of you start to think about baptism classes soon. Spring will be here before you know it, Easter, and the *gmay*."

He turned, back stiff, and stalked away.

Leila exhaled, realizing for the first time that she'd been holding her breath. Leroy had said as much as he could say, truth be told. All of them were still in their rumspringas. The parents might not like what they did, but mostly they didn't interfere as long as no one rubbed their noses in their activities.

Which didn't amount to much out here in the middle of nowhere, south Texas. They had neither the money nor the means to do much more than ride into town now and then to listen to music and play pool at the bar and grill that served truckers passing through Beeville to and from Mexico.

She couldn't imagine how it must be to have a bishop as a father. If it were her, she might feel pressure to always do the right thing. Not that she didn't feel that now. Every day.

Mudder's favorite admonition fluttered in her ears. *Gott is watching.*

"Go on, Leila. It's okay." Will seemed a lot calmer than she would be under the circumstances. "Lots of mouths to feed up at the house."

"If she wants a walk, she should take a walk." Jesse jerked his head toward the path that meandered through the brown weeds that passed for grass. "What with the folks from Tennessee and Missouri, there's more women up there than fit in the kitchen. They're elbow to elbow and nose to nose."

"Will's right, they'll be wondering where I am—"

"Let them wonder for a few minutes." Jesse started walking. "I'll go with you."

"But your daed—"

"He did his duty. He won't interfere with my rumspringa. Or yours."

Was this rumspringa? Or was it courting? Both? The thought made Leila's head swim. She hesitated. Leroy had spoken, but Jesse knew his father better than she did.

Will stepped in front of her. His blue eyes were dark in his tanned face, his expression troubled. "It's nasty and muggy today. Wouldn't you rather be inside?" He swiveled and glanced toward Jesse, who continued to walk as if confident she followed. "With the women."

"Why didn't you tell Leroy the cigarettes were yours?" Her tone was more accusing than she intended, but she couldn't help it. What kind of friend was he? "You let Jesse take the blame."

"He doesn't care." Will's face reddened. "But you're right. I'll fix it. Don't worry."

"You coming?"

It might have been a question, but Jesse said it as if he already knew the answer.

"I have to go."

Will's mouth worked. "Be careful."

"Of what?"

Will gave her a halfhearted smile, then brushed past her. "Sometimes things aren't what they seem."

With that cryptic statement, he disappeared around the corner of the barn, leaving Leila exasperated but no less determined. "Wait, Jesse."

A litter of kittens doing belly flops in her stomach, she tromped through the knee-high grass and weeds to catch up with Jesse. Her chance had finally arrived, one she'd hoped to have months ago. Here it stood, within her grasp. She waited to speak until they reached the gully that passed as a creek bed beyond the clusters of nopales bigger than some of the mesquite trees. "Why didn't Will tell your daed the cigarettes belonged to him?"

"Because he knew I didn't want him to get on Daed's bad side."

"But it's okay for you to get in trouble?"

Jesse snatched up a straggly blade of grass and twisted it. "I won't get in trouble. I haven't done much of anything that would shame him during four years of rumspringa. A cigarette behind the barn is slim pickings."

"But you weren't smoking."

"Will is my cousin and he's my friend."

"A good friend doesn't let his friend take the blame for something he did."

"I owe him."

"Owe him what?"

"That's between him and me." Jesse pulled back the low-hanging branches of a live oak and waved Leila toward a downed trunk graying with decay. "Sit. You look like you're about to heave."

"I won't heave. I'm fine." The wind whipped through the tree branches, lifting the ribbons on her kapp. She shivered. "I feel like stretching my legs, that's all."

"Your legs are awful short. They could use some stretching."

His tone had a teasing quality that surprised her after the scene with his father. "My legs are fine."

"Jah, they are."

He couldn't actually see her legs under her long skirt. Still, heat mixed with a chill that ran up her arms, goose bumps popping up in its wake. "I'm-I'm," she stuttered, making the heat burn white hot. "That's not—"

"I'm just teasing you." He held out his hand, his fingers wiggling. "Sit. You need to smile more. You have a fine smile too."

"My smile's been around here for a while now." Mesmerized by Jesse's sudden grin that brought out dimples in his tanned face, she took his hand. He had calluses. His fingers gripped hers in a warm, sure hold. "So far you haven't seemed to take particular notice of it."

He led her to the trunk, his face so close she could see the curls of his black hair under the back of his hat. She inhaled. He smelled like burning mesquite. He plopped down next to her and leaned close, eyes the color of burnt caramel, intent and amused. "Well, I'm noticing now, aren't I?"

Leila ducked her head, her thoughts jumbled by his closeness. After a few seconds, he leaned away and plucked blades of grass. He began to braid them together, his blunt fingers nimble. She cast about for a subject—any subject—that didn't involve her legs and him noticing them. "Do you think the district will fail?"

"Gott's plan."

Leila had heard that response her entire life. How did a person know? "That's what your father says. What do you say?"

He added more blades of grass to his braid. Soon it would be a rope. "I say Gott's plan could be that we are meant to go somewhere else or be somewhere else. Some of us, anyway."

"My family just moved here over a year ago." To her horror, tears pricked at her eyes. She blinked them away. The move from Tennessee had been hard for all of them so soon after her father's death, but they'd adjusted. They'd made friends. And now, Mudder had married again. Deborah had married. They had put down roots. "Can you imagine Phineas or Mordecai living anywhere else?"

Jesse's chuckle sounded hard and dry. "You can raise bees anywhere." He shrugged. "But I see your point. Mordecai might thrive up north or even back in Tennessee, but take Phineas away from this place, he'd wither."

"You sound like you don't think leaving would be a bad idea for you."

"I never said that." He handed her the braid as if giving her a gift. She took it. Their fingers touched, his calluses rough against her skin. "I do think we can plop this district down anywhere and our folks will worship the same way they do here. Only living will be easier."

"So what were you and Will arguing about?"

Jesse studied his empty hands. Something in his expression flickered. A sadness mixed with fear or anger, she couldn't be sure. "We weren't arguing, just talking."

Leila had imagined riding in a buggy next to Jesse many times. It had never been like this. They'd have light conversation. They'd laugh. He'd smile that smile. Instead, here she sat next to him in broad daylight a stone's throw from her brother-in-law's house, the sunshine breaking through clouds that scudded across the sky as if driven by God's breath, and Jesse looking like he'd just lost his best friend. Maybe he had. *Let it be. Let Gott's plan unfold.*

Maybe he'd only offered to walk with her to escape his father's wrath. Maybe he had no intention of courting her, or he would have asked under better circumstances.

"I haven't seen you leave the singings with anyone." He dusted his hands on his pants as if ridding them of dirt she couldn't see. "I mean, leastwise, not with one of the fellows."

"Nee."

"Me neither." He chuckled, a halfhearted, embarrassed sound. "I mean, with a girl, me, I mean."

He sounded as nervous as she felt. She folded the grass braid and made a knot, forming a crooked cross. "I know what you mean."

"Have you ever been to a movie in a real movie theater, you know, with the big screen and the sound system and all that?"

Of course not. "Nee."

"You know, it takes two to have a conversation, and you're not making this any easier."

Now he sounded like a little boy much aggrieved that he didn't get that one thing he longed for on Christmas Day. "I don't know what to say." She had no experience being alone with a man, making conversation with him. She cleared her throat. "I've never been to a movie—any movie."

"I've been a few times. It's fun, if it's a good movie. Loud and silly, if it's not. I have an Englisch friend who wants me to go to the movies. In George West."

Leila mulled over his words, trying to interpret the unspoken message woven into those she'd actually heard. "Are you asking me to go with you?"

"Would you?"

"Why me?"

"Because I'm asking you."

"You walked out here with me to get out of talking to your daed."

"In part."

"What's the other part?"

"I always wanted to ask you to take a buggy ride with me. I didn't for reasons you won't understand. But neither did I ask another girl."

What reasons couldn't she understand? She hadn't been a great scholar in school, but she had some book-learning smarts. Jesse wanted to ask her to the movies, but he wasn't doing a very good job. Did she want to go to the movies? So far, her rumspringa had been a series of gentle forays into the Englisch world. Letting her hair down in town. Wearing a thin necklace of fake pearls when she, Sally, and Patty ate tacos at the taquería on the highway and then watched friends play pool, a game she couldn't seem to master.

"If it takes you that long to figure it out, I'm thinking the answer is no." Jesse didn't sound surprised or even disappointed. "It's only a movie."

"It's not the movie."

"Ah. It's me."

Leila chewed her lip, seeking a response that wouldn't offend.

"My daed is the bishop, but that doesn't make me any different than you."

"He doesn't watch you closer?"

"Nee. He worries same as any other parent, but he's determined not to interfere."

"Still, being the bishop's son must weigh on you sometimes."

He wrinkled his nose as if assailed by a bad odor. "You have such a sweet, innocent face."

So he didn't want to think about the truth of the matter. Everyone was equal in their faith. All were to be humble and obedient, even the bishop. Yet how could it not weigh on him, son of the bishop and grandson of the founder of this district? Jesse had been the anchor of the group of young men who attended the singings. Always listening to the younger ones. Showing up when surely he had tired of their silliness and shenanigans. He and Will were the oldest. "What's that supposed to mean?"

"You surprise me, that's all."

Did men like to be surprised? Leila couldn't wait to ask Deborah. Her sister had more experience with men. At least with men like Phineas, and it appeared God had broken the mold when He made that man.

"You think I'm addled or stupid? You talked to me a couple of times at a singing, said you were going to take me for a ride some-time, and then decided I wasn't worth knowing and moved on."

"It wasn't like that."

"What was it like?"

"Other stuff happened. Stuff you wouldn't understand."

"See there, you think I'm not smart because I'm a little . . . *doplisch*."

"A little? You knocked into the table and broke three glasses at the singing last month."

"Once. That happened once. You've seen me play volleyball and baseball. I'm just fine doing that." How could she explain to this man how she felt every day, like a chubby goat stumbling around in a meadow filled with a herd of sleek horses? "It's social stuff that . . . Anyway, if you hadn't been teasing me about the burn on my apron, I wouldn't have done that."

"I like teasing you. It makes your cheeks turn pink and you giggle. Since that first time I saw you in the store, I've always thought you were sweet."

Leila remembered that day too. The memory made her

cheeks heat even in the fall air. He'd been working for his father, unloading baskets of fresh squash, beets, and okra, sweat beading on his forehead, his tanned face flushed, biceps bulging under the rolled-up sleeves of a shirt washed so many times the cobalt had faded to a pale blue. "I liked you too."

More heat. Should a girl say such a thing aloud to a man?

Jesse snorted but said nothing for a long moment. Maybe she had said too much. How did a girl know? Would it always be this hard?

His breathing sounded harsh. "So go to the movies with me."

Maybe she'd done it right. But a movie? The goose bumps reappeared. Mudder wouldn't like it. But wasn't that the point of rumspringa? To find a special friend? It might be her only chance to know Jesse and for him to want to know her. "If we go in a buggy, it'll take half the night to get to George West."

His smile flashed. He did indeed have a nice smile, all white teeth and full lips. "Who said anything about a buggy? Just be ready when I shine a light in your window."

"When?"

"I don't know exactly when. We have company now and next week, the auction. Maybe the weekend after that. Saturday night in a week's time before we get too close to Thanksgiving." He slapped a hand on hers, clasped in her lap. His fingers were icy now. "Don't look so worried. How much trouble can you get into with the bishop's son?"

Indeed. Exactly how much?

THREE

The creak of the rickety lawn chair on the front porch gave his daed away. Jesse ducked his head against a night breeze just cool enough to suggest fall might be about to show its face in Bee County. He strode across the yard and up the three steps that led to the porch and front door of his family's home. The brash light of the full moon had disappeared behind a cluster of clouds thick as a pile of winter quilts. Which meant he couldn't read the bishop's expression.

He often thought of his daed that way. As the bishop. His daed drew the lot when Jesse was twelve, and everything changed. His mudder said it wouldn't, but it had. Sermons and gmays and weddings and funerals and disciplinary actions. How could it not?

Not that Jesse begrudged the district its bishop. Daed made a good bishop. Fair, even-keeled to the point of cool under pressure. He had a keen mind and a methodical nature. Which gave Jesse hope that this exchange would be a peaceful one.

"You're back."

"I am."

The clouds drifted and the light of the moon spilled over

them, giving an odd shine to Daed's glasses, masking his expression. "Sit a spell with an old man."

It wasn't an invitation, as quietly as it was delivered, but an order. Daed had a way about him. He rarely had to ask twice, a quality that served him well as bishop and as head of his family. Only Mudder dared argue with him, and then only for a minute or two before she gave in. Jesse endeavored to see his father's face as he eased into the nearby hickory rocker that squeaked worse than the lawn chair. Heat and humidity had warped it, making the rockers off kilter.

Daed held a flashlight resting on his thigh. With his other hand he stroked his beard. Dark circles hung like bruises under his eyes. Officiating a wedding and all that went with that important role had taken its toll. His wire-rimmed glasses sat low on his long nose, meaning he'd been deep in thought, too deep to remember to slide them up with the flick of a finger as he so often did while making a point during a sermon. He'd been ruminating on something important.

Jesse leaned back and waited.

"Talked to Will." An innocent enough beginning, but Daed's tone left no doubt that there was more to come. "Saw him at the house with the others."

With the other unmarried men, sitting at a table across from the unmarried girls. This long-standing tradition offered a chance to pair off after the singing and games. A chance Jesse had missed. "Jah."

"He told me the cigarettes were his. Is that true?"

"Will doesn't lie."

"You didn't say anything."

The wind kicked up and a fine mist dampened Jesse's face.

They would have rain before dawn. Coupled with the downpour of the previous day, it heralded at least a start to the end of a painful summer drought. Maybe the fall and winter vegetables would do better. Maybe hard times would ease up a bit. "Nothing to say."

"I don't care about the cigarettes." Daed drummed his thick fingers on a stack of upside-down bushel baskets that sat between them. "I do care. They're a waste of money we can ill afford and bad for you, but what I mean to say is, don't flaunt your rumspringa in my face."

"Didn't mean to do that."

"See that you don't."

"I will."

Daed started to rise. Then he sank back in the chair and leaned forward, his elbows on his knees, the flashlight rolling from one big hand to the other and back. His suspenders strained against his broad, barrel chest. "I know there's been talk."

The ever-present band of guilt and worry tightened around Jesse's chest, causing a hitch in his breathing. "Talk?"

"About whether we'll survive another year here."

"Jah."

"What are your thoughts?"

Daed wanted his thoughts. A year ago that idea would've brought Jesse a certain measure of satisfaction. Daed valued his opinion, not son to father, but man to man. Now, he stumbled, trying to order his thoughts in a way that wouldn't reveal his turmoil. "This district's been here going on twenty-five years. It's survived this long."

"Andrew's considering moving back to Tennessee. His mudder is ailing and his daed wants to retire to the *dawdy haus*."

Will had been right. Two families had moved to Missouri the previous year. Scholars at the school had dwindled to fifteen. Church fit easily into their house now. Moreover, his Onkel Andrew had been chosen by God to lead as minister. "He drew the lot. He'd ignore that?"

"He's praying on it."

"What does *groossdaadi* say?"

"You know him."

Jesse did. His grandfather Solomon had ridden through Texas on the way to Mexico to pick up cheap materials. He'd decided he liked the wide-open spaces. Tennessee was too crowded for his taste. He liked the humidity. He didn't mind the isolation. He never batted an eye in the face of year after year of drought that turned green fields into brown dust that caked a man's face and left grit to grind on his teeth. "No turning back."

"No turning back. Every man must put his shoulders into the work here. The crops. The greenhouse. The store. Breaking the horses. Selling honey and the milk from Abram's cattle."

As if Jesse hadn't done that his whole life. "Understood."

"Sometimes I'm not so sure."

A chill crept up Jesse's arms and curled around his neck. Thankful the dark hid his face, he leaned forward and rested his hands on his knees to hide sudden trembling. "I don't work hard enough?"

"You got something stuck in your craw, something you want to say?"

"Nee."

"You ain't been yourself of late."

"Did Will say something?"

"Does Will know something?"

Not a question Jesse dared answer. "Is my work around here and at the store not pleasing to you?"

"Your work is fine. It's . . . your face . . . I see it in your face at Sunday service when I'm up front. You look . . . disagreeable."

"Mostly I'm tired on Sunday morning."

"Get yourself home earlier on Saturday night and that will take care of itself."

"Jah."

Daed fiddled with the button on the flashlight. It flickered, casting a weak light over the mesquite, hackberry, and live oak trees in the front yard. "When you didn't partake of the baptism classes this summer . . . again . . . your mudder and I didn't say anything."

As well they shouldn't. The point was for a man or woman to be ready to take that next step without cajoling or coercion. A decision for a lifetime. No going back. No second thoughts. Jesse couldn't do that.

Not yet. Maybe not ever.

"I appreciate that."

"You're twenty. Now you're stepping out with Leila . . ."

Jesse's walk with Leila was a private matter. "It's the first time. Nothing may come of it."

He shouldn't have asked her to the movies. He'd thought for a fleeting second that he might find what he was looking for in her. Sweet Leila. The very first time he'd laid eyes on her in the Combination Store more than a year ago, he'd known she was something special with those bright, inquiring blue eyes, wheat-colored hair, dimples, a figure that filled out her faded cotton dress, and full lips made to be kissed. She might be a bit awkward and not much interested in baking and sewing, but he liked the way she looked at him—as if she suspected he could make her happy. She didn't deserve to be hurt.

What had he been thinking when he asked her to the movies?

He hadn't been thinking with his head, but rather with his heart.

Which more often than not led to trouble.

"I thought it had been longer." Daed turned the flashlight on and off again as if making sure it still worked. "You've been gone a lot of evenings, coming home late and all. We figured, your mudder and I, well, you were . . . courting."

Again, not something to be discussed. "Out and about."

"Be that as it may, we'll start classes in January to be done in time for baptism before the gmay and Easter services."

"I'm aware."

Daed stood. This time he didn't hesitate. He clomped past Jesse, his boots making squelching sounds on the wet wood, and pulled open the screen door. "Dawn comes early."

Indeed it did. Jesse thanked Gott that he could count on that, if nothing else.

Daed let the screen door shut with a gentleness that spoke of a houseful of sleeping people accustomed to rising early. "Get some sleep. Tomorrow's another day."

Jesse didn't bother to argue. He followed his daed into the house, knowing his knees were in for another long night on his bedroom rug.

FOUR

A piece of pie was good for what ailed a person, no matter what it might be. Leila swiped at piecrust crumbs on the table with a damp washrag, then arranged the paper plates with slices of pecan pie, apple pie, and lemon meringue pie in what she hoped served as a pleasing, appetizing array. She slapped away flies determined to make the slices their home. She'd been helping with auction fund-raisers her whole life, but she'd never been more aware of how important this auction, this year, was to everyone.

Mordecai and Mudder talked about it, their voices lowered, faces somber, after evening prayers. Mudder, with her darning in her lap, her glasses perched on her nose, Mordecai, *The Budget* newspaper spread across his knees, matching glasses slid down his nose. They needed a good turnout, and they needed good sales.

If cars were any indication, the turnout couldn't have been better this first Friday of November. It seemed all of Bee County congregated in this little strip of land for a few hours. Monster pickup trucks, vans, and cars as far as Leila's eyes could see along the road. The sight made her itch for a ride somewhere. Anywhere. This wanderlust confounded her. Did it have something to do with Jesse and his promise to take her to the movies next Saturday night? In a car. What kind would it be? A big pickup truck or one of those little cars that looked like a ladybug?

No, to take them and the Englischers, it would have to be a regular-sized car. Maybe a minivan. Did Englisch teenagers drive minivans? Her cousin Frannie claimed to have driven a station wagon on a dirt road outside of Jamesport, Missouri, where she lived now with Onkel John and *Aenti* Eve. Leila would've liked to have seen that.

"Stop daydreaming, child. Here comes another customer." Mudder nudged Leila with a gentle elbow. "When the line slows down, you can wipe off the tables and pick up trash."

"I'm not daydreaming."

Nor was she a child. Leila clamped her mouth shut as Mudder offered an Englisch lady dressed in a neon-orange T-shirt and blue jeans the menu of a meatloaf plate, hamburger, or barbecue sandwich. Fighting the urge to argue with her elder, Leila wiped the vinyl tablecloth a second time with more elbow grease.

The lady made the smart choice of the meatloaf plate. The entire day before had been spent making meatloaf, green beans, baked potatoes, and coleslaw for the plates. A veritable feast that made Leila's mouth water. If there were leftovers, they'd all get to share in them. She hadn't eaten meatloaf in a month of Sundays. Ground beef was expensive these days.

"Wheat bread or white?" Rebekah sounded so timid it made Leila want to giggle. Her sister acted like a kernel of popcorn in a skillet of hot oil most days, but she didn't have much experience with Englischers. "It comes with the meal."

The Englisch lady balanced the plate in one hand and adjusted her leather bag's strap on her shoulder, her gaze fixed on the pie, which Leila agreed was much more interesting than bread. "Wheat. Does the pie come with it too?"

"It does." Leila's department. "What kind would you like?"

"Leila, Leila, there you are!"

The high voice with its Texas twang sounded familiar, but it took Leila a second to register the source. Rory Beale, now Rory Chapman, their neighbor from down the road. Before she'd had her baby, Rory often rode her horse to the Combination Store. She bought honey and teased the Glick boys and stopped to chat with Leila every chance she could. Now that she balanced a baby with finishing high school, her visits were sparse.

Leila slid a plate of apple pie toward the lady, who smiled and moved on. She squeezed toward the end of the table, hoping Mudder would be too busy making plates to notice the interruption. Rory zigzagged through the crowd, little Trevor bouncing on her hip.

"Hey, Leila, just the person I wanted to see!"

"Trevor is getting so big." Leila smoothed her hand over the baby's silky brown tufts of fine hair. He cooed and smiled a toothless smile in response, slobber sliding down his chin into a strategically placed bib. "He's as sweet as ever."

"Yeah, except when he's keeping me up half the night fussing because he's teething on the night before I have a biology test." Rory's wide smile said she really didn't mind all that much. She'd made it perfectly clear to Leila that she stayed in school because her father insisted. "I have a proposition I've been dying to make to you. Just dying. How I wish you had a phone, girl. There's an opening at the day care where I work after school. Little Angels. I immediately thought of you. You're so good with babies and you said you wanted to get a paying job."

Leila ducked her head, not wanting to see what curious glances like darts her mudder might be hurling her way. She'd been in a *wunderbaar* mood since the wedding, but that didn't mean she wouldn't be on guard as she always was at these auctions. Her girls were not to draw attention to themselves. Or they stayed home.

Furthermore, Leila had talked to an outsider about their hardships. Mudder wouldn't like that either. The conversation about jobs had been an idle one, the idea she hadn't shared with anyone else but Rebekah, who thought she had a better chance of being allowed to drive a car than get a job in town. Leila returned to the other side of the table and began cutting another pie. "I don't know." She kept her voice low, forcing Rory to bend toward her. "I'd have to get permission from the bishop."

"Ask!" Rory shifted Trevor to her other hip and held out a five-dollar bill. "I have to have some of that pecan pie. It looks yummy. The job pays nine dollars an hour. It's full-time. We could pick you up every morning. We have to drop Trevor at the day care anyway. Then I come over to work after school and we leave together at six thirty. It's perfect. I told my boss all about you. She says Amish girls are great workers. She used to live in Pennsylvania."

Rory did talk up a storm. Mudder moved their direction, the wrinkles on her forehead deepening. Leila shoveled another piece of apple pie onto a paper plate and wiped the spatula against the pan. "We're different from the Lancaster County Amish."

"You work just as hard, right? And you take care of lots and lots of babies and little kids because your families are *muy* big."

Muy big. Rory was studying Spanish in school, a fine skill to have so close to the Mexican border. Leila had been to the border a couple of times but was not yet allowed to cross since she had no photo ID. How did Rory define *muy* big? Leila couldn't help but giggle. She caught sight of Mudder's concerned expression and wiped the smile from her face. "I'll have to let you know."

"No *problema*. The lady who's retiring still has another two weeks to go." Rory scooped up her piece of pie, ignoring Leila's attempt to give her change for the five-dollar bill. "I have to find Dad. He's looking at some rototiller thingamajiggy. As if his job at the prison doesn't keep him busy enough, he wants to plant a big vegetable garden next spring."

Trying to keep busy so he wouldn't think about the passing of Rory's mother. Leila had watched her own mother do that when Daed died. "Good for him. You and your little brother could use some fresh vegetables on the supper table."

"I'd rather buy them at the Combination Store—then I'd get to see you more." Rory wrinkled a nose covered with a smattering of freckles. "Gotta go. A certain little boy has a dirty diaper. I can smell it. Call me—I mean, come find me when you know when you can start. We're gonna have so much fun."

She slipped past a knot of people putting ketchup and mustard on their hamburgers at the condiment table before Leila could contradict her. Not that she wanted to disagree. Working at the day care would be perfect until she could have her own children. They needed the money and she loved taking care of babies. It was a perfect fit. Getting Mudder and now Mordecai to see it that way and convince Leroy—that would be a challenge the size of the state of Texas.

"We keep ourselves apart."

Startled, she turned to see Mudder frowning as she brushed piecrust crumbs from the table. "What do you mean?"

"We keep ourselves apart. Especially from folks who aren't living according to Scripture."

"Rory's married to Trevor's father."

"Now."

Mudder didn't need to elaborate. Trevor's daddy still lived at home with his own parents. He was a senior at the high school in town and worked at an auto parts store on weekends. Nobody seemed too happy about the arrangement. Rory didn't seem to know how lost she was, and Leila longed to tell her friend about God's grace and provision, but it wasn't the Plain way. Besides, Rory seemed determined to make the best of her choices. She said she loved Dwayne and one of these days, when they both finished school, they'd get a house together and live happily ever after. "Sometimes folks get things out of order, I reckon."

"Not if you stay on the straight and narrow path. That's why you have Andrew to guide you in the baptism classes."

Unless Andrew decided to take his family and move back to Tennessee.

Maybe Mudder didn't know about that possibility. This was simply her way of asking when Leila would begin taking instruction. "I know. I'm looking forward to going."

"Why don't you take a plate to Caleb?" Mudder knew better than to push on this topic. Leila had to make up her own mind. "Knowing him, he's starving or thinks he is."

"I thought you wanted me to wipe down the tables and pick up the trash." Leila followed Mudder's gaze. Rory had found her father, and they seemed to be arguing over something near the entrance to the shed that doubled as a restaurant today. "Caleb can wait a little longer."

"I'll have Rebekah do it. See that you come right back." Mudder's frown eased as she handed Leila a plate of green beans, coleslaw, baked potato, and corn. No one got to eat meatloaf until customers bought their fill. "Try not to dally in the barn. I know it's all very exciting, but you'll be in the way of the customers actually trying to buy something."

It was nice to know Mudder hadn't forgotten how exciting auction day could be—even at her age. Holding the plate close to her body, Leila dodged customers wandering about, deep in conversation about doohickeys they wanted to buy, mostly not watching where they walked. In the few dozen yards from the shed to the barn, she almost collided with four people. Flies buzzed around her face. The smell of the chickens, ducks, and pigs in the livestock section nearly knocked her back a step. She held the plate up, hoping to breathe in the enticing scent of food instead, and walked faster.

Looking much older than his ten years, Caleb manned the soda table at one of the side entrances to the barn. Business was brisk given the dank air and lack of the slightest breeze. The tip of his tongue poised in one corner of his mouth, her brother counted out change for a ten-dollar bill and then counted it again, much to the amusement of a tall man in a white cowboy hat, red plaid Western shirt, and jeans so worn they had a round, white circle on the back pocket. When he smiled, he showed off teeth brown from chewing tobacco.

Caleb handed him a Dr Pepper dripping with condensation and nodded at the man's thanks. He turned and grinned at Leila. "It's about time. I was ready to chew off my arm up to my shoulder."

"Don't be so dramatic." She slid in behind the table and plopped the plate on the crate behind him. "It's barely noon."

"I've sold three cases of water." Caleb slapped the metal box shut, a satisfied expression on his face that made him the spitting image of Daed. That face gave Leila a chance to remember what her father looked like. He'd loved auction day. "The Englischers really like their water."

"Eat your lunch. I'll man the booth." That wasn't what Mudder had in mind, but Leila wanted to extend her stay a little longer—until Leroy or Andrew noticed—then she'd hustle back to the food shed. "I can handle it just fine."

"Leroy will see." A mouth full of green beans muffled Caleb's words. "Or worse, Stephen. You know how he's always picking at us, now that Mudder chose Mordecai instead of him."

"I don't know why. Everyone knows he and Ruth Anne are courting. Let me do this just for a minute."

She had to yell to be heard over Leroy's voice and the shout of the spotters who were keeping track of bidders on one side while the Englisch auctioneer kept up a steady patter on the other side, simultaneous auctions that no one seemed to have trouble following. On Leroy's side, they were bidding on a nice cedar chest. It would be handy for storing quilts in the summer. Englisch folks milled about everywhere. If Leroy let her take the job at the day care, she'd surely see some of these people on a regular basis. On their territory, not hers. What a different life she would lead—at least for a little while.

She grabbed a bottled water and handed it to a lady who used her free hand to mop her face with a huge flowered handkerchief. "That's a dollar."

"Worth every penny." The lady tucked her handkerchief in a canvas bag covered with fancy embroidered flowers in purples and reds. "At this rate they won't get to the livestock until midnight."

"They move along pretty fast—"

"Hey."

Jesse stalked up to the table as the lady rushed past him, her gaze intent on some item on the other side of the barn.

That's all he had to say after not speaking to her since the day of the wedding? *Hey?*

He glanced at Caleb, who grinned and kept shoveling food into his already-full mouth. "Help me with the horses?"

Leila shook her head. Mordecai would notice for sure. He never missed a thing and he stood not ten feet away, jawing with a man about a double rocking chair he'd built special for the auction.

"I have to check on them." Jesse glanced at the platform where Leroy never missed a beat, calling out numbers and pointing at folks as the bids for a hand-carved leather saddle shot up. "Come with me."

"I thought you were helping Leroy spot the bidders and showing off the items."

He shrugged. "Daed gave me twenty minutes to get something to eat."

"Then go eat."

"I will." He glanced at Caleb, whose spoon hovered between his plate and his mouth, cheeks bulging like a chipmunk storing his acorns. "In a minute."

He slipped through the open double doors without looking back. So sure of himself. Leila chewed on her lip. Maybe he'd changed his mind. Maybe he wasn't coming for her after all. She needed to know. "I'll be back for your plate."

"Leila has a special friend," Caleb sang, grinning as if he'd just opened a birthday present. He still had food in his mouth. "Leila's in *lieb!*"

"Don't talk with your mouth full." She squeezed from behind the table. "And just you never mind."

"I won't tell."

He wouldn't tell, but he would tease her about it every chance he got. Sighing, she dodged a lady with a double stroller filled with roly-poly twins dressed in matching pink-checkered dresses and two men carrying dented milk cans as if they were priceless. She made her way around to the back of the barn where the horses were lined up waiting their turns. Jesse patted a butterscotch-colored filly and whispered something in her ear.

"Do you always talk to the horses?"

"They're good listeners."

What would Jesse think of her working in town? She wanted to ask, but the matter of their impending date took precedence. If he didn't want to go out with her, what she did with her time would be of no interest to him. "They look fine to me. They don't know they're about to be sold."

"I know." He slid his fingers through the horse's mane, untangling the hair. She shook her head and whinnied, apparently not happy with his ministrations. "I don't think we should go to the movies after all. For your sake."

He added the last three words in a stammered mess. Leila had been right. He'd had time to think about it, time enough to realize asking her had been a big mistake. She swallowed a sudden knot in her throat as big as a Texas Ruby Red grapefruit. Her eyes stung. Just the dirt and hay dust in the air from all these folks traipsing around, nothing more. "That's fine. It's fine."

She lifted her hand to her mouth to hide the painful red burn that scurried up her neck and across her face. She whirled and headed toward the food shed.

"Wait, wait, it's not you, it's me." Jesse's voice had turned hoarse. Somehow Leila doubted that. She should've known better than to think a man like Jesse, so sure of himself, so good at doing what men do, would be interested in a girl so doplisch.

She would not make a good fraa, surely he saw that. His hand clamped on her shoulder. "I said wait."

The heat of his fingers permeated the thin cotton of her dress. The burn wrapped itself around her throat, spread to her chest, then to the pit of her stomach. Her breath caught. His fingers were strong. *Stop it.* She forced herself to tug free of his grip. "It's fine. I have to get back to the food tables. Mudder will miss me. She'll make me go to the back and stay with the little ones."

"I don't want to . . . lead you down the wrong road."

She turned to face him, planting her black sneakers so hard in the dirt that puffs of dust floated around them. "I'm not a horse to be led anywhere. I have a mind of my own." Not necessarily a quality Plain men looked for in a fraa. "I mean I know what's wrong and what's right."

He stood so close she could see tiny beads of sweat on his nose and flecks of green in his dark brown eyes. His hand came up as if to touch her again. She fought the urge to lean in. His hand dropped. "I know you do, but you haven't been exposed to some of the things I have."

Her breathing came in short, painful spurts. "Like what?"

"Like . . . I don't know . . . you wouldn't understand."

What she didn't understand was this. Him. The on and off again. "I'm not stupid."

He ducked his head so she stared at the top of his straw hat. "I know that."

"What is it that you don't want to tell me?"

"If I tell you, you'll have to tell someone and I can't have that."

"So I'm stupid *and* you don't trust me."

"I want to. I want . . . I need . . ." He lifted his hat from his head and smacked it against the hitching post. The horses tossed their heads and whinnied, jostling each other in their anxiety. "Sorry, sorry, sorry."

Leila couldn't be sure if he directed the refrain at her or the horses. "Tell me, please tell me. You're scaring me. What is it?"

His Adam's apple bobbed. "I'm—"

"Hey, y'all, what's going on?" Will's voice, normally a soft drawl, had turned to a growl. He stalked across the yard, his arms straining under the weight of a huge box of Ball quart canning jars. "Leroy is looking for you, Jesse, and he isn't happy."

FIVE

Only the weight of the box of canning jars in his arms kept Will from surging forward. He was supposed to be delivering them to Molly Carter's minivan. The sight of Leila and Jesse out here in public arguing, Jesse's hand on her shoulder, had sent him spiraling off course. He swallowed, his anger tight in his gut. He'd always thought of Jesse as the smarter one among his many cousins. Not anymore. He seemed intent on dragging Leila down with him as well. He knew better than to put his hands on her, especially at such a public event. Everyone in the county milled around at this auction, whether to buy something or simply because they wanted to socialize with their neighbors and take home a bit of gossip, along with a jar of Mordecai's honey.

Every member of the district knew best behavior was expected, and punishment for stepping out of line would be quick and severe. He and his brothers had made only one trip to the woodshed for a whupping to understand that. He was nine at the time. Jesse was old enough to know better.

Will took a breath and tried to smooth his expression. "Leila, you should get back to the food shed. Your mudder is looking for you too."

Leila's already pink cheeks darkened to a radish red. She looked as guilty as he had felt that day in the woodshed when his daed asked him why he'd been playing shoot the trash cans using BB rifles with the Englisch boys instead of manning the water table. "Did you tell her where I was?"

"Nee. I didn't know until I saw you here . . . with Jesse." He shifted the heavy box again and shot Jesse a meaningful glance. His cousin's whiskerless face reddened. He turned his back and smoothed the mane of the closest horse. Will had to remind himself that Plain men didn't resort to physical violence. "Guess I should've known."

"What's that supposed to mean?" Jesse whirled and muscled his way past Will, forcing him to take a step back. "Isn't none of your business, for one."

Jesse was right, except Will knew too much to let him go without a struggle. Too much was at stake. Drawing Leila into it would only make matters worse. "I know. I just don't want there to be a scene here in front of all the folks from town."

"Nobody's making a scene except you." Jesse ducked his head. "Besides, I was just leaving."

"Don't go." Leila squeezed past Will. He could smell her scent of soap and vanilla, so light and sweet after the smells of livestock and sweaty men. She didn't even look at him. "What were you going to tell me?"

Jesse shook his head. "I'm—"

"Not here. Not now." Will shoved forward into the small space that separated his cousin from a girl Will wanted to protect from something he didn't understand. "Think about what you're doing to her."

"Doing to me—"

Jesse shoved forward as if to close the gap between Leila and him. His arm swung out and smacked the box between them. Will lost his grip and it tumbled to the ground, jars clanking against each other, the sound of breaking glass ominous in his ears.

"Now look what you did." Will squatted and righted the box. At least three jars were broken and two cracked. "Molly Carter already paid for these."

"I'm sorry. I'm really sorry." Jesse backed away, both hands in the air. He shook his head, the pain on his face so acute it hurt Will to look at him. "I didn't mean to do that."

Consequences were consequences, regardless of the intent. Will would suffer the consequences for his actions, coming out here instead of delivering the box to its new owner. "That's the problem. Sorry isn't enough, not for this and not for the other thing."

Jesse stared down at Will, his chest heaving. He backed up, whirled, and stomped away.

"Jesse, Jesse! Now look what you did." Leila shook a finger at Will, the picture of righteous anger. "He was going to tell me why . . ."

The pique in her face faded. She sighed, dropped her hand, and knelt next to him. "Never mind." She picked up a jar and set it upright in the box. "It's not your fault, I reckon."

"I'm sorry. I didn't mean to interrupt something important." Could she be more oblivious to his feelings? Not that it was her fault. He'd never stepped up and said anything. Everyone knew he'd been interested in her sister Deborah, who'd also ignored him, such was her preoccupation with Phineas. No one wanted to be second choice—especially to a sister. He didn't think of Leila that way, but she surely would. "I just don't want y'all to get in trouble."

"That's sweet of you, but I reckon we can both take care of ourselves."

Sweet? His emotions, normally so even-keeled, seemed to billow like smoke from a raging grass fire on a windy day every time he encountered Leila. He'd never felt that way with Deborah. "Not really. It's no fun for anyone if things go wrong at the auction. It's supposed to be a good day."

She stared at the empty space where Jesse had stood. Probably not even hearing Will's voice. Jesse had been going to tell her his big plan, the plan that would break his mother's and father's hearts. Making her privy to it would only put Leila in a precarious position as well. She was such a pretty girl with a sweet nature—how could Jesse do that to her? He was being selfish, that's how. On the other hand, Leila might be the one person who could hold Jesse, keep him here. Will couldn't stand in the way of that. "I'm sorry, but you know how Leroy is. Everyone is to be on their best behavior."

"Stop saying you're sorry. Jesse talking to me isn't good behavior?"

"Don't be dense. He had his hand on you. I saw it. If I could see it, others could too." Will wanted to brush a bit of straw from her cheek and run his fingers down the small patch of white skin exposed on her neck. How could he judge Jesse when all he could think about was touching the very same girl? *Think about something else. Anything else.* "That kind of behavior is frowned upon at any time, but especially in the middle of the auction with all the folks from town here."

"It wasn't what you think." Her voice quavered. "He was . . . unasking me out."

Her expression bereft, she wiped at her nose with the back of her sleeve. The girl never had a hankie when she needed one. So Jesse had managed to hurt her already. Will needed to do something. Something physical. A long evening chopping fire-wood loomed in his future. "I'm sorry."

Her forehead wrinkled and she shook her head. "Why do you care?"

Will studied the horses beyond her. "I don't like to see you sad."

More than that, he wanted to be the one asking her out. He would never unask her.

She sniffed and smiled a determined, if watery, smile. "That's nice of you."

He took a jar from her hand and settled it into the box. "I don't ever want to see you . . . hurt."

The sadness faded, replaced by bewilderment. "What are you saying?"

What was he saying? He had no right to horn in on his cousin's intended. But how could Jesse pursue Leila knowing what his attentions might cost her? The dilemma tightened around Will's throat in a stranglehold. He coughed and sucked in air. "I'm saying there's something you should know—"

"Will, what are you doing?" His daed marched across the yard, Molly Carter behind him. "Molly is looking for her box of jars. She said you were to carry them to her van."

"I was. I stopped . . ." How to explain this to his daed? "I mean, I . . ."

"I got in his way and the box fell," Leila jumped in. "I'm sorry, Molly, some of the jars are broken."

The Englisch lady frowned, her pudgy face full of disappointment. "I already paid for a full box. I plan to can pickles next summer. I paid a fair price."

Daed's expression scorched Will. "We'll refund your money, and you can keep whatever jars can be salvaged. Will, take the box to her van while I settle up with her."

"I'm sorry."

The woman nodded, but the pique didn't fade from her face. "Just see that you don't break any more in the two hundred yards between here and the van. I don't see how you ended up back here with my jars when the van is out there on the road."

"I don't either." The growl in Daed's voice didn't bode well. "Be sure I'll have a word with him about learning his directions."

They started back toward the barn just as Leila's mother flounced across the yard, her usual smile turned down in a worried frown.

Leila ducked past Will. "Mudder—"

"Go." Mudder's gaze flicked over Will. "Now."

"I'm sorry, I was just talking to Will."

Funny how she didn't mention Jesse. Will moved out of Abigail King's way. She was a woman on a mission. She slapped both hands on her hips and bore down on him with a withering glance. "You know better. I'm sure you have a duty assigned to you. Get to it and stop keeping Leila from her duties. You both know better."

"Yes, ma'am."

Leila rushed away, head down, her mother marching behind her, skirt swishing in a determined rustling sound. Will picked up the box with its broken contents. An all-around fiasco. His daed would not soon forget this incident. Leroy would surely hear about it. Abigail King would tell Mordecai. It would be the talk of the district.

About Leila and Will. Not Jesse. Jesse came out smelling like one of Mordecai's beeswax candles. All Will had wanted to do was help. Instead he'd caused a major incident. How had that happened? He shook his head and started walking. The road to hell was paved with good intentions, that's how.

SIX

Now or after supper? Leila mulled the question as she deposited a basket of hot cornbread on the table next to the enormous cast-iron pot of venison chili. The mingled aromas of onion and garlic made her mouth water. She inhaled and brushed crumbs from her apron, trying to ignore the stains where the chili had dripped in her haste to carry the steamy concoction from the kitchen on the previous trip.

She stole a glance at her mother. Mudder busied herself correcting Hazel's enthusiastic, if haphazard, attempts to lay out the spoons and butter knives. Mudder had been wordless during most of the preparations for supper. In fact, she'd said little to Leila in the three days that had passed since the auction. No mention of Will. Which was good, because Leila had no idea what he was trying to accomplish. Leila wanted to tell Mudder her assumptions were incorrect, but to do so would involve explaining about Jesse. She had no desire to explain him, even if she could.

If Jesse wasn't interested in her, the job at the day care became all the more important. She wanted to broach the subject, but nothing in Mudder's silence suggested she would be open to that idea either. No other woman in the district had done such a thing—thus far. If she couldn't convince Mudder, she'd never have the opportunity to try to convince the bishop. If Leila waited much longer, surely the position would be filled and the opportunity lost. She straightened the silverware next to her soup bowl. Then she began to pour water into the glasses at each place. *Gott, give me the words. Soften her heart.*

Now. Say something. Go on.

"Whatever's on your mind, spit it out." An amused smile on her face, Mudder added a jar of pickled jalapeños to the table. Mordecai liked some extra heat in his chili. "You've been wiggling around all afternoon like you have a splinter in your behind. You've got something to say, best say it."

"Rory, you know the Englisch girl—"

"The one with the *bopli*?" Mordecai clomped into the room, drying his hands on a dish towel as he went. He tugged his chair from the table and plopped down. "I talked to her daed at the auction. He bought a rototiller. He mentioned he's interested in the mare Andrew's selling."

"Poor man, he hasn't gotten over his fraa's death yet." Susan set a pitcher of water on the table and wiped her hands on her apron. The concern on her face made her look the spitting image of her brother Mordecai. They were two peas in a pod when it came to feeling deeply for others. "He needs to work the earth. It'll do him good."

"Rory says he's planting a big garden this spring." Not the opening Leila was looking for, but she'd take what she could get. She helped Hazel climb into her chair and picked up the ladle to start serving. Caleb dodged his stepbrothers, Samuel and Jacob, racing to beat them to the table. She raised her voice to be heard over their good-natured squabbling. "Anyway, she says there's an opening at the day care where she works after school. A full-time job. She asked the director if she would consider me. The director said she would. She said Amish girls are good workers."

She said it all in a rush, then stopped, dropped into her chair, and stared at her bowl, afraid to look at Mudder's face. The scent of chili, so tantalizing a few seconds earlier, turned her stomach now. Mordecai was the deacon. He could have a word with Leroy. He would have a say in the decision. And he was the head of the household now. Mudder would have to listen to him and acquiesce to his decision.

"What has gotten into you, *dochder*?"

Leila looked up to see a forlorn expression on Mudder's face. Not the disapproval she'd expected. Mudder looked disappointed in her. Why? "I want to help. It's a chance to earn some money to help us make ends meet, that's all." Leila kneaded her napkin in trembling fingers. "I'd be taking care of babies. Little *kinner*. All the workers there are women. What harm could there be in that? Rory's daed would give me a ride. It's during the day only, weekdays only. It pays nine dollars an hour."

That last fact drew a collective *aah* from the other young folks in the room. Susan, Mordecai, and Mudder didn't share in their enthusiasm.

"You would be taking care of Englisch folks' kinner all day." Esther passed the cornbread to her brother Samuel, who extracted a huge chunk and plunked it on top of his chili. "Wouldn't that make you nervous? I know it would me. They raise their kinner differently."

The banns for Esther and her special friend Adam Glick had been announced at the service on Sunday. She need not worry about what her future held. Soon she would be married. She would have her own babies to raise. Unlike Leila, who'd been dumped by Jesse before they even had their first date.

Leila gripped the ladle and filled her bowl. "I love boplin. I know I can do it. I take care of them around here all the time."

"I know you could do it." Her shoulders hunched, Mudder sat across from Mordecai, her gaze fixed on him. "The question is, should you do it?"

"A question that will need to be answered by Leroy." Mordecai smiled at his fraa as if giving her reassurance. "This is a conversation best had with him."

Mudder's returning smile faltered. "You would go to Leroy with this?"

"Leila's desire to help us and the district is good." He gripped the edge of the table with long, calloused fingers, his gaze bouncing from one family member to the next. "Gott will provide for us. He always has. When an opportunity is placed in the road right in front of us, do we take it or do we try to find a detour?"

"But she's just a girl."

"Nee, she's a young woman in her rumspringa." Mordecai lifted one hand as if to silence Mudder. "This is the time for her to learn what's out there and what's important to her, don't you think?"

The look that passed between the newlyweds left Leila wondering how she would learn to be an obedient fraa. She was glad Mordecai saw her request as a good thing, but a rush of guilt rolled over her, guilt for putting her mother in this position. She would accept Mordecai's decision even if it wasn't to her liking.

"If Mudder doesn't—"

Mordecai bowed his head. "Food's getting cold."

Leila bowed her head, but she couldn't keep her mind on

praying for the food. Thoughts milled about like cattle waiting for slaughter. Chagrin at causing a rift between her mother and Mordecai. A kernel of delight that Mordecai saw her side of the situation. Nerves at the thought of talking to Leroy about the job. Even more nerves when it occurred to her she might see Jesse when she visited Leroy. She sighed and scrunched her eyes tighter. If ever she needed to pray, now would be the time.

SEVEN

Leroy's house. Jesse's house. Leila smoothed her apron with damp hands. She wrapped her fingers around the soft cotton material to still their shaking. Her first visit with Leroy in his capacity as bishop, and the possibility existed her supper might end up on his boots. It didn't help that she might encounter Jesse here. Jesse with his on-again, off-again approach to courting.

She sideswiped Mordecai with a glance. He nodded, his expression somber but his eyes kind. He seemed certain Leila could be trusted to comport herself well in the Englisch world, a vote of confidence that surprised her. That Mudder had chosen not to accompany her on this trip did not surprise her, however. She'd stood at the kitchen sink, back to the door, when Mordecai announced they were leaving. She hadn't turned around.

"Go on." Mordecai tugged open the Glicks' screen door and stood back to let her pass. "Leroy won't bite you. Leastways, not as long as you don't irritate him too much."

He chuckled and Leila felt the nerves that whirled in her stomach settle, at least temporarily. So far, so good. No Jesse in sight. Before she could pass through the door, Will Glick strode out. A toothy grin stretched from ear to ear on his smooth, whiskerless face. "Hey, Mordecai." His gaze dropped to Leila and the grin disappeared. "Leila."

His voice held a wary note. Maybe because of Mordecai. As far as Leila knew, Mudder had said nothing to her new husband about seeing her with Will. She nodded and inched back on the porch to let Andrew and him pass.

His daed clomped down the steps as if in a hurry to get on with things. Will paused, then turned back, his grin reappearing. "Leroy said yes. I can work at the nursery."

"He said yes." She forgot to whisper. A momentary sense of hope coursed through her. Nee. Men were different. Leroy would surely see it that way. "Good for you."

Will's gaze went to Mordecai, who had one hand on the screen door as he looked back, his expression benign, then back to her. "I hope you get what you want too."

Was he talking about the job or something else? With men, who knew? She settled for a quick wave, but Will had already jumped the steps and headed for the buggy.

Gott's will. Gott's plan. The men in their district worked with the Englisch all the time. Building buggies for those who had a hankering to stick one in their front yard like an ornament. Making their saddles, harvesting their crops, breaking their horses. Women, that was another cup of *kaffi*. At least, that's what Mudder said. Still, it was Leila's rumspringa. She could push a little harder. She wanted this. She needed it, now that Jesse had rescinded his offer to take her to the movies. Will kept giving her those strange looks and leaving things half said or unsaid, but he had yet to speak up and he probably wouldn't, given that he thought Jesse was interested.

He was wrong about that.

After taking a deep breath, she slipped through the door, inhaling the scent of fried potatoes and onions that hung in the air in Leroy's front room. He sat in a hickory rocker, his big hands still in his lap. Without so much as a howdy, he nodded toward two straight-back chairs, arranged side by side across from the rocker.

Leila sank onto the closest one, thankful her legs hadn't betrayed her. She glanced around. No Jesse. Naturally, Leroy would want privacy for these meetings. Jesse likely was doing chores outside. *Please, Gott, let him stay outside.*

Mordecai removed his hat and settled it on his knees. His thick, curly black hair stood up all over his head, giving him a wild mountain-man look that would've been funny if Leila didn't feel as if she'd contracted a sudden case of the flu. "Leila came to Abigail and me with an idea that bears looking at. Requires your approval."

Leroy plucked at his long gray beard. "It's getting late. Let's not belabor this."

Leila held her breath. Did he mean her or Mordecai?

"We think it's a good idea." Mordecai picked up his hat and planted his elbows on his thighs. "She wants to try her hand at taking care of boplin at Little Angels Day Care, there in Beeville. They've said they'll take her. Forty hours a week. Nine dollars an hour. Nolan Beale is willing to give her a ride to and fro."

He leaned back and gave the hat an expert twirl on one finger. Leroy's eyebrows rose and fell like thick strands of gray yarn escaped from their skein. "You and Abigail think this is good." He grunted and sniffed. "In what way is it good for our girls to be exposed to the shenanigans of those folks?"

"She's in her rumspringa. Better she get this itch taken care of now, so she can be baptized and get on with business here."

Mordecai didn't flinch at Leroy's perturbed expression. "You know as well as I do we're going into the winter low on provisions and funds."

"Gott will provide."

"Indeed. Maybe this job is one way He's doing that. She didn't seek it out. It came to her. Makes me think Gott's hand might be moving in it."

Leroy pursed his lips. His gaze whipped from Mordecai to Leila. She fought the urge to shoot from the chair and flee. Leroy stared at her, wordless, for seconds that seemed to stretch into months. He sniffed. "Cat got your tongue? What do you have to say for yourself?"

She swallowed and glanced at Mordecai. Leroy shook his head. "Mordecai said his piece. I want to know how you think you're going to do this."

"It's taking care of little ones. That's all." Her voice quavered. She sucked in air and let it out, steadying herself. She wanted this. She wanted to feel those babies, warm and sweet smelling in her arms. She might not have her own, but she could do the next best thing. "I'm good at that. There's not much chance of problems. They're just boplin."

"Who have mudders and daeds." Leroy crossed his arms over his rotund belly. "You'd be talking to them every day. I imagine they have all manner of fancy appliances and such there at the day care. Piles of stuff for those babies."

"I'll only talk to the Englisch folks about their boplin. I'll change diapers and fix bottles and play with them, rock them to sleep when they fuss." She could see it now, their tiny little bodies snug against her chest. "You don't need fancy appliances for that."

"What if something happens to one of those boplin? Something they blame you for. Then what?"

"I would take care of them just like I take care of the little ones around here. Like they were my own."

"Only they won't be."

Leroy couldn't know his words were like vinegar poured on an open wound. "Boplin are boplin. Not much to it."

Leroy tapped his work boot on the faded linoleum, still tugging at his beard. The hard lines around his mouth didn't dissipate. Leila steeled herself for the inevitable no. Why had they wasted their time on this? He would never allow it.

"We've had no trouble from you in the time you've been in Bee County."

"Nee." Not much trouble a girl could find in a place so barren and so sparse of people.

"We best pray on it." He rose. Mordecai did the same. Leila scrambled to her feet. Did he mean now? She peered at Mordecai. He didn't bow his head. Leroy headed to the door. "Andrew, Mordecai, and I will pray on it."

So the answer wasn't no. Relief made Leila's legs and arms feel like wet towels. She scurried to keep up with Mordecai, who paused at the door. "Time with the Lord on this will make things clear."

Leroy nodded. "Gott's will."

"Gott's plan."

Leila took one last look around. No sign of Jesse. She couldn't be sure, truth be told, if she was happy or sad about that. She wished she knew just exactly how these wise men figured out what God's plan was. She didn't have a clue.

EIGHT

"Whatcha doin'?"

Leila jumped, shrieked, and dropped the tiny mirror she'd been attempting to use to see her face. It clunked with a thud on the wooden floor. She didn't believe in luck, but breaking a mirror didn't bode well, especially when it belonged to her new stepsister Esther. "Rebekah! Don't you know you shouldn't sneak up on a person like that? You'll give me a heart attack."

"Mudder sees you preening in front of a mirror, she'll give you a heart attack herself." Rebekah giggled and flounced on the quilt-covered bed Leila shared with Hazel and her. It was squeezed up against the wall in the tiny bedroom the sisters occupied in Mordecai's house—their new home. After living in three different houses during their first year in Bee County, it was good to have a permanent home. "'Course she's probably doing a little preening herself, seeing how she spends every waking minute thinking about what new shirt to sew for Mordecai, what Mordecai wants for breakfast, dinner, and supper, when he'll be back from working the apiaries, and when he'll be leaving her again."

"I'm not preening, and stop talking about Mudder and Mordecai. She's his fraa. She's only doing what's expected of her because she loves him." The word *love* stuck in her throat. What girl wanted to think about her mother loving a man besides her father? Even a man as kind and funny as Mordecai. Leila veered away from that thought, instead focusing on trying to smooth the wrinkles in her dress. No good. The dress was a hand-me-down, also from Esther.

Leila didn't know why she bothered to look at herself in the mirror. Obviously, Jesse didn't see what he was looking for in her. She didn't look ugly, but then again, she wasn't as pretty as Deborah or Rebekah. The plain middle sister. She scooped up the mirror, which had survived intact, and stuck it facedown next to the kerosene lamp on the crate that served as a table of sorts. "Don't you have cookies to bake for the service tomorrow?"

Rebekah rolled from the bed and pulled back the curtain hanging on the room's only window. No breeze wafted through it. For November, it was downright warm. "Cookies are done. Kitchen's clean. We've swept, mopped, and dusted. Everything's ready for us to move the furniture and set up the benches in the morning."

Leila chewed her lip. She should've been helping her sisters and not mooning around in the bedroom. Leila didn't want to be selfish, but she'd been listless since the meeting with Leroy. No trip to the movies, and so far, no permission to work in town. She wanted . . . something . . . something to which she could look forward. Mudder would say she should be looking forward to baptism. And she did, but first she wanted . . . an adventure. She wanted her rumspringa to be something she'd remember when she was married and the mother of her own children.

If that ever happened.

She turned her back on her sister and picked up a dress of Hazel's that needed the hem let out. The four-year-old was growing like a weed. "I thought Mudder said you should finish cutting down the hand-me-down dresses for Hazel that Sadie gave us. And the hems in Caleb's pants. He can't keep going to school in pants that are two inches too short."

"Well, if it ever decides to really rain and fill up the pond, he'll be able to go wading without getting his pants wet." Rebekah logic. Sewing was not one of her favorite chores. "Besides, Mudder said you were supposed to help."

"Only one sewing machine."

"You're just trying to get rid of me. Why are you mooning around in our room all the time? There'll be a singing again next week. Maybe you'll get an offer for a buggy ride then."

Rebekah had already experienced her first ride, and she was a year younger. But then, she was prettier than Leila, with her blue eyes and dark hair and fair skin. Plus she was taller and had a slim build. Not a roly-poly bug like Leila.

Pretty is as pretty does. That's what Mudder would say. Men needed fraas who could cook and sew and take care of babies. They didn't care about looks. Which must be true. Look at Deborah. She'd married a man with a disfigured face and she doted on him. So why didn't anyone look at Leila the way Phineas looked at Deborah?

"Leroy Glick just pulled up in front of the house." Rebekah pulled her head back from the window and whirled. "What do you think he wants? Do you think it's about you working in town? Do you think they made a decision? Mordecai didn't say anything about it at supper. You know he talked to Leroy and Andrew about it. They decide everything—"

"Rebekah. Rebekah! Enough already." Leila clutched her hands to her stomach and swallowed against sudden nausea. A bitter bile swelled in her throat. "There's no point in getting all worked up. Whatever he wants, we'll know when we're supposed to know."

"Let's go downstairs and see what they're doing." Rebekah scurried to the door, her face a study in curiosity. "I could serve some cookies and sweet tea."

"If they want us around, Mudder will let us know."

"Since you started courting, you've been no fun at all."

"Who said I was courting?"

"Sally says Patty saw you walking with Jesse at the wedding, and then you were talking to him at the auction and Caleb said—"

"Caleb doesn't know what he's talking about." How she wished he did.

"Jesse is easy on the eyes and everyone likes him. But still, it's strange that he hasn't asked anyone to go for a ride in a long time. He's getting old; he must be at least twenty. Esther says if he doesn't settle down soon, he may never do it. All the girls will be married off. There won't be a soul left."

Only Leila and he wasn't interested in her. Leila slipped past her sister and headed out the bedroom door. She inhaled and exhaled, willing the frolicking kitties in her stomach to take a nap. Wiping her damp hands on her skirt, she proceeded down the stairs at a steady pace. No need to look in a hurry.

Mudder came into view. She stood in the front room, a pitcher of tea in one hand. Leroy and Mordecai were seated in the two oak rocking chairs Mordecai had made himself.

The other kinner were nowhere in sight. Maybe Susan and Esther had taken Hazel for a walk to wear her out before bedtime.

Leroy set his glass of tea on the table and looked up, his gray eyes stern behind his glasses. He nodded without speaking.

Leila breathed.

Her mother turned. She looked flustered. "Leroy wants to talk to you about the job at the day care."

Leila sucked in a breath. "Jah." She managed to stutter that one syllable.

Leroy gazed up at her, his dark eyes piercing over his glasses. "Sit."

She sank onto the one remaining chair in the room.

"I was just telling your mother we'll start the baptism classes in January." Leroy picked up his glass, sipped, and returned it to the table. "That will allow us to finish them before Easter."

"Jah." Nothing more to be said. She would begin the classes. Gott called her to commit to her faith. Her life would be barren without Him to give it meaning. She had no doubt about that. Other things, but not about her faith.

"Mordecai, Andrew, and I have thought about this. We've prayed. We've talked."

"Jah."

Leroy eased back in his chair, the rockers squeaking on the linoleum. He folded his beefy arms over his chest. "I don't make this decision lightly, is what I'm telling you."

"I understand." Her voice failed her, instead the barest of whispers. Her anxiety had stolen it. "If I can't work—"

"You may work at the day care. For now. Until you are baptized, whenever you decide that will be."

Leila's mouth dropped open. After a few seconds, she managed to shut it.

Leroy stroked his beard. "It's up to you to make good decisions. You know how to behave in a way pleasing to Gott. That won't change because you work with Englischers' kinner. This is a part of your rumspringa. It will help you make your decision. I pray it will be the right one. And that it will come sooner rather than later."

Leila managed a nod. "I won't disappoint you."

"Don't worry about disappointing me. It's Gott's judgment you need to be concerned with."

She nodded.

"Never forget you are the first young woman from our district to be allowed to do this. How you behave will affect the others who might also want to help their families by earning money in town."

"I understand." The weight of the responsibility made her neck hurt. "I won't let them down."

"I wouldn't say no to a refill of that sweet tea now, Abigail." He leaned back in his chair, making it clear the women had been dismissed. His gaze encompassed Mordecai only. "The Millers over by George West came by today. Asked me to break another horse for them."

"Good news." Mordecai's voice was a vague rumble in Leila's ears as she eased toward the stairs. Business accomplished, they would settle in for a long, rambling conversation about horses and honey and the drought. "Are you headed there Monday then?"

"Jah. Jesse will run the store for a few days."

"Let me know if you need me to take a turn. I'm happy to do it. We're done with the hives until spring."

"I will do that."

Leila made a beeline for the stairs. She could rest now, knowing what her future held. Knowing Jesse wouldn't be in it. She would be like Susan, who taught at school and seemed content with her lot as a single woman. She had her scholars. Leila would have her Englisch boplin to love. Best get some sleep and begin again tomorrow.

Leila was almost to the stairs.

"Don't let Gott down."

She'd almost made it. She glanced back at Leroy. The flickering lamplight glinted on his glasses, making his expression hard to read. "I won't."

"See that you don't."

———

Jesse felt warm and cold at the same time. He leaned back against the headrest and let the cool air from the open window rush over him. Why had he let Tiffany and Colton talk him into this? He'd had the guts to tell Leila he couldn't take her out and now here he was, changing his mind again. The poor girl would think he was an idiot.

"There's nothing to be nervous about." Colton craned his neck from the front seat of the Impala, then snapped his attention back to the dirt road. The tiny evergreen-tree air freshener hanging from the rearview mirror bounced, along with a cross on a chain of beads. "It's just a movie. It's not like you're getting married or something."

Tiffany snorted, not a ladylike sound, but one that she often employed when her boyfriend said something she found silly. "Jesse will never get married if he doesn't start doing something about his love life. Like dating for example."

"I'm not looking to have a wedding." Leila's sweet face the afternoon of her mother's wedding presented itself front and center. He hadn't told Colton and Tiffany about the discussion behind the barn that day or the encounter at the auction. The way he changed his mind and hurt Leila. The look on her face. The look on Will's face. His cousin had reeked with disapproval. Will need not sit in judgment. Jesse knew he'd caused that pain, that disappointment. His friends would want to stop and pray about it, and he'd already covered the topic thoroughly. *Gott, are You listening?* "I shouldn't be asking out any Plain girl right now."

Tiffany wiggled in her seat until she faced him, her chin resting on the rust-colored seat cover. "Why? This isn't wrong. We're not wrong. There's nothing different about what we believe and what you believe."

She was right. But a world of difference existed between how the Amish lived and how his Englisch friends lived. He would never judge. It wasn't his community's way. But one look at Tiffany's getup, the tight jeans, the glittering green goop on her eyelids, the pink lipstick, and the dangling earrings, proved that. "It's not that simple."

"I know that." She blessed him with a smile that let her true self shine through all the goop. "Which is why you're in my prayers every single day."

Much as it embarrassed him to think of her praying about him, it also touched him. "Appreciate that."

"It'll all work out in the end." She gave him a thumbs-up that featured a long bubble-gum-pink nail and turned back toward the front. "That's what my dad says. If it isn't working out, it isn't the end yet."

Jesse swallowed the lump in his throat, glad she couldn't see the morass of emotion that battered him. Tiffany might be the daughter of an Englisch minister, but she couldn't really understand his situation. She couldn't understand the consequences of choosing not to be baptized. Of not joining his church. Eventually he would have to leave his family and his friends and his life. His community's faith encompassed a way of life.

Leila would understand. Not only the consequences for him, but for her, should she do more than just go to the movies with him. If, by God's grace, something came of their courting, she would lose her family and friends. Which made this whole thing unfair to her.

Which brought him back to the original question. What was he doing in this car headed toward her house?

Her innocence. Her eagerness. The pink of her cheeks and the simple, plain beauty of her round face. No goop. No jewelry. No painted-on jeans. Something told him Leila had a beauty inside her of which he'd seen only the merest of glimpses.

He wanted to see more. Jesse didn't understand it. He didn't even want to think about it. His desire to see Leila kept growing, no matter how he tried to stifle it. He simply hadn't found a way.

Or he'd lacked courage. Nee, he had courage. The courage not to ask her, knowing she would end up hurt. It took a man to do that. He would have this date and maybe that would get this hankering out of his system. They'd both realize they weren't right for each other and it would be done. A person so often wanted what he couldn't have. Having it took the mystery and suspense from it. He'd be able to move on and so would she.

Tiffany smacked her hand against Colton's arm. "Hey, watch out. Buggy alert."

The car slowed and Colton eased farther to his right. Sure enough, a buggy kept a steady pace toward them, its battery-operated lights bobbing in the deepening dusk. Who would be leaving Mordecai's this late in the evening? On a Saturday night with services tomorrow. Jesse leaned his head through the window, squinting against the lights, trying to see.

The clouds parted and the moon beamed down on them. His father's disgruntled face, his hollow cheeks sculpted in the moonlight, stared at him behind wire-rimmed glasses as they passed. Jesse's stomach lurched. He sucked in air, afraid the butter noodles and fried chicken his mudder had prepared for supper would end up on the floor of Colton's newly vacuumed car. "Ach."

"Who is it? Someone you know? Will they tattle on you to your dad?" Tiffany knew all about Jesse's conflicted feelings about Leroy Glick. "You're not doing anything wrong. We're just going to the movies. Even if whoever that was says something, it's no big deal, right?"

"That was Leroy Glick." He kept his tone light. "My father."

Colton pulled the car to the side of the road. "We can talk about this."

"There's nothing to talk about."

"Pray then."

Prayer seemed the only option left these days, and Jesse's knees ached from spending so much time on that bedroom rug. "Sure, prayer would be good."

———

Leila stood at the window, letting the cool night air waft over her warm skin and listening to Rebekah snore, a soft, gentle rumble that seemed to have lulled Hazel to sleep. The little girl had her chubby hands clasped around her big sister's right arm. The two looked so peaceful. Leila longed for such sweet repose. She'd tried to sleep after her conversation with Leroy, but she was too keyed up. She wanted to grab the buggy and race to Rory's house to share her good news, but Mudder had said no, not until after services tomorrow. Time ticked by so slowly. Everyone had to have gone to bed now that Leroy's buggy had pulled away from the front steps. If she could just sleep, tomorrow would come sooner.

She turned from the window. Time for her nightgown and her pillow. Dawn would creep into the bedroom before she knew it. Lights flickered on the road, casting beams against the dark night. She hesitated, then leaned on the windowsill, trying to make out the bearer of that light. A car. A car coming up the drive to Mordecai's house after dark on a Saturday night.

It could only be one person.

Nee. Jesse had uninvited her. He'd been clear about that.

She waited, her heart a hiccup in her chest. The car stopped and the engine died, leaving the same silence as before, yet different in the knowledge that someone sat in the car, someone who would get out any moment and everything could change for Leila.

A car door opened. Butch began to bark. Nee. He would wake Mordecai and Mudder. Leila flew down the stairs and out the door. The dog stood at attention on the narrow front porch, a low growl emanating from his throat. "Hush, Butch, hush." She grabbed his collar and tugged. "Settle down."

The growl died to a soft whimper in the back of his throat. He was simply doing what he did. "Good dog, it's okay, it's okay." Leila strained to see in the darkness. A new light appeared, quivering against the black night. A flashlight held by a nervous hand. She swallowed and breathed. The light approached, dancing and bobbing. She put her hand to her forehead to shield her eyes as she strained to see. The light hit her in the eyes. "Hey, hey, stop it. Who is that?"

"Leila, it's me."

The loud whisper filled up the night. A distinct male voice. Jesse. "Shh, you'll wake everyone. It's the middle of the night."

"It's nine thirty. Come on, let's go."

"Go where?" She dropped her shoes on the porch. "What are you doing here?"

"Taking you to the movies."

She straightened and crossed her arms. "Are you telling me you didn't pull me aside at the auction to tell me you were uninviting me to the movies?"

"I had a . . . what my friends call a . . . momentary lapse in judgment."

"Those are some awful big words for saying you acted like an idiot."

"Agreed."

"So I'm just supposed to forget that and jump in some strange car with you?"

"It's not a strange car. It's an Impala."

"You know what I mean."

"I do. I don't know that I think this is a good idea." He flipped off the flashlight. "I'm pretty sure it's not. But nothing ventured, nothing gained. That's another thing my friends say."

"They're sure full of lots of sayings."

"They're full of other things, too, but I think you'll like them. Get in the car and you'll find out."

"I'm just supposed to trust you now."

"Come on, get in the car."

"You sound more like an Englischer than you did before."

"So will you when you start working at the day care."

"How do you know about that?"

"My daed was here this evening, wasn't he?"

"Jah."

"He saw me coming up here."

The hiccup was back in her heart. It twisted, all out of whack. "And you still came."

"He knows what we do during rumspringa is not for him to judge. This is our time, so come out with me."

As much as her head said no, her heart said yes louder. "Are you sure you want me to come?"

"Let's go."

Ignoring the naysayer in her head, she shoved her feet in the shoes. "What took you so long?"

NINE

Leila sat still, sunk into the plush padded seat that felt like velvet under her fingers, her gaze glued to the enormous screen that lit up the dark theater with bigger-than-life images. She inhaled the mouthwatering scents of buttery popcorn and chocolate. She couldn't contain a small sigh. The movie told a beautiful story. So beautiful. What could be so bad about a movie like this? The lion protected the children and stood strong against evil forces and taught his followers the difference between right and wrong. A parable. That's what it was. A story with a meaning. She liked that. If all movies were like this, what could be the harm?

Jesse leaned close to her and scooped a handful of popcorn from the enormous bucket he'd handed to her before the movie began. His fresh scent of soap mixed with the peppermint on his breath. He smelled good. Leila tucked a handful in her mouth and chewed, trying not to think about how close he sat. Trying to think about the popcorn and the movie and the cool air that brushed her face from vents overhead. Not the way the muscles in his arms bulged against the sleeves of his shirt and his teeth shone in the flickering light.

It was almost too much to take in. This movie probably cost a pretty penny. Jesse refused to let her pay for anything. It was a rerun, he said, showing at the all-night dollar theater. A bargain in her book, but one she gladly would've paid for herself.

The salt burned her chapped lips. She longed for a sip from the large soda Jesse had nestled in a cup holder in the chair arm between them. Was it meant to be hers too? He hadn't offered any to her. The enormous cup held more than one person could drink, surely. But did a boy and a girl share a cup? Germs didn't scare her. Overstepping and sharing something more did.

The music thundered from the speakers, pummeling her from all sides. The figures on the screen seemed poised to leap on top of her. She jumped. Why did it have to be so loud?

She sneaked a glance at Jesse, who tossed the popcorn in his mouth and wiped his hands on his pants, his expression unperturbed. He had more experience with movies than she did. He looked almost morose for a man in the middle of courting. The Jesse who'd stood outside her house, flashlight in hand, had disappeared somewhere along the highway into George West.

She looked beyond him. Colton and Tiffany were snuggled together, her head resting on his shoulder. Colton leaned down and landed a kiss on Tiffany's forehead. She responded with a kiss on his cheek. She giggled and he shushed her.

Her cheeks burning, Leila jerked her head back toward the screen. Plain folks didn't go for that sort of thing. Kissing in public. She hunched her shoulders and tried to delve back into the movie.

"What's the matter?" Jesse leaned into her, his deep bass a whisper in her ear. He picked up the cup, slick with condensation, and offered it to her. "Don't you like the movie?"

She shrugged and took a long pull from the soda—root beer, icy cold, bubbly, and sweet. The liquid helped her swallow the lump in her throat. Grateful, she took another sip to give herself time to form a response. The couple next to him acted in a shameful manner. How could it not bother Jesse? He sat right next to them.

Or maybe he wished he could kiss her too. Did Plain folks kiss on the first date? Surely not. Despite the chilled rush of air from the overhead vents, Leila felt flushed and sweaty. If Jesse did like her, would he want to kiss her? Did she want him to kiss her?

If her heart and lungs had a vote, it would be yes, because both seemed to be off kilter at the thought. Nee. Nee. A girl didn't do that, especially with a man so on again, off again.

She should've asked Deborah. Deborah would know and she wouldn't laugh at Leila for asking.

"Well?"

Jesse was waiting for an answer.

"It's . . . good . . . nice," she whispered. Her voice quavered. "I like it."

"Good." He slumped back in his chair, one hand on the chair arm between them.

Leila took another sip of the soda, trying to swallow her anxiety. Enough. She didn't want to hog Jesse's drink. She slid the cup back in the holder. Jesse's hand caught hers before she could return it to her lap. His long, calloused fingers grasped hers, warm and strong. They enveloped hers as he pulled her hand toward him. Leila jerked back. "What are you trying to do?"

"Shush, shush!" He let go and sat forward, head ducked toward her. "I just wanted to—"

"You know better." Was this what Will had been talking about?

Was Jesse falling into the Englisch ways? She didn't know what those ways were. Or if they were bad. "This is our first . . . time."

"I'm not trying to kiss you or anything." His hoarse whisper carried embarrassment and the same uncertainty she felt. "I didn't want you to think I didn't . . ."

She stood, aware the people in the row behind them were fidgeting. "Let me out."

"Where are you going?"

"Hey, some of us are trying to watch the movie," a group of girls chorused almost in unison. "Come on, we can't see."

Jesse stood and squeezed past Colton and Tiffany, who patted Leila's arm, her perplexed expression clear in the flickering images on the screen. "Hey, you guys, come back. It's just getting to the good part."

Leila doubted Tiffany had been paying enough attention to know. Her stomach rocking with nausea born of embarrassment and shame, she tromped past them. Jesse waited at the end of the row and then led her down the dark aisle to the exit. She pushed through the door and into a hallway empty except for a man in a theater uniform sweeping popcorn into a dustpan with a long handle.

"What's wrong? Where are you going?" Jesse caught her elbow with an iron grip. "What are you so mad about? I only thought I would . . . hold your hand. Is that bad?"

"It's just that I've never done this before. Never been someplace with an Englisch couple who thinks it's okay to . . . do that kind of thing in public."

"What thing? You mean kiss?"

Heat drenched Leila from head to toe. She glanced at the man with the broom. His shaggy eyebrows lifted over black-rimmed glasses, his cheeks covered with painful-looking, swollen acne. He pivoted and scooted down the hallway, leaving them to their argument. He probably thought it was a lovers' quarrel. Another wave of heat washed over her. She planted her hands on her hips and looked Jesse in the eye. "Jah, kiss."

"I had no plans to kiss you, if that's what you're worried about." The scorn had turned to a rough whisper as if someone might still hear the conversation in the now-deserted hallway. "Not in public or anywhere else."

"*Gut.* Because I don't want to kiss you either. I don't know why you asked me out in the first place if I'm so . . . so . . . unlikable."

"That's not what I mean." His voice rose. Pretty soon the people watching the movie would be able to hear them over the booming dialogue and thunderous music. "I mean not yet. I know that's not what you would want."

"Why did you ask me to come with you?"

"I told you before. I like you."

"Then why are you acting like this?"

"Like what?"

He couldn't be that dense. He'd been like an irritable bear late for hibernation all evening. "From the minute I got in the car, you've acted like I did something wrong. Like you wish you hadn't asked me. Then you try to hold my hand. Why would you do that?"

"It doesn't have anything to do with you." The words were almost a growl. "I'm just . . . You wouldn't understand. Maybe after working at the day care, maybe then you'll be able to understand."

"Understand what? The only reason Leroy said yes is he wants us to be able to stay here. To stay in our homes. We're not making enough to keep food on the table."

"He said that? We might have to leave Bee County?"

Jesse's expression puzzled Leila. He didn't look so much concerned as . . . excited. Maybe *excited* was too strong a word, but he didn't seem to mind the idea. "Not in so many words, but that's what he meant. I heard Mordecai and my mudder talking about it."

Jesse stared at a point somewhere beyond her shoulder. "My daed told me we're staying. Groossdaadi told him we have to stay the course."

"I hope so. We uprooted ourselves once to come here. I don't want to do it again."

"Right." He chewed on a nail already bitten to the quick. "We should go back into the movie. I promise to keep my hands to myself."

She stared at his face. The words said one thing, but his expression said another. He looked . . . sad. She wanted to wipe that look off his face. How? By letting him kiss her? Courting was harder than she'd ever imagined. "I really want to go home." Surely they'd seen enough of the movie that the two dollars wasn't a total waste. "The story was a book first. Couldn't we just read the book instead?"

His dimples appeared even when he frowned. More a scowl than a frown, really. "Colton's driving. It's his car. And Tiffany loves this movie. She's seen it at least twenty times."

Twenty times. Twenty dollars. Forty if she saw it with Colton, which, of course, she had. Now *that* seemed a waste of money. "Then she knows how it ends."

"I suppose you're right, but I don't think it's fair for us to ask them to leave early because I did something to get you all worked up."

"I'm not worked up." She wanted to stamp her foot and shake her fist, but she wasn't worked up. "Not much, anyway."

For the first time, the corners of his mouth turned up. If she didn't know better, she'd think Jesse was laughing at her predicament. She felt a tiny tickle of a giggle burble up in her. She slapped her hand to her mouth to keep it prisoner. He couldn't know how much looking at his lips made her wonder what they would feel like touching hers.

"I promise I won't try to hold your hand again." He took a step toward her, despite the studied intent of his words. "Ever, if that's what you want. I promise to never, ever kiss you."

She took a step back and felt the wall nudge her shoulders. "That's not what I want." That sounded all wrong. "I mean, I want to do things the right way. Don't you?"

"I do. I think." He rubbed his forehead with two fingers and grimaced. "Jah. Most of the time."

"Most of the time?"

"Don't you ever wonder if there's a different way to do things?" Something in his eyes begged her to contemplate the question with care. He cocked his head and shook it as if doing that very thing himself. The sadness deepened and carved lines around his mouth and eyes, making him seem older than she knew him to be. "A way that isn't bad, just different?"

Leila had a terrible but fleeting urge to give Jesse what he wanted, anything and everything he wanted, anything to wipe that forlorn, pleading look from his face. But she couldn't lie. She was Leila Lantz, a Plain girl who believed Gott to be good. He provided. His will be done. "I like the way we do things. I like the rules. I like knowing what I'm supposed to do. Don't you?"

"You like knowing what to do. Good for you. I wish I knew

what to do." He tucked a curl of her hair back under her kapp with one calloused finger. She swallowed, sure she would sink to the floor and dissolve into a puddle. His gaze traced her features. "Sometimes the rules don't feel right. Sometimes the rules only tell us what not to do. Not what we should do. What would be so wrong about holding my hand?"

"I would like to hold your hand . . . someday." The words whispered themselves over her insistence they stay quiet. She wanted to reel them back in. Her body quivered with embarrassment. Perspiration trickled down her temples, and she shivered in the refrigerated air. "When the time is right."

"What about kiss me? Would you like to do that too?"

Let the ground open up and swallow me now. Please, Gott.

Again her heart fought with her mind and all she knew to be right. Her heart had survived the death of her father and the move from Tennessee to barren south Texas. It was strong, far stronger than her head. "Someday. Jah."

A smile broke across his face like dry lightning, sudden and jagged, then gone from the dusty, flat south Texas horizon. "Let someday come soon then."

He started down the hallway.

"Where are you going?"

"To tell Colton you need to get home. You have a service at your house in the morning—later today."

"You do too."

"We'll see."

The sadness returned. His gaze enveloped her. She couldn't help herself. She reached for his hand and caught it before he could move away. "Don't be so sad. The Sunday services aren't that bad. Your daed is a good preacher."

His Adam's apple bobbed. "I like the shape of your lips."

She had to lean in to hear his whisper. He leaned closer yet. His lips brushed hers. Soft and warm. A kiss so fleeting she didn't have time to close her eyes or protest or kiss him back.

"Sorry." The painful smile came and went again. "I didn't mean to do that. I guess someday came sooner than you expected."

"It was . . ." She couldn't find a word. Her pulse pounded in the hollow of her throat. Her breathing sounded loud in her own ears. She licked her lips, wishing she had balm. "I'm . . . it's . . ."

"Leila Lantz is speechless." He smiled for real then, the dimples appearing, making him look younger and somehow, for a second, carefree. "Maybe I should help you find the words."

He kissed her again, this time letting his lips linger on hers. His hands settled on her shoulders. His lips trailed across her cheeks and then her forehead, leaving behind a strange sensation like floating on a lake, the only sound the water dashing against the shore. "Now?"

"Nice. It's . . . nice." She couldn't seem to control her breathing. Her words fluttered between them. Whether they should kiss no longer presented itself as the question. When would they kiss again—that question planted itself foremost in her mind and refused to budge. "Maybe . . . maybe we should stay for the rest of the movie."

Jesse wrapped his long fingers around hers and held on tight, his grip grounding her, comforting her. "Maybe it would be better to take you home before you get into any more trouble."

Leila closed her eyes for a second and concentrated on drawing one breath, then another, then another. How much trouble could she handle? If tonight were any indication, she had set a course right into the heart of that very question. "I want to see how the story ends."

TEN

They'd stayed out too late. Jesse put his hand on the car door, ready to open it the second Colton stopped in front of Mordecai's house. Leila would likely meet her mudder or one of her sisters as they rose to begin preparing for church. They should've come back sooner, but Tiffany had insisted on donuts and hot chocolate after the movie, and then a drive along the back roads and a stop to count the stars. He was too enthralled with Leila's hand in his to protest. Next time, he would take her out on his own where he had control over the situation.

Next time? He shouldn't be thinking of a next time.

Leila shifted, her body warm against his shoulder, making it hard for him to concentrate on what he should and shouldn't do. She'd drifted off to sleep somewhere between the highway and the dirt road that led to Mordecai's. Her eyelids fluttered. A second later, she straightened. Her hand went to her mouth, her eyes wide, cheeks stained cherry red. Their gazes met. Her uncertain smile quivered.

She didn't need to be embarrassed. They hadn't done anything wrong. At least, not in his book. His father's book? That was a different story. "It's okay—"

"Here we are." Colton braked and brought the car to a stop in the yard in front of the house where buggies would soon be parked. Hay stanchions were already in place for the horses. "I hope we didn't keep you out too late."

"It was fun." Leila rubbed at her face with both hands as if trying to rub away the sleep. "It was nice to meet you."

"Wait, wait." Tiffany, who'd been half asleep in the front seat, popped up and swiveled so she faced Leila and Jesse. Most of the goop had migrated from her eyelids and eyelashes to the area under her eyes, creating dark circles, and her hair fuzzed up around her face. "We have to pray."

"Pray?" Leila's gaze skipped to Jesse, her eyebrows raised over bloodshot eyes. "Now?"

She wouldn't understand. It was too soon to explain. Jesse didn't want to scare her away, even though far away would be the best place for her. "It's been a long night, and Leila has to get inside. We're having church service at her house today."

"Oh, come on, we need to give thanks for the great time we had and we got home safe and sound and you had a great time with your new girl—"

Not his girl. Leila couldn't be his girl. Tiffany would never understand the sacrifice a Plain woman would be required to make if she chose to follow him down the road Tiffany represented. "Don't you have to get to church too?"

"We go to the late service. We've got lots of time—"

"Leila needs to get inside. Her mother will be up soon, if she's not already."

"So we'll pray she doesn't get in trouble. Come on. Hold hands. Leila, you can go first if you want."

Leila's hand hovered in the air. Her look beseeched him. He

knew exactly what she was thinking. They didn't recite their own public prayers. The Lord's Prayer was best. Jesus' own words were best. Otherwise they prayed silently. "Why don't you pray, Tiffany." He made it a statement, not a request. "We'd rather pray silently."

Tiffany's eyebrows popped up and down. "Whatever. He'll hear either way."

Nothing could stop Tiffany when it came to praying. It was one of the things Jesse admired about her from the first time he met Colton and her when they came into the tavern where he and Will and a few others were playing pool and watching TV, the big rumspringa activities available to them in such a small town. She'd handed each of them a flyer for a youth group at her church. The others had chuckled over it, finding it funny that this Englisch girl would try to convince Plain men of the gospel, something of which they had more than a passing knowledge.

Something about the couple had stuck with Jesse. So much so, he'd taken them up on their offer. Just once, he'd told himself, just out of curiosity. No one had to know.

No one could know.

One time had turned into two and three and four. Now he counted Colton and Tiffany as friends who'd shown him another way to worship.

Jesse bowed his head and prayed his real, true community would never find out.

ELEVEN

"Coming or going?"

Leila dropped her sneakers. Taking a quick breath, she forced herself to turn back from the foot of the stairs. Deborah stood in the kitchen doorway, a dish towel in her hands. She looked crisp and clean and wide awake. Which only made Leila more aware of her rumpled clothes, disheveled hair hanging out from her kapp, and a face that felt greasy from buttered popcorn and a stop at an all-night donut shop. "You're here early."

"So are you." Deborah draped the towel over her shoulder and smoothed her apron. "We came to help get ready. What's your excuse?"

The question made heat race along Leila's neck and scorch her cheeks. She rubbed eyes gritty with fatigue. The first rule of rumspringa: A person didn't let it interfere with carrying her weight at home. Parents might turn a blind eye to late-night activities, but they still expected their kinner to contribute, same as always.

"Just let me freshen up and I'll come help you with the bread."

"At least get a cup of kaffi first." Deborah turned, her hand still rubbing her belly as if it hurt. "Come on, *schweschder*, I don't go anywhere anymore. Share."

"Kaffi sounds wunderbarr."

How much could she tell Deborah? Leila chewed her lower lip and followed her sister into the kitchen. The fragrance of baking bread wafted around her. It smelled so fresh and sweet and so . . . like home. She breathed it in. She belonged here. Not at a noisy movie theater in George West. How could she get so turned around in a foreign place like that?

She felt as if she'd awakened from a long, troubled dream in which no familiar landmarks existed.

Deborah handed her a chipped blue mug filled with coffee that looked strong enough to take the enamel off her teeth. That her sister didn't drink coffee was apparent in the way she prepared it for others. "Who was that in the car?"

"You saw it?"

"Phineas did, from the front window. He said Jesse got out, but he couldn't see who was driving."

"Friends of Jesse's."

"Don't worry. Phineas keeps things to himself. He's a big believer in folks learning from their own mistakes."

"It's not a mistake."

"I imagine it's too soon to tell. Don't you?" Deborah waddled to the wood-burning stove and opened the oven door. The heat made her cheeks rosy. She pulled out a pan of bread and set it on the top of the stove. When she turned, her forehead was creased, her mouth down in a frown that made her look like Mudder, with their matching wisps of blonde hair always peeking from below their kapps. "I've heard some things about Jesse."

"Like what?"

"Not to gossip."

"Nee, of course not."

Deborah slapped pot holders creased with age onto the counter. "It's his rumspringa. Has been for an awful long time."

"Better he wait and be sure."

"I know." Deborah's hands flew up in the air, signaling her concern. The more agitated she got, the more her hands moved. "He spends a lot of time with Englisch kids."

This was not news to Leila. "Like you said, his rumspringa."

"I'd hoped you might take a shine to his cousin, actually."

"You mean Mudder hoped."

"We all hoped."

"He hasn't asked and Jesse did." She sank into a chair at the pine prep table and spooned four tablespoons of sugar into the coffee. "Will tried to warn me off Jesse."

"Will's a good man."

"So is Jesse."

Deborah shook a finger at Leila as she sank into a chair across the table. "Then tell me why did he take you courting into town with his Englisch friends instead of a proper ride in a buggy?"

"Maybe he thought that would impress me."

"Did it?"

Maybe it did. Maybe she wanted to know what it felt like to be someone else for a few scant hours. Maybe Deborah, with her happy marriage and impending motherhood, couldn't remember that feeling.

"I'm still in my rumspringa too." The memory of Jesse's lips on hers sent another wave of heat cascading through her. Followed by the memory of Tiffany's bent head as she prayed with an openness and abandon that Leila had never heard before. Like she was talking to a close friend. Leila could use a friend she could talk to like that. "I'm trying to figure things out too."

Frowning, Deborah stood and lumbered across the room. She manhandled a huge cast-iron skillet onto the stove and began cracking eggs into it. Maybe it would be easier to talk to her with her back turned. Leila opened her mouth. Deborah turned. "You sound . . . like you're feeling guilty about something."

"Can I ask you a question?"

"Anything." Deborah picked up a fork and began to whip the eggs in a frenzied motion. Her scrambled eggs were always the lightest and fluffiest. "Except how babies are made. You'll have to figure that one out on your own."

"Deborah!"

"Shush, you'll wake everyone in the house. What is the question?"

"Did you and Phineas kiss?" It was easier, somehow, to ask about the physical part than the praying. "I mean, not to get in your business or anything."

"Jah, we kiss." Deborah's cheeks, already red from the heat of the stove, turned a beet color. "Married folks do that now and then."

"Nee. Before. When you first started . . ."

"Things were different for me and Phineas. He's different." Deborah ladled pancake batter in small beige puddles in a second cast-iron skillet. It sizzled and the aroma made Leila's mouth water. All the same, her stomach clenched. Deborah turned and faced Leila, her expression thoughtful. "He never thought anyone would want him, because of his scars, the silly goose. So he never let me get close. Not until . . . not for a long time."

"Do you think it's wrong to kiss someone the first time you go out with him?"

"Jesse kissed you?" Deborah's hands batted the air again. "Already?"

"Is that bad?"

Her head bent, Deborah wrapped the bread in a towel and laid it in a basket. "Sometimes we get ahead of ourselves. Phineas wasn't the first man to kiss me."

"Nee?"

"Nee. Remember, I courted before we moved here."

Leila searched her memory. "Aaron. Aaron, right?"

"Right."

"You kissed Aaron?"

The blush spread across Deborah's face, blotches decorating her neck. "I've always regretted that I didn't save that for Phineas."

"Does he know?"

"Nee, he never asked." She picked up a spatula and flipped the pancakes with an expert flick of her wrist. "I just hope you don't experience the same regret."

Leila tugged the spatula from her sister's hand and waved it toward a chair. "Take a load off your feet. I think I already do. Jesse is so . . . He runs hot and cold. He can't seem to make up his mind."

"He's probably as new at this as you are. It's not like we get a lot of advice on how to treat men. Men don't get much in the way of advice either." Deborah waddled back to the chair and sank into it, her hands rubbing her hips. "You're a good girl. Daed raised us all to be good girls. If something doesn't feel right, most likely it isn't right. You'll know it in your heart and you'll step away."

Only Leila hadn't stepped away. She'd stepped into that kiss. "It's hard to think about what's right in the middle of it all."

"I know." Deborah sighed, her light blue eyes somber. "My advice? Don't go places in cars with Englisch folks. Makes it hard to walk home."

A day late and a dollar short, as Mudder was wont to say.

Still, good advice. Deborah might have good advice about praying with Englisch folks too. How could praying ever be wrong? Leila couldn't put her finger on it. Her district didn't have Bible study or Sunday school. They got their needs filled through Sunday services and private prayer. They didn't judge how anyone else worshipped, but their Ordnung was clear on how the Bee County district would do these things. Worship as a district kept them together as one big family.

Still, at the childlike enthusiasm of Tiffany's prayer, the abandon with which she shared her feelings with the Lord, and the joy in her face as she prayed, Leila felt something precariously close to jealousy. How could it be jealousy? She walked a righteous road, a road carved by Mudder and Mordecai and the bishop and all those Plain folks who came before her.

She needed to talk to Jesse about all this. His palms had gone clammy when they held hands with Colton and Tiffany during the prayer. He'd barely said good-bye before he slid back into the car and slammed the door, leaving her standing there waving.

He'd be back for church soon. She slid the pancakes in a stack onto a nearby platter and dropped the spatula on the counter. "I should get cleaned up."

"Was there something else?"

"Nee. Why?"

"You looked like you were mulling over something. Is it about the job? I heard Leroy said you could go to work at the day care."

The events of the long night had overshadowed this astonishing development. "I'm so excited. If I can't have my own bopli, I can take care of others."

"You will have your own." Deborah rose and went back to the stove. She sniffed a huge pot of corn mush, picked up a ladle, and stirred. "Especially if you keep going like you did last night. Schweschder, do take care."

"I'll be back down to help with the cookies."

"Are you sure you couldn't see your way to spending time with Will?"

"He hasn't asked."

"Maybe because you haven't shown an interest."

"He's Jesse's cousin."

Deborah dropped the ladle on the counter with a bang. "You can tell a lot about people by the company they keep."

Was she talking about Jesse or Leila? "It was one date."

"Kisses lead to more. Think with your head and not just your heart."

Her heart shouted, drowning out her head. "I know."

"Hurry up." Deborah made shooing motions. "If the boys get down here before you, there won't be anything left except a *schmier* of peanut butter on yesterday's bread."

Leila trudged from the room, Deborah's words chasing her. *"Kisses lead to more. Think with your head."*

Kisses couldn't be taken back, any more than words could.

TWELVE

The belligerent *a-oo-gah* of the horn sent Leila racing out the front door, a slice of bread, peanut butter, and honey clutched in one hand and the cooler containing her lunch in the other. She did a two-step and narrowly avoided stumbling over Butch, who sat in front of the door keeping guard. She would have to learn to manage her morning rituals better. She'd spent too much time helping with breakfast, doing dishes, and getting the younger ones ready for school.

Her fourth day of work at the day care. Her stomach clenched as she remembered the look in Mordecai's eyes at the breakfast table on Monday. *"Take care,"* he'd said. *"Remember where you come from."* So far, she hadn't seen or heard anything that made her feel any more than a simple Plain girl. No one beckoning her to a life of sinful easiness. No one luring her into any dens of iniquity. What exactly was a den of iniquity, and where did a person find one?

Not at a day care, obviously.

Or little Beeville, Texas, at the corner of Back Road and Nowhere.

"Leila."

Mudder's voice stopped her in her tracks. She turned. "I don't want to keep Nolan waiting."

Mudder pushed open the screen door and stuck her head out. She had patches under her dark blue eyes, smudges of deep purple. Red spots deepened under her high cheekbones. "I know. I just want to tell you I'm praying for you."

Her mother had never said that to her in her whole life. Plain folks didn't talk about such things. "I know."

"Keep your eyes lifted to Gott."

"I will."

"He sees and He knows."

"And I know." Mudder should trust her. "I have to go."

"Have a good day and . . . be careful."

"I will."

Sighing, Leila tripped on the steps and caught herself just as Rory pushed open the door on her father's enormous diesel pickup truck and scooped up the cooler so Leila had a free hand to pull herself up and into the double cab. *"Danki. Guder mariye."*

Nolan nodded and smiled, but his gaze traveled to the silver watch on his wrist. He couldn't be late for his shift at the prison. His consent to provide her with transportation had been contingent on her not making him late for work.

"Sorry, I'm here, I'm here." Leila squeezed into the tight space next to Trevor's car seat and struggled with the seat belt stuck down in the cracks of the seat. With Rory's little brother, Sawyer, on the other side with his backpack and lunch box, they were like a family of birds snug in a nest. The baby cooed, bubbles of drool posed for liftoff on his pursed rosebud lips. "He's chipper this morning." She tickled his cheek and planted a kiss on his silky brown hair. "No fussing?"

"Only all night." Rory turned sideways in the front seat. "Kept me up. I'm going to bomb on my history test for sure."

"Keeps me up at night too." Sawyer, a miniature Rory with freckles and dark-rimmed glasses, grumbled. "I can hear you singing and carrying on."

"Just trying to get him down so I get two minutes of sleep." The dark smudges under Rory's eyes revealed she hadn't been successful. "I don't know how I'm supposed to keep up at school on three hours of sleep a night."

"No excuses." Nolan's frown revealed itself in the rearview mirror. "You and Dwayne went out last night on a school night. It's wrong of you to expect your Aunt Cheryl to watch the baby, especially when he's in day care all day long."

"We were studying, Daddy. Most of the time." Rory's smile disappeared. She wiggled in her seat, her expression suggesting this wasn't a new argument. "Besides, we hardly see each other at all. If you would let Dwayne live with us, we'd see more of each other during the week. He could spend more time with Trevor too."

Sawyer snorted. Leila glanced his way. The boy's hat was on backward and his coat buttoned wrong. He stared out the window, his expression sour. Poor child, he must feel like he'd heard these squabbles a thousand times and he had no one he could tell. No mother. "Did you get your homework done, Sawyer?" She squeezed the question in quick, hoping to end the battle in the front seat. "You have a test in math today, too, don't you?"

Nolan hit the horn in a long, angry *a-oo-gah*, drowning out his son's response. He hit the brakes and the truck fishtailed and then righted itself. "Deer in the road again." His fingers drummed the wheel. "I'm not supporting that boy."

Inhaling the scent of pine air freshener and Nolan's spicy

aftershave, Leila tried to make herself small in the corner of the backseat. Sawyer continued to look out the window, the back of his head a silent barrier. Trevor whimpered. She hushed him. She didn't want to be privy to this argument between father and daughter any more than Sawyer or Trevor did.

She didn't understand why Englisch kids went to school so long, especially if they were going to have jobs like working in a hardware store or a day care. Book learning wasn't much use when it came to diapering a baby or loading a truck with baling wire.

On the other hand, she didn't understand having a baby before becoming mann and fraa either. Her district frowned on that, as did Scripture. Nolan didn't look too happy about it either. Yet she saw no sign he'd turned to the Lord for help. There had been a time the Beale family had attended church. Without Lois Beale to guide them, they seemed to have lost their way. She longed to remind them Gott was still there.

Was it her place to do that? Leroy would say to hush up and lead by example, not to judge, and not to be so prideful as to think she knew the way.

The sound of sniffles wafting from the front seat told her Rory was crying. Her friend's head swiveled toward her father. "You wouldn't have to support him. Dwayne works." She sounded as if she were begging him for something. "He wants to be a good husband and father."

"Twenty hours a week, minimum wage isn't going to support a wife and baby."

"If you'd let us quit school—"

"No one quits school." Nolan's face turned brick red. His gaze met Leila's in the rearview mirror. "That was the deal when you got married. This argument's done been had."

"You started it." Rory sounded like Leila's sisters, picking at each other while washing dishes and cleaning the kitchen after supper. "Not me."

"You could be studying for that test right now."

"I'm ready for it." Rory scooted around in the seat to look at Leila, her tone suggesting the argument had indeed come to an end. Tears stained her red cheeks. "So tell me, have you heard any more from Jesse since your big date?"

Ever since Rory had first met Leila at the Combination Store, she'd been on a mission to help Leila find true love—just as she claimed to have done at the age of sixteen. She'd been suitably impressed with Leila's story of her first outing with Jesse and pooh-poohed Leila's concern about the kiss. Everyone kissed on the first date, according to Rory. Leila suspected that attitude had been the one that sent Rory on the road that had her juggling motherhood with history tests.

"Come on, give. What's up on the Jesse front? Give it up!"

Leila took a bite of her bread and chewed, trying to ignore the sudden heat that bloomed on her cheeks when she thought of that first date.

"You're blushing!" Rory chortled so loud Trevor's lower lip curled down and his chubby face scrunched up in that look that often preceded loud squalls. "Spill it. Come on!"

"You're okay, you're okay." Leila rubbed Trevor's tiny chest. She glanced at the back of Nolan's salt-and-pepper hair cropped short on his head. He seemed consumed with the market reports on something called hog futures and milo and wheat recounted by an announcer with a gruff voice. "No, not a word. I think he decided I wasn't worth the trouble. After all, we argued on the first . . . date."

"Men! They're such pigs." Rory's short brown curls bounced as she wiggled in her seat. "Not Dwayne. He's the best. He took me to a nice restaurant last night in George West for our first anniversary."

"What he spent on you yesterday should've been spent on diapers." Nolan, like Mudder, seemed to have the ability to do five things at once and still follow three conversations. "That's how it works when a man becomes a father. Whatever money you have goes into putting food on the table and clothes on your children's backs."

Here we go again, Leila wanted to say. But she didn't. Not her place. Besides, Nolan should know. He was supporting his daughter and his grandson.

"You never liked Dwayne. You could at least give him a chance."

"I should never have let you go out with him. I knew he was nothing but trouble the first time I saw him."

"Don't you love Trevor?"

Nolan's hand slammed against the wheel. "Don't make it about the baby. I'm no monster. I'm disappointed. That's what it is. Disappointed."

"You've told me that a million times. No way to change it now."

Silence ensued, broken only by the drone of the announcer on the radio talking about the chances of rain—slim and none.

Rory swiped at her face with the back of her hand and turned toward the window. Leila stroked Trevor's rosy cheek. She worked hard at not envying her friend, but when she held Trevor the day Rory introduced her to the day-care director, his warm body snug against her chest, his sighs like music in her ears, she caught herself imagining he was her bopli.

She was nineteen and ready to be baptized, ready to be a fraa, ready to be a mother. Far more than this Englisch girl with her high school classes and her dreamy plans for going to dances with her husband who went to high school, practiced for wrestling matches, and worked in a hardware store. She tried to imagine her mudder's reaction, should she come home one day and announce a bopli on the way.

Unimaginable.

But not unforgivable. Her community believed in forgiveness for all sin.

But actions had consequences. What would they be?

She never wanted to find out.

Should it be this hard? Mudder would say the answer to that question was yes. Things that came easy weren't appreciated. Hardship honed character and developed faith.

Hers should be honed by now. Daed's death. Leaving Tennessee to come to this dirty, windswept place. Trailing after Mudder from house to house while she tried to figure out God's plan for herself. It had not been an easy time.

"For someone who went on her first real date, you don't look happy." Rory had turned in her seat so she faced Leila again. She had a smile pasted to her face despite red eyes and a red nose. "Is Jesse not the one?"

"That remains to be seen, I reckon." Love at first sight didn't exist, only a love that grew and blossomed over time. That's what Mudder said. Leila never argued, but she couldn't help but look at Deborah and Phineas and wonder if there could be more than one kind of love. They'd known each other six months when they married, and now they had a bopli on the way. Not that either one of them had mentioned that precious little fact. "He's nice, but I don't really know him yet."

Other than kissing him and holding his hand. Her cheeks burned at the memory. She wiggled in her seat, her palms sweaty.

She knew of Jesse. She knew what she saw, but she didn't know what he thought about, what he dreamed about, what he cared about. Knowing those things about a man made him a husband and not just another friend. Until she did, no more kissing and holding hands.

"Mind your ways, dochder. Gott is watching." Her mother's voice reverberated in her ears.

Gott had received an eyeful at the movie theater.

Nolan maneuvered the truck into the circle drive and under the portico that sheltered the day care's double-door entryway from the blazing sun and hot south Texas wind in the summer and rain in the winter, saving Leila from trying to explain all this to the man's wayward daughter.

Rory made quick work of removing Trevor's car seat while Leila climbed down on the other side. She adjusted the blue crocheted blanket around his roly-poly body and gave him a quick smack of a kiss on his forehead. "Be good for Miss Leila, little one. I want a good report this afternoon."

Tears welled in Rory's eyes as they had every day so far. "See you this afternoon. They have my cell phone number—"

"She knows, she knows," Nolan growled just as he had every day so far. "I'm gonna be late."

"All right, all right. Here's his bag. There's five bags of my frozen milk in there, and a new bag of diapers."

"She knows." Nolan tapped on the gas, making the engine rev. "Let's go."

"Be sure they put the bags in warm water until the milk is warm. He doesn't like my milk cold."

"I know." Leila tugged the diaper bag from her friend's hand as she had every day so far. She could only imagine having to leave her bopli in the care of others all day. As a Plain woman, she would never have to know how that felt. If she ever had a baby. "Go on before your daddy leaves you in a cloud of fumes. Have a blessed day. Trevor will be fine. I'll take good care of him."

Rory sniffed and swiped at her face with the back of her hand. "I don't know why I'll ever need to know about Texas history—"

"Rory Anne Beale."

Nolan still called his daughter by her maiden name, which spoke volumes about his acceptance of the path his daughter had chosen—or had been thrust upon by her own actions.

"It's Rory Chapman, Daddy, and you know it."

"Rory Anne."

"Yes, sir. Aye, aye, Captain!" She scurried back to the truck, pulled herself in, and slammed the door. A hairbreadth of a second later, the truck took off, leaving Leila standing in a cloud of nasty diesel fumes.

Coughing, she turned and lugged the car seat, diaper bag, and her lunch toward the door. Trevor was getting heavier by the day.

"Guder mariye."

Leila halted.

Will Glick pushed away from the red brick wall and straightened. With his blue shirt, black hat, and black pants and suspenders, he stood out like a turnip stuck in the middle of a basket of tomatoes. Parents pushed past him—women in suits, women in medical scrubs, women in prison guard uniforms, women in all manner of dress, rushing to drop off their children and get to their jobs. "I need to talk to you."

THIRTEEN

Timing was everything. Contemplating the man who towered over her, the brim of his hat hiding his eyes, Leila let the car seat rest on the sidewalk in front of the day care, her lunch box next to it. She took her time rubbing the muscle in her forearm. She needed a moment to gather her wits. What possessed Will to show up at the place where she worked simply because he needed to talk to her? Could they not talk at her house? In the evening? "What are you doing here? Shouldn't you be at the plant nursery by now?"

"I had Bob drop me off here with enough time to walk to the nursery."

Will took a step back to let Janine Martin pass, her one-year-old on her ample hip and her four-year-old trotting behind her, a tattered teddy bear clutched in her arms. The mother who ran a local real estate office nodded and Leila nodded back. Janine had forgotten to wipe toothpaste from her upper lip, her skirt appeared to be on backward, and she wore only one earring. Such was the life of a working mom in the Englisch world. "I have to get inside. The parents are dropping off. I can't be late my first week—or ever for that matter."

"Can we talk over there?" Will pointed to a cluster of spindly live oaks that shaded a fenced playscape, all bright reds, greens, and blues in the dreariness of the cloudy morning. He picked up the cooler and the diaper bag, having the good sense to know that Leila was in charge of Trevor. "I promise to make it short."

"What's this about?" She followed him as far as the cedar wood fence. "I have to clock in by six fifteen."

"I know." He settled her things on the dewy grass and took off his hat. He rubbed his fingers along the brim. "I just wanted to tell you . . . I mean . . . warn you . . . just be careful."

"Careful? Of what?"

"Of Jesse."

Jesse. What did Will know about her date with Jesse? Had the cousins talked? Had Jesse shared the intimate details of that first evening? Of the kiss? Heat blasted through her. He wouldn't. Jesse wouldn't do that to her. "What are you talking about?"

"I'm saying there's no stopping the grapevine in Bee County. I'm saying I know he took you into George West to the movies and all . . . with those *Englischers*." His Adam's apple bobbed and the cords in his neck stood out as if he gritted his teeth. "Just be careful."

And all? "Jesse is your cousin. And your friend."

"He is both."

"And yet here you are warning me off him." Anger replaced the embarrassment, equally warm on her face despite the early-morning chill in the air. "It's wrong to talk behind a person's back. I'm surprised you would do it and call yourself his friend."

A loud squawk emanated from the car seat. Apparently Trevor agreed. Or he was getting hungry already. "I have to get Trevor inside. He's likely hungry."

Will squatted and tickled the baby's cheek with his long fingers. "He's so little."

"He is and he's hungry." Trevor cooed and gurgled. Traitor. Men stuck together, at any age. "I have to go."

"I got dropped off five miles from my job to do this." Will straightened and stood, once again towering over her. "I will do it and you will hear me out. For your own good."

Will spoke like a Plain man who had a right to tell a Plain woman what to do. He wasn't her father or her husband. Or even a brother. Yet his tone commanded. She opened her mouth, then shut it.

"Jesse has strayed."

So had she. "None of us is perfect. It isn't right to judge."

"I'm not judging." Red stained Will's whiskerless cheeks like beet juice on a white towel.

"I'm warning. I don't want to see you, I mean, I don't want you, it's just that . . ."

He sounded an awful lot like she did whenever she tried to talk to Jesse about something. Tongue-tied. Words twisted. He sounded nervous, like a boy who liked a girl.

Leila stared up at him. Surely Will didn't want to step on his own cousin's territory. He couldn't have Deborah, so he settled for the middle sister? If she said no, would he try out Rebekah for size? The idea stung like a drove of bees. "Have you no shame? I have to go in. Now."

———

Will fumbled for words. He was messing this up. Just like he always did. He'd planned to simply say his piece and go about his business. He didn't expect Leila to look so much like a mother sparrow in her beige dress, black tights, and black kapp. Even with peanut butter on her face and what appeared to be a splotch of honey on her apron, she looked as if she knew what she was doing. Put her out on the field for a game of baseball or a volleyball match and she was in her element. But singings and such? She tripped over the bench leg or hit a high note whenever everyone else sang low. She always had a stain on her dress or a wrinkled kapp. Not like her sisters, Deborah and Rebekah, who always looked so pretty and neatly put together. Leila might not be the most social girl, but she knew the important stuff. How to hush a baby.

Maybe she didn't need his advice or his warning. Maybe he had the wrong idea about her.

She undid the straps on the car seat and lifted Trevor into her arms. Will had never seen a woman look more . . . motherly as she cooed and shushed the fussy baby. Instead of searching for words, he found himself mesmerized by the dimples that appeared when she smiled at Trevor and the soft timbre of her voice as she uttered the silly baby language all women seemed to know instinctively. She might not be the fairest of the girls who came to the singings, but there was something about her. Something about her nature. He couldn't quite put his finger on it. She made him want to do . . . something.

She glanced up at him, the fact that she'd caught him staring obvious in her startled expression. "I said I'm going in."

"You have peanut butter on your cheek." The words came out in a stutter. He raised his hand and dabbed at the spot. The rosy red of her cheeks deepened. Her skin was soft and warm. "Got it."

"I was in a big hurry." She swiped at her face with the back of her hand. Now she looked downright miserable. He hadn't meant to embarrass her. She wouldn't meet his gaze. "I didn't want to keep Rory's dad waiting."

"It was just a smidgen. If you're planning to spend more time with Jesse, be careful." He jumped in, wanting to save her any more explanation. "He's a little . . . lost right now and it would be easy to get lost with him."

"He wasn't the one smoking behind Leroy's barn after the wedding." She tucked the blanket around Trevor's tiny feet clad in apple-red socks. "He's not the one who kept silent when the bishop asked what was going on."

"I know, I was there." She didn't know the whole story and Will couldn't tell her, not without betraying the confidence of his best friend. "I've said my piece. Just be careful."

"Jesse's nice." She laid Trevor back in the car seat and picked it up. "Careful of what?"

Jah, Jesse was nice. But he trod on a dangerous path. One that could take him away from his family and his community, and that included Leila. "Just what I said. Be careful."

"Of what?" She was back to being peeved at him. "Come out and say what's on your mind instead of hippity hopping around it like a jackrabbit on a bed of coals."

She had a way with words. "I can't tell you anything more. Just be careful."

"Will Glick, you've said that about five times now. You're not making any sense." She slipped past him, her shoulders slumped against the weight of the car seat. "If I didn't know any better, I'd think you were jealous. What kind of man tries to wave a girl away from his best friend?"

"That's not what I'm doing."

"Sure looks that way. Why do you feel the need to warn me about a man you went to school with all the way through eighth grade?"

"I can't explain. I promised." Stupid promise.

"Promised what?"

"Not to tell."

Without another word, she tugged the diaper bag from his hand, looped the strap over her shoulder, and relieved him of her lunch cooler.

"Leila."

"I have to get this baby inside and I have to get to work. You should do the same."

"Just do me one favor."

"What?"

"I may not be able to tell you why I'm so . . . worried, but Jesse can. Ask him one question."

"Ask him what?"

"Ask him where he goes every Wednesday night. Ask him if he plans to be baptized this spring."

"That's two questions."

"They're part and parcel of the same thing."

She chewed her lip. "Where does he go on Wednesday night?"

Will shoved his hat down to shade his eyes from the sun. "Just ask him."

"Maybe I will. Or maybe I'll mind my own business. Like people should." She shoved through the door with her shoulder and disappeared from sight.

Will glared at the door. A skinny man dressed in a prison guard uniform with redheaded, toddler-sized girls dangling under both long arms jostled past him, forcing Will to move from the busy sidewalk.

He'd done what he could, but it didn't feel like enough. Leila wouldn't want anything to do with him anytime soon, and if she told Jesse about it, his cousin most likely would feel the same.

Sighing, he started the long walk to the nursery. His daed would call this a fool's errand and Will had played the role of fool. A Plain man who took a Plain woman aside in broad daylight outside an Englisch day care didn't have his head on straight.

This thing with Jesse had him off kilter. He had to do whatever it took to get Jesse back on track. He wasn't just his cousin; he was his friend. That was more important than his feelings for Leila. Jesse liked Leila. That made her out-of-bounds.

Period.

It couldn't be allowed to matter that Will had a picture of Leila in his head, the likes of which he couldn't shake.

Leila Lantz with a baby in her arms and peanut butter on her cheek.

FOURTEEN

No fuss, no muss. Leila grabbed baby Kaitlin's kicking feet with one hand, tucked the diaper under her, and quickly fitted it around her rotund belly. These disposable diapers had a knack to them. They were easy to use. But they cost a pretty penny. More than a Plain woman would spend when she could wash diapers and reuse them again and again.

"You're too cute for words." Inhaling the scent of baby wipes and diaper-rash cream, she blew raspberries on the white patch of belly above the diaper. "Did you know that, pumpkin?"

The baby crowed with laughter, her tiny hands flailing.

"You have a way with her."

Leila turned at the low voice. Kaitlin's father stood a few feet from the changing table, one hand on a Bee County EMS cap with the bill twisted to the back. His words held a hint of something she couldn't fathom. Like the sudden, unexpected pain of accidentally touching a hot stove. She forced a smile. "All babies love to have their tummies tickled."

He didn't return the smile. "I suppose."

"She's fed and changed. Is she headed home early today?"

He lifted the hat from his head. Tufts of his dark brown hair stood at attention. "Yep. I had a thing at the courthouse. No sense in going back to the station this late in my shift."

Tom Fletcher was an emergency medical technician, according to Rory, who felt it necessary to give Leila the life story of every parent and every child every chance she got. Tom's wife had skipped town when Kaitlin was a newborn. Rory claimed she suffered from a bad case of postpartum depression, which made her leaving a good thing for Kaitlin. Leila couldn't imagine how a mother leaving her baby could be classified as a good thing, ever.

"Kaitlin's very happy to see you."

She held the little girl out to her father. Kaitlin immediately began to wail.

"Funny, that's mostly what she does at home. Cry." His frown belied the word *funny*. His fisted hands slipped into the pockets of jeans washed enough times to be a pale blue. He took a step back, leaving the baby dangling in Leila's hands. "I keep hoping I'll get better at it, but I guess that's wishful thinking."

His crestfallen look hurt Leila's heart. "Don't you worry. All babies fuss. It doesn't matter who takes care of them, mother or father—"

"We'll never know, I guess. Kaitlin doesn't have a mother, but I guess you probably already knew that. The grapevine is lightning fast in this town."

"She still has a mother even if she's not—"

"She's never coming back and it doesn't matter if she does. A judge just gave me sole custody." His voice broke on the last word. He shook his head, his almond eyes dark with emotion over the black stubble of a five o'clock shadow. "I'm it and I don't have a clue."

Leila held Kaitlin to her chest, pressing her close to her heart, feeling for the baby and for the man in front of her. What did a woman say to something so heartbreaking? This job taking care of babies appeared to require more of her than she'd thought. "I don't know, Mr. Fletcher—"

"Tom. Mr. Fletcher is my father."

He swiped at his face with the back of his sleeve. He seemed to be waiting for her to explain to him how he would do this. How would he do this? "Babies just want to be loved. They want their diapers changed, they want to be fed and warm, but mostly they just want to be loved." She held up Kaitlin. "From the looks of this little roly-poly pumpkin, she's getting everything she needs."

He cocked his head. "She does look healthy, doesn't she?"

"And happy." Leila held her out again. "Go on, take her. She wants to do some loving on her daddy."

Kaitlin cooed this time, right on cue. Leila breathed a sigh of relief when Tom took the baby, her head resting in the crook of his arm. She giggled and burrowed into his shoulder, trying to pull herself up. "She acts like she has ants in her pants."

"She's six months old. She's ready to explore the world."

He nodded. "Thank you."

"For what?"

"For listening. And for taking care of my baby girl."

"It's my job."

"Yeah, but you seem to take extra joy in it." He rubbed Kaitlin's Onesie with a hand almost as big as her back. "Maybe you could help me out."

"Help you out?"

"Yeah, it seems like she always gets a rash on her bottom. I wonder if I'm doing something wrong, you know, and she spits up a lot after her bottle, and should I be giving her cereal right now? I've heard the mothers at the park talking about giving their babies cereal at night so they sleep longer. The good Lord knows I could use more uninterrupted sleep—"

Leila held up a tube of diaper-rash ointment and her hand at the same time, hoping to stem the rush of his words. "Be sure to change her before bed, and every time you feed her, check to see if the diaper is wet. It's about prevention, that's what I always say." A squawk from behind her told her one of her other babies was waking up. "As far as spitting up, all babies do that and my mother always said wait until the baby can sit up on his own to feed him cereal, but you folks usually ask your doctor that kind of question."

"Good, yeah, that's good, true."

He started toward the door, Kaitlin on one hip. Leila leaned over to pick up Joshua, who had creases on one side of his face from the sheet and smelled like he needed his diaper changed.

"Do you do house calls?"

Startled, she scooped the fussy baby up and turned. Tom had padded back across the room, his sneakers soundless on the tile. He stood within arm's reach. She took a step back and settled Joshua against her chest. "Sorry, what?"

He shifted Kaitlin to his other hip and tucked the strap of her diaper bag on his shoulder. "I could use someone to watch her at the house while I get some things done. It seems like I never get the dishes clean or the laundry and I haven't had a decent night's sleep since Diane—that's Kaitlin's mother—left."

His hangdog expression ate at her heart. "I'm sorry, Mr. Fletcher—"

"Tom, please."

"Tom, I can't. This is a full-time job and my mother needs me at home when I'm not working. I reckon Miss Sally could refer someone to you—"

"Kaitlin already knows you."

"That's nice of you to say—"

"Leila?"

She looked beyond Tom to Sally, the center's director. She looked none too pleased. "Yes, ma'am?"

"Just checking in. Tom, is there something I can do for you?"

"No, no, Leila was just giving me some advice about Kaitlin's diaper rash."

Sally pursed thin lips, her expression sharp behind blue-rimmed glasses with lenses so thick, her eyes seemed to bulge. "Leila is new and she still has a lot to learn, but she does seem to have a knack with the babies."

"Kaitlin sure likes her."

Sally wrinkled her nose in disapproval. She did that a lot. How could being good with babies be a bad thing for a day-care worker? Sally gave Tom a bright smile. "Did you need anything else?"

"No, no, just headed out."

He smiled at Leila and strode past Sally without looking back.

Sally waited, arms crossed, head cocked, until he was gone. "Keeping a professional distance from our parents is an important skill to learn." She straightened and picked her way through jumpers and Bumbo seats to where Leila stood. "Do you understand what that means?"

Leila tugged Joshua's pants down and unbuttoned his Onesie. "Yes, ma'am."

"That means when one of the children's fathers comes on to you, you back off and let him know you're not interested."

"Comes on to me?" Heat toasted her cheeks. "Tom just wanted some advice, that's all."

"*Mr. Fletcher* is a lonely man in a stressful situation. He's drowning and he's looking for a life preserver."

"I don't even know how to swim." Leila kept her tone firm but polite as she made quick work of removing Joshua's sodden diaper. She glanced up at her new boss. "Changing diapers and burping babies, that's what I know how to do."

"Good." Sally tapped the lever on the diaper pail with one white sneaker-clad foot. Her nose wrinkled. "Your pail needs emptying. And make sure you sanitize it after."

"Yes, ma'am."

She waited until Sally marched from the room to take a deep breath and let it out. Tom Fletcher hadn't been "coming on to her" as her boss put it. He'd been sweet and sad and he needed her advice. He needed a friend and he loved his baby. They had that in common. She wouldn't be rude to a man so sad. She would pray for him, for Kaitlin, and for Kaitlin's mom.

Any woman who could run away and leave behind a baby needed lots of prayers.

FIFTEEN

A trailer park was the last place Jesse expected to be on a Wednesday night. He leaned through the open window of Colton's Impala and stared at the rusty double-wide resting on cinder blocks. It had a set of spindly wooden steps pressed up against the edge under a dinted door, with a gap between them big enough for a toddler to fall through. A naked overhead bulb did little to throw light on the narrow gravel drive where a gray van sat, its windshield cracked and paint bubbling.

He pulled his head in and swiveled in his seat to look at Colton. His friend had a fox-ate-the-chicken look on his thin, acne-scarred face that warned Jesse. Colton, who had said he needed to make a stop on the way to church, was up to something no good. "What are we doing here? I thought we were headed to youth group. Are we picking up Tiffany here?"

Colton shoved the gear in Park and turned the key. The engine ceased to rumble, leaving behind a soft *tick, tick* sound. He leaned back in his seat and tossed the keys in one hand, *jingle-jingle* joining the *tick, tick* in an annoying melody. The scent of his cologne mixed with burnt oil and exhaust fumes. "We'll meet Tiffany at youth group later. We have a meeting here first."

"Here where?" They usually met at Tiffany's or Colton's house and then went to the Dairy Queen to give pamphlets to the other teenagers who were busy gobbling down ice cream so fast they always whined about brain freezes. The youth group meetings were fun, but he hadn't gone any further than that. He hadn't attended a service. Not yet. "One of the guys lives here?"

"Not exactly. This is Matthew Plank's place. His father, Levi, is one of you folks—"

"I know who he is." Jesse smacked his fist against the door frame. "I can't."

"He and his family have been coming to services. Not regular, but now and again. Y'all need to talk."

"No. I can't."

"Just because the rest of your folks aren't talking to him and his brother doesn't mean you can't. Hear his side of the story."

"I can't. It's not permitted. He's shunned."

Meidnung was an act of love. An intentional act designed to bring a wayward child back into the fold. That's what his daed said. It wasn't punishment, even if it felt like it. It was also meant to protect the other members of the community from being led astray by that wayward child.

Colton picked up his Bible from the dash and smoothed one hand over the leather cover. "He loves Jesus enough to leave his father and his mother and his other brothers to follow Him. Luke 14:26–27." He offered the book to Jesse. "See for yourself."

Blood pounding in his ears, Jesse hunched down in his seat. Colton loved to do this. Pin him against the wall, challenging him, knowing he didn't have the knowledge of Scripture his friend did. He had his own Bible, with its English and German translations, but he didn't need to study it. He'd been attending church services his whole life. His daed shared the Word, along with Andrew, when it was his turn. "I don't need to see."

"'If anyone comes to me and does not hate father and mother, wife and children, brothers and sisters—yes, even their own life—such a person cannot be my disciple.'" Colton recited the verse without opening the book. "Look it up."

The unspoken question hung in the air.

Did Jesse love Jesus enough? That's the way Tiffany and Colton looked at it. Jesse's Plain district didn't have Sunday school. They did things differently. Who was right? Did God care about their human-made rules? Jesse inhaled and caught the acrid scent of trash burning in a barrel somewhere nearby. "I don't hate my mother and father. I thought we weren't supposed to hate anyone."

"I asked Pastor Dave about it, and he said that was Jesus' way of saying you have to put God first above everything else." Colton laid the Bible on the console between them. "Be willing to give up everything, even family."

"We put God above everything. Joy—Jesus first, others second, you third. It's one of the first things children learn in our community." As usual, Jesse found himself grappling for words. Why couldn't he be more like his father, who never faltered in those endless three-hour sermons? "Look at the way we live. Just so we don't slide into the evil ways of the world."

"And what about being fishers of men? Winning the lost and making disciples?"

Sometimes it seemed as if Colton spoke a foreign language. English was hard enough, but this stuff, Jesse couldn't fathom. "What?"

"Your people don't evangelize."

This Jesse knew how to answer. He listened—most of the time—to his daed's sermons. "We set an example by our ways. We are light to His feet and a lamp unto the world."

"And that's very good. I respect that." Colton touched the Bible again as if looking for words there. "But sometimes it's not enough. Sometimes people need to be invited in. They need someone to reach out and say, 'Hey, come on in.' That's what we do. Jesus calls us to be fishers of men."

Just as Colton and Tiffany had done for Jesse. They'd invited him in. Jesse didn't want to argue with Colton. Colton would win. He had years of practice and a way with words far greater than Jesse, who'd never had to defend his faith or his way of life in what felt like a physical fight. "I know you're trying to help, but you're putting too much pressure—"

"It's a big deal. There are people out there who need saving. It's the most important work you will ever do."

"I need time."

"Just listen to what Matthew has to say. He really wants to see you. Talk to you."

"He could come home. Then we could talk whenever he wants. The community will take him and his family back anytime. He knows that."

"He just has to repent of his sin and promise never to do it again?"

"Something like that."

"He hasn't sinned. He's closer to God than he's ever been."

"When he was baptized, he committed himself to our way of life, our rules. He drives a van and uses electricity and sends his kids to public school. His fraa—wife—doesn't even cover her head anymore."

"And that's sinful? You think we're sinful—me and Tiffany and Greg and Sophie and Louis and the other guys in youth group?"

Jesse struggled with the question. He was no bishop. He'd read more Bible and talked more Scripture since walking into the first youth group meeting two months ago than he had in his entire life. He'd always relied on his daed and Mordecai and Andrew to steer him in the right direction, to steer all of them toward a godly life. They had the Ordnung. If they followed the rules and kept God at the center of their lives, they would be fine. They were obedient and humble and hardworking, asking nothing of others, doing no harm to others. "Electricity and cars are not sinful themselves." He could say that much. "But the more we're connected with the world, the more we become like it. That leads to sin."

According to Daed.

"Do you know that for sure, or did someone tell you it did?"

Colton liked asking questions to which he already knew the answers. Jesse breathed in and out, in and out. Maybe this was his chance to talk Matthew into coming home. Maybe this was God's way of sending him into the fray. "Fine. We talk for a few minutes and then you give me a ride home or I'll hitchhike."

"I would never let you do that." Colton grinned, his face alight with the thought that he'd won this particular scrimmage. "What kind of friend do you think I am? Besides, we still have youth group after."

The kind of friend who had the best of intentions but didn't know how to let up.

Colton shoved his door open and loped around the car as if he had known all along Jesse would capitulate. He hated to think he was that predictable. With much greater hesitation, he opened his door and slid out. He marched up steps so wobbly he put out his hand to steady himself. Colton already had the door open.

Little Sarah, Matthew's youngest girl, peeked out, her eyes wide, curly blonde hair snarled in a rat's nest, face smeared with what looked like blueberry jam. She waved with both hands and then stuck a thumb in her mouth.

"Sarah, get back! You know better. Scoot, girl." Matthew scooped her up with one arm and held her football style, legs dangling, as he waved them in. "Welcome. Jesse, it's good to see you."

Feet planted on a welcome mat crowded with an assortment of work boots, Jesse said nothing. The darkness of the trailer, lit by only one electric lamp and a bulb over the kitchen sink, was at odds with the smell of chili and fresh-baked bread. It still smelled like home. His father wouldn't agree. It couldn't be their true home. Daed's disapproving face hovered in his mind's eye. Not following the Ordnung cost them a great deal. It cost them their community.

It had to be that way, Daed had told him on more than one occasion. The terrible possibility existed that others would be infected by this rebellion, by these worldly ways. Then they would all succumb.

That was the word Daed had used. *Succumb. Wither and die.*

"It's okay. Come in. Have a seat." Matthew waved his hand toward a sofa covered by an orange and red crocheted comforter. His four boys, stepping-stones a year apart from five to nine, scooted down, their freckled faces bright with anticipation and curiosity. They wore T-shirts and faded jeans and assorted colors of dirty sneakers. Jesse sank onto the edge of the couch, not leaning back.

"Are you our cousin?" the oldest asked, his face turning candy-apple red at his own impertinence. "Are you a Plank?"

They didn't know. It had been so long since their parents left the community, they didn't know their own family's members. The Planks had since moved back to Ohio, only returning to Bee County once to try to talk some sense into their two sons. To no avail. Their stoic faces as they loaded into the van that would take them to the bus station in George West were still burned on Jesse's brain.

"No, he's not a Plank. This here's Jesse Glick." Matthew rescued Jesse. He plopped into a plastic lawn chair, leaving Colton to squeeze into a rocker, the only other chair in the long, narrow living room that ended in a kitchenette on one side and a dark hallway on the other. His boys might dress Englisch, but Matthew still wore a blue work shirt, suspenders, and black pants. The exterior hadn't changed, but the interior of the man had. "He's family, all the same."

Jesse cleared his throat. Words clogged it. And an emotion that surprised him. He had liked Matthew. They'd played together as kids. His absence had been keenly felt by all of them. He nodded at the boys, then ducked his head to study the matted carpet of no particular color under his scuffed boots.

"Colton wanted me to talk to you." Matthew didn't sound any fonder of the idea than Jesse felt. "I told him you can't push a person into this. A person has to come willingly. He has to be willing to pay the price."

Jesse forced himself to meet Matthew's gaze. He sucked in air and nodded. "On that, we agree."

"I know you think we must be suffering something awful." Matthew tugged at his ragged beard with a big, calloused hand.

"But we're not. We have Jesus. He's all we need. We've gotten used to the other."

Used to the other. The not having family anymore. How did a person get used to that, exactly?

And what did it mean to have Jesus? Didn't they all have Jesus? They had the Bible. They had Sunday services. They prayed. What made Matthew and Ruth special? Jesse gritted his teeth and studied the carpet. It had a rip right at the spot where the sofa leg punished it under his weight.

"You're not going to hell for looking at me."

The amusement in Matthew's voice did nothing to improve Jesse's mood. He jerked his head up and let his friend—ex-friend— see his scowl.

Matthew smiled, but the sadness in his eyes relayed another message.

"It's not something I can explain. It's not knowledge." He touched his chest with two fingers in the vicinity of his heart. "It's something I experienced. I'm at peace now. Me and Ruth, we're at peace with our decision."

Peace. That sounded good. Jesse tried to remember the last time he felt at peace. The memory came to him with quick, painful clarity. The darkness, the rush of the wind through the cracked window in Colton's Impala. Leila's hand in his, her eyes closed, her head against his shoulder, her expression peaceful and trusting in sleep. His throat ached at the thought. He stood. "I shouldn't be here."

"I know you're torn." Matthew rose as well, Sarah still dangling from one arm. She wiggled so she could bury her face in her daddy's shoulder. He nuzzled the top of her head with his beard. "But you haven't been baptized yet. It's different for you. You won't be shunned."

"No, but if I choose not to be baptized, my family will be shamed. My father is the bishop."

"It's a hard road, but it's worth it to be able to think freely and worship freely."

"I do that now."

"You think you do, but you don't. They tell you what to think. They tell you to be quiet. They tell you not to think on your own."

His daed did say it was better to listen more and talk less. Nothing wrong with that. "That's not the way I see it."

"Angus and I are doing good with our carpentry work. We have more houses to fix up than we can handle. We can always use another set of hands and a strong back."

"I have a job at the store."

"That pays you nothing. How will you raise a family?"

The same way his father and grandfather did. Sharing in the work and in the profit. He shook his head at Colton, hoping his friend could read his thoughts. He never should have come here. He put his hand on the doorknob.

"Don't go yet!" Ruth hustled from the hall at the other end of the narrow room. She carried a baby in each arm. "I was just changing Esther and Mary, our newest additions."

Ruth looked the same. She still wore a long gray dress and an apron, but her hair hung down her back in one thick braid. If they were going to drive cars and use microwaves, why not dress like the Englischers? She smiled up at him, still a pretty woman despite the dark smudges under her eyes and a roundness that spoke of giving birth recently.

"Congratulations." His tone sounded churlish, even to him. "They're healthy?"

"Almost five pounds apiece. And their lungs work real

good." Matthew laughed. "Keep us up half the night with their caterwauling."

Ruth chuckled. One of the babies began to fuss. She handed one bundle to the oldest boy, pulled the other one up on her shoulder, and began to pat her back. "I just wanted to say hey. Tell your mama I miss her pecan pie. No one makes it like her." Her caramel-colored eyes seemed to beseech him. "I make it all the time, but it's just not the same."

Did her words hold a hidden message? Jesse couldn't be sure. He did know he couldn't tell his mudder about this visit. She would have to tell Daed. The bishop. He'd have to explain why he'd come here and talked to these folks who were shunned. He nodded and touched the brim of his hat.

Ruth's smile faltered. "She's well? Everyone's good?"

He nodded.

Her features dimmed into something he did recognize. He'd seen it on his own face reflected in the mirror behind the bar at Carl's Grill, where Colton and Tiffany liked to go for burgers, fries, and pool on Saturday night. Resignation. The baby in her arms yawned, her pink rosebud lips opening wide. "It was good to see you, Jesse. Real good. Come on, boys. Time to get ready for bed. Ten minutes till prayer time."

The boys popped off the couch in quick succession without so much as a murmur. They traipsed past Jesse, grinning, the two younger ones pushing and shoving while the older one sang "Jesus Loves the Little Children" off-key to the baby. The youngest boy plowed to a stop. "Do you ride a horse to work?"

He shook his head. "I drive a buggy."

"I like horses."

"To bed." Matthew set Sarah down on her feet, gave the boy's bottom a playful slap, and sent both on their way. "They like horses. No place to have one around here."

They would never be close to horses, not as long as they lived in a trailer park. Most likely they would never be farmers. Matthew must've followed his train of thought. "I figure they'll make up their own minds about what to do with their lives once they're older."

"You'd let them come home, then, if they wanted?"

"They are home." Matthew held the door open and nodded at Colton as he passed through first. "But I am for people making up their own minds about how they live their lives and about how they worship."

"Even if they decide to worship as Plain folks?"

"As long as they get a chance to make that decision for themselves."

"Isn't that what rumspringa is for?"

"That's what they say. But if you make the so-called wrong decision, look what happens." He waved his hand around the trailer. "I ain't heard from my parents in three years. I sent them a card to tell them about the twins. They never answered."

"They can't." Jesse clomped down the stairs, hoping they didn't collapse under his weight, and turned to look up. "It's not because they don't love you. It's because they do."

"My point exactly." Matthew put one hand on the door frame and leaned against it. "It doesn't make sense. I believe all the same things you do. I live by the gospel. I believe Jesus is my Lord and Savior. Why shun me?"

Jesse stared up at the other man. Why? A reason existed, surely it did. At this moment, with only a naked lightbulb illuminating the soft mist that had begun to fall, wetting his face, he couldn't think what it was. "Good-bye."

He folded his legs into the car and locked the door as if whatever pursued him would try to squeeze in next to him.

No locks could keep his thoughts out.

SIXTEEN

Of all the holidays, Thanksgiving had the best smells. Leila eased the pumpkin pie from the oven, the heat singeing her eyebrows and toasting the tip of her nose. The aroma of turkey fresh from the second oven mixed with the pumpkin spices. Her mouth watered. She turned and displayed the pie with the golden, fluted crust to the dozen or more women crowded into the kitchen her mudder and Susan now shared in Mordecai's house.

This was the first year Mudder had let her be in charge of the pies. Deborah had the potatoes and gravy, and Rebekah helped with the breads. The cranberry sauce belonged to the younger girls who took turns cranking the hand grinder attached to the table. For some reason they found the sight and sounds of squishing cranberries, apples, and oranges hilarious. Mudder had them washing the prep pots and pans now to keep them out of trouble.

"That looks beautiful." Aenti Alma leaned over and sniffed, her long nose dangerously close to the hot pie tin. "Smells delicious too. Are we making whipped cream?"

"Already on it," Susan volunteered. "Can't have pumpkin pie without whipped cream."

"I need more flour for the gravy." Deborah stood at the stove, a wooden ladle in one outstretched hand. The size of her baby bump kept her from getting any closer. "We had plenty of drippings. It should have a nice flavor."

Leila set the pie on the pot holders Hazel had made and given to Mudder for Christmas the previous year. It looked lovely sitting next to the two turkeys shot by the men earlier in the week, now baked to a golden brown and ready to be carved. She reached for the canister filled with flour, opened it, and slid it toward her sister. Something smacked her in the back of the head and thudded on the floor behind her.

"Hey! Ouch!" She whirled, rubbing the spot just below her kapp. Hazel and her little cousin Emma shrieked with laughter as Hazel scrambled across the room and scooped up an apple that rolled around on the floor at Leila's feet. "Did you do that?"

Giggling, Hazel and Emma slapped their hands over their mouths, eyes wide, looking like twins. Muffled nees emanated from behind their plump fingers.

Leila grabbed an orange from the basket on the table and tossed it in the air. "Playing catch with our food?"

"Juggling," Emma piped up. She grabbed two oranges from the basket and tossed them in the air, her hands flailing. One piece of fruit stayed aloft, while the other plummeted to the floor.

Hazel grabbed it and tossed it to Leila. "Think quick."

Laughing, Leila snatched it up midair and still managed to catch her own orange. "You girls are silly willies."

"Catch, catch!" The other little girls joined in, grinning as they grabbed fruit and tossed apples and oranges around the room. "First one to let it drop loses."

"This isn't a game!" Mudder didn't sound at all cross as she caught an orange just before it hit the floor and tossed it to Esther, who neatly forwarded it in the same motion to Aenti Alma. "We have a lot of food to serve. The men are getting hungry."

"A little game of catch will help us women work up an appetite." Susan caught the toss from Alma and whirled to throw it to Deborah. "Seeing as we haven't done any work today."

Leila ducked in the same direction. Her sister had her back turned. She was busy with the gravy—and hot oil on the stove. Leila stuck out her hand and deflected the orange. The fruit slammed into the open container of flour. It plopped on its side and spilled its contents, flour blooming in a white fog that coated the counter. And Leila.

She breathed in flour and coughed.

"Let me help you!" Deborah dropped her ladle and grabbed a towel. She dabbed at the mess, spreading it down the front of the apron and adding to the layer on Leila's shoes. "Oops, maybe you should go outside and dust yourself off."

"We could hang you from the clothesline and beat you like a rug." Rebekah offered this suggestion, her face contorted with mock concern. "We'll have you cleaned up in a jiffy."

The women's giggles turned to gales of laughter. Leila looked to her mother for help. Mudder's cheeks were red and tears of laughter trickled down her face "It's not that funny."

"Dochder, you should see yourself. You look like a ghost or a snowman or a giant marshmallow."

Leila looked down at her dress and apron—all covered with flour. "Ach!" She grabbed her apron and shook it. Flour puffed into her face. More coughing. "What a—"

"I've been sent to see what all the commotion is about." Will strolled into the kitchen. He halted, mouth open for a few seconds. "I've heard of pancake makeup, but I've never seen a Plain woman going in for it."

"We were just . . ." Leila searched for words to explain such a mess. "Cooking."

"So that's the secret. The more flour on the cook, the better the food?" His gaze slid around the room to the other women. He grinned. "How come you're the only one with flour all over you?"

"The orange was about to hit Deborah so I batted it away." The words sounded ridiculous in her ears. Emma and Hazel tittered. Even *Mudder* grinned. "I mean, we were—the girls were having some fun, that's all."

"Nothing wrong with that." Will scooped up an apple from the table and tossed it in the air. It fell neatly in his enormous palm. "I just hope you made the gravy before you used all that flour on your face. I really like gravy." He turned and strode from the room, still grinning.

"Someone is in lieb." Esther nudged Susan, a grin as big as Will's on her face. "Don't you think?"

"He's not!" Leila turned her back on the other women and began sloshing water from the tub in the sink on her face and hands. It did little to cool the burn that roared across her face. He couldn't be, or she had an even bigger problem than the insurmountable one presented by Jesse. "You're imagining that."

"Nope, and from the way you're hiding your face, so are you." Susan joined in the chorus. "You've been doing a real good job of keeping it private. I didn't know y'all were courting."

"We're not." She and Will had been too busy waiting for Jesse to make up his mind. At least that's the way it looked from her perspective. "He hasn't asked me. Maybe he's never gotten over losing out to Phineas for Deborah."

Deborah laughed so hard she snorted, which made the rest of the women laugh. "It's not funny." Leila flapped a dish towel at her sister. "You have your husband."

"Will never even asked me out."

"He didn't get a chance."

"Or he wasn't all that interested. He can't ask you because he thinks his cousin is interested, that's what it is."

"Nobody is courting anybody at the moment."

"I think that's about to change." Susan, a short, round version of her brother Mordecai, swept the floor with short, hard strokes. "A man who has lost out once is not going to want to do it again, that's for sure."

Leila turned to study her. "From a one-minute conversation, you could tell all that?"

"That boy has it bad." Susan whipped the dustpan into position and swept up the flour that surrounded Leila's feet. "I suspect he'll be visiting a whole lot more."

"How can you tell?" Leila blurted the words before she could think about how they would sound. She'd let Jesse kiss her in the movie theater. How could she be thinking of Will? It was too confusing. "How do you know which person is right for you?"

"There's no hurry." Mudder smiled as she poured a quart mason jar of bread-and-butter pickles into a bowl, the pungent smell of vinegar and pickling spices adding to the piquant bouquet already floating in the air. "Just remember that. Don't let teasing from these girls sway you. You'll know when you know."

"How did you know with Mordecai?" Leila would rather know how her mother had known with *Daed*, but she didn't want to cause her pain. "I mean, how did you know it was . . . Mordecai and not Stephen."

Mudder shrugged. "I felt it in my heart. As much as I'd like to advise you differently, it doesn't matter what makes the most sense. I wish it did. It would be so much easier. It's what you feel in your heart. Like this is the person you want to commit to for the rest of your life. In fact, you couldn't do anything else."

Deborah waved her hands in front of her face, damp with a sheen of sweat, as if to cool herself. "Believe me, schweschder, you'll know. Maybe not at first, but it grows on you until you can't ignore it. You think about the person more than you want to. You look for him when you should be doing something else. He'll irritate you to no end, but you still can't get enough of his company."

Leila thought about Jesse because he'd plowed his way into her life, planted the seed with that kiss, and then bailed out on her. That wasn't love. That was meanness. Will, on the other hand, had shown up at the day care to warn her about Jesse. He wanted to protect her heart.

Or he wanted it for himself. Maybe Will acted as if he wanted to say something, but he didn't because he was too honorable to horn in on Jesse.

Which left her alone at the singings. Caught between cousins, neither of whom had made his intentions clear.

"Doesn't sound like much fun," Alma observed, saving Leila from having to speak. "I'm thinking I'll do like Susan and become a schoolteacher."

Susan, with her book-learning smarts and keen sense of humor, seemed perfectly happy never to have married. She taught her scholars and took care of her brother, Mordecai, and his kinner after his first fraa died. Then Mudder came along and took her place. Leila examined Susan's face for signs she regretted her life. Not an iota. "It's not up to you." Susan emptied the flour into the trash can and balanced the broom against the wall next to it. "Gott's will, Gott's plan."

Leila tried to find it in her rebellious heart to accept this fact. She gritted her teeth until her jaw ached.

"Amen." Esther smoothed back black hair that had escaped her kapp, a dreamy look on her face as if she were seeing something none of the rest of the women could share in. Another shorter, rounder version of Mordecai. "I can't wait to become Adam's fraa."

She only had a few weeks to go. Without moving, Leila swatted away the ugly green bugs of jealousy that bombarded her at the thought. *Praise Gott for Esther and Adam's happiness.*

Praise Gott. Through hardship and suffering and pain. *Praise Gott.*

"Fun is making Leila dump flour on herself." Hazel took a bite of her apple, her nose crinkling, chewed with a crunch, and swallowed. "That's the most fun."

Everyone laughed. Except Leila. She wasn't having much fun at all. This love thing was a thorn in her side. She longed to pluck it out.

Gott wasn't known for plucking thorns from sides.

Give me a sign, Gott—please give me a small sign.

SEVENTEEN

Oh, for a wheelbarrow and someone to push her to her bed. Leila patted her full stomach and eased onto the front step. *Thank You, Gott, for such bounty.* A puff of flour settled around her, reminding her of the fun they'd had preparing the food. *Thank You, Gott, for family. Every day, not only today.* Even with the painful turn in the conversation, she was blessed to have family and friends. The rest of her problems would have to wait. Today was a day for enjoying family and counting blessings.

By the time they had the food on the table, she'd been hungry enough to eat a cow by herself. Or maybe she ate to console herself. Mashed potatoes and gravy were called comfort food, after all. Fresh air might help her overcome the desire to nap. Otherwise, she'd lay her head down on the prep table in the kitchen and go to sleep in half a second. Turkey, two servings of cornbread stuffing, mashed potatoes, gravy, corn, green beans, beets, a roll, and a gigantic piece of pie would see to that.

"You have flour on your kapp."

Leila slapped her hand on the back of her head. She raised her other hand to her forehead to shield her eyes from a gorgeous afternoon sun that took the November chill from the air. Will Glick towered over her. She dropped her hand and switched her gaze to the corral. "What are you doing out here? How come you're not playing kickball with the others out back?"

"Twisted my ankle the other day." He plopped down on the step next to her, a little too close for her liking as a matter of fact. She leaned away. He grinned. "Besides, if I run around after eating all the food, I'll probably hurl."

"Nice."

He shrugged. "It's a day for being lazy."

"A day for being thankful."

"I am thankful." He dug at his front teeth with a toothpick, his expression thoughtful. "Thankful my daed accepted the invitation to have Thanksgiving with the Mordecai Kings."

Leila hadn't been so keen on the idea after her strange encounter with him at the day care not so long ago. After Susan's observations in the kitchen, Leila couldn't help but feel even more awkward. Was Mordecai's sister right? Did Will have intentions toward her? How she wished she could come right out and ask him. Life would be so much simpler. "It's nice to share a meal, isn't it?"

"Especially when the Mordecai Kings include you."

The tiniest bit of hope fluttered through her. Maybe Susan was right. Will hovered around the edges at the singings. Sometimes she caught him staring at her with a look she couldn't decipher. Almost like worry. He was worried for her.

Jesse, on the other hand, hadn't been to a singing since their trip to George West to the movies. He hadn't made a single appearance at her door either. Not a word after church services. Not even a note. Heat scorched her cheeks. She'd given Jesse her first kiss. She should've saved it for someone who thought she was special. Someone she considered special.

Maybe that man was Will.

Will's shoulder touched hers. "Are you cold?"

She leaned away. "What?"

He cocked his head, his forehead wrinkled, eyebrows lifted. "Your face is all red. It's not that cold out. Cold for south Texas, but that's not saying much."

"Nee. I just ate too much."

"Me too. Want to take a ride?"

"What?"

"Is your hearing going?" His face was the one red now. "It's hard enough to ask once. Don't make me ask twice."

"You're asking me to take a buggy ride with you?"

"Actually, I brought the two-seater. I came on my own today. If you don't want to, that's—"

He'd planned to ask her out. He brought his own ride just so he could ask her to step out with him. If her face had been red before, it surely was the color of an overly ripe tomato now. "I do, I do, I'm just surprised. What about Jesse?"

Again with the blurting out of words. When would she learn to hold her tongue?

Will looked around with exaggerated care. "I don't see him here. I ain't seen him anywhere near you in two weeks."

"You've been watching?"

He ducked his head and picked up a stray twig, which he proceeded to worry with both hands. "Not trying to mind the business of others or anything."

"Nee, why were you watching? Why don't you just ask him? Did you ask him?"

She wanted to know what Jesse was thinking. More than anything, she wanted to know.

"We're not talking much right now."

"Why?"

"It's—"

"Personal, I know."

Leila swiped a side glance at him. His pulse pumped in his temple as his jaw jutted. He had a nice, strong jaw and white, even teeth. And he was here, now, and asking her to take a ride with him. "Jah."

He tossed the twig on the ground and swiveled his head so their gazes met. "Jah what?"

"I'd like to take a ride with you."

"Jah?" The consternation fell away, replaced by a genuine smile. "Are you certain?"

"Better hurry before my mudder notices I'm not in the kitchen cleaning up."

"There's at least a dozen women in there. You won't be missed." He stood and swept a hand toward the row of buggies on the other side of the dirt and gravel road that cut in front of the house. "I'm ready to roll."

———

The *clip-clop* of the mule's hooves on the pavement ringing in his ears, Will contemplated the endless farm-to-market road that stretched before them, brown fields of stubble on either side, sun low in the western sky. A wispy cloud huffed and puffed across the sky as if in a rush to escape the sun. He had Leila Lantz in the seat next to him, a dwindling autumn day before him, and a blank mind. Absolutely, utterly blank. He had a dark void where thought should be. He'd been planning this moment for days, since he'd come to the realization that he couldn't wait for Jesse to make up his mind. If Jesse continued down his current path, Leila would get hurt, and Will couldn't have that.

Even if it cost him his friendship with his cousin.

If Jesse chose to leave the community, Will would lose him anyway. He didn't want to lose Leila too.

As if he had her. Which of course he didn't. Not yet.

And he never would, if he didn't open his mouth and say something interesting or funny. What did girls think was interesting or funny?

"Beautiful day. Mite warm for so late in the year. Hard to believe Christmas is only a month away."

Resorting to weather. He sounded like an old man making conversation with another old man at his uncle's store.

Leila nodded and brushed back a tendril of hair that had escaped her flour-caked prayer kapp. She was such a funny girl, not caring at all about her appearance. That flour would still be there at the end of the day. He found that appealing. And her hair was the color of corn silk. He'd like to see the rest of it. Down around her shoulders.

Mortified at where his thoughts had taken him, he clamped down on his tongue until he drew blood. "Ouch."

She swiveled and gave him a look of grave concern. "What happened? Did a bee get you?"

"Nee. Bit my tongue, that's all." A feeling akin to the panic he'd felt one time when the tide almost carried him out to the Gulf from the beach at Port Aransas burbled up inside him. *Think. Think.* "I like to hunt. Deer mostly. But dove and quail too. No alligator though. Too big. And the license is expensive. What's a man gonna do with all that alligator meat and skin? Some folks make belts and boots, I reckon, but me, I . . ."

He stopped, certain the heat of embarrassment would cause his skin to burst into flames and his whole body would burn to a crisp.

Leila giggled. She slapped a hand to her mouth, but the giggles came louder. Her blue eyes widened and tears formed in the corners. "I'm sorry," she gasped. "I'm sorry. That just sounded . . ."

"Funny, I know." Will laughed too. He couldn't help it. Her laugh was contagious. So all he had to do was say stupid stuff to make her laugh. "I'm no good at this."

"Me neither."

"You do fine with Jesse."

Her smile disappeared, taking the warm, balmy sun with it.

"Sorry." Will kicked himself with an extra-large work boot. "That was a . . . stupid thing to say."

"Nee." She leaned back against the seat, staring straight ahead. "Will Glick, what are we doing?"

"Taking a ride." Determined to salvage the moment, he stuck his hand under the seat without taking his gaze from the road. He fumbled around until his fingers found the handle and he was able to produce the prize he sought. "With music."

She took the old-fashioned boom box in both hands as if it might shatter in her grasp. "Where'd you get this?"

"At the secondhand shop next to the feed store. I had my first paycheck in my hands and I thought, why not just look around a minute or two?"

"So you bought a radio?" She slid her fingers across the row of black buttons on the top with a soft, almost loving touch. Will couldn't rip his gaze from her fingers. She looked up, frowning. "Something you know you can't keep?"

He had wanted to do something a little reckless during his rumspringa, but he'd never found that thing. He didn't feel comfortable around the Englisch teenagers the way Jesse did, and he had no desire to tag along to the youth group meetings. The words *slippery slope* kept buzzing in his ears every time he thought about it. "I can keep it in the barn until I'm baptized."

"As long as your daed doesn't find it and throw it away."

"He'll do worse than throw it away; he'll stomp on it real good."

They both laughed, an uneasy sound in his ears. She nestled the radio in her lap and studied it, the tip of her tongue slipping from the corner of her mouth. "How does it run? Do you have to plug it in?"

"Nee." Delighted at the obvious interest on her face, he pointed to the Play button. "Just push that button. I already put new batteries in it. You can't get a lot of stations out here. But there's one that plays country music. The others are mostly in Spanish."

She did as he said, and sure enough, a song in Spanish blared, accompanied by the brassy sound of trumpets and accordions so loud they both jumped and laughed. The singer sounded as if he had a bellyache with all those *ay-ay-ays*. Will had heard this music before, blasting from the stores on the strip that led to the border crossing when they had to go to the doctor or the dentist. It sounded like a raucous party to him. Even though he couldn't understand the words, the songs sounded happy.

Leila grinned at him and twisted the knob until a country music song wafted from the radio, a little staticky but definitely a fine bit of music for a sunny afternoon. "Better?"

He nodded and turned left onto a dirt road that led to property belonging to one of their Englisch neighbors. He pulled the wagon into the first shady spot near a stand of gnarly mesquite trees that provided almost no shade with their fine, feathery leaves.

"What are you doing?"

"I thought we could sit and talk a little bit."

Leila tilted her head, the sparse leaves of the tree making a dappled pattern on her face as the sun played hide-and-seek in the branches overhead. Before he could get down, she hopped from her side and spun around. "What do you want to talk about?"

He hauled himself down and wrapped the reins around a branch, his back to her as he tried to think of a topic of conversation. He was awful at this. He squeezed his eyes shut and concentrated. Nothing. A fierce void.

"We have music." Her voice held a note of something . . . giddiness. He'd never thought of her as giddy. She tugged the boom box from the wagon and set it on the bedraggled grass between them. "We could dance."

Dance. He'd never danced. He had no idea how to do it. Why that? Why did she want that? He turned and faced her. "I'm not like Jesse."

Her smile disappeared once again. "Didn't say you were. If you don't want to dance with me, fine. Let's go."

Will stepped between her and the two-seater. Maybe he needed to offer her something exciting, something a little bad, like Jesse had with the movies. "I just mean, I'm not looking to experiment or anything. I just want to get to know you."

She nodded, but her eyes were bright with tears.

"What's the matter?"

"Nothing."

"You're crying."

"Am not!"

No doubt about it. A tear trickled down her cheek. She brushed it away, her lips twisted in a defiant smile.

"It's not that I don't want to dance with you—I don't know how."

"Me neither." She wrapped her arms around her middle. "Does it ever make you sad to think of all the things we won't do?"

"Nee. I'm happy thinking of the things we will do." He grasped her hands in his and placed them on his shoulders. Her eyes widened and she sniffed. She had to stand on her tiptoes to reach. "I think about getting married and having . . . kinner."

She nodded, her gaze fixed on his. Swallowing hard, he laid one hand on her waist with the same care he used when asked to hold a bopli. Her startled intake of breath forced him back a step.

"Nee." She took a quick step forward. "I think that's right."

It felt right. The curve of her hips. Her warmth. "I think so too."

The song on the radio died away, but still they swayed to the sound of the wind rustling in the trees, their gazes locked. "We're dancing," she whispered. "I think we're dancing."

"I think you're right."

She stared up at him, then slid her hand down his chest and inclined her head until it nestled against him. No doubt she could hear the hammering of his heart. It might burst through his rib cage any second. He couldn't breathe. They were dancing. He and Leila.

He moved one foot, then the other.

"Ouch!" She jerked back. "That was my foot."

"Sorry, sorry!"

"It's okay." She hopped on one foot for a second. "I don't think my toes are broken."

He let go and backed away. "Sorry. I'm a big oaf."

"No, don't stop!" She caught at his hands, placed one on her waist, and wound her fingers in the other. "Another song is start-ing. We're dancing."

So they danced, one, two, three songs. Mostly, they swayed. He was afraid to move his feet for fear of doing more damage. They didn't talk. After a while she let her forehead rest on his chest again. He memorized the top of her head dusted with flour and the curve of her cheek and savored her scent of vanilla and soap.

"What are you thinking about?" Her voice was soft, barely a whisper. "You're so quiet."

"I'm thinking about you."

She raised her head. "What about me?"

"I like the way you smell." If he could melt into the earth, he would. "I mean—"

"Thank you. It's just soap."

"You smell clean and sweet."

She leaned her head against his chest again. "I can hear your heart."

"I wish you could feel what it feels."

"What does that mean?" She kept her head down now, for which Will was eternally grateful. "What does it feel?"

"Content. Like this is how it's supposed to be."

"Dancing?"

"Nee, you and me, together."

"How do you know for sure? How does anyone know?"

"It feels good, like we could just do this forever, go on and on."

"Except we can't."

"Nee. We can't."

"Danki for this. It's nice." She tilted her head back to look at him, her face glowing in the dwindling light. "We should go back. Mudder will be looking for me."

He swallowed. He didn't want it to end, but he didn't want to spoil the moment either. Step by step. That's how these things were done. Forging a bond a little at a time. *Gott, give me enough time. Please.* "Maybe we can do it again sometime."

"Jah, I'd like that." Her cheeks turned pink again. The poor girl couldn't hide her feelings—her face gave her away every time. Her gaze drifted over his shoulder to the horizon. "I like slow. Let's just go slow. Can we go slow?"

"Slow is good." Especially when it came to dancing. He didn't want to break her foot. And he didn't want to get his own heart broken. He grabbed her hand and squeezed. He didn't want the contact to be lost. He didn't want to be far from her for any length of time. This was bad. He had it bad. Someone needed to tell his heart to go slow. "That's not a problem."

She nodded, but her gaze slipped beyond him. The soft contentment in her face fled. "Someone's coming."

Will shifted to follow her gaze. They weren't doing anything wrong. So why did his throat constrict and his lungs stop working? He leaned down, reaching for the volume knob on the boom box. They weren't doing anything wrong. He flicked the Off switch. The music died, leaving behind an odd, hollow silence broken only by the rustling of leaves in the wind. "Who is it?"

Her hand went to her forehead. She squinted against the setting sun. A deeper pink bloomed on her cheeks. She took a step back, then another. "It's Jesse."

Will's mind contemplated the words, but his body continued to think about the space that had opened up between them. So much space. He forced his gaze to the road.

Sure enough. Jesse.

EIGHTEEN

Leila smoothed her apron, sure it somehow held evidence that she'd been pressed against Will's body only seconds earlier. She would not turn a fiery red. She hadn't been doing anything wrong. Jesse never came calling a second time. Weeks had passed. He had no hold on her. She lifted her chin and waited until the buggy drew near, then graced him with a wide smile and quick wave. A normal, everyday greeting for someone she'd known for a long time now. A friend.

Jesse reined in his horse and buggy and stopped. He didn't return her greeting. He studied Will first, then her. His hands remained wrapped around the buggy reins. "What are you two doing out here?"

"None of your business." The words barreled from her mouth before she could stop them. So much for the high road. "I mean, we're stretching our legs. We both ate too much."

Will picked up the boom box and tucked it under the seat. "We were just headed back."

"Stretching your legs?" A doubtful tone mixed with a painful attempt at nonchalance in his gruff voice. "It's funny. From down the road, it looked like dancing."

"What do you care?" Again with the ugly, spiteful tone. Heat rushed through Leila. How could she be so angry with Jesse when a moment ago she'd been dancing a lovely, sweet, swaying dance with Will? Was she that shallow? Nee. She wouldn't have thought so, not until this moment. She breathed, unable to meet Will's gaze. "We were enjoying the afternoon and getting some fresh air, that's all."

Will's hand squeezed her elbow, then dropped. "Like Leila said, we were—"

"I know, stretching your legs." Jesse jerked his head toward the road. "Where everyone can see you."

"Rumspringa—"

"Doesn't mean you rub people's noses in it."

"What are you doing out here?" Will's tone was even, but the red blotches on his neck and chin crept across his face. "Just riding around on Thanksgiving Day or headed into town to see your Englisch friends?"

Jesse's face darkened to the color of an overripe tomato. "You said you wouldn't say anything."

"I haven't." Will jerked his head toward Leila. "Not a word. But I won't stand by—"

"I'm not asking you to—"

"Then go about your business and leave her out of it. Otherwise, she'll pay the price."

Leila felt like a spectator, watching two men spar. Plain men didn't spar. Not even with words. Will's words sank in. "Leave me out of what?"

Neither man looked at her, but Jesse's shoulders sagged. He ducked his head and stared at the ground. "You're right, but there's no need to rub my nose in it."

"I didn't think you'd be out here gallivanting across the country-side on Thanksgiving Day." Will didn't look at Leila either. He sounded ashamed. Ashamed of what? "It wasn't my intent to cause you . . . discomfort."

Jesse's head bobbed. "I know. It's pure happenstance."

"Or Gott's way of pointing us in a certain direction."

Jesse's face contorted in a painful grin. "Gott's will, Gott's plan."

"Right about what? What plan?" Leila studied Jesse's face, then Will's. They didn't sound angry anymore. Will looked as if he'd just lost his best horse, and Jesse grimaced as if he had a pain in his chest. They were staring at each other like they were saying good-bye forever. "Somebody tell me what's going on, please!"

Without another word, Jesse jerked the reins and guided his buggy back onto the road.

"You don't want to know." Will untied the reins from the mesquite. "Get in. It's time to go."

She climbed into the two-seater, feeling as if she no longer stood on solid ground. "I don't understand. What just happened?"

Will hopped in next to her and snapped the reins. "Some things aren't meant to be understood. Let it go."

"I can't."

"Why?"

"He kissed me." Why had she said this to Will, of all people? Because she couldn't hide her feelings from this tall, thin bundle of muscles whose hands were strong and who would never take her to a movie theater and then kiss her in an empty hallway that smelled of stale popcorn and hot dogs. He would do things in the right order and show her how to do the same. She'd never felt more sure of a fact. "I'm sorry."

Will halted the two-seater in the middle of the road. He stared at Jesse's buggy disappearing into the distance. "He shouldn't have done that."

"We shouldn't have done it. I didn't mean for it to happen. It was wrong."

"Nee." Will leaned closer. So close she thought he might touch her. "I've wanted to do nothing else all day."

Leila shrank back on the seat. She'd made this mistake once, not again. "I can't. I'm sorry."

"I wouldn't. Just because a man wants to do such a thing doesn't mean he should." He straightened and snapped the reins again. "Don't be sorry. You're right. Everything in its time."

And this wasn't the time. Not with Jesse still visible in the distance, a tiny shrinking speck on the horizon. Not with the sound of his name still on her lips.

"Our time will come."

Will whispered the words so softly she almost didn't hear them. Yet they sounded as if they were a promise.

NINETEEN

Jesse gritted his teeth and tugged on the reins. If he didn't slow the buggy down, he'd end up on his head on the side of the road. He wasn't a child, to throw a tantrum because he didn't get his way. He wanted as far away from Will and Leila and the two-seater as possible. But no amount of distance would relieve him of the image of the two of them, arms entwined, swaying in broad daylight in the thin shade of a mesquite tree in an empty corn-field along a country road. What was Will thinking?

The same thing Jesse had been thinking in that movie theater hallway or out behind the barn at the auction. Not thinking. That was the problem. A man didn't find it easy to think in certain sit-uations. He was finding that out. Feelings drowned out thoughts. It was dangerous. The green snake slithering across his shoulders and down his back belonged to a man who wanted something he couldn't have. To a man who didn't want to see his friends happy if he couldn't be happy too.

Gott, forgive me.

He had no claim on Leila Lantz. One trip to the movies. A kiss. He hadn't even taken her for a ride after that. What must she think of him? Her first kiss stolen by a man who didn't appear to care about how important it was.

His stomach roiled. He pulled off onto the dirt road that led to Phineas's place. They'd all be at Mordecai's for Thanksgiving. He needed wide-open space to burn off the ugliness that enveloped him the second he saw Leila with one hand on his cousin's shoulder, the other clasped in his.

Forcing himself to inhale a deep breath of cool November air, Jesse eased up on the reins and let the buggy slow some more. Had he really expected Leila to sit at home and wait for him to come to his senses?

Nee. Not courting her was the right thing to do. He had to stand firm on that decision. And stop acting like a boy denied the opportunity to hunt on the opening day of deer season.

He eased around a bend in the road, contemplating the future as he did a hundred times a day. Time to concede the truth. Time to give in. He couldn't live a Plain life, not when every fiber of his being ached with a sense of being called. Called to what he wasn't exactly sure. Not yet. But called to something more. Something bigger than himself or his feelings for a woman.

A harsh screech filled the air, deepened, and became a scream. Jesse jerked the reins and stopped. He stood, searching the surrounding area. What was it? The angry sound, much like that of an unhappy, hungry baby, emanated from the other side of a stand of live oaks and nopales. "Who's there?"

Nothing. No one could hear him over that ruckus.

He eased back on the seat, pulled to the side of the road, and stood, craning his head to see over mesquite and scrub brush.

There. Phineas.

Phineas?

Leila's brother-in-law bent over a mesh of netting attached to an old, abandoned chicken coop. Despite the cool air of a fading fall day, he'd shed his jacket on the ground. Exertion and sun had made the thick, ropy scars that marred his face stand out in stark relief against red skin. He didn't look up at the sound of Jesse calling his name. "Phineas! What are you doing?"

"Hang on! I'm rescuing this bird." Phineas made it sound like the most common thing in the world. While his brethren hunted birds, he spent a good part of his free time watching them. For him, this most likely wasn't an unusual occurrence. "He's stuck in this netting and he's not happy about it."

The bird was unlike any Jesse had noticed before, but he wasn't one to notice a bird unless he planned to shoot it and eat it.

Phineas worked at the netting, which apparently had the bird gripped around its neck. The more it struggled, the tighter the noose. "There you go," Phineas cooed, as if singing to a baby in a hoarse voice that had never been the same after his accident. "You're fine. You're fine. Almost there. Got it. Go on, get out of here."

The bird did just that, gone, leaving an impression of a flash of red on its head and a golden-yellow patch on its forehead that stood out against its black-and-white-barred back.

Jesse watched its headlong flight. He longed to join the bird, to get untangled from his predicament. To escape. Not thoughts he could share with a man like Phineas. "Different-looking bird. Kind of pretty like."

Phineas slid a pocketknife into the green canvas knapsack lying on the ground next to his tattered black coat. "Golden-fronted Woodpecker."

Huh. "The ones that make such a racket smacking the chimney in the spring?"

"That would be the one." Phineas raised a hand to his forehead, squinting in the glare of the setting sun. "Only two kinds of woodpeckers in this part of south Texas. The Red-bellied Woodpecker and the Golden-fronted Woodpecker."

That would be Phineas, a fountain of interesting if useless information to Jesse's way of thinking, just like his daed, Mordecai, who knew something about everything, it seemed. "Why are you out here instead of visiting with family?"

"I visited."

That was Phineas, a man of few words. He would do his duty with family, but he preferred the solitude of tending his bees and watching the birds.

"Yeah, me too."

"I don't reckon you're out here bird-watching."

"Nee."

Phineas squatted and picked up his jacket. He frowned and swatted leaves and twigs from the wool. "You know why I started bird-watching?"

It had something to do with the accident that claimed Phineas's mother's life and left him disfigured. "I reckon it gave you something to do when you were . . ."

"Healing."

"Jah."

"I used to wish I could fly away with the birds. Grow wings and take off. Downright fanciful, ain't it?"

The hard knot in Jesse's chest loosened. "Not so much."

"You learn there's no easy way to escape." He threw his arms out in a flourish, north and south, the coat plopping on the ground. He retrieved it yet again. "You have to decide to walk away."

What did Phineas know? Had Will said something to him?

Phineas had never been a rabble-rouser. He'd kept his own counsel, married a woman any one of them would've been glad to call his fraa, and now seemed an example of the obedient contentment every Plain man strived to attain and maintain. "It's a long walk."

"Too far to come back?"

What were they talking about? Jesse chewed the inside of his cheek. "Did someone say something to you?"

"A man has eyes in his head."

"I'm trying to figure some things out, that's all."

Phineas shrugged on his coat and picked up the knapsack. "I wouldn't say no to a ride up to the house."

"You walked all the way down here?"

"Don't see a lot of birds on horseback."

"You're welcome to ride."

Phineas climbed in. Jesse waited for him to settle, then took off. The man next to him whistled in a soft, tuneless way for a few seconds, his hands laced and relaxed in his lap. "So what are you really doing out here?"

Running away from home. Getting his heart broken. Deserved though it might have been, it still hurt worse than having an arm chopped off. "Fresh air."

Phineas chuckled, a hoarse sound more like a cough. "You've never struck me as the fresh-air type."

He liked the outdoors as much as the next farmer. "I intended to see about . . . a girl."

"Ahh."

"Jah."

"Didn't turn out like you expected?"

Jesse snorted.

They rode in silence for a while, the *clip-clop* of the horse's hooves thudding against the dirt. Jesse contemplated the streaks of gold and pink in the clouds, bright against the darkening sky. Phineas had stepped up to be baptized right after his eighteenth birthday. He hadn't hesitated, even after what had happened to him. The house came into sight. A small, compact structure, newer than the wind-and-sun-battered homes that dotted the land owned by the Plain folks of this settlement for almost twenty-five years. Jesse pulled on the reins and stopped short. Phineas straightened. "I don't mind walking." He put a hand on the running board. "Happy Thanksgiving."

"Wait."

Phineas leaned back, his thick eyebrows raised, the beard he'd started growing a scant year ago bobbing. He looked so much like Mordecai. "You got something on your mind?"

"Before you were baptized, did you have any . . . thoughts about . . . not doing it?"

Phineas rubbed his hands together and then stuck them under his arms as if to warm them. "Can't say that I did."

"Even after what happened to you?"

"Maybe because of what happened." He stared at the horizon, not meeting Jesse's gaze. He'd never been one to talk about the accident. "I survived."

"Jah, but . . ."

His gaze swung around and met Jesse's head-on. "Maybe a merciful Gott would've let me die?"

"Nee, I didn't mean that."

"I've had a lot of years to come to terms. I'm the man I am because of what happened. Honed by the fire. The thorn in my side will never go away, but Scripture says Gott's power will be made great in my weakness."

"I know."

"You got doubts, you should talk to your daed."

"I can't."

"He's the bishop."

"Exactly."

Phineas cocked his head and pulled the bill of his hat down so the brim shaded his eyes. "What about my daed?"

"I think . . . I've walked down a road and there's no going back."

"There's always a way back."

"I'm not sure I want to come back."

"What is this road?"

"I'm trying to understand some things. Scripture that says we should win the lost and make disciples."

"Evangelism. So this is about the way we practice our faith?"

"I've made some friends."

A look of comprehension spread across Phineas's mangled face. "Englisch friends."

"Jah. They have Bible studies and they meet at the Dairy Queen and talk to people about what they believe. They pray a lot. Aloud. Prayers they make up in their own words."

Phineas studied the horizon, quiet for so long Jesse feared he'd gone too far, revealed too much. The other man hopped from the wagon in a quick motion, turned, and looked up. "Come in. Deborah's still at my daed's. I have a few minutes before I go for her."

"Forget I said anything."

"I'll not forget. Neither will you. What you're talking about is complicated. We believe in the same Gott as your Englisch friends. We take our beliefs from the same Bible. But we live our lives differently and they don't understand why. You don't have to justify our beliefs to them. We're held accountable by Gott, no one else. Come in."

Jesse blew out air. His chest felt tight and his ears rang with Phineas's stern lecture.

For a man of few words, he'd exhausted an enormous supply on Jesse. He slid from the wagon and walked next to the taller man, feeling small and chastised. His feet didn't seem to want to cooperate. He didn't want to choose. He wanted to live in both worlds.

Every Plain man and woman had to make this decision. Why was he any different? Irritated at his own inability to navigate the prickly thicket, all thorns and burrs, that was his mind, he stomped up the steps and held the door for Phineas, who entered without comment.

In a neat, clean kitchen that still harbored the tantalizing aroma of fresh bread and pumpkin pie, Phineas filled a kettle with water and set it on the wood-burning stove. He took two green ceramic mugs from cabinets that had no doors and added a tea bag to each one. "Milk?"

"Nee."

Phineas settled into the chair closest to the stove and rubbed his hands to warm them. "I'm not the thinker my daed is."

"But you understand my . . . situation."

"I'd be lying if I said I don't understand how a person can get turned around, a little cattywampus, when it comes to trying to understand the whys and wherefores of our faith. But don't let those folks keep you from making up your own mind about what you believe."

"We believe the same things, but we don't do things the way they say the Bible says we should."

"It's not for them to interpret Gott's Word for you. Any interpretation should come from our entire congregation, our community, our district. That's why we have the Ordnung and the gmay every year to discuss any possible changes."

"Why don't we pray like they do?"

"We don't try to improve on Gott's Word. Jesus remained mute in the face of mocking taunts. Silent prayer models His behavior. And He taught us how to pray, gave us the very words we are to use when we pray."

For a guy who wasn't much of a thinker, Phineas knew what he thought.

The words of the Lord's Prayer echoed in the silence around them. Jesse had heard them every morning and every night of his entire life. He'd heard them at Sunday services, weddings, and funerals. The same words over and over. He slapped his hat on the table and ran both hands through his hair. "I've been going to Bible study."

Phineas didn't flinch. He held his hands close to the stove, his expression serene. "And look how divisive it's been for you already. You're questioning your beliefs. You're losing your sense of community, your family. People are giving you their own inter-pretation and trying to convince you to see it their way. You're being torn apart, not unified with other believers."

That was exactly how Jesse felt. Ripped apart. Torn in two directions.

Phineas stood and poured the hot water into the mugs, cov-ering the tea bags. He handed one to Jesse and nodded toward the table. "Honey's there."

Jesse took his time doctoring the tea, waiting, hoping for words that would knit together what had been ripped asunder.

Phineas stirred his tea and stared at the flames leaping behind the open door. "What it comes down to is that our faith is focused more on how we live our lives than on what we believe. We live by example. We surrender to Gott's will. We believe in discipline and obedience and humility. We don't judge others on how they worship. We hope they'll give us the same leeway."

"I know." Jesse did know, so why was this so hard? "You know what to say, how to answer people's questions. Maybe someday you'll draw the lot."

That he might also draw that lot was not lost on Jesse. Gott's will, Gott's plan. Could he wait until that day? It would only come when his daed or the other men who served as deacon and minister were too old and weak to perform their responsibilities—not a time that Jesse wanted to see come anytime soon.

Colton would say the better question would be, should he wait?

And could he live with the limitations that came with that responsibility?

Phineas's face reddened around the ropy, white scars. He ducked his head. The thought of standing in front of his family and friends and speaking surely terrified him. It would Jesse, and he didn't have a bent nose and dangling ear and scars that split his face forehead to chin. Phineas raised his head and shrugged. "Gott's will be done."

Jesse had heard those words every day of his life as well. He still didn't know how a man knew what God's will was. "This girl . . ."

Phineas's face deepened into a frown. "You steer clear. Until you get yourself straight, you have to steer clear."

"I know."

"It's not right to lead her astray."

"I know."

"Gott's will."

"Gott's plan."

Phineas stood. "I need to fetch my fraa."

Fetch my fraa.

Jesse stood as well, every bone in his body aching with the knowledge that he might never say those words.

TWENTY

Hunting had never been so much fun. Will fought the urge to hum under his breath as he stepped over a fallen mesquite and slogged through underbrush and brown cornstalk stubble. The tune wouldn't scare off the deer, but his father wouldn't cotton to the noise. Especially since the tune sounded a lot like one of the songs to which he and Leila had been dancing on Thanksgiving Day. Definitely not a hymn. In his head, Will still felt as if he were dancing. He'd been dancing for two days now. What an odd thing for a Plain man to think, yet he couldn't help himself. He could still feel the sway of her body and the way one of her small hands gripped his while the other pressed into his shoulder. The look on her face. Delight married to guilty pleasure.

He ducked behind a huge snarl of nopales, sure the grin on his face would give him away. "Straighten up," he muttered.

"You say something?" Daed stalked between the trees, his shotgun at the ready in his hands. "Did you see something?"

"Just talking to myself." Will surveyed the open field. Not a deer in sight. They'd been tromping across pastures and through stands of straggly trees since dawn and had seen nary a one. "The deer sure are making themselves scarce."

"Yep. With the drought, a lot of them have moved on to look for water."

"We need a deer blind."

"We need to keep moving."

The early-morning chill of a late November day had given way to a bleary sun that hid itself behind dull gray clouds every chance it got. Sweat dampened Will's shirt. His boots felt heavy as bushel baskets of potatoes. "Mind if I take a load off for a minute?" Will tugged his water jug from the strap that held it over his shoulder. "I'm parched."

"You coming down with something?" Daed rubbed at his face with his sleeve, his expression sour. "Your heart doesn't seem to be in this. We need to stock up on venison. Your mudder's waiting to start canning."

Will could've asked Daed the same question. His expression reminded Will of a child who thought he was about to eat vanilla ice cream and instead found himself with a mouthful of sour cream. "I'm fine. Just thirsty." He held the jug out. "You could probably use a swallow yourself."

Daed took the jug and settled himself on the stump that Will had been eyeing upon which to rest his own weary bones. Keeping his grumble to himself, he squatted instead. Daed's gulps were loud in the silence. He wiped his mouth with his sleeve again, then handed the jug back.

"As good a time as any to give you the news." He burped, a prolonged affair that made Will smile at the ground. "I've made a decision. We're moving back to Tennessee."

Will's smile slid into the pit that had just opened in front of him. "When?"

"We're headed home after the new year."

Will had been to Tennessee a dozen times or more to visit family. Usually for a week at a time. He always enjoyed it, but he was always glad to come home. "Home isn't in Tennessee for me. I was born here."

"We can't make ends meet here anymore. We never really have."

"We don't need much." A piece of dirt to farm. A woman to call his fraa. Leila. "We have what we need."

"We have family there, too, folks who will be glad to see us. It won't be much different than it is here, except the ground is meant to be farmed. You'll feel at home." Daed's color darkened under a fading tan. "It's time you settled down. There's more young women there ready to do the same. Slim pickin's here."

"Not so slim." Will straightened and stood. He let the sun, now shining full-on overhead, warm his face. He closed his eyes, but he could still see the light burning through his eyelids. Tennessee might be more fertile and the climate more forgiving, but south Texas had Leila. He couldn't tell Daed about her. "I'm grown now, though, and I reckon this is my home. I'll make my own way."

Daed stood as well. "And I reckoned you might say that, but your family needs you."

"I'm ready to farm my piece of dirt here." He had roots here. Deep ones. "Sell it to me and I'll make my way on my own."

"If that were the plan, I'd give it to you. You're my son. But your mudder wants her family together in one place."

"Kinner grow up and move on. It's part of life. She'll get used to it."

Daed put a finger to his lips and jerked his head. Will swiveled at the hips, slowly, without moving his feet, just enough to look behind him. A buck meandered through the tall, brown grass on the other side of the dirt road that separated their property from the Planks'. He stopped, lowered his long neck, and munched on a clump of weeds. Will eased into a crouch. His daed lifted the shotgun.

The boom of the gun shattered the silence. The buck jerked, stumbled, went down.

Will knew exactly how the animal felt.

TWENTY-ONE

Sometimes babies simply needed a distraction. Leila plopped Duncan into the closest jumper and pushed the button so the animal sounds of monkeys and elephants would play and lights flash yellow and green. The toddler reached both chubby hands for the red parrot dangling in front of him. He crowed and giggled. A second before, he'd been inconsolable over his empty bottle. Leila couldn't help giggling with him. "You are such a cutie, little chunky cheeks."

"Hey, you'll scar him for life if you tell him he's fat." Rory strolled into the room, Trevor on one hip, toddler Sophia Cramer on the other. "You'll give him a complex."

"What are you talking about?" Leila picked up Alyssa, who had a smell wafting from her behind that overpowered. A diaper change was in order. "His chunky cheeks are adorable, and I love Alyssa's thunder thighs."

"You do now. But just wait, she's not going to want thunder thighs when she's in high school and headed to cheerleader tryouts."

Having seen the skimpy cheerleader outfits worn by the high

school girls, Leila hoped Alyssa chose choir or the school news-paper instead for her extracurricular activities. "She'll run off the baby fat when she starts walking."

"I can't wait until Trevor starts walking."

"You'll have to race to keep up." Leila laid Alyssa on the changing table and tugged a diaper from the basket with the baby's name on it. Alyssa cooed and grabbed her foot, tugging it to her mouth. "You'll chew on anything, won't you, bopli?"

She glanced back at Rory, who bounced the two babies on her hips as adept as any older woman. "Why aren't you in Miss Rachel's room, helping her?"

"I just came to tell you that Daddy called. He picked up a second shift, filling in for some guy who went home sick, so he can't pick us up."

"How are we getting home?"

"I called Dwayne. He's headed this way as soon as wrestling practice is over."

Leila mulled over this information. Mudder wouldn't be happy to see her show up in Dwayne's rust-decorated pickup truck with its big rumbling engine, but what could she do? Spend the night at the day care? "Okay, but we have to go straight home."

"Sure, sure. No problem." Rory adjusted Trevor on her hip, her tone airy. "Sawyer is taking the bus home from school and Daddy doesn't want him at the house by himself too long."

The day care didn't close until six thirty. Sawyer got out of school at three and the bus ride took at least an hour. He was at the house alone every day for a couple of hours. But he was ten, plenty old enough in the Plain way of thinking. "See you out front in half an hour."

By the time she cleaned the room and handed off her charges

to their parents, Leila felt as frazzled as they looked. She loved taking care of babies, but it was a nonstop proposition. Her arms ached and the muscles in her shoulders were tied up in knots. The late fall sky had turned dark. Another day and she'd missed the sunshine.

She pushed through the front door and sure enough, Dwayne's primer-gray, fumes-spewing pickup rumbled at the curb. Rory had beat her to the punch. She sat in the front seat, close enough to be in her husband's lap. Trevor's car seat was wedged into the backseat of the extended cab. Suppressing a sigh, Leila squeezed in next to it, the other side being taken up with a gym bag, a pile of books, half a dozen greasy, stinky fast-food bags, and a variety of mismatched sneakers that reeked of boy feet.

"Hey, Leila." Dwayne gave her a half salute under hair still wet from a shower, his usual semi-amused stare greeting her in the rearview mirror. "What's shaking?"

"Not much."

He pulled away from the curb with a jerk, tires squealing. The driver of a minivan laid on his horn, the sound adding to Leila's throbbing headache. Dwayne saluted the man with a different finger than the one he'd used with Leila. She swiveled and glued her gaze to the passing scenery, trying not to inhale the odor of stale French fries and old hamburger.

A couple of turns later and she knew one thing for certain—two things—Dwayne drove with reckless abandon despite having his baby son in the truck, and they weren't headed out of town on Highway 59. "Where are we going?"

"Just a little detour. Don't you worry, it'll be fun."

She didn't want fun. She wanted supper and bed. "I have to get home and help clean up after supper."

"All work and no play makes a girl a sad sack."

He grinned at her in the rearview mirror, his teeth white and his cheeks dimpled. She could see the resemblance to Trevor, even though the baby had Rory's curly brown hair and eyes the color of milk chocolate, whereas his daddy had sandy-blond hair and green eyes. "I like work."

He chuckled and swerved to avoid a pothole. The force sent Leila against Trevor's car seat. He began to fuss.

"Hush, little guy," Dwayne hollered. "We're almost there."

Trevor's fuss turned to an outright cry. "Shhh, shush, shush." Leila patted his cheek and dangled a pacifier over him. Trevor's fat little hands grasped at it and a second later he quieted, except for the *thwack-thwack* of the pacifier in his mouth.

"There" turned out to be a park. Leila liked parks just fine, when it wasn't cold and dark and her stomach growling for its supper. "Rory—"

"Just for a few minutes, Leila, please. I never get to spend time with Dwayne during the week." Rory already had her door open. "Please, pretty please with sugar on top of it."

She didn't wait for Leila's answer. She popped from the truck and ran across the dried, brown grass to the lone swing set illuminated by tall streetlights, leaving Leila to deal with getting Trevor from his car seat. With the truck door open, a gust of cool, damp night air wafted through the car, making Leila shiver.

"Let's go, sweet pea." She unsnapped the straps and tugged his chubby arms out. Rory hadn't thought to put his jacket on him before taking him from the day care. Leila rummaged in the diaper bag stuck on top of the pile of books until she found his coat. "Just for a little bit, and then I'll convince your mommy to go home. I'll steal her cell phone if I have to. Your granddaddy will set her straight."

Hopefully it wouldn't come to that. She lugged Trevor across the grass and settled into a swing. The baby crowed with laughter when she pushed off and sent them sailing through the air. She liked to swing too. Except when she was cold and tired and hungry.

Rory and Dwayne seemed to be engaged in a game of hide-and-seek. Rory ran from tree to tree, pretending to hide behind fat trunks while Dwayne danced around on the other side. When he pulled her out into the open, she collapsed to the ground and he followed suit. They rolled around, giggling and snuggling as if they weren't in the middle of a city park on a cool autumn day that had already turned to night in the middle of Beeville, Texas.

"Your parents are a little strange," she told Trevor as she tightened her grip on his roly-poly body and pushed back from the ground to reach new heights. Then again, she was a grown woman enjoying herself—she could admit that—by swinging. "I reckon they're allowed to act silly now and again."

Most folks did. Like her and Will with their dancing in broad daylight. Or her and Jesse, kissing in a movie theater hallway.

Will or Jesse. Will or Jesse. The refrain echoed in her head in time to the squeak of the swing's long chains. *Up and down. Up and down. Squeak, squeak. Will or Jesse. Will or Jesse.* Will with his blond hair and blue eyes and broad shoulders and his simple, straightforward approach to life. Or Jesse with his stocky body and barrel-shaped chest and curly black hair and brown eyes. Jesse with his strange disappearing acts and his sad face when he thought she wasn't looking. So different.

How could she like them both? Will tried so hard to do the right thing, while Jesse couldn't seem to make up his mind what the right thing was. Something about his ferocious gaze had embedded itself in her heart. It wasn't the kiss. The intensity of his questioning gaze held her pinned to a wall of emotion. He wanted something from her, but she had no idea what it was. Will might give her what she needed, but Jesse might give her what she wanted.

Stop. Stop. Stop. The squeaking of the swing chains kept time to the refrain in her head. *Stop. Stop. Stop.*

She needed to do the right thing, even if Jesse couldn't. *Gott, forgive me. Gott, help me keep my eyes on You. Gott, Thy will be done.*

So easy to pray. So hard to do.

Mordecai said once during evening prayers that sometimes faith was an act of will. She hadn't understood then. She did now.

Will could help her do the right thing. Maybe Gott had planted this man in her path to help her do what was right. He wanted to help her. He'd made that obvious.

Doing the right thing surely didn't involve hanging out in the park instead of getting herself home. She didn't need anyone's help to know that. She slowed the swing, digging her heels in the dirt where the grass had worn away under the sneakers of a steady stream of carefree children.

"Time to go," she yelled as she strode toward the couple. Now they were involved in a kiss the likes of which she'd never seen. Right there in front of her. "Rory, time to go. Sawyer's home all by himself and it's way past dark."

Dwayne threw himself back on the grass, gasping for air. "Can't go yet."

"Why not?"

"Friends coming."

His long arm wrapped around Rory and pulled her against his chest. She giggled harder and buried her head in his jean jacket.

"Rory!"

A car painted the color of pickled beets pulled in behind Dwayne's truck. The doors flew open before the engine died and a jumble of people exited. All boys with leather jackets that featured big fuzzy *B*s on the back and little medals pinned to the front.

"They're here. They're here." Dwayne sat up, bringing Rory with him. "Dude, did you bring the stuff?"

Apparently *dude* referred to a specific guy in the group of half a dozen boys. The one with red hair and pale skin covered with freckles produced a brown paper sack with a bottle neck sticking out the top. "Straight from my daddy's liquor cabinet."

"Yee-haw."

Rory slapped her husband's arm hard, then added a second whack for emphasis. "Dwayne Chapman, you know better. You can't drink and drive. Not with our precious little bundle of joy in the car."

Dwayne scowled. "I suppose you're right. You could drive and then I could—"

"Daddy will have my hide if I drive after that last accident. He took my license."

"How 'bout you, Amish girl?" Dwayne dangled the keys on a bottle opener key chain in the air. "Wanna drive us home after we have some fun?"

His idea of fun didn't jibe with Leila's. "Amish folks don't drive cars."

"Right. I knew that." Dwayne flopped his baseball cap on the ground. "This being a daddy is no fun sometimes."

"Well, excuse me, you think it's so much fun for me, changing diapers and getting up to feed him every three hours?" Rory hauled herself to her feet and dusted leaves from her jeans. "And then getting up to go to school and then to work and then do homework. Guys have got it easy."

"No fair. If we lived together, I'd get up with him."

Leila didn't bother to try to get a word in edgewise. At least Rory had the good sense to know better than to let Dwayne drink and drive. Rory took off, Dwayne in close pursuit. His friends invaded the swings and the monkey bars, hooting and hollering like a bunch of first graders. She chewed her lip, eyeing them. *What now?* She shivered. The night air had taken on a sharp chill.

"Hey, who are you?"

Leila forced her gaze from the teenage boys acting like children loose at a rodeo carnival. A tall, thin guy wearing a cowboy hat, skintight, faded jeans, and well-worn, scuffed cowboy boots plopped down on the merry-go-round. He had dark, kaffi-colored eyes and the wispy beginnings of a beard. She forced a smile. "A friend of Rory's."

"I'm Shawn. A friend of Dwayne's. And Rory's. We have that in common, I reckon." He shoved his cowboy hat back, revealing dark brown curls that dangled just above his eyebrows. "How do you know Rory?"

"She buys honey at our store sometimes, and now we work at the day care together."

He tickled Trevor's cheek and smiled at the baby's gurgling attempt at conversation. "I can't imagine having a baby right now." His gaze traveled to Rory, still jawing at Dwayne, hands flailing to make her point. "I mean, I still have geography tests and book reports, you know?"

"I know."

"Could I hold him for a second?"

Leila contemplated Shawn's face. He reminded her of Caleb, even though he was much older. "Have you ever held a baby?"

"Sure, I got cousins and a nephew." He held out his hands and wiggled his fingers. "I know what I'm doing."

She handed Trevor over. "Support his back—"

"I know, I know." He held Trevor up to eye level. "What's up, dude?"

Trevor spit up, liquid running down his chin and onto the front of his jacket and Shawn's hand.

"Dude!"

Leila wanted to laugh at the horrified look on his face. "It's just milk."

"Warm, regurgitated milk!" He held the baby up, legs and arms dangling. "All yours."

She pulled a burp rag from Trevor's diaper bag and wiped him down. "You said you were an expert."

"No, I didn't." He laughed, a deep chortle that made Leila want to laugh too. He plopped Trevor into her lap. "All I know about babies is they poop, eat, sleep, and cry."

"Yep."

"You have any babies?"

"I'm not married."

"Well that doesn't mean anything these days."

"It does to me."

"Good for you." He tugged a red bandanna from his hip pocket and applied diligent elbow grease to the thick puddle of spit-up white against his jeans. "Can I give you a ride somewhere? You look cold and it's getting dark."

She was cold, it was getting dark, and the way Trevor kept

rubbing his eyes and fussing told Leila he was as tired as she was. "That would be nice, but I can't leave Trevor."

"His momma's right over there."

They turned in unison to look at Trevor's parents. Dwayne had Rory pinned against the bright-yellow plastic slide, his long legs covering hers. Apparently the apology had been accepted and followed by the usual kiss-and-make-up routine. "I think they're gonna be awhile." A few bars of a country music song wafted in the air. Shawn tugged a slim cell phone from his front pocket, frowned at something, and shoved it back in his jeans. "My mom's looking for me. She's got supper on the table. Let me take you home. I have to go anyway."

By the time he drove all the way out to Mordecai's, his supper would be cold and his momma mad. Trevor's whiny fuss turned into an outright cry. Leila snuggled him to her chest and began to rock. "Sorry, little one, sorry." She shook her head. "You go on. Your supper's waiting and I'm not leaving Trevor."

"You're a good friend to watch out for Rory's baby." Shawn cocked his head, studying her with a surprisingly serious expression. Leila was reminded that a person should never judge another by appearance. "I reckon having a baby doesn't make a person a grown-up."

Leila glanced back at Rory and Dwayne. The lip-lock continued. How did they breathe? "Making babies has nothing to do with being a good parent."

"At least get in my car. It has a good heater. You and Trevor can keep warm until they cool off. I also have an excellent sound system. What kind of music do you like?"

Shawn didn't know much about Plain folks, that was obvious.

"I like . . . church music and country music some. But it doesn't matter. I don't want your supper to get cold."

"I'll warm it up in the microwave. I like country music. I've got Lee Brice and Blake Shelton and Jason Aldean on my iPod. Come on, I promise to be a gentleman—"

A horn cut the air in a long, fierce blare. Leila whirled. Colton's silver Impala pulled up to the curb, Jesse hanging out the window. "Leila! What are you doing here?"

"I have to go." She stumbled away from Shawn, her heart hammering in her chest. "It was . . . nice to meet you."

"I thought y'all drove buggies." Shawn followed after her, his long legs eating up the ground. "You'll take a ride from somebody who just randomly pulls up?"

"Friend of a friend," she hollered without looking back. "Thanks for the offer, but I'm fine now. I promise."

He halted, his expression confused, hands on his hips. "Take care then."

"You too." Trevor clasped tight to her side, she scurried across the grass to Colton's car. "What are you doing here?"

"That's the question I asked you." Jesse's jaw worked. His face had that same expression it had on Thanksgiving Day when he'd driven up on Will and her. How dare he look hurt? "Who's that guy you were talking to?"

Once again, what right did he have to ask? "A friend of Rory's. Why are you here?"

"We were on our way to . . . Colton happened to notice you. We were just driving by."

A dull shade of red crept across his face. "We'll take you home, okay?"

Colton revved the engine, then let up. "We don't have time to go out to her farm and still get back in time for—"

"She shouldn't be here with these guys," Jesse cut in, his tone brusque. "I'm not leaving her here."

She didn't want to stay, but she didn't need Jesse to tell her right from wrong. He hardly knew himself. Who was he to judge her? Trevor's warm weight against her hip and side reminded her that she wasn't the only one stuck. "I can't leave the baby."

"He's not your baby." Jesse blew out air, inhaled. The fierce emotion etched across his face seemed to abate. "His mother should take responsibility. Take the baby to her."

He was as bad as Will about telling her what to do. They didn't have a right. Neither one of them. Not yet. Maybe never.

Colton shoved open his door. "I'll help."

He took Trevor from her arms and together they trudged to the slide. Dwayne and Rory stood on the top step. She waved, hooted, and together they whipped down it on their behinds, a single unit. "Wahoo!" she screamed and laughed. "You gotta do this, Leila, it's fun. Hey, Colton, what are you doing here?"

So they knew each other. Of course, from school. "I have to go now. Colton will give me a ride. You should get Trevor home. It's time for his bath and bed. And Sawyer's waiting."

Rory wrinkled her nose, her gaze on Colton. "How do you two know each other?"

"Colton's the one who took Jesse and me to the movies that time I told you about."

Rory picked herself up from where she'd landed at the bottom of the slide and brushed off her hands. "I wish you'd told me, girl. Colton is famous."

"Not famous." Colton didn't seem fazed by her teasing tone. "Committed to standing on solid ground is all."

"Don't you know, Leila, he's a Jesus freak? He's always trying to convert people," Dwayne chimed in, his tone exaggerated with false friendliness. "Careful, he'll convert you."

"Hey, be nice." Rory smacked Dwayne's shoulder with the back of one hand. "To each their own."

"I don't need to be converted." Leila wasn't sure exactly what they meant, but she wouldn't allow her faith to be questioned. "I know Jesus."

More than Rory and Dwayne did. The thought made her sad.

Colton's expression mirrored her feelings. He stuck his hands in the pockets of his faded jeans and shrugged. "Good for you, Leila. I want everyone to have the chance to know Jesus, that's all. I imagine you do too." He took a step toward Rory and Dwayne. "Y'all are welcome to stop by youth group any Wednesday. You know where Tiffany's house is, right?"

Dwayne snorted, but Rory smacked him again before he could speak. "Thanks for the invite, but with a baby and school and work, my schedule is full up every night, including Wednesdays."

Wednesday nights. Will had told her to ask Jesse where he went on Wednesday nights. Leila glanced back at Colton's car. Jesse sat in the front seat, his expression bleak and distant. "Take Trevor home, please, Rory. I don't feel good about leaving him if you won't promise you'll get him home right away."

"Don't you worry about him. I got my baby." Rory tugged on Trevor, whose little fists gripped Leila's apron straps. The baby squawked and let go, his arms flailing. "Come on, little man, come to Momma. We're going now."

"We are?" Dwayne pulled his Texas Rangers ball cap down

over his face and leaned back against the slide. "What if I'm not ready yet?"

"Cowboy up, buddy." Rory kicked his leg with the point of her red boot. "Move it. Sawyer will call Dad and complain for sure."

As soon as she was certain Rory would actually get in the truck and take her son home, Leila started toward Colton's car. Something like shame swept over her. Colton had gone out of his way to help her, and Dwayne had insulted him over something he obviously didn't understand. She should've stood up for him more. "I'm sorry Dwayne talked to you that way."

"It's okay. I'm used to hecklers."

"Why do you do it then?"

He opened the car door for her with a tiny flourish. "Because I have the truth."

Colton had the truth. Did Jesse think he had the truth? Did Leila have the truth? If she did, why didn't she tell Rory, a friend so obviously lost and in need of such a powerful truth?

Leila plopped into the backseat and leaned forward so her words would reach Jesse's ear only. "It's Wednesday night. Where are you going?"

TWENTY-TWO

Maybe Gott didn't intend for men to understand women. Or vice versa. Jesse tugged open the car door and bent down to look at Leila. She sat bolt upright, back stiff, in the backseat. Her frown said it all. She didn't have any right to be peeved at him. He hadn't been cavorting in a park with a bunch of Englisch teenagers. Most likely they'd been drinking, knowing that crowd. It struck him as ironic that he would be criticized for the company he kept when his circle of Englisch friends walked the walk when it came to being Christians. They didn't drink or do drugs or have wild parties. They liked Bible studies, softball games, and movie nights. They had paintball parties or went hunting for fun.

"Where are you going?"

Her question reverberated in his ears the entire length of the drive from the park to Tiffany's house. No more than a mile, but it seemed to last an eternity. Colton had made small talk, but Leila didn't bite, and neither did Jesse. The electricity in the air crackled and popped until even Colton looked uncomfortable, and nothing fazed that guy.

Jesse hadn't answered her question because he couldn't. He

didn't know. He could show her this place, he could show her his Wednesday nights, the road he now traversed. No turning back. The choice he had to make. No, it wasn't a choice. Not really. It was a calling that he couldn't ignore.

"What are you looking at?" She stared up at him, her face full of concern. She didn't look mad. She looked sad and confused and nothing like the girl he'd kissed in the hallway at the theater. She looked scared. "What are we doing here?"

"You want to know what I do on Wednesday nights; I'm showing you." He didn't finish the sentence aloud. *I'm trusting you.* "I'm answering your question."

He couldn't keep pretending. If he wanted her in his life, she had to know. She had to decide. She would be the one Plain person, aside from Will, who knew what Jesse faced. She might even understand, if God blessed him to such a great extent. She hadn't moved. Her frown melted into a puzzled look. "Are you sure?"

She knew this was important.

"I want you to know because it explains how I've treated you." He kicked at a scraggly weed sticking up in the crack in the sidewalk. "I know it's confusing. But it's not you. It's me."

"Where are we?"

"This is Tiffany's house."

"You come to Tiffany's house on Wednesday night. Why?"

"Come in and you'll see."

He stepped back. She slid from the seat and slipped past him. Colton pounded up the steps ahead of them. She followed without looking back. With each step, the strap around Jesse's chest tightened. What if she told Mordecai? What if she told his daed? Was he ready to tell them about this?

Colton held the door for them. "Head into the family room. I'll get Pastor Dave."

His throat dry, tongue stuck to the roof of his mouth, Jesse nodded and tried to swallow as he turned to Leila. He cleared his throat. "This way."

"Who's Pastor Dave?"

"The youth minister from Tiffany and Colton's church."

"Youth minister—"

"Just follow me, okay?"

He led her to the family room where Tiffany and her sisters had shoved back a sofa covered with crocheted blankets and arranged folding chairs in a large circle on a tattered carpet in need of cleaning. Card tables lined one wall under shelves covered with family photos. One table featured sodas, bottled water, cookies, brownies, rice crispy treats, and other snacks that made his stomach rumble despite its queasiness. He hadn't been home for the noon meal, and the corn mush, eggs, and toast he had for breakfast were long gone. They'd loaded another table with flyers about mission trips, brochures, devotionals, and Bibles available for the taking. In one corner, some of the guys tuned electric guitars and checked a portable sound system.

"What is all this?" Leila's voice shrank to a whisper. "Is this some kind of meeting?"

"It's their Wednesday night youth group."

Their youth group. His group. After three months, he could not deny he felt a part of this group. They made him feel at home, not like an outcast. They teased him about his suspenders and his straw hat and his haircut, but they also listened to him and offered kind words of encouragement. They included him in their pranks and asked his opinion about their own quandaries.

They were his friends.

He followed Leila's gaze as it traveled to a cluster of girls sitting cross-legged on the floor making posters. Tiffany looked up, grinned, and waved. She had glitter on her nose and a slash of neon marker above lips bright with pink lipstick. "Look who's here! Glad y'all could make it." She popped up like a jack-in-the-box and padded toward them in feet clad in pink polka-dotted slippers. "You finally had the guts to ask Leila, that's so great. I'm totally psyched!"

"She was at the park and she needed a ride." The words sounded lame in Jesse's ears, like he didn't really want Leila here. He did want her here. Dread tightened in a noose around his throat. "I'm hoping she'll see her way clear to stay for a while."

"I don't know." Spots of red darkened Leila's cheeks. "No offense to you, Tiffany, but I don't think I'm supposed to be here. I don't think Jesse is either."

"You're gonna love it. Oh, there's Samantha. She hasn't been here in forever. Grab a brownie and have a seat. Music starts in five." Tiffany catapulted past them toward the door where a girl, presumably Samantha, stood looking equally as uncertain as Leila did.

Quelling the urge to hurl, Jesse pointed to the first chair. "Like she said, have a seat. They'll get started any minute."

Leila shook her head and leaned close. "Get started with what?"

"Give them a chance."

"A chance to do what?" Suppressed anger made her blue eyes spark. She looked pretty. Jesse dropped his gaze to the carpet that sparkled with the flotsam and jetsam of glitter from meetings gone by. Leila's voice rose slightly. "This is wrong. It feels wrong."

"Not to me. They sing songs. They talk to each other about

Scripture. They pray. And then they go talk to other people about Jesus."

It felt right to him.

"They talk to people about Jesus." Her voice had softened. "To strangers?"

He raised his head and nodded.

Her eyebrows rose and her mouth closed.

"People do that, you know?"

"Have you?"

"No. Not yet. I'm too tongue-tied." He couldn't tell her how sometimes the words burbled up in him and threatened to spill out in a mumble jumble of the sheer joy of knowing God loved him. Even him. Jesus died for him. To save him.

Why, he couldn't imagine. Most days he didn't feel worthy of being a speck of dirt. Then he came to these meetings and he felt awash in love. What Pastor Dave called *agape* love. Brotherly love. He could hold his head up because he was a child of God along with all these other children.

His gaze met Leila's. She cocked her head, her expression quizzical.

"What?"

"You look happy. I've never seen you looking so happy."

"I guess I am." He let his gaze wander to Tiffany, talking Samantha's ear off while trying to foist a brownie on her. Jack and Ricky tuning their guitars. Alison throwing popcorn at poor Luke, on whom she had an obvious crush. They were good kids who liked Jesus and liked talking about Him. How could it be wrong? "I think maybe you could be happy too."

She shook her head. "You think I don't understand what this means? I do understand."

"Just hear them out. For one hour. Just one hour."

After a long moment in which he contemplated spending the rest of his life alone, she sank into the chair and clasped her hands in her lap. "One hour. Then you promise to take me home?"

"Promise."

She clasped her canvas bag in her lap as if someone might steal it. "Okay, but you have to sit with me."

He sank into the chair next to her, sure his legs were about to give way. She hadn't run from the room screaming. "Gladly."

———

Leila's hands were slick in her lap. The others clapped and sang at the top of their lungs. What they lacked in musical talent, they made up for in volume. When she'd asked Jesse to bring her, she'd been so sure she could handle it. Jesse's truth. She tried to focus on the lyrics, but Jesse's presence next to her threatened to consume her every thought. The intensity of his desire for her to understand and accept his friends and what they were doing confounded her. In this living room with its shabby couch and recliner and mismatched coffee tables, he looked different. He looked like his friends. He hadn't changed his clothes and he still wore his hat, but he sounded like them when he talked. He had an assurance about him that made him all the more appealing.

For these few moments, he seemed at peace.

In the almost two years she'd been in Bee County, she'd never seen Jesse Glick at peace. In perpetual motion, yes, as if chased by wolves or his own thoughts. Now, in this room, the motion had stopped and a content man sat next to her. He sang with his shoulders thrust back, head held high, smiling. He had a nice baritone and he knew all the words. He tossed her a tentative grin and sang louder.

She sank deeper into the chair, aware of all the eyes watching her, full of curiosity, full of something else. They wanted something from her. They wanted her.

The music died away. Every head bowed. They began to take hands, all around the circle, without hesitation or embarrassment. Girls held hands with boys. Jesse's hand came out. Leila stared at it, then up at him. "It's okay. I promise."

She dashed her palms on her apron and took his offering. His hand felt cool in hers. On the other side, a girl with a diamond stud in her nose and a tattoo of a pink rose on her neck offered a hand. Leila took it. Her fingers were sticky with rice crispy treats.

Leila squeezed her eyes shut and prayed that nothing else would be required of her.

Pastor Dave, who'd turned out to be a mountain of a black man dressed in faded jeans and a white T-shirt that stretched across a broad, muscled chest, had a deep voice with a soft Southern cadence. "Lord, I pray for these young folks, that You would guide them and keep them safe and lead them in Your ways. That Your will be done in their lives. Show them what You would have them do and where You would have them go and what Your plans are for them. Each one of them. Lord, I pray for Jesse, who has decisions to make that will affect his family and his life. It's a rocky road ahead for this young man . . . and for the people he loves . . ."

Leila didn't hear the words after that. Jesse's hand tightened around hers. She tried to jerk away, but he refused to release her. She stood. He followed suit. Everyone looked up, looked at her, at them. "I'm sorry. I'm sorry."

She pulled away from Jesse. He let go, the peace of a few

seconds before slipping from his face. She stumbled from the room, through the foyer, and out the front door. The clear, cold night air greeted her. She gulped it down, like a baby starved for her mother's milk.

"Leila. Leila!" Jesse stormed onto the porch and let the screen door slam behind him. "Don't go."

"I'm going home if I have to walk."

"You said you'd give it an hour."

"You didn't tell me you're leaving us. You're leaving your community." To her horror, tears made her voice crack. She swallowed against them and cleared her throat. "Leaving me."

"I haven't committed."

"But you've talked to Pastor Dave about it."

"I have."

"Why?"

Jesse sank onto the step and patted the spot next to him. "I want to try to explain, but you have to hear me out."

She debated, her head telling her to *go, go, go. Get away.* Her heart demanded she *stay, stay, stay.*

She couldn't drive herself.

Face burning, heart pounding, she plopped down next to him, leaving a gap the size of Caleb between them. "Make it snappy. Mudder will be worried about me."

"Snappy?"

"That's what my boss says at the day care. I have to go home."

"This isn't easy."

"I reckon not. Why would you do this to us?"

To me?

"To know more, to be closer to God, to be able to pray the way I want and talk to people the way I want." He slapped his big hand across his barrel chest. "I feel something here that I don't when I'm at our services. Don't you?"

"I feel . . . different. I feel like I don't belong." She contemplated her hands in her lap, trying to identify feelings that hurled themselves about and then collapsed into a jumbled heap. "I feel far from home."

Too far and getting farther all the time. She stood. "I want to go home. You said you'd take me home."

He stared at her, his dark eyes mournful. "You don't feel it?"

Leila had felt . . . something big and warm and welcoming, but it couldn't matter. If she let it matter, everything would change. Her whole life would change, and in that change came loss. Terrible loss. Her bones ached at the thought. Her skin burned with fever. She shivered. "Come home. Talk to Mordecai. He can help you figure this out. It's not too late."

"I already talked to Phineas."

Phineas might not have his father's way with words, but he had a certain calm to him that Leila had always liked. "And it didn't help?"

"What we believe isn't different. Can't you see?" He slid closer to her and put his hand over hers. His fingers were so strong. The ache subsided. A warmth spread that overcame the chill. He leaned in so his shoulder touched hers. "It's how we practice our faith that's different. I want to shout about Jesus from the rooftops. I think I may be a minister someday."

She wanted to pull away, but somehow she couldn't. Their fingers were entwined, the bond tangible and physical. She could see him standing in front of the room sharing the Word with her family and friends, his family and friends. It could happen, but not because he wanted it to be so, only if God decided. "If you draw the lot."

"I don't believe I have to wait for that. I believe I'm being called."

The ache returned. She peeled her fingers from his. "Gott chose your father when he drew the lot. It could be the same for you. It's up to Gott."

"My father has done God's will all these years. He's done right by his responsibilities. I believe I can do the same. I don't have to wait for some sort of holy slot to open up. Sometimes God speaks to us directly."

"That's so prideful."

"In your way of thinking."

"In our way of thinking. It's yours too. Humility. Obedience. Jesus first, others second, you third."

Jesse captured her hand again and rubbed his fingers over her knuckles. Heat shot up her spine and spread across her neck. She couldn't breathe. *Breathe. In and out.* "I won't try to convince you, even though I know I'm right, because I would never take you from your family. I don't have to save you. We believe the same things. Plain people are godly people. So are these folks. They just want to share the good news of Jesus Christ with people who are lost. Do you understand?"

She closed her eyes and concentrated on the feel of his fingers on hers. She felt at peace when she sat on the bench on Sunday morning with Mudder and Esther and Susan and Deborah and Rebekah and little Hazel. She felt at peace when they sang those long, slow hymns and Leroy spoke the Word. She felt at peace when they said the Lord's Prayer as she had done every day twice a day as long as she could remember.

The feelings she had here and now on this porch with Jesse holding her hand, these feelings were real too. And powerful.

They rocked her to the bone. She felt alive. She felt Gott's presence all around her. So close. So inviting. *Gott, forgive me.* How could she want both? "I don't understand anything. Come home and talk to Mordecai. Please."

Jesse's hand dropped and the cold closed in around her. He leaned in until his lips brushed her cheek, soft, soft, so softly. "I will, but not tonight."

"You can't do that. Please don't do that." She backed away, trying to put a physical space between them. It didn't help. The bond forged between them held, as if their hands still touched, as if his lips still warmed her cheek. He didn't play fair. "It's not right."

"I can't help it." He shrugged, his smile bittersweet. "I think about kissing you all the time."

"You want this too." She waved toward the house. "You throw this at me and then ask me to choose you."

"Not just me. Don't just choose me. Choose to believe in what we're doing here. I've watched you. You feel your faith deeply. It's personal to you too. You want to help. You want to share your faith. I can tell." His hands reached for hers. She drew away. He stared at her, his gaze fierce and imploring. "I never meant to put you in this position. I saw you at the park with that guy, and I realized I might not have the chance to tell you the truth and ask you—"

"That guy was a friend of Dwayne's who was concerned about the baby being cold. He was kind. That's all. A kind person."

"Okay, so I overreacted." Jesse clutched his hands together in his lap, his knuckles white. "I'm the kind of person who has strong feelings about a lot of things."

That, they had in common. "About me?"

"About you. About my faith in God. I think you do too."

She'd always felt God's presence in her life, but never more so than when her father died and they'd moved to south Texas to start a new life. Every step of the way He'd held her hand as surely as Daed had when she'd learned to walk as a toddler. But this was something entirely different. The consequences too enormous to contemplate. She would drown in them. "I can't. It's too much."

"At least give it time. Think about it. Listen to what they have to say. Before you turn your back on me and choose another."

"I told you. I only just met the boy at the park. I don't even know him."

"But if it's not him, it'll be Will."

He made it a statement, not a question. Leila closed her eyes, the image of Will's face floating in front of her as he put one hand on her waist and clasped her hand with the other. The dancing had been about this. Will knew about this. He thought he had to compete.

No one had to compete. She had to choose what her life would be. "I should go."

Jesse's Adam's apple bobbed. "Are you sure?"

"You said you'd never take me away from my family."

His gaze dropped to his big hands now limp in his lap. "And I won't." His gaze lifted to her face. "If that's what you choose."

Swallowing hard against hot tears that burned her throat, Leila edged away from him. "How will I get home?"

"I'll take you." Colton stood in the doorway, car keys dangling from his hand. How long had he been there? "Jesse promised you a ride home. We won't abandon you."

So why did she feel so lost?

TWENTY-THREE

A propane pole lamp blazed in the front window, signaling to Leila that she must tread carefully in all things. No chance of slipping in unnoticed.

She inched the car door forward until it closed with a soft click. She didn't respond to Jesse's good-bye. She couldn't. She had no words left to say to him. They'd been silent on the ride home from Tiffany's, yet her ears rang with the raucous argument that raged in her head the entire way. She wanted to slap her hands to her ears and block out all sound, all thought, all memory of Jesse's hands and his lips. Everything about him. Pain ripped through her heart at the thought of never feeling his touch again.

What is the right thing, Gott? I'm only a simple woman. How do I know?

No answer floated down to her from on high, no matter how she strained to hear.

She should be thinking about what awaited her in the house and not the way Jesse's gaze sent heat spiraling through her from head to toes. Her hopes that she could postpone any confrontation with Mudder until morning had disappeared when Colton pulled his car onto the dirt road in front of Mordecai's house. Folks were still up. They should be in bed by now. Instead she would have to greet them and explain why she was so late getting home from work. Why she arrived home in Colton's car, Jesse in the front seat.

She pushed open the screen door and let out a gusty sigh. How did she explain her day to Mordecai? Or worse, her mother?

"You're home." Mudder stood in the doorway to the kitchen, her face glowing with a sweaty sheen. She clutched a pile of towels to her chest. "I was about to send Caleb to the Beales' to track you down." She smiled despite the irk in her words.

"What is it?" Leila dropped the cooler and her canvas bag on the braided rug. "Did something happen?"

"The baby's coming."

"The baby? The baby! It's early, isn't it?" Because she'd been gallivanting about in town, she'd almost missed it. The birth of her sister's first child. Leila bolted toward the stairs. A scream echoed from above. "Oh, Deborah, I'm coming."

"She's been at it for hours." Mudder scurried after her, her bare feet close on Leila's heels. "It's about time for her to push."

"Where's Phineas?"

"Out back. I reckon he couldn't stand the screaming."

Leila raced down the hallway, slung open her bedroom door, and barreled through. Deborah lay on the bed, her chest heaving, her face covered with sweat and tears. "Leila, Leila, help me. I have to get this baby out." Sobs punctuated the words. "I'm trying to be brave, but it feels like it's breaking me in two."

"You're fine, child." Mudder's tone was the calm one Leila remembered from childhood bouts with fever, chicken pox, and influenza. "I've had five babies and it always feels like that toward the end. It means you're almost done."

Leila squeezed between Rebekah, who stood wringing her hands, and Esther, who held a load of dirty towels in her arms. She had the bemused look on her face of a girl who was watching her own future unfold. Unlike Leila, she would soon marry the man she loved, have babies, and settle down in her Plain life as a wife and mother. Leila batted the thought away. This was Deborah's time. Nothing must spoil it.

Susan sat on the far side of the bed, a basin of water and a damp rag in her lap, her face serene. Between Mudder and Susan, the two women had helped deliver dozens of babies into this world. Deborah would be fine. "What can I do to help? Is that water cool?"

Susan smiled up at her. "We're doing fine. Sit with your sister. She could use some company. Rebekah can bring fresh water."

She handed the basin to Rebekah, who scampered toward the door without a word.

"Bring her a glass of water too." Leila scooted onto the bed and grabbed another rag to wipe her sister's face. "I'm so excited for you. Just think, any minute now you'll hold your first bopli in your arms. You and Phineas will be parents. What a blessing."

She was running on at the mouth, but she couldn't help it. Deborah had what Leila wanted. A man who loved her, married her, and gave her a child. That it hurt to bear that child was a given. It would be worth it.

Deborah chuckled, the sound weak and weary. "It doesn't feel like it right now, but I'm sure you're right. Where have you been, schweschder? I needed you."

Those last three plaintive words shot daggers into Leila's heart. She'd been where she never should have gone. She gallivanted about in Beeville when her sister needed her. Mixing with the Englisch, being a part of their world. Shame burned her cheeks.

"It's a long, stupid story. I'll tell you sometime. You'll laugh." Leila glanced up. Mudder and Susan exchanged concerned glances. "No harm done. I'm here now. Let's have us a baby."

Despite those optimistic words, the minutes dragged on. Deborah's screams weakened and turned to whimpers. Phineas appeared in the doorway, his scarred face white and drawn, then disappeared.

Deborah's screams rose again. Leila held one hand while Susan grasped the other. Leila prayed silently as Deborah gathered the last of her waning strength and screamed through another push. The sound of a baby wailing filled the ensuing silence. A plaintive sound. "He took his sweet time getting here, this little one. Has a mind of his own, he does." Mudder made quick work of cutting the cord and wiping down the baby, flailing arms and legs included. She wrapped him in a towel and held him out to Deborah. "He's a little bag of bones, but he won't break."

"A son," Deborah whispered, wonder wending itself around the two words. "A boy."

"Jah. He's breathing good and his skin color is nice and pink. He'll do."

"Get Phineas."

Leila did as Deborah asked. Phineas stood outside the door, head bent, eyes closed. Praying.

"He's here, Phineas, he's here. Your son is here."

Phineas's jaw worked. His lips trembled as he nodded, but he said nothing. Leila wanted to wrap him in a hug, but he'd never accept such a comfort from anyone other than his own fraa. She slipped out of the way and let him enter the room first.

Deborah tilted her precious bundle so her husband could see his son's face. A red, wrinkled face stared back at them, damp black hair spiking around it. The baby's lips puckered; he opened his mouth and wailed once again, this time with greater vigor.

"Hush, hush." Deborah smiled, then kissed his tiny forehead. "He looks like you."

Phineas grunted, a sound that might have been an attempt at a laugh. He kissed his wife and took the baby from her. "I'd like to introduce him to his groossdaadi."

"Do that. I want a word with Leila." Deborah's smile drifted away and she focused on Leila, who tried not to look guilty. She already expected a discussion with Mudder, but Deborah too? Now? At the door, Phineas stopped and turned. "We'll name him Timothy, then."

Mudder made a faint sound, a soft sigh. Deborah nodded. "For Daed."

Leila swiped at her cheeks, hoping they wouldn't see the sudden tears that refused to stay put. "That's a good, strong name."

Mudder hugged Deborah hard, then straightened. "You must be famished. I'll bring you some soup."

"I'll get some clean sheets." Susan followed Mudder to the door.

Deborah eased against the pillow. "Danki, y'all, for everything."

"All in a day's work." A smile blossomed on Mudder's face. "I'm a groossmammi. Who would've thought?"

She bustled from the room, Susan behind her. They were both still smiling. Leila found more tears threatening. She now served as little Timothy's aenti. "We're all grown up, aren't we, schweschder?"

"I don't know about you . . ." Deborah winced and rubbed her belly. She closed her eyes for a second, then opened them. "Come brush out my hair for me? I'm a mess. Where's my kapp?"

Leila picked up the brush from the crate and crawled in bed

next to her sister. "Who cares about your hair. How does it feel to be a mudder?"

"Wunderbarr. Unimaginably wonderful." She scooted up so she could lean against the pillows propped on the wall and bent her head forward, letting Leila take out the mangled mess of a braid hanging down her back. "I was in labor all day. When you didn't come home from work, Mudder was worried. She worries about you a lot, much as she tries not to show it."

"I know. It was a mess. Nolan had to work a double shift, so Rory's husband, Dwayne, was to give us a ride home."

"Unless I'm touched in the head after all that labor, I believe it's still the same distance whether it's Nolan or Dwayne driving. Did he get lost or something?"

"Or something." Leila worked her fingers through a nasty snarl, glad her sister couldn't see her face. "He insisted on going to the park instead of coming home. Some of his friends showed up. They brought alcohol."

"Did you drink?" Deborah's tone was matter of fact. She hadn't done much in the way of running around, but she'd never been one to judge others. "You didn't let him drive you home after that?"

"Nee. I didn't drink and I didn't come home with them."

Deborah swiveled. She grimaced and her hands went to her belly. She breathed, a high, aching sound. "Tell me."

"Now's not the time."

"It'll take my mind off my aches."

Leila told the story with no embellishment. She couldn't see her sister's face, but an occasional clucking sound told her Deborah listened. When she finished, the hair was neat and tidy in its bun, so unlike Leila's own messy life. "Well?"

"Ach." Deborah tucked her kapp over her hair and eased back

on the pillows. "My sweet schweschder, the can of worms you've opened."

"I didn't open it. Jesse did."

"Now you know."

"What do you mean?"

"Now you know what Jesse's secret is. You can't pretend ignorance."

"I know."

"That means you have to choose."

Leila plucked at the threadbare sheet. She couldn't tell Deborah—not even Deborah—about the pull she'd felt in Tiffany's living room. The intensity of the worship. The sense that Gott had been there. Right there in the midst of their praise of Him. Near to her. Even her. Little Leila Lantz. So much more of a choice than Deborah could imagine. "I want Jesse to choose me. At least I think I do. There's Will too. He's steady and strong and not taken to flights of fancy."

"It's not just about you."

"I know."

Deborah patted the pillow next to her. Leila snuggled up next to her big sister, aware of the seconds ticking by. Anytime now, Phineas would return and this moment would be lost. This happy time in her sister's life should not be marred by this discussion. "It's okay. Don't worry about it. I know what I have to do."

"Do you?"

"I have to make the right choice."

"Jah."

"That's always been true though."

Deborah closed her eyes, her breathing soft and even. "Jah, but never more than now. You have to decide what you believe, and you have to choose how you want to live."

"You never had any doubts?"

"Nee." Her eyelids fluttered. "Tell Phineas to bring me our baby."

Leila kissed her cheek. Deborah didn't move. "Danki, big schweschder."

She slipped from the bed, careful not to jostle her sister. Rubbing her eyes, shoulders aching with exhaustion, she trudged down the stairs. She'd sleep in Esther's room for the night. The soft, worn cotton of sheets and a pillow called out to her. Tomorrow would be another day. First she needed to eat. Her empty belly rumbled in agreement. It had been too many hours since her PB&J sandwich and oatmeal cookies. Food and then sleep. Choices would have to wait.

Phineas passed her on the stairs, his gaze fixed on the steps as if he feared a wrong step in his new role as daed. She smiled at the fierce concentration on his face. He would be a good daed. She heaved a sigh and started through the front room.

Mordecai stood between her and the kitchen. His grave expression caused her fatigue to flee. Her mother stood behind him, her arms crossed, shoulders bowed. "It's time we have a talk."

"Could we do it in the morning?"

Mordecai shook his craggy head, his beard swaying. "Everyone will sleep better if we do it now."

He turned and disappeared into the kitchen. Leila shuffled after him, inhaling the mouthwatering scent of frying onions. Her stomach growled. Mudder moved between the cabinet and the stove. When she turned, she held a plate piled with fried potatoes and onions, stewed eggplant, and a venison patty with a chunk of sourdough bread on the side. "I reckon you didn't get supper."

Leila accepted the plate and slipped into a chair across from her stepfather. Funny to think of Mordecai that way. Their relationship was so new, yet he held so much authority over her. "I didn't, but it won't happen again. It's not what you think. Nolan had to work a double shift—"

"We think you working in town was a mistake." Mordecai spread his long fingers in wide fans over the rough pine table that separated them. "It's become more and more clear that you're drifting into ways that aren't ours."

"Nee. I'm not."

"Where were you tonight?"

"At the park in town." She blurted out the words without considering her story. They were true enough. Was she willing to lie for Jesse about the rest of her evening? Even if it was a lie of omission? She swallowed against bile that burned the back of her throat. "Dwayne was supposed to bring us home, but he wanted to stop at the park first. Rory was . . . distracted. I didn't want to leave the baby unattended."

Telling Mordecai about her forced visit to the park because of Rory's teenage husband would only reinforce her stepfather's opinion that she'd been led astray, but she couldn't bring herself to share her experience with the youth group. Everything would change. So much was at stake. For Jesse. For her. Even for other girls in the district who might set their sights on a job in Beeville to help their families survive here. Rebekah and Hazel who would come after her.

Mordecai tugged at his beard. His gaze shifted to where Mudder stood, hands in a tub of soapy water, her expression filled with concern. "How did you get home then?"

"A friend of Jesse's gave me a ride."

"Jesse was there." Mordecai's thick eyebrows bunched as his forehead wrinkled. "What was he doing there?"

"He was with a friend who drove by the park. They stopped when they saw me."

"And he brought you home."

"Jah."

"Gut. That's gut."

It was the truth. She let her gaze sink to her hands, bunched in fists on the table. Not telling the whole truth protected not only Jesse, but herself. Jesse's involvement with this youth group was already causing her trouble. Her involvement. She had gone willingly into that room. But she hadn't known what lay ahead. Now she did. Lying was a sin. Not telling the whole truth was a sin of omission.

She couldn't tell the whole truth. She didn't know it yet. Choices remained to be made.

Gott, forgive me. Help me understand these feelings. She had been touched by what she saw. The depth of their fervor, the joy in their beaming faces. She could admit it, now that she was away from Jesse's prying eyes. Something in her had embraced their expression of their faith, loud and noisy and exuberant. Faith so alive, she could almost touch it. No wonder they wanted to tell people about it.

Would she give up her family to experience that feeling all the time? Nee. Nee? Although at this moment in time, she would give much to escape the paralyzing examination of Mordecai's eyes. It was as if he read the very words written by God on her soul. She willed herself not to squirm.

"You're not to get in a car with this Dwayne again. If Nolan can't bring you home, use the phone at the day care to call the store."

Not a problem. "I understand."

"You'll let her go back to work then?" Mudder squeezed her hands together in front of her as if in supplication. "But we—"

"She's not to blame for Nolan's inability to give her a ride." Mordecai tapped his fingers on the table in a restless beat. "She showed good judgment in not leaving the baby alone with young folks who were drinking. She was brought home by a friend of Jesse's."

The goodwill in Mordecai's voice made Leila's face burn. He had faith in her. He trusted her to tell the truth and do the right thing. She wanted to do that so badly, but she couldn't reveal Jesse's secret to the deacon. He would have to take her revelation to the bishop. Jesse's father. She now understood Will's dilemma and the pain it caused him. To be caught between right and wrong on behalf of a friend and cousin. For her, a man for whom she had feelings. Strong feelings.

"Will came by the house this evening."

Leila started. Mudder had many attributes, but reading the minds of her kinner was not one of them. Thanks be to Gott. Her mother's voice held a soft, pleading note, whether for her or for Mordecai, Leila couldn't decide.

"What did he say?" She took a breath. "I mean, what did he want?"

"He *said* he came to tell us Andrew is firing up the cement mixer tomorrow to help Jacob finish the slab for his milk storage house. Wanted to know if I was headed out to help." Mordecai tugged his glasses from his nose and polished them with his shirtsleeve. He yawned. "I am. While we have the mixer going, we'll work on the honey storage house and make some sidewalks up by the store. Make a day of it. Time for sleep."

He rose and stretched his arms over his head. "Eat your supper. You'll sleep better. Tomorrow is another day, Gott willing."

She picked up her fork. Mudder set a glass of water by her plate, wiped her hands on her apron, and then squeezed Leila's shoulder.

"Mudder?"

"Don't forget your prayers." Mudder trudged to the door. Her tone was soft, sad. "Gott sees and Gott knows the whole truth. Not just the bits and pieces we choose to share."

"I know."

"Whatever went on tonight, He knows. Ask Him for guidance. Trust in His will for you." She disappeared through the doorway.

God's will. Leila forced herself to eat the food in front of her because she couldn't bear to waste it, but the venison and sourdough bread tasted of nothing. Her mouth was so dry she had to gulp water to force the food down. Finally she dropped her fork on her plate, rose, and carried it to the sink. Her stomach roiled as she stared down at the tub of soapy water. She balanced on the edge of an abyss, teetering on the edge of everything she'd ever known and a world so fathomless it seemed a bottomless pit.

Any second, she would fall.

TWENTY-FOUR

All those illuminated numbers on the dash meant something. Aware of Colton's waning patience, Jesse stared at them. Despite the cool early December air wafting through the open window, his palms were hot and slick on the wheel. His dry mouth made it hard to swallow. He forced himself to put one hand on the round knob of the gearshift and look through the dust, bird droppings, and splattered insects on the windshield of Mr. Wise's ancient Ford pickup truck.

The dirt road on the Wise ranch wound its way as far as the eye could see across flat, brown fields barren of vegetation in winter. A good place to learn to drive. No one he could hit and nothing he could damage within miles. And no one to see him do this thing, which by all accounts a Plain man should not do. "Do you really think I'm ready for this? I mean, what's the hurry?"

"The hurry is I can't keep hauling you all over the place." Colton slurped from a sixteen-ounce Big Red bottle and then settled it into a plastic cup holder dangling from the passenger side door. "If you're gonna help us by leading meetings and doing hospital visits and such, you have to learn to drive. It's time to put up or shut up."

The hint of sarcasm in Colton's voice told Jesse they weren't simply talking about driving. Colton had made it clear he wanted Jesse to dive headfirst into this new life, holding back nothing, not looking back. Colton understood the price Jesse would pay, but he believed their mission to be worth it. Jesse agreed, but that didn't make it easy.

Not with Leila still out there. He'd seen something in her face that night at youth group. She'd felt it. She wanted it. She simply wasn't ready to admit it. Not yet. That hope kept him going.

Or maybe he saw what he wanted to see.

"Earth to Jesse." Colton tapped the dashboard in double time. "Now would be good, dude."

"I don't have a car, so what does it matter if I can drive?" To own a car. To drive. Those things meant freedom to travel in a way not dependent on anyone else. Freedom and independence. Not words often used in the Plain vocabulary. "It's not like I can afford to buy one. I don't even have a license."

"One thing at a time, my friend. License is next on my list. My dad raised four boys. We have half a dozen old junk cars on the ranch. That's how we all learned to drive." Colton waved a hand at the dusty interior of the truck with its ripped upholstery and Hawaiian dancer bobblehead on the dashboard. "Logan learned in this very vehicle last year. We fix them up and drive them. That way if we have an accident—which my dad says all teenage boys will do—it's no big loss. Plus you learn to repair cars. Very important skill for guys to have. Girls like it. You can drive this one or one of the others, it doesn't matter. Next we'll teach you how to change the oil and replace the battery. All the basics."

He sounded genuinely happy about the situation, as if he were passing on to Jesse a family tradition important to him. Not a tradition Jesse had ever expected to share. If his family could see him now. His daed. Leila. They would never understand. He didn't really understand himself.

Jesse studied the gears on the tiny diagram on the knob. 1, 2, 3, 4, 5, R. PUSH IN THE CLUTCH WITH YOUR LEFT FOOT, HIT THE GAS WITH THE RIGHT, AND SHIFT—ALL AT THE SAME TIME. Who had that kind of coordination? How could he watch the road and manage all this shifting stuff too? Buggies were so much easier. Horses did all the work. "Why does it have to be a standard?"

"'Cuz my dad always says a guy needs to know how to drive a stick first. If you can do that, you can drive anything. Farm equipment, pickups, sports cars. Besides, girls like a guy who can drive a stick." Colton leaned against the door and stuck his elbow on the frame of the open window. For a guy about to put his life in Jesse's hands, he looked mighty relaxed. "We're not getting any younger, buddy. Let's do it. Stop stalling. Start her up."

Groaning, Jesse wiggled the stick to make sure it was in Neutral and turned the key in the ignition. The old truck rumbled to life, its engine sounding smooth and silky despite its rusting hulk of an exterior. The smell of exhaust wafted through the windows. A thrill ran through him so acute the hair on his arms bristled. He inhaled. He was driving.

Jesse Glick was driving.

What if Leila could see him now? What would she think? She danced with Will. Would she let Jesse take her for a ride?

"Push in the clutch and the gas at the same time as you go from Neutral to First. Gently. Smoothly." Colton's voice was soft and patient. "Relax, just take it slow, real slow."

Jesse shoved the stick in First. Gears screeched in a horrible grinding noise. The truck jerked. The engine died.

Or not.

"It's okay, it's okay." Colton slapped a hand over his mouth, but it didn't muffle his chuckle. "Everybody does that at first. It takes some coordination."

"No kidding."

It took twenty minutes and a dozen or more attempts, but Jesse got the hang of it. He was determined to do it, if for no other reason than to show Colton he could. If every Wise brother could do it, every Englisch man could do it, Jesse Glick could drive a stick. Somewhere in the second half hour, they made it to the end of the dirt road, much to Jesse's surprise. He stopped at the intersection where dirt and gravel met asphalt.

"Go on, you know you want to." Colton pointed toward the west. "Hit the highway. Let her rip. Get some speed up."

"Are you kidding? The speed limit is like sixty-five out there."

"That's the great thing about a standard. Once you get in gear, if you maintain your speed, you're good. You don't have to downshift until you're ready to slow down."

"I don't have a license."

"You think anybody out here is checking?"

Driving a truck on the highway. He'd watched them sail by for so many years, leaving him and his horse eating dirt, plodding along, five miles an hour. Jesse looked left. He looked right. He slapped the turn signal on. "Here we go."

"Attaboy!"

Jesse jabbed the gas, worked the gears, and made it onto the highway in a wide turn that wasn't half bad. Air rushed through the open windows, bringing with it the smell of winter and damp earth. He inhaled and tried to relax. Thirty, forty, fifty, sixty. They were sailing down the highway. He was driving. Never in his life had he imagined such a feeling. He had control of this one little piece of his life. For these few seconds.

"Feels good, doesn't it?" Colton sucked down his Big Red. "Nothing better than being your own ride."

"It does feel good." He could admit it to Colton. His friend understood about these things. "I don't know exactly why, but it's good."

"It's a guy thing. Every guy wants to drive a truck."

"Not every guy."

They came up over an incline and rounded a deep bend in the highway. A second later an enormous SUV blotted out the road ahead. It blocked the entire lane. Its crumpled front end faced Jesse head-on. A massive truck with welding equipment hanging off its mangled sides blocked the opposite lane.

Beyond it were more cars, smaller, more crumpled. Jesse didn't have time to count them. His foot went from the gas to the brake.

"Easy, easy!" Colton hollered as he fumbled the Big Red bottle. It tumbled down his front, soaking his white T-shirt. "Easy!"

Tires screamed, the brakes squealed. Jesse tried to control the skid, but the truck seemed to have a mind of its own now. Its front end missed the SUV by a hairbreadth. He twisted the wheel and avoided some kind of smaller car turned so it faced the wrong way on the road. The truck bucked and shimmied. Tires screeched, brakes ground. The smell of burnt rubber filled the cab. They careened across the oncoming lane, slammed into the ditch, bounced up the embankment, and smashed into the posts of a barbed-wire fence.

Finally, they stopped moving.

It might have taken all of fifteen seconds to reach this blessed resting place, but it seemed hours had passed. Jesse panted. His lungs couldn't seem to suck in air. Blood pounded in his ears. Black dots floated in his peripheral vision. His legs and arms shook inexplicably. His brain searched the far extremities of his body. No pain except for the bruising hold of the seat belt across his chest.

His hands still grasped the wheel. He couldn't release the white-knuckled grip of his fingers, hard as he tried. He managed to turn his head toward Colton. His friend had both hands wrapped around his seat belt as if willing it to hold him in place. "You okay?"

"Yeah, but those folks aren't." His breathing ragged, Colton flipped off his seat belt and shoved open the door. "Looks like it just happened. Let's go."

Spurred by the urgency in his friend's voice, Jesse did the same. He hurled himself from the truck, surprised to find his legs still worked. He darted across the field and onto the highway. A lady stumbled toward him, blood trickling from a cut on her forehead under bleached-blonde bangs. "My girls, my twins, they're hurt. Help us, please help us."

A man hoisted himself from the welding truck's open door and trotted toward the woman. "You better sit down, ma'am, before you fall down. That was a nasty head-on."

The woman's legs collapsed and she crumpled to the ground, hands covering her face.

"I've got her." The man waved Jesse on. "Check on the others."

Jesse kept moving toward the Tahoe. A tiny blonde girl stared back at him from the backseat. Her face crumpled and she began to whimper. The other girl's eyes were closed, her mouth slack. "Colton, they're little girls. They're hurt."

Colton already had his cell phone to his ear. "Help's on the way. Just talk to them. Keep talking to them."

"Hi, I'm Jesse. It'll be fine. Help is coming." He squeezed his head into the opening, avoiding shattered glass. The girls were dressed in matching jean jackets and blue corduroy pants. They were still belted in. "What's your name? What's your sister's name?"

The girl's whimpering subsided. "I'm Hannah. That's Hilary. She won't wake up."

"We're gonna help Hilary. Don't you worry." The prayers welled up in his head, silent entreaty to the Great Physician. Sirens began to scream in the distance. *Thank You, Jesus.* "Where were you headed?"

"Into town to buy Christmas presents for Daddy." Hannah's voice quavered. "We're gonna get him a new charcoal grill. He burned out the bottom of the old one. Mommy likes it when he grills. Then she doesn't have to cook."

"You'll still have plenty of time."

"Hold my hand?"

Hannah's small hand crept toward Jesse's on the window frame. He stuck his out to meet hers. It was clammy. "Help's on the way."

The quiet of the countryside disappeared into a cacophony of ambulances and fire trucks. An EMT jumped from the first ambulance. Jesse squeezed Hannah's hand one last time and let the man do his job, starting with Hilary, who stirred and mumbled when the EMT touched her face with a purple-gloved hand.

Jesse took a breath, sure he'd been holding it for days. *Thank You, Jesus, thank You.*

He eased back and turned around. Seven cars in all. A chain reaction of some kind. He lurched around in a bad dream. If only it were a bad dream. One minute he cruised along the highway, driving a truck, and the next he was confronted with carnage on the road. Little girls hurt and bleeding.

What did that mean?

Colton trotted toward him. The Big Red soaking his shirt made him look bloody. They stood together on the edge of the road, watching the emergency responders assess injuries, prioritize, and transport the injured. Hilary and Hannah went first to the medical center in Beeville. Minutes later the *whop-whop* of the Halo-Flight helicopter blades filled the air. It landed right on the highway, scattering dust and debris. Its presence only served to add to the surreal nature of the afternoon.

"They're transporting the couple from the Neon. They're hurt bad. They'll go to Corpus." Colton fingered his cell phone as if itching to call someone. "The one little girl's injuries are minor. The other one, they need to check her out more. She might have a head injury. The mom needs stitches and she has two broken wrists—air bags, you know."

"Driving was a bad idea."

"You didn't have an accident."

"No, I ran into one."

"And you handled it just fine."

"I wrecked your truck."

Together they turned to survey the pickup. From a distance it looked fine, but the front end was wedged against the fence. Colton stalked through the weeds. "Hardly a scratch. I bet it will start right up."

"The keys are in it."

"You need to do it."

"I don't think so."

"Come on, I'm not asking you to drive anywhere. Just start her up. It's like getting back on a horse after you're thrown."

Only one of them had actually experienced being thrown from a horse, and that was Jesse. The pain of his bruised behind would never be forgotten. "Easy for you to say."

"Y'all the ones who reported this?" A tall state trooper with skin the color of licorice strode toward them, a clipboard in one hand. "I'm looking for witnesses."

"I think a bunch of folks in the cars reported it." Colton leaned against the side of the truck. "We didn't really see anything. The accident had already happened when we drove up on the scene."

The trooper's gaze flitted to Jesse. He seemed to study his attire. Jesse fought the urge to fidget. What if the guy wanted to know who was driving? "You see anything?"

"No. We came around the bend and there they were. He drove off the road to avoid them."

We. He.

The trooper made notes, his pen making a scratching noise on the paper. "I'll need your names and contact information."

Colton recited his number. "You can reach Jesse here through me. His family doesn't have a phone."

The trooper's eyebrows did push-ups, but he didn't comment. "Do you need a tow?"

"Naw, I'll call my dad if we need help."

"Thanks for getting involved. Folks don't always want to do that anymore."

"We do. We're all about getting involved." Colton's gaze encompassed Jesse and the trooper. "That's what life is all about, getting involved."

After the trooper moved away, Jesse brushed past Colton and

got in the truck. His friend was right. He'd spent a lot of time standing on the sidelines. Helping people felt good. It gave life meaning. He needed to remember that.

Colton plopped into the seat next to him. "Big Red will never come out of the seat. But in this truck, who cares?"

Jesse turned the key. The engine rumbled. Then it died. And refused to be coaxed into starting again. He blew out air and settled against the seat, his damp shirt stuck to his back. "Now what?"

"Now I call my dad. He'll have my uncle bring his tow truck out. They're at an auction this afternoon, so it'll take him a bit to get here." Colton scrounged around in the space behind the seat and pulled out a small cooler. "But that's okay. I got food."

"How can you eat at a time like this?"

"You can't?"

His friend was right. Jesse was always hungry.

Colton made the call. It didn't sound as if his dad was too upset about the situation. Jesse had met the man a time or two, and he had an easygoing way about him that matched his lumbering size and genial grin. "He says it'll be about an hour. We'll eat and take a nap, how about that?"

The fade of the adrenaline had left Jesse weary beyond measure. "Sure."

Colton rummaged in the cooler and brought out two sandwiches. He handed one to Jesse, said a quick blessing, and then began unwrapping the other one. "Do you know the story in Genesis where Jacob wrestles all night with the Angel of God?"

Here we go. Jesse picked at the wrapper on his sandwich and nodded. "Sure. Who doesn't?"

"Lots of folks in this world, which is why we do what we do, but that's not where I'm going at the moment."

Jesse couldn't wait to find out where Colton was going now. He kept that sarcastic thought to himself. The guy knew his Bible inside and out and had no fear when it came to approaching strangers with the best news possible. Whatever Colton had to say, he said out of a love for Jesus and because he cared about Jesse. Why, Jesse didn't really understand.

"Watching you talk to Leila the other night reminded me of that story."

The bite of ham-and-cheese sandwich in Jesse's mouth lost all flavor in that moment when his mind's eye ran through the images. The anger and the tears and the confusion and the sadness, sometimes one after another, and then mixed together as Leila tried to understand what he was saying. "All I did was make her feel bad and put her in a terrible position of having to either rat me out or lie to her family and my family. I don't feel good about what I did to Leila."

"Jacob didn't want to give it up and give God control of his life. He was fighting Him every step of the way. The Angel of God wrestled with him all night and then finally touched his hip and made it come out of the socket."

Jesse knew the story as well as he knew the story of Adam and Eve or Noah and the ark or Jonah and the great fish. "What does that have to do with me?"

"Give in. God could have caused that hip problem right at the beginning, but He didn't. He wanted Jacob to relent on his own. Instead he wasted a whole night fighting God's will. Let God have control over your life. You're either in or out. You can't keep sitting on the fence."

"I'm not sitting on the fence. I'm all in." Even as he said those words, Jesse knew he hadn't demonstrated to anyone, not Colton, not Leila, not God, that he truly was committed. He'd wavered. It was time to take a stand. "I've been working through my faith and figuring out how to make this change without hurting people. But I will make it."

"I understand that. I never had to make the choices you have to make. That's not lost on me." Colton contemplated his sandwich, took a bite, chewed, and swallowed. "I respect you for doing what you're doing. But you can't make the decision based on your feelings for Leila. If she doesn't have the same calling, you have to come without her."

Jesse shoved the remainder of his sandwich into the plastic bag. He rubbed at his face with the back of his hand, trying to hide the emotions that battered him. He cleared his throat. "I'm just—"

"Crazy about her, I know." Colton tugged a bottle of water from the cooler and twisted off the cap. "That's tougher than I can begin to imagine. I'm blessed to have a girlfriend who's on the same page with me. It's a God-thing that Tiffany and I found each other so early on. So I can't claim to know how you feel about any of this. Leaving your family or Leila. But you're making it worse by prolonging the agony. Make a decision and then make a clean break."

"Did I have to learn how to drive a stick to do that?"

"I guess it's all connected in my mind—wrestling with a stick shift, wresting with an Angel of God, wrestling with your conscience, wrestling with a decision that will change your entire life." Colton squeezed the plastic bag from his sandwich into a ball. It blossomed out again. "Jacob was a new man when it was over. God gave him a new name. He started a new life. You can do that too."

A new man. A new name. A new life. Jesse wanted those things. He wanted them badly. But he also wanted Leila. Whether he could have both was up to God. God's will. "You're right, but I still have to figure some things out, so give me time."

"I hear you, dude. I'll try not to be so obnoxious about it." Colton pulled a bag of Oreos from the cooler and held it out. "Here. Cookies make everything better."

"I think that's peanut butter."

"You do love Leila, don't you?"

Jesse took two cookies, then thought better of it and went back for three more. Even that wouldn't be enough. "Yeah, I do."

"Then don't give up on her."

"It's not fair to her."

"Dude, if you're the man God has chosen for her, then you need to do everything in your power to make her see that." Colton pulled a cookie apart and licked the white frosting in the middle. A look of pure bliss spread across his face. "Don't you see? You could be the love of her life *and* help her have a closer relationship with God. It's a win-win."

"She has a close relationship with God. She's a believer. If she chooses me, chooses us, she loses her family and the only life she's ever known. Not a win-win."

"Nobody said it would be easy." Colton tossed Jesse the bag of cookies. "Somehow I don't see you living your life much different than you do now. A simple, plain life. A good life. One you can share with a good woman. It's a God-thing, dude. If you really believe in what we're doing, you can't do anything else. You have to try. For her sake and yours."

"How can you claim to be so sure of what God's plan is?"

"It's all in the Good Book."

"We—my folks—live by the same Good Book."

"People like to pick and choose the parts of the Book they want to live by. Sometimes they ignore other parts because it's more comfortable or easier or whatever."

Jesse dropped the bag of cookies and shoved open his door. He needed to think. He needed space. "That's not the case with my folks. There's nothing comfortable or easy about our lives."

"I know, I know. I'm not judging. Believe me. I have nothing but respect for the way your folks live their lives. I'm just saying it's not for you. You're called to something else. It's possible Leila is too. Maybe that's why the two of you feel such a pull toward each other."

"If this is you not being obnoxious, we're in trouble." Jesse rubbed his face with the back of his sleeve. It smelled of asphalt and sweat. He hopped from the truck and looked back at Colton. "I'm gonna walk up to the road and wait for your uncle."

"Sorry, dude, I've only got one setting, I guess. Full tilt. Think about what I said, will ya?"

How could Jesse think about anything else? He started toward the road. Colton's voice carried through the open window. "Tomorrow we go to DPS so you can take your driver's test. Get a haircut. You want to look good for the photo on your license, don't you?"

Jesse closed his eyes against the pale, lackluster sun. A haircut. A driver's license. For every action, there was a reaction. Little pieces of his old self chipping off and falling by the wayside until a new man was born.

A man his family wouldn't recognize. But God would. God knew what was in his heart. The desire to tell the world about the love of Jesus and the promise of salvation.

He couldn't cover his ears and block out the voice calling him.

He didn't want to ignore it.

Gott, I'm yours. I surrender all to You.

Now could I talk to You about Leila?

TWENTY-FIVE

Shivering in a cool, early-morning breeze, Will hopped from the buggy and tied the reins to a fence post at the Glick corral. The mid-December sun shone bright, but the purpose of his visit took the edge off his natural inclination to be buoyed by the light. If Jesse had noticed his arrival, he didn't show it. He had his hands full with a Morgan intent on breaking free of its halter. The horse whinnied, tossed its head, and tried to nip at his own belly. Jesse hung on to the lead with both hands and urged the horse to walk, his tone gentle and cajoling.

Will had seen this behavior before. He felt for the animal and for the Glicks. Colic could be a deadly thing in a horse. He climbed over the fence and dropped into the corral, his weight causing puffs of dust to billow around his scuffed boots.

"Hey."

Jesse looked up, his expression dark and distracted. "Hey."

"Walking him?"

"Jah, but it's been fifteen minutes. Daed said no more than fifteen, twenty at the most. We don't want to wear him out if he's got it bad."

"Colic?"

"Worse, I think. Daed talked to the vet this morning and we gave him some Milk of Magnesia. It didn't help. Looks to be twisted gut."

The worst kind of news. "Vet's been out?"

Jesse shook his head. "Daed talked to him on the phone. We thought we could doctor him ourselves, but it isn't getting better so he went back to the store to call the vet to come out—"

The horse reared up and bucked, hooves flying. The reins whipped from Jesse's hand. He stumbled back, dropped to his knees, then scrambled sideways. The horse careened around the corral as if trying to escape his own pain.

Will threw himself out of the way, rolled, and came up against the fence, the breeze on his face telling him how close he'd come to getting a hoof in the face.

"Grab him, grab him!" Jesse yelled. "Don't let him roll."

Rolling, the horse's first instinct, could exacerbate a twisted gut. Will shot after the animal and scooped up the trailing reins. "Whoa, whoa, hold on, Sugar, come on, boy, slow down."

A series of hard tugs brought the horse under control, but sweat lathered his flanks. His lips curled as he tossed his long, lean neck and whinnied again and again.

"It's okay, boy, it's okay. Easy does it."

Jesse edged closer and snatched the reins from Will. They were both sweating despite a nippy wind that spoke of winter and December finally arriving.

"What are you doing here?" Jesse panted. "You didn't come to see about a horse."

Will leaned over and planted his hands on his dirty pants, trying to catch his breath. He didn't take his gaze from the horse.

In his current condition, the animal could bolt again and again until the pain became too much and he sank to the ground, or by some miracle, the medicine took hold and the blockage dissolved. Will tried to gather his thoughts as Jesse smoothed his hands over the horse's back, whispering sweet nothings to the animal.

They'd been friends as long as Will could remember. More than cousins. More like brothers. He couldn't be sure how they'd arrived at this moment. But this would be the moment. He was determined. He wanted to do more than hold Leila's hand and dance with her. He wanted to be the one standing in front of the district one day, promising a lifetime of commitment. Jesse couldn't have it both ways. Living with one boot in this world, one boot in that one.

Right now, he looked the picture of a Plain man, soothing a sick horse and praying that it was enough. That they didn't lose an animal vital to their survival and costly to replace. A deceiving picture, indeed.

Will inhaled and exhaled. The smell of dirt, manure, and straw filled the air, familiar and calming. "Did you go to your youth group thing this week?"

"Jah."

Jesse's tone said he didn't want to talk about it. Will ignored it. "And have you decided what you'll do?"

"I'm working on it." Jesse smoothed his hand over the horse's nose, his touch gentle. The animal's head dipped and he whinnied, long and low. "Come on, Sugar, come on. You're needed around here, boy."

"Vet will be here soon." Will straightened and heaved another breath. They needed calm as much for the horse as for themselves.

"He can give him that mineral-oil treatment and something for the pain. He'll make it."

Jesse wrapped his fingers in the silky hair of the horse's mane. His head dropped until his forehead rested against the mammoth animal's sweaty neck. "If it's more than colic, if it's a twisted gut, he'll need surgery."

This wasn't Will's first go-round with severe colic. The horse would have a fifty-fifty chance of surviving surgery, and where would the money come from? "Cross that bridge when we come to it."

"I could do without the judgment. Daed says we're not to judge others."

The flip-flop of topics didn't surprise Will. "I'm not judging. I'm worried for you."

Jesse raised his head. His face was gray with fatigue, and smudges darkened the skin under his eyes like fresh bruises. "You're worried for Leila."

"I don't deny that." Will tugged the reins from his cousin's hand. "But you're my family and I see you drifting—nee, running—in a direction that takes you far from us. I don't understand it."

"Come to a few meetings and I promise you will. These folks are the real thing. Their faith and devotion are real."

"You'd try to suck me in too?" Will shook his head, baffled by his cousin's inability to see the consequences of his actions or more, his inability to stop himself from going down this road. What hold did these people have on him that was stronger than the faith and community with which he'd grown up? How could he contemplate a road that would shame his entire family? "I feel like we've lost you. You're not Jesse anymore."

"I'm not the Jesse I used to be. That's true." Jesse faced Will, his expression lighter. He smiled for the first time. "This is a good thing. I'm closer to Jesus than I've ever been before."

"And you won't be close to Jesus if you're baptized and worshipping with your community?" It seemed as if they were speaking different languages. "I don't understand. We worship every other Sunday. Leroy does a good job with the sermons. What more do you need?"

"I need to talk about it, study it, share it."

"So it's about you?"

"Nee. It's about making sure everyone gets the good news."

"The good news?"

"That Jesus loves them."

"And it's your job to tell them?"

The horse bobbed his head and swiveled it, his bared teeth yellow against his dark mane. He strained and nipped at his belly. Jesse tugged at the reins. "Nee, nee, Sugar, you'll only hurt yourself."

Could he not hear his own words? "Jesse—"

"Spreading the good news is my job and your job and everyone's who knows about God's saving grace."

Will stood, boots planted in the dirt, staring. He had no words for this argument. He only knew what was in his heart. A sense of loss. Sadness. An ache. The man standing before him was a stranger, not the cousin and best friend who had shared every good memory in Will's entire life. The first time fishing. The first time hunting deer. The first swim in the Gulf. Rumspringa. That boy-turned-man had disappeared down a path Will couldn't see, let alone follow. "And your parents?"

"They don't know yet."

"There's no changing your mind?"

Jesse's sigh mingled with the horse's snorts of pain. "I pray every night for a way to stay. That God will soften hearts and open ears to my words."

"Your words. Do you know how prideful that sounds?"

"It's not pride."

"And Leila?"

"She says she can't do it."

Relief washed over Will. He wouldn't lose them both. "Then I ask you not to stand in my way."

"Leila's a grown woman. Her choice will be her choice, not mine or yours." Jesse's voice quavered. "I may have lost the skirmish, but not the war."

"Are you talking about us or her faith?"

"Both. I told her I wouldn't try to convince her, knowing it would mean she would lose her family, her life here." He turned and faced Will. "But then I prayed on it and talked to Colton and I realized I was wrong. Her faith in God's saving grace through Jesus Christ is the only thing she needs in order to find eternal salvation, whether it's here or with me."

Will refused to debate religion with his cousin. Even if he could. He didn't have the fancy words used by Jesse's Englisch friends. "Here she has her family, her community."

"I know." Jesse's jaw worked. "I know what coming with me would mean for her. The loss. But also the gain of a community of believers who read the Bible, study it, talk about it, draw closer to God in every way."

"You want to have your cake and eat it too. You'll tear her away from her family in the name of Gott so you won't have to go on in your new life alone." Will took a step back, then another. An enormous lump formed in his throat. He was losing this battle, losing his best friend. Words seemed to have no effect. Perhaps because he couldn't find the right words in the midst of his own morass of emotion and fear. He was failing Jesse. He must not fail Leila too. "It's selfish and you know it."

"I'm not tearing anyone away. It will be her decision."

Influenced by her feelings—feelings Will recognized—for Jesse. "Stay away from her."

"I can't."

"You won't, you mean."

"It's between her and me."

Will stared at him. Jesse stared back. The impasse festered in the scant few feet between them. Everything had been said.

The sound of an engine rumbling broke the silence. Will tore his gaze from a man he didn't know anymore. A stranger walking in his cousin's boots. Jesse swiveled. A familiar, dusty green SUV bounced on the dirt road, gravel spitting behind it. The vet.

"I'll go and let you tend to the horse." Will brushed past Jesse without looking at him. He didn't dare or he would do or say something he shouldn't. "I hope Sugar makes it."

"Will!"

One syllable full of a million emotions.

Will kept walking.

"Come to a youth group meeting. You'll see. You'll understand."

He whirled. "You'd try to convert me too? Have you no shame?"

"I have only . . ." Jesse's voice was low and so full of emotion it hurt Will's ears. Like gravel scraping skin. "I care about what happens to you."

Plain men didn't talk of such things, but Will understood the inclination. His heart felt as if Sugar had stomped on it. "If you cared about any of us, you'd come to the baptism classes in January and forget this nonsense."

Jesse's face whitened. The dark bruises under his eyes deepened. "I can't. Not if it means keeping my mouth shut about things I know are important."

A door slamming told Will the vet would soon approach. One last-ditch effort. "We'll be baptized in time for Easter and the gmay. It could be you, me, and Leila up there, answering the questions, feeling that water on our heads."

Jesse's Adam's apple bobbed. His jaw worked. "I'll keep praying."

"You do that." Will turned and opened the corral gate for Dr. Martinez, who strode toward them, a huge leather bag in one hand, his gaze already fixed on Sugar. "So will I. For healing for you and for the horse."

"I don't need healing."

Jesse's voice chased Will from the corral and up into the buggy. He sounded so sure of himself.

Will found himself sure of nothing.

TWENTY-SIX

Stepping with care so as not to spill her cup of hot black tea, Leila squeezed between the coffee shop tables, thankful for the warmth of the heavy mug in her hands. It was only mid-December, but already they were experiencing unusually cold winter weather for south Texas. She didn't mind. Crisp, cold air served as a nice change from the hot humidity of the long summers in Bee County. She set the cup on the square Formica-topped table for two by the long window framed by red-checked curtains on either side.

She liked to watch the sporadic traffic go by in downtown Beeville while she ate her lunch. She always chose a small table so as not to take up space for customers buying lunch. Marie Diaz, the coffee shop owner, allowed her to eat her peanut-butter-and-jam sandwich in here, even though she never bought more than a tea or an occasional soda when she could afford it. She had one hour for lunch, and she tried to get out of the day care and away from her sweet babies so she'd have plenty of patience for them during the long afternoon that would follow.

Inhaling the mouthwatering scent of Marie's cinnamon rolls, Leila pulled her waxed-paper-wrapped sandwich from the mini cooler and contemplated the plastic container of cold macaroni and cheese. She should be content with her lunch, made with loving hands by family. For some reason, even Mudder's gingersnaps couldn't cheer her up today. Two weeks had gone by since her discussion with Jesse on the front porch of Tiffany's house and not a word from him. He hadn't come by to talk to Mordecai. He hadn't shone a flashlight in her window and asked her to come away with him.

Not that she wanted him to do that. She wrestled with that thought. Sometimes when she lay in bed at night and stared at the ceiling, with Rebekah's soft snores tickling her ears, she did want it. She could admit it in the dark of night. But in broad daylight, sun shining, Hazel giggling at the table, the smell of okra gumbo wafting through the air, Caleb and Esther arguing over the last biscuit, nee, she couldn't imagine another life for herself.

She couldn't have it both ways.

She had to choose. But that had always been the case. One day soon she would stand before her community and be baptized. Or she would walk away from this life. She'd been given a choice, just as Jesse had.

Just as Will had. More choices. She hadn't seen hide nor hair of Will either. One minute he was dancing her around an open field, the next he'd made himself scarce. He came by the house when she wasn't there but couldn't find his way to the door when she was. The story of her life.

"Hey, it's you."

She jumped and hot tea splattered on her hand. "Ouch!"

Tom Fletcher towered over her, his face lighted with a smile that brought out dimples in both cheeks. He wore a fleece-lined leather jacket and faded blue jeans and the usual Texas Rangers ball cap. Not working today. So why was Kaitlin back at the day care instead of with him? Leila stifled the question. He paid for a full week whether or not his child attended every day.

He held a tray laden with a wrapped sandwich of some kind, a bag of chips, one of Marie's slices of chocolate meringue pie, and a large glass of milk. "Sorry, didn't mean to startle you."

"Just daydreaming." Determined not to stare at his handsome face, she settled the mug on the table and dabbed at her hand with a napkin. "It's not your fault I was in never-never land."

"I'm surprised they let you out of your room. Who's watching my baby girl?"

"Don't worry, Shelby has her." Why wasn't he watching her? "It's only for an hour and she's had her bottle, so she's probably down for a nap anyway."

"I was just kidding. I know you have to eat like the next person." He glanced around the coffee shop. Despite the fact that it was lunchtime, a few tables were still open. His gaze landed back on her. "Mind if I join you? I have a couple of questions you might be able to help me with."

The heat on her face had nothing to do with her tea. Leila let her gaze drop to the sandwich in her hand. Lunch with an Englisch man. What would Mudder say? Or Mordecai? Tom was the father of one of her scholars, so to speak. If she were a teacher. She was a babysitter. They were in a public place, many folks around. What harm could there be? Mordecai and Mudder didn't want her around Dwayne and his friends. Tom was different.

"It's okay. If it takes you that long to think of an excuse not to let me sit down, I should move on." Tom balanced his tray on a thick book that looked like something he'd use if he were in school. "I have some studying to do anyway."

"Nee, nee, I didn't mean to be impolite—"

"You're not. If you want to eat alone, I totally understand. You spend all day with crying babies."

"They don't always cry. Just this morning, Kaitlin giggled."

He set the book on the third chair at her table, settled the tray on it, and slapped his ball cap on top of the book. "She doesn't giggle much around me. Her aunt and her cousins can make her laugh though."

Leila set her cooler on the floor and made room for Tom's food. "Try a little squeeze on those thunder thighs. She's ticklish."

"She is." He looked delighted. Then the smile faded. "So was her mother."

"And you're not?" Leila kept her tone light, teasing. "Not even your feet?"

He grinned. "I suppose so."

"Try it. Her laugh is so sweet."

He unwrapped his sandwich—pastrami on rye from the looks of it—and took a bite. She did the same and they chewed in companionable silence for a few seconds.

"You're not working today?"

He shook his head and tapped the mammoth textbook. "I'm studying. I want to be a physician's assistant."

Leila didn't know for sure what that was, but it sounded important. "You have to have a lot more schooling for that?"

"Yep. But it would mean I could do a lot more for sick or hurt people, not just pick them up in an ambulance and turn them over to someone at the ER."

"Do you have to work a lot if you're a physician's assistant?"

He shrugged as he licked a spot of mustard from his thumb. "I work a lot now. Fortunately my sister takes Kaitlin when I work night shifts. She's got three older boys, so she's happy to have a little girl now and again. Working any job in the medical field means odd hours, nights, weekends."

"So why do you want to do it more?"

"Because I help people." His gaze didn't meet hers. "And it keeps me occupied."

And away from his baby daughter. Tom was running from his responsibility. He feared not doing a good job, so he was shirking the duties altogether. "Kaitlin needs her daddy too."

"I know that." He frowned. "Like I said, I have family to help out."

She could understand that. Plain families raised their children as families. "What were your questions?"

He wiped his mouth with a paper napkin and laid the sandwich on his paper plate. "She isn't crawling yet. Shouldn't she be crawling? The book I read said six months."

"She just turned six months, and boy howdy, is she ready to crawl."

"How can you tell?"

"Do you lay her on a blanket on the floor at night?"

"Yeah, sure."

"Does she stay in one place?"

"No. She rolls around from one corner to the other and does this silly bucking thing like she's trying to look behind her by throwing her head back."

"She's a wiggle worm through and through, that girl." Leila couldn't help it. She grinned. "If you put her on her tummy, she does this thing with her legs like she's revving up to start moving. All of this stuff is the start of crawling. She's so close, she's almost there."

"That's what Sam said, but I wondered if the baby was confused or something. She can't seem to get it."

"She will. Who's Sam?" Not that it was any of Leila's business. She was glad Tom had a man friend to whom he could talk.

"My partner." He took another bite, his expression thoughtful. He chewed and swallowed. "I guess I should start baby proofing."

"What do you mean?"

"You know, put plugs in the sockets, locks on the cabinet doors, and such."

Leila nodded. Plain folks didn't have sockets to worry about, and mostly the older children kept an eye on the younger ones to keep them out of trouble. "Probably a good idea."

"How old are you?"

Startled by the question, she dropped her sandwich on the waxed paper and wiped peanut butter from her fingers on the napkin she'd brought from home. "I'm nineteen. Why?"

"Diane and I were nineteen when we got married. My folks said we were too young, but we were in love and we wanted to be together. I thought we were doing the right thing. Getting married all proper and such."

How did a person know if love would last? That's what he was asking. Leila didn't know the answer. How she wished she did. "You were."

"I don't know. Divorce isn't proper."

"Nee, it's not."

"Don't sugarcoat it." His smile took the sting from the words. "Not my choice. I never thought I'd be divorced at twenty-five."

"I know."

"You're the expert. Come over and baby proof the house for me."

"I'm no expert. We don't have sockets."

"'Course you don't." His nose wrinkled. He had a nice nose. "But you work in a day care."

"And then I go home to my family."

"You have a boyfriend?"

The bite of cookie in her mouth turned to sand. She didn't know how to answer that question. Jesse or Will? Did either qualify as a boyfriend?

Tom held up one big hand. "It's none of my business. Sorry."

"I don't know."

"How could you not know?"

"Two men have courted me. Sort of."

"Two? That's progressive."

"That's not how it is. Neither has . . . staked a claim."

"You Amish women aren't much for feminism." He chuckled, a deep, rich sound, and held out a fork. "Help me eat this pie. No way I'll be able to finish it by myself."

"I have a cookie." The stutter in her voice sent more heat waves through her. Sharing a piece of pie on the same plate with the same fork. It was something a couple would do. "But thank you."

"I'm not trying to embarrass you." He dropped the fork on the plate with a sharp ping. "The truth is . . . I'm just lonely."

For a man such as this one—tall, broad shouldered, pleasing to the eye, with a job and a child and family—to say such a thing to her, it made her heart seize up. She inhaled but no relief came. "I'm sorry."

"Not your fault. I shouldn't have said it. It's just that you're easy to talk to." He shoved the plate away, pie untouched, and leaned back in his chair. "They keep saying I should read to Kaitlin. She just wants to grab the book and chew on it. She tears the pages. Is it all that important?"

"It helps them learn words and it's something you do together." Back on solid ground, Leila breathed again. "Get the heavy cardboard books. Then she can't tear the pages. If she gets slobber or spit-up on them, you just wipe them off."

"She does plenty of that. I mean the spit-up and slobber. It's everywhere."

"I reckon she's teething. I felt a couple of buds on her gums this morning when she was fussy after her nap."

"Teething already. Right." He scratched his head, looking perplexed. "How's a guy supposed to keep track of all this?"

"You'll get the hang of it." He had no choice.

He picked up a toothpick and rolled it between his fingers. "Anyone ever tell you you're pretty?"

She squirmed in her chair. Not a soul. Plain folks didn't set much store by looks. "No." The word came out a whisper.

"Even prettier when your face gets pink like that." He grinned, teeth white and even. "I didn't mean to embarrass you. A guy just doesn't meet a lot of women like you. So without adornment and artifice."

She would have to look up those words in the dictionary. Neither got used much at her house. Unable to think of a thing to say, she nodded.

"So do you know which guy you'll choose?"

She watched his long fingers work the toothpick. No calluses there. No scars. Hands that did inside work. Healing hands. "I don't know."

She must've whispered again because he leaned forward, full lips parted, as if straining to hear. "What?"

"I don't know."

He picked up the book on the chair. "You're fortunate to have choices. I keep thinking Kaitlin needs a mother. I'm not equipped for the job. But the idea of getting out there and trying again . . . that scares me. And where does a guy with a baby and a full-time job and studies meet a woman? It's not like I have time or the inclination for bars."

"Have you tried asking someone out from your church?"

He opened the book, then shut it, his fingers smoothing the cover. "My church . . . I haven't been to church since me and Diane split. I guess I feel like God let me down. He let me marry a woman who left the first chance she got."

"He didn't choose your wife for you. You did."

"Thanks for pointing that out."

"Sorry. We believe in taking everything to God. He has a plan for us. His will be done."

She'd heard those words hundreds of times. Now she spoke them to another. She believed them, heart and soul, even as she said them to this troubled, sad, lonely man in need of succor that a simple woman such as herself could not provide. How was that so different from what Jesse wanted to do? A bite of cookie lodged in her throat and she coughed and choked.

"You okay?" Tom rose and smacked her on the back with a big hand, nearly knocking her from her chair. He didn't know his own strength. "Breathe, breathe!"

She coughed again and gasped. "I'm fine, I'm fine."

From someone who wasn't sure of anything anymore.

TWENTY-SEVEN

Surely she knew better than to do such a thing.

Jesse slammed to a stop in the middle of the sidewalk underneath the flickering neon sign that read MARIE'S COFFEE SHOP. Leila sat at a table by the window, big as you please, where everyone who passed by could see her talking and smiling with an Englisch man. The man was tall, dressed in jeans and a leather jacket. He was smooth shaven. He leaned forward as if hanging on Leila's every word.

Someone bumped Jesse from behind, knocking him forward a step. An elderly man, dressed in a long wool overcoat far too heavy for south Texas's mild winters, stumbled back and shook his cane, his grizzled face red. "Watch it, buddy—you don't own the sidewalk."

"Sorry, sorry." Jesse sidestepped the man and allowed him to pass. "I'm sorry."

Still muttering, the old man hobbled on, the cane clacking in a brisk staccato against the cement, the scent of mothballs and spearmint mouthwash wafting behind him.

Jesse pressed himself up against the brick exterior of the

squat one-story building and then hazarded a peek inside. If anyone saw him, they'd think he'd lost his mind. Like a spy or something. A spy in suspenders, work boots that had seen better days, and a straw hat. The man's face looked familiar. A second passed as Jesse grappled with memories. The EMT from the accident. That was it. How did Leila know an EMT?

Hurt mixed with anger raced through Jesse like a stampede of javelinas. What was she doing in public with yet another Englischer? This one was no boy like the one in the park. He was a man. Letting her work at the day care had been a mistake. He would tell his daed and Mordecai. He drew a painful breath, his heart thumping in his chest, and closed his eyes against the bright afternoon sun that took the December nip from the air. What a hypocrite he was. He'd been the one to take her to the movies. He'd been the one to kiss her on her first date in her entire life. He'd been the one to confuse her with his waffling, his inability to pick a world and stay in it. What was she to think?

And who was he to judge her? He was doing something far worse in the eyes of their community. He didn't just share meals with Englischers; he worshipped with them. Something he planned to continue to do. Something he wanted her to do with him.

And she knew it. Yet she said nothing.

Gott, forgive me. Help me. I don't know how to do this.

He had no right to interfere. His heart might be clenched in painful hurt, but his brain shook a finger at him, reminding him. He had no right.

"Hey, Jesse. What are you doing?"

He opened his eyes to find Matthew Plank leaning out the window of a rusty, faded-blue minivan with a series of long aluminum ladders strapped to a rack on top. A vinyl sign stuck to the side read PLANK HOME IMPROVEMENT. Underneath was a rough sketch of a pile of wooden planks with a hammer on top. "Nothing, I'm doing nothing."

Matthew slapped his hand on the passenger door. "You look a little peaked. Are you sick or something? Do you need a ride?"

"Nee. Nee." Jesse straightened and swallowed the bile in the back of his throat. He coughed. "I'm just, I mean, I have to go . . ."

Matthew's gaze bobbed toward the coffee shop, encompassing the window and the occupants at the table so unaware of passersby. "Ah."

"Nee."

"Get in. We're headed over to the Corn House for a quick bite before we get back to work. Come on, join us." Matthew jerked his head toward the driver. His brother Angus, four years younger, twenty pounds heavier, and whiskerless, had both hands on the wheel. "Angus here is a good driver. He's been practicing. He even has his license now. Come on."

Jesse chose not to share with Matthew that not only did he know how to drive, but he had taken his test and received his license earlier in the month. He hadn't used it yet, but it was only a matter of time. "I need a part for the generator. I just came in for it. Mr. Cramer's meeting me at the hardware store later this afternoon to give me a ride back."

"We'll get you there. I promise." Matthew grinned. "Hop in."

Something about Matthew's grin invited Jesse to leave this quagmire behind. Even if only for an hour. Ignoring the voice in his head that said he would soon drown in the quicksand of his own making, he tugged open the sliding door and hauled himself into the back of the van where tepidm warm air from the heater grazed his face. Rubbing his cold hands together, he settled back in a seat that featured coffee and grease-stained upholstery.

The interior of the van smelled of an acrid mix of varnish, paint thinner, grease, and man sweat. Next to him was a box of doorknobs and other assorted hardware. He swiveled his head and encountered an assortment of tools and wood stacked in the back. The last row of seats had been removed to make more room for buckets, paintbrushes, and a folded stepladder.

"My company on wheels." Matthew seemed to read his mind. "I don't have a garage so I keep everything in the van, ready to roll."

"Makes sense."

Something about the van felt homey. Jesse settled into the seat and tried to leave behind the miry pit that was his quandary over Leila. A few minutes later they pulled into a spot in front of Jesse's favorite drive-by restaurant. The Corn House sold roasted corn, nachos, Fritos pies, flaming hot Cheetos covered with cheese, and pickles. Nothing good for a person, in other words. The best kind of restaurant.

"What'll it be? It's on me." Matthew already had his billfold out. "I'm all about the Fritos pie myself."

"Roasted corn with chili and lime would be good, but I'll pay for mine." Jesse removed his straw hat and dug behind the thin band inside it that held his tiny savings, trying to remember how much money he had. It wasn't much, but enough to cover his own lunch. "I wouldn't mind a Fritos pie too."

Matthew waved away the money. "My treat. I've been wanting to talk to you for a while."

Everyone seemed to want a piece of him these days: Colton, Will, Matthew. His appetite waned. *Peace, Gott, all I want is peace.*

How to get there?

A few minutes later the van filled with the aroma of roasted corn. Jesse's mouth watered. It had been a long time since breakfast. He took the white paper sack Matthew offered and sank his teeth into the hot corn. Juice ran down his chin. He sopped it up with a paper napkin, ignoring Matthew's grin.

"We're headed to the old Driscoll place. We're restoring both the interior and the exterior." His voice full of undisguised enthusiasm, Matthew scooted around in his seat so he half faced Jesse. "It's a sweet Southern Colonial with big columns in the front. It was built in the original Beeville home district around the mid–eighteen hundreds."

Jesse nodded and tried to look interested. Most of the words didn't mean much to him. Matthew didn't seem to mind. "We have to rebuild the columns in front. They're basically shells wrapped around six-by-six beams. Once they're repaired, we'll put them back in place, just like the originals. It's slow going, but we're getting there. Ain't that right, Angus?"

Angus's shaggy-haired head bobbed. "We're getting there."

Staring out the window at the businesses and then houses that flashed by, Jesse finished his corn, ignored the greasy melted butter on his fingers, and started on the Fritos pie. Angus made a turn onto Jackson Street and then Washington. In minutes they pulled into a drive behind a house that faced Washington. Scaffolding adorned the columns across the front.

"We're here." Matthew balled up his paper sack and threw it into the pile on the floor near Jesse's feet. "You interested in a job by any chance?"

"I have a job at my daed's store."

"Jah, but I can pay you. Restoring old houses pays a decent wage." He chuckled. "Good thing. Ruth is expecting again."

Matthew had left the old ways behind in every sense. No Plain man would make such an announcement. Jesse squirmed in his seat.

"Jah, it's soon after the twins, but God is good. We are blessed."

"Jah."

"So who's the girl?"

"The girl?"

"At Miss Marie's."

"I have to get back."

"You have time. Tell me why you were gawking at a Plain girl sitting in Miss Marie's with some guy."

Jesse shrugged. "I didn't mean to gawk."

"Sure you did. If I hadn't come along, I reckon you'd have gone in there and said something to her. Who is she? I don't recognize her. Must be new since I left."

"She's just a girl. I'm sort of courting her." Only not. "I mean, I took her to the movies once."

"Once?" Matthew's thick black eyebrows rose and fell. "Then you realized you were in a bit of a pickle over staying or going?"

"I already knew that. It was a mistake. Taking her."

Matthew ran his hand through hair already sticking up all over the place. "You gotta go for it." Exactly what Colton said. "So you *are* leaving?"

Since that moment after the crash when he'd bent over little Hilary and Hannah, he had known. God called him to do this. No going back. The questions that remained involved his heart and the girl who'd stolen it. "Yes, but I'm still figuring some things out."

"Like the girl?"

"Jah."

"Does she have a strong faith?"

"Jah."

"Then neither of you has anything to lose and you have so much to gain."

He was worse than Colton. "I have to go."

Matthew tugged a toolbox from the foot well. "You have time. I want you to see the work we're doing. You'd be good at it."

"How do you know?"

"Plain men work hard." Matthew shoved open his door. "My brothers Phillip and Solomon are coming down from Ohio."

"To visit?"

"Nee. Me and Angus have been talking to them about what we're doing. They're thinking about joining us."

"Joining you in the business."

"The business and our way of life."

Even long distance, Matthew could be convincing. "You'd do that to your parents?"

"I'm not doing it to them. I wish they would see the light too. We could all fellowship together. We could start our own worship services."

"You'd have taken four sons from them, if you include yourself."

"They still have Jacob and Silas. Those two will never leave. Jacob drew the lot. He's a deacon now."

"Why are you telling me this?"

"I want you to know you have a place to come, if you decide to do what you're thinking about doing."

Jesse studied the naked beams, waiting to be covered again. They still supported the weight of the porch roof, but they had no beauty. Function, but nothing to shroud their ugliness. The families in his district, including his own, didn't paint their houses or gussy them up in any way. They lived a bare-bones existence and they didn't mind. They didn't care about the junkyard by the Combination Store. They didn't care about the rusty siding on the houses. External beauty didn't matter.

Were his feelings for Leila about the way she looked? Or a deeper beauty? In her Plain dress, her apron, and her kapp, she still looked beautiful to him. Her lips felt beautiful when he kissed them. If he went to work for Matthew, he likely wouldn't be allowed to see her again.

Ever.

His heart contracted in a painful hiccup. He couldn't stay for her. Yet he didn't want to live without her.

Matthew hopped from his seat. A minute later the van door slid open. "Feel like slinging a hammer for a few minutes?"

Maybe he could pound out his frustration. Jesse swallowed and nodded, unable to form the words.

Matthew paused, hand on the door. "I've been where you are. I know this isn't easy. It shouldn't be easy. Our faith is honed in the fire. God is with you always."

"Isn't He with our families also?"

"He is. And He will carry them through this. Do what you have to do. He will ease their pain, just as He bears yours."

"And Leila?"

"The decision is hers." Matthew handed him a hammer. "But that doesn't mean you shouldn't make your case."

"I've tried."

"Try again. Keep trying."

He was right. "I need to go back to the coffee shop."

"Not right this minute. Choose the time and place well. Take her for a buggy ride."

Jesse took the hammer Matthew offered him and hauled himself from the van. He landed on solid ground for the first time in months.

TWENTY-EIGHT

The thud of a horse's hooves on the dirt road outside her window brought Leila straight up out of bed. She hadn't been able to sleep or slept fitfully, her dreams full of strange uneasiness, since the night of little Timothy's birth. She slid back the curtain and peered out, careful to keep out of sight in her nightgown. A buggy, battery-operated lights flashing and bobbing when the buggy hit ruts in the road, approached.

She closed her eyes. She had to choose. That's what she'd told Deborah. Every night since that conversation with her sister, she'd lain in bed, trying to piece together the quilt of thoughts that would cover her with a peaceful solution.

Always it led her to a place where she felt at cross-purposes with Gott. He knew her name before she was born. He knew how many hairs were on her head. He provided for her just as He provided for the sparrows. Why could she not simply trust that He had a plan? When the time came, she would make the choice He'd planned for her all along.

The way her family worshipped, it was right and good in God's eyes. She believed that. So why had she felt this deep welling of blessedness as she sat next to Jesse in Tiffany's living room? As if God had taken her hand and led her to this place Himself.

Why did she feel completed every time Jesse put his hand on hers?

How could she love her family so much and yet feel so convicted by Jesse's words?

They were stuck at cross-purposes when they were both trying to get to the same place. *What would Gott say about that?* Surely their puny human brains could no more fathom Gott's greater plan than a ladybug or a hummingbird could.

She leaned from the window, staring down. Butch didn't bark. Maybe he only barked at cars. Buggies meant friends. She squinted, trying to see beyond the bright lights to what the darkness held beyond them. The person who hopped from the buggy was tall. Too tall for Jesse.

Will.

Light blinded her. It bobbed and skittered away. "Will?" She kept her voice low, hoping not to wake Rebekah and Hazel.

"Jah."

"What are you doing here?"

"What do you think? Come down here."

"Did you come to warn me off someone or something?"

"I came to ask you to take a ride with me." His tone made the words a challenge. "It's a nice night. I have blankets in the buggy if you think it's too cool."

"I'm not dancing anymore. Ever." She couldn't allow herself to be confused by the comfort she found in having his arms around her. "No more boom box."

"I didn't even bring the thing. The batteries are dead."

"Wait there."

Fingers shaking, all thumbs, she scrambled into her clothes. She fumbled in the dark, bumped the crate, and stubbed her toe on the bedpost. Rebekah stirred and muttered in her sleep. "Shush, shush, you'll wake Hazel," Leila whispered. "Go back to sleep."

"Stop talking." Rebekah groaned and rolled over, arm thrown over her little sister. The rest of her words were lost in a mumble laced with sleep.

Leila took another minute to smooth her hair and slap on her kapp. She tiptoed down the stairs, shoes in her hands. At the door, she stopped and listened. Nothing except a house settling and creaking in the night wind. *Gott, help me make the right decision. Heart and head hand in hand.*

On the porch, Will squatted next to Butch, one hand on the dog's back, the other holding the flashlight, creating skittish blobs of light on the floor beneath his boots. He straightened, slipped down the steps, and turned. "Let me help you up."

Knowing full well she didn't need his help, Leila took his hand. His fingers were warm, the skin rough. Gaze on the buggy step, she hauled herself up and forced herself to let go. Her hand wanted to stay wrapped in his. She sighed.

"Why the sigh?" He slid onto the seat next to her and picked up the reins. "Is my company that onerous to you?"

"Nee. Confusing, that's all."

Will didn't answer. The buggy jolted forward, headlights blending with the light of a half-moon to cast elongated shadows on the pitted road. He slapped the reins and the horse picked up his pace. Maybe she had offended him with her honesty. One thing she knew for certain, the relationship between a man and his wife had to be based on honesty. She was confused. How could she have all these feelings for Jesse and yet enjoy Will's company?

Because he made her feel safe. She had to give up nothing to be with him. He was steady and true to their faith. With Will, she could have everything she'd ever wanted. The life her mudder and daed expected her to live.

With Jesse? The abyss opened at her feet and left her breathless with a fearful anticipation. She couldn't see the future with Jesse, only what it didn't hold: her parents, Deborah, Rebekah, Hazel, Caleb, her new nephew.

She saw a gaping hole where her family had once been.

She shivered.

"You're cold. I should've brought more blankets."

Will transferred the reins to one hand and used the other to pull the fleece blanket up around her chest. He turned the buggy onto the road—more of a path than a road—that led to the back side of Mordecai's property. Where the apiaries dotted the landscape during the day. The bees were down for the winter.

Leila tried to relax. She inhaled cool, fresh air that stung her nose and her lungs. White puffs clouded the air with each breath she took. Stars hung crystal clear in the night sky. "It feels good. We spend so much time being hot and sweaty around here. I miss winter."

"I've never experienced a real, cold winter with snow."

So they would talk about the weather again. As they had done before dancing. Will was no conversationalist, but then, neither was she.

"You should visit Tennessee at Christmas one year." Images of Daed throwing snowballs at her, missing, and knocking an arm off the snowman they'd all made together assailed Leila. She hadn't thought of that in a long time. Warm memories despite the cold of that day. "You can have fun playing in the snow and then go inside for cocoa and s'mores."

"We have fun here too."

"Once in a blue moon."

"Often enough."

"Did you come out here to argue with me?"

"Nee. Daed has decided to move the family back to Tennessee."

So Will wouldn't be visiting Tennessee at Christmas. He'd be living there, a thousand miles away. She swallowed the sudden knot that threatened to choke her. "When?"

"After the first of the year."

"So you'll experience winter. The snow and the cocoa and the s'mores."

He jerked on the reins and brought the buggy to a sudden halt. "That's all you have to say?"

"What do you want me to say?"

"That you have a horse in this race."

Leila shoved the blanket away, suddenly warm. "Do I?" It was a stupid question. Of course she did. It wasn't fair to Will to imply otherwise. "I mean, I don't know what to think. You run hot and cold. You show up and then you don't. Do I have a horse in this race?"

Will hopped from the buggy and stormed down the middle of the road, arms flapping. "You tell me."

"You dance with me and then run away." Leila sprang down on her side and marched after him. "You're the one who's been wishy-washy. I have no idea what you think."

"I think it's wrong to horn in on a cousin's girl." He faced her, his white teeth glinting in the moonlight. "I think it's wrong for a girl to kiss one man and dance with another."

Leila slapped her hands on her hips. "Maybe a girl wouldn't do that if someone would speak up and make his intentions clear."

"I just did."

They glared at each other. Leila refused to let her gaze drop. Will's jaw worked. His hands went to his hips in an unconscious imitation of her pose. He sniffed, whirled, and marched away.

"Will Glick, get back here."

He kept walking.

"Fine."

He turned and marched straight at her. He kept coming, not stopping. The look on his face made Leila's fingers flutter to her cheeks. His big hands engulfed hers, drawing them away from her face with that same gentle touch he'd used to wrap her against him in a dance. His face hovered over hers. "I'm here now."

Leila closed her eyes and leaned into him. His fingers left her hands and made their way to her neck, cupping her face so she couldn't move. She stopped breathing.

He let go and she plummeted back to earth.

She opened her eyes. Will towered over her, glowering, his breathing harsh. "I'm here. I may not . . . show how I feel the way some men do, but I'm here."

"I know you are." Did she feel relief or disappointment that he'd stopped short when she'd been so sure he would take one more step forward in this strange dance they did? He was here and being with him cost her nothing. Except Jesse. Jesse. What did it say about her that he crowded her thoughts at this very moment? "I'm . . . I'm . . ."

"You're what?" Will crossed his arms. "You have to make a choice."

Perhaps the choice had already been made for her. *Gott, forgive me.* "I know. I know I do."

"I choose you."

Her heart did that jerky thing again. If he left, the choice was made for her. The coward's way out. She wasn't a coward. "You're not going to Tennessee then?"

"This isn't about whether I'm going and you know it. This is about what you'll do with all this." He flung his arm toward her and then back so his hand rested on his chest. "With you and me."

She cleared her throat. The pounding of her heart made it hard to think. She didn't want this power to hurt him. *Gott, take this cup from me.* "It's just that I'm . . . I can't . . . I mean, I have to figure out something."

His hands went back to his hips. "Jesse?"

"Jesse."

"Do what you have to do." He brushed past her. "Time to go home."

She couldn't tell him about the Wednesday night group. Or the way she'd felt when she suggested Tom go back to church to assuage his loneliness. This wasn't only about Jesse. Leila followed Will to the buggy on shaky legs. "Nothing has been decided yet."

"And if he chooses the district, it'll be because he doesn't want to lose you. He gets you."

"Those are two separate things."

"You need to stay away from him before you get sucked in too."

How could she tell him it was very possible his admonition came too late? She caught his sleeve and tugged. He turned. His expression wasn't the anger she expected. He looked fearful—for her. She wanted to wipe that look away. "I'm strong in my beliefs."

Which was at the root of everything. For Jesse and for her.

"So is Jesse. That's how he got sucked in."

"He was looking for something, or it wouldn't have happened." She accepted Will's offer of a hand and tottered into the buggy. Grateful to be seated, she searched for words to ease his concern. "Give me time."

He settled into the seat next to her. A pulse beat in his jaw. "You have unfinished business. Finish it." He snapped the reins and the buggy jolted forward. "I'll be here one way or another. I'm not going anywhere."

The words hung in the air like a promise. He'd asked for none in return. A gift.

They made the ride back to Mordecai's in silence. Leila kept reliving the look on Will's face when he bent over her. Such determination. Such intent. Such a struggle to abstain.

Such love.

She searched her heart. Did she feel the same? Her hands shook and her legs felt like wet noodles. It was one thing to react to a man's touch. Another to take his heart and give hers in return. Jesse's face hovered in her mind's eye. She couldn't be certain she still possessed her heart to give. Her feelings for Jesse, as muddled as they were, traveled far beyond the kiss they'd shared so long ago in that movie theater.

"You have company."

Will's voice startled her from the painful consideration of her own inability to separate the two. A figure did indeed huddle on the front step. Leila peered through the darkness, unable to make out a face. A baby's wail pierced the dark serenity of the night.

Trevor. Rory, with Trevor wailing on her lap, sat on Mordecai's front porch. No ride home in sight.

TWENTY-NINE

Between the crying baby and the crying mommy, the noisy waterworks filled the dark night. Leila pushed aside Butch, who seemed intent on providing some sort of doggy comfort to Rory or investigating the contents of the diaper bag, she couldn't be sure which. Leila shoved aside a pile of stuff that turned out to be two duffel bags, a folded baby stroller, and an overflowing diaper bag. She sank onto the porch step next to Rory and tugged Trevor from her friend's arms. To her surprise, Will had jumped from the buggy right behind her and stood nearby, a comforting presence.

"Hush, baby, hush, hush," she cooed to Trevor as she inhaled his familiar scent of baby wipes and diaper-rash ointment. "You'll wake the whole house."

The sound of the baby's cries receded, only to be replaced by sniffles that emanated from his mother. "What's the matter?" Leila snuggled Trevor against her chest with one hand and patted Rory's shoulder with the other. "Did something happen?"

Silly question. Of course something happened.

Rory laid her head in her arms and sobbed.

"What can I do to help?" Leila rubbed the girl's back. "Do you need a ride home? Will and I can take you."

"Daddy kicked me out." The words were muffled against the girl's arms. "He called Dwayne and told him to come fetch his wife. He stuffed the baby's Pack 'n Play into its bag and set it out on the front porch."

That didn't sound like Nolan. "Did you argue with him?"

The girl raised her head. Tears soaked her face and her eyes were rimmed with red. "I don't know what I'm going to do." Her lower lip quivered and a fresh batch of tears rolled down her cheeks. "I'm pregnant again."

Lord, have mercy.

Leila glanced at Will. Eyebrows raised, he shrugged. A person didn't have words for such a thing. To have kinner was to be blessed in every circumstance. Rory and Dwayne were man and wife. Still, Leila could see why Nolan would be upset, considering he supported his daughter and grandson, while the husband and father did neither. Still, to throw out his grandson . . . he must be heartsick. "And what does Dwayne say?"

"He says it's too soon. He says it's my fault." Rory's voice rose to a shriek. "He says he can't support me and Trevor, let alone another baby."

Rory wailed. Trevor joined in. A regular concert. Any minute Mudder or Mordecai would be at the door to see what the ruckus was all about.

"Hush, hush, both of you." Leila tucked Trevor's pacifier in his mouth and began to rock. "How did you get here?"

"Dwayne got mad and I started yelling and he was yelling and the baby was crying so I told him to let me out of the car."

Rory swiped at her face with her jacket sleeve. "At first he said no, but then I yelled at him that he wasn't my boss or my keeper or nothing like that. I could raise our babies by myself just fine. To dump me by the side of the road. We'd be just fine."

"But he wouldn't do that," Will interjected. "No man worth his salt would."

"He brought me here instead." A sound like crickets chirping burst from the cell phone in her hand. She flashed it at Leila. "He's been texting me every five seconds, but I'm not answering."

Leila tugged Trevor's blanket up around his face. The *slurp-slurp* of the pacifier had stopped. He slept. She rose. "You'd best come on in. It's cold and it's late."

"I didn't mean to invite myself to a sleepover. I tried calling my friends from school, but everyone's asleep." Rory sounded relieved despite her words. "I'll get one of them to pick me up first thing in the morning. Pam or Alison can give you a ride to work when they come for me."

"Let's see what the morning brings."

"Nothing will be different in the morning." Rory stumbled to her feet. "I have a Spanish test just like always."

Leila opened the screen door and waited for Rory to go in. Will scooped up the bags and strode through the door behind her. "You don't have to do that."

He paused inside the door. "You'd best have a word with your mudder right quick." He settled the bags on the floor and held out his arms. "Give me the baby while you let your folks know they have company."

Mordecai's house. His guests. She eased the sleeping baby into Will's arms. He corralled the child against his chest. He looked as at ease with this task as he had carrying the bags. She hesitated. He looked up from the bundle in his arms. "What?"

"Nothing."

"Then go. Rory looks tuckered out and this baby needs a bed."

"We have a cradle. We'll put him in it so we don't have to set up the Pack 'n Play right now. Rory can have my spot in the bed. I have a sleeping bag."

"I can't put you out of your bed." Rory pointed to the couch. "I'll sleep here."

Not where Mordecai and the boys would pass by in the morning. "I'll be right back."

Leila paused at the closed door that led to Mordecai and Mudder's bedroom. She put her hand on the doorknob, then let it drop. She raised it again to knock. Before she could, the door opened and Mudder peered out. "What's the matter?" Her voice was the barest whisper. "Are you sick?"

"How did you know I was out here?"

"You knocked."

"Nee, I didn't."

"A mudder knows when her child needs her."

"It's Rory. She's here with the baby."

Mudder disappeared from sight. Leila lingered in the hall, not sure what to do next. Was Mudder telling Mordecai? A few seconds later Mudder returned, her hair covered by her kapp. Her nightclothes replaced by a dress. She squeezed through the door and shut it behind her. "Is Rory all right? Is the baby sick?"

"Nee."

Leila waited for her mother to notice that she was already fully dressed, but Mudder brushed past her and trotted on bare feet toward the front room. "She'd best spend the night then. It's too late for her to be gallivanting around the countryside with a baby."

"Mudder."

Her mother paused and looked back. "What is it, child?"

"Her father kicked her out because she's expecting again. He said her husband should take care of her."

"As well he should. Where is this husband?"

"They argued—"

"We'll worry about it in the morning."

Mudder trudged ahead of Leila into the front room. Will had turned on the kerosene lamp and taken up a spot next to the dark fireplace. He'd given the baby to Rory, who huddled in a rocking chair, her sleeping son on her lap, her face wet, head down in the flickering light.

Mudder didn't hesitate. "Will, you'd best get on home now. It's late."

He made his way toward the door without speaking. At the last second, he turned and nodded at Leila. She managed a quick nod back, knowing Mudder missed nothing. He pulled the door closed behind him with a gentle tug that made no sound.

Mudder bustled across the room. "Leila, put the cradle in your room. Rory's a tiny thing; she'll squeeze in next to Esther. It's time everyone was in bed."

Leila started toward the closet that held the cradle, blankets, quilts, and towels. Outside, an engine raced. A horn shrieked again and again. The sound of splintering wood filled the air, along with ferocious barking and a horse's whinny. Rory bolted from the chair. "Dwayne—he's come back for me."

Trevor wiggled in her arms and began to wail as his mother dashed for the front door. With a fierce frown, Mudder marched after the girl. Leila slid in behind them.

Will's voice rose above the rumble of the engine, Butch's

barking, and the shrieking horn. "Stop honking! You almost hit me. You hit the buggy. You could've killed my horse."

"Butch, hush, hush!" Leila squeezed past her mother and raced down the steps. "Are you all right, Will?"

The honking ceased. Butch sat down on the porch, but his jagged teeth remained bared in a snarl.

The buggy lay crumpled against the porch, back wheels bent and broken, one side crushed under the bumper of Dwayne's pickup truck, which looked none the worse for wear. Will slapped his hat against his leg as if removing dust and debris. "I am, but the buggy is destroyed."

"What is going on here?" Mordecai shoved through the screen door and slammed to a halt on the porch. Leila had never seen him angry before, but at this moment, he looked peeved. "A man deserves a decent night's sleep."

"That's what you get for not having porch lights." Dwayne staggered from the truck. The word *porch* came out *pooch*. "I come for my woman." He stumbled and fell flat on his face.

THIRTY

A fall like that had to hurt, but surely the man had it coming. Will squatted next to Dwayne, who sprawled nose down on the ground. He grabbed one arm and shook it. Dwayne didn't move. His head lolled to one side. The smell of alcohol and tobacco wafted from the inert body, making Will long for a clothespin to clip on his nose.

All the commotion had awakened everyone in Mordecai's house. The girls were crowded at the windows, and Mordecai's sons milled on the porch with Leila's brother. It was like a Sunday service in the middle of the night.

"I take it this is your husband." Will glanced toward Rory, who bounced Trevor against her chest and sobbed, tiny, breathless sobs. She nodded and hiccupped as she dropped to her knees next to Dwayne. "I reckon he's in no shape to drive you anywhere."

"Is he all right?" She patted the man's dirty, stubbled cheek. "Dwayne, wake up, babe, wake up, honey."

"From the smell of him, he's drunker than a skunk. He's passed out, that's all."

"How do you know he's not hurt? He just wrecked his truck."

"No, he wrecked my buggy." Will forced himself to keep his voice level. This girl cared for the man on the ground, that was obvious. "That big pickup truck broke it like it was a toothpick. It didn't hurt the truck or him, you can be certain of that."

"It's my fault. I'm so sorry for this. I'm sorry for your buggy. I'll pay for it. I'll find a way, I promise." Tears trailed down Rory's face. Her nose was bright red and running, yet she still managed to look pretty. "I shouldn't have told my dad tonight. I should've waited. We could've done it together."

"Don't worry about the buggy." Will saw no point in rubbing salt in the poor girl's wounds. "Sometimes it just takes people awhile to adjust to new things, I reckon."

"Daddy was so mad. I never seen him so mad." She took a shuddering breath. "Not since I told him about Trevor and me and Dwayne getting married."

"But he got over it the first time." Will couldn't keep his gaze from Leila. What did she think of him giving advice to an Englisch girl about family matters? He couldn't mend things with Jesse or with her. Instead he'd come within a hairbreadth of kissing her. And she knew it. Even thinking about it only muddied the waters more. She stared back at him, eyes wide and unblinking. "Things will work out in the end. They always do."

"Everybody, back in bed. All y'all." Mordecai waved at Esther and Rebekah and shook a finger at his boys. Everyone melted back into the house as quick as they'd appeared. Mordecai stomped down the steps and halted next to Leila, who had one hand on Rory's shoulder. "We'll drag him out to the barn. Let him sleep it off." He jerked his head toward the buggy, his beard bobbing. "Will, you might as well bed down for the night out there as well. We'll see what we can do with this mess come first light."

"I'm obliged." He straightened. Exhaustion weighed on him like stones on his shoulders. He'd like nothing more than to lay his head down and sleep. The expression on Leila's face told him nothing. Would she be aggravated or embarrassed if he stayed? "But I can take the horse and get myself home if you'll loan me a saddle. Mudder and Daed will wonder where I am come morning."

"True enough. Help me with this boy and I'll rustle you up a saddle."

Will hooked an arm under Dwayne's armpit and Mordecai did the same. Together, they heaved him from the ground. He mumbled something unintelligible, but his head drooped, eyes still closed.

"Wait, wait." Rory rose, her sleeping baby's legs flopping against her. "Dwayne, honey, wake up, baby, wake up."

"He won't wake up." Mordecai kept moving. Will followed his lead. "You'd best get some sleep. He'll be crabbier than a cougar in a cage in the morning."

Rory trailed after them. "He'll be sorry, you'll see. He's a good guy. He really is."

"Go on in the house. Leila will help you get situated."

Will waited until the women were in the house, then snorted. "A good guy? Driving so drunk he ran into my buggy. If I'd been in it, I'd be the one on the ground."

"But you weren't. Gott is good."

Indeed. They half dragged, half carried Dwayne into the barn, too focused on the task to say any more. Inside, they lowered him onto a pile of hay in the first unoccupied stall. Breathing hard, Will brushed his hands together and turned away.

"Long night." Mordecai grabbed a rake and began to fluff more hay into the pile. "Sure you don't want to stay?"

"I'd better get home."

"Because of Leila?"

Will froze, one hand on a saddle that lay across the wooden posts that separated Dwayne's new bedroom from the horse next door. "Come again?"

"That's the only reason I can think for you to be here at this hour."

That Mordecai would speak so openly of this surprised Will. "What are you getting at?"

"A man hears things."

"I know I do."

"Abigail's girls have had a rough row to hoe."

"They have."

"You know what you're doing?"

Will snorted. "Does anyone when it comes to this stuff?"

"Can I give you a word of advice?"

"Might as well."

"Pray about it. Put Gott at the center of your life, and everything else will follow."

"Is that what happened with Abigail?"

Dwayne emitted a snore loud enough to wake the horses. Mordecai shut the gate to the stall and headed for the barn door. "It took twelve years for Gott to bless me with another fraa after He took the first one home, but I always figured if it was meant to be, it would come in His time. Lots of folks tried to get me to marry sooner, but it never felt right."

"Until Abigail."

"Until Abigail."

"And you had no doubts?"

"I didn't say that. She came here to marry another man. I had doubts."

Leila might not have been joined to Jesse by the banns, but he had courted her. Will fell in step next to Mordecai, breathing in the cold night air. "She was intended for another. How could you even approach her knowing that?"

"Circumstances brought us together again and again, until it couldn't be denied. She couldn't deny it. I didn't want to deny it." Mordecai brought his big hands to his face and blew as he rubbed them together. "Cold tonight. Wouldn't a little snow be nice?"

Now that was dreaming. Will slipped a blanket onto his horse's back and then heaved the saddle over it. "The whole thing has me a little discombobulated."

"Trust in Gott." Mordecai patted the horse's long neck. "Then trust your heart. When it comes to Leila and when it comes to Jesse."

Will's heart slammed in his chest. His throat ached with the effort not to pour the story out to this man who had been a fixture in his life for as long as he could remember. "I don't know . . . I mean . . ."

"Don't say anything. Just listen." Mordecai cinched the saddle snug under the horse's belly and stepped back. "I ain't blind. Neither is Leroy. The time will come when choices will have to be made. Very soon. We're praying each one of you makes the right choice."

He gestured toward the pile of wood that had been the Glicks' best buggy. "Come over in the morning and we'll see if we can salvage that thing."

"Bright and early."

Mordecai looked back and grinned. "I imagine we could make quite a ruckus in the morning long about sunrise. Roust a guy off his pile of hay."

For the first time all evening, Will had the urge to smile. "Sounds about right."

"Abigail makes a fine pancake. Kaffi too."

"Crack of dawn then."

Will waited until Mordecai was inside and the light in the front room was extinguished. Then he mounted the horse and turned him toward the road and home.

The undercurrents of his conversation with Leila's stepfather most likely would carry him home, but he no longer feared drowning in them. Mordecai was a wise man. Pray. Make God the center of his world. Everything else would come after that.

———

Leila rolled over and covered her head with her arm, wanting to block out that rustling sound. As tired as she was, she couldn't sleep. Every time she closed her eyes, Will's face hovered over her as he bent toward her. Heat rolled through her. She'd been so sure he would kiss her, but then he didn't. Thank Gott, he hadn't. It would only muddy the waters further. So why did she keep thinking about the look on his face as he leaned in?

Even the thin sheet seemed too hot and heavy. She tossed it back. The box springs creaked and the mattress rose and fell around her. She rolled back over, raised her head, and opened her eyes to the black of night. She rubbed them with her fists and tried to focus on the figure tiptoeing away from the bed.

Rory slipping away in feet clad in thick, woolly socks.

"Where are you going?" Leila didn't need Rory traipsing around the house at night. Mordecai had the ears of a hound dog. "You need to get some sleep."

Rory glanced back and put a finger to her lips. She shook her head and kept moving.

Sighing, Leila pushed herself from the bed and followed. In the hallway Rory sped up as if pursued by a pack of javelinas. Leila wrapped her housecoat tighter and scurried after her. "Rory, wait, where are you going? It's the middle of the night."

"I need to talk to Dwayne."

"Dwayne is sleeping it off."

Rory stopped. Her head dropped and her shoulders began to shake. She slapped her hands to her face.

"It's okay, it's okay." Leila sped up so she could lay an arm around her friend and squeeze her shoulders. "You need to get some sleep. Everything will look better in the morning."

"How can it? I mean, seriously, how can things get better?" Rory shook free and marched toward the front room. "My dad's furious with me. My husband thinks the way to solve our problems is to get drunk, and I'm a high school kid with a baby and another one on the way. What was I thinking?"

Her wail was enough to wake everyone in the house. Leila grabbed her arm and tugged her toward the kitchen. "Come on. You need a cup of chamomile tea to settle you down. You're expecting. You need to stay calm for your baby."

Rory wailed louder.

"Hush, hush, everyone just got back to sleep. We don't want to wake them again."

"I can't believe I'm having another baby. I just did this."

Leila couldn't answer that one. Not without asking questions that would embarrass both of them. "You've done a good job with Trevor. You'll be a good momma to this new baby."

"I'm so tired all the time." Rory plopped onto a chair and laid her head on the table. "I throw up my breakfast every morning and sometimes lunch too."

"That will pass." So Leila had heard. She put the teakettle on the propane stove and turned up the flame. "You have some time to figure things out. Tomorrow you can go say you're sorry to your dad."

"He was so mad. So mad." Rory straightened and ran her fingers through hair already wild from repeated rakings. "And he has a right to be."

That admission was an important one. "Tell him that. Tell him you're sorry you're putting them through this again. An apology goes a long way."

"You're so lucky." Rory looked around the kitchen. "You have a big family and you all do everything together. You have three sisters and a mother and y'all go to church together and have meals together."

"You don't go to church?" Leila had never dared ask the question before. It wasn't any of her business. They didn't judge other folks' ways of worshipping. Which made her think of Jesse. He'd think her a bad friend for never talking to Rory about her beliefs. "I don't mean to stick my nose where it doesn't belong."

"We went to church when my mom was alive. Every Sunday." Rory's eyes shone and her whole body perked up. "We went to Sunday school and to church picnics and the fall festival and the chili cook-off and the Easter egg hunt."

Leila poured hot water over the tea bags in two big mugs. She carried them to the table and took a seat. This was a conversation friends had where they could see each other's expressions and know what their hearts said. "And when your momma died, everything changed?"

"Totally." Rory spooned enough honey into her cup to sweeten a pitcher of tea. "Daddy barely went out of the house for weeks, except to work. People kept coming by, bringing food and checking on us. He told every single one of them we were fine."

"But you weren't."

"We weren't fine. We aren't fine now."

Letting the fragrance of chamomile, like sweet flowers, envelop her, Leila sipped her tea. It burned her throat all the way to her stomach. Maybe it would burn away the terrible ache that throbbed in her chest. She, too, remembered the days and weeks and months after her father's death. A smile fixed on her face, Mudder went about her business as if nothing had changed. She tilled the land and planted the garden and fixed the meals and sewed clothes until late in the night, never once shedding a tear in front of her children.

"We weren't fine either, when my father died."

"I thought you Amish folks believed in God's will and God's plan and that people's days are numbered on this earth."

A touch of sarcasm permeated Rory's words, but Leila understood where it had come from. Sometimes a thing happened that was so inconceivable, it was impossible to imagine God meant for it to happen.

Sacrilegious. That's what Mordecai would say. He lost his wife in a horrible van accident that left his son scarred for life. Yet he didn't shake his fist at the sky.

But that didn't mean he hadn't wanted to do it.

"We do." Leila reached across the table and squeezed Rory's hand. "But we're only human. There's a hole in my heart where my daed should be. Gott will fill it up. I know He will. Seek Him out and He will do the same for you. You only have to ask."

Rory laid her head on the table and sobbed. "I want my mom."

Every fiber in Leila's being screamed to join her. "I know you do." She brushed the girl's hair from her face and stroked her head. "It'll get better, I promise."

"When? I need her now. I can't do this by myself anymore."

"You're not alone. You have Gott and your daed and me and Dwayne. I pray for you every day and I know my mudder does and I imagine your daed does too."

The crying subsided and Rory raised her head. "You pray for me?"

"Yes."

"Do you pray Dwayne and I work it out? Or that I come to my senses and realize he's never gonna be a good father? That's what my dad prays, I imagine."

"I pray Gott's will be done in your life, that Dwayne grows up sooner rather than later, and that Trevor will be loved and cared for by both his parents. That you and Dwayne bring Trevor up in a godly home."

Rory smiled through her tears. "You're a good friend."

Surprise blossomed in Leila. She had talked about God to Rory and it had worked. Her friend needed God in her life, and if Leila were truly a good friend, she would help her find Him.

No wonder Jesse felt called. It felt good.

THIRTY-ONE

Traffic this early in the morning could only mean one thing. The familiar rumble of a truck engine sent Leila scrambling from the breakfast table, through the front room, and out the door, her cup of kaffi still in her hand. Nolan Beale had come. And early, at that.

She'd dragged herself from bed at dawn to send Caleb to the store to call Mr. Carson to take her to work and Rory to school. Late-night crisis or not, they all had obligations to fulfill in the early-morning light. The money would come from her meager savings, but she had no choice. She couldn't miss work and Rory had to go to school.

Nolan pulled the truck in next to the pile of boards and hardware that had been the Glicks' buggy and turned off the engine. For a second Leila thought he would stay in the truck. After a bit of hesitation he opened the door and emerged, his head covered by a thick wool cap and his coat buttoned up to his neck. He ducked his head against the brisk breeze. Butch sniffed at his hand once, twice, and then settled back at his post on the porch. The dog knew a good man when he saw him.

"What happened here?" Nolan motioned toward the buggy remnants. "Looks bad."

"No one was hurt. Thanks to Gott." She leaned on the railing and stared at the broken wheels piled one on top of the other. Mordecai, Andrew, and Will were on their way to the store to talk to Leroy. He was the best at building buggies. If anyone could restore it, he could. "It got hit by a truck."

Dwayne's truck, which no longer sat in their front yard. Apparently he'd left without trying to talk to Rory. Too ashamed? Too hungover? He hadn't even looked in on his son. She couldn't fathom such an attitude in a father. Still, Nolan already thought poorly of his son-in-law. She hated to heap coals on the boy's head.

"I was looking for Rory." He cleared his throat. "I went by her . . . Dwayne's house. His mother said she hadn't been there. In fact, she hadn't seen Dwayne either. I couldn't think of another place, unless they did something stupid like run off. I'm hoping they didn't run off . . ."

"They didn't run off." Leila shut the door behind her to keep the cold from permeating the house. "Rory's here. She's still getting dressed."

"I can wait."

Leila peered past him to the back of the truck's extended cab. "Where's Sawyer?"

"I dropped him off with my sister. She'll make sure he gets to school on time."

It must all be so confusing for the little boy. "Why don't you come in for a cup of kaffi?"

"I don't want to trouble anyone."

"It's no trouble." Leila held open the door. "Kaffi's hot and so are the pancakes."

Nolan peeled off the wool cap and squashed it in oversized hands. "I ate breakfast."

Leila doubted that, but she kept her mouth closed as she led him into the house and to the table where the women were still cleaning up from breakfast. Mudder looked from Leila to Nolan, then wiped her hands on her apron. "I'll fetch Rory. Esther, you finish up the dishes. Leila, get Nolan some kaffi."

She bustled out and Leila did as she was told. Nolan shifted from one foot to the other, then plopped into a chair that creaked under his large frame.

Hoping the scent of coffee and fresh-made biscuits would soothe the man in some small way, Leila poured him a big mug of coffee and set it in front of him. "Milk? Sugar?"

"No, thanks." He took a sip and his expression eased for a second. "Good coffee. Hits the spot. This is the coldest December we've had in a while."

Men always took refuge in talking about the weather.

"Hot kaffi on a cold day is truly a blessing." She refilled her own cup and returned the pot to its pot holder. "Help yourself to a biscuit. They're hot, too, and we have molasses."

"Y'all must think I'm the worst kind of father."

Leila let the silence after those abrupt words linger for a beat or two, trying to summon a response. "We don't think any such thing. We don't judge people. We have enough planks in our own eyes."

"I surely love that girl, but she's driving me to the edge of the cliff." Nolan grabbed a napkin from the table and swiped at his face. "Without her mother to guide her, she's lost."

"She has you." Leila plopped two biscuits on a plate and set them in front of Nolan. She shoved a saucer of butter and a jar of honey toward him. "Rory loves you and she cares what you think. She's made her share of mistakes, but I reckon we all do."

"Those mistakes don't end with another child to raise and to care for and to teach right from wrong." Nolan twisted a napkin in knots, ignoring the biscuits. "I don't begrudge her the food or the money it takes to raise a baby. It's the responsibility. Without her mother, I'm . . . I've messed this up with Rory. How much better will I do with my grandchildren?"

"They say practice makes perfect." Leila eased into the chair across from him. "I'm just a girl, but it seems to me a father's love goes a long way toward raising a child right."

Nolan's Adam's apple bobbed, but he managed a halfhearted smile. "You've met Dwayne. Tell me you think he can be a father to those children."

"He's the one who ran into our friend's buggy and squashed it." Leila couldn't help herself. Nolan already knew what he was up against. "He was upset. I think he came to apologize to Rory."

"But he got drunk first." Nolan broke off a piece of the biscuit and popped it in his mouth without the benefit of the butter or honey. "I love that girl more than life itself, but when it comes to him, she doesn't have the sense God gave a gnat. He's a kid; he's not cut out to be a father."

"He will be. Give him time. Teach him what he needs to know."

"That's a tall order."

"I reckon you'd best get started so he'll do a better job with the next one."

"Daddy?" Rory stood in the doorway, Trevor on her hip. "I'm so glad you came." She shot across the room, Trevor crowing as he bounced on her hip. "I'm sorry. I'm sorry. I'm so sorry."

Nolan stood and held out his arms. Rory barreled into him

so hard, he took a step back and knocked into his chair. "Easy, girl, easy."

"I didn't mean the ugly things I said. You're the best dad ever." The flow of tears had returned once again. "I don't know how you put up with me."

"You're my kid." He wrapped her in a hug that included Trevor, who squealed and shrieked something that sounded a lot like "Poppy." "And this is my grandson."

"Take me back?"

"We have to talk about some things. It can't be like it's been."

"I know, I know. I'll tell Dwayne we're done."

Nolan peeled her arms from his waist and took a step back. "Dwayne's your husband. He's Trevor's father. He has to man up and take responsibility. We'll have a conversation when everyone has calmed down a little."

"Daddy? That's the first time you've ever called Dwayne by his name."

Or admitted that his daughter was married to the man. Leila hid her smile. Indeed, a big day for Nolan Beale and Rory Chapman.

Change was possible. Anything was possible.

THIRTY-TWO

Every dollar counted. Especially when they came in two, three, or four at a time. Jesse collected the four dollar bills, two quarters, and two dimes Thelma Doolittle laid on the glass-top counter and slid them into the open cash register drawer. The coins were sticky as if the lady had been eating some of the honey she'd just purchased. The smell of her perfume, like an overgrown row of rosebushes, permeated the store. Ignoring the temptation to hold his breath, he smacked the drawer shut and glanced out the store window. The sun had dropped in the west. This day would soon be over and he still hadn't done what he came to do.

"You don't have any okra?" Thelma's white-haired head tilted over a body shaped like an oversized pear as she surveyed the store crowded with all manner of homemade soaps, candles, jars of honey and jams, books on raising bees, saddles, rocking chairs, quilts, and piles of stuff that could only be described as junk— until someone bought it and declared it treasure. "No produce at all?"

"Too soon for the greenhouse crops, and the fall crops are all gone."

She sighed, a long, drawn-out, gusty sigh that made her triple chin quiver. "It's only December and I'm ready for spring and fresh produce." She picked up her jar and waddled to the door, her cane clacking on the cement floor and her ankle-length, purple-flowered dress rustling around her. "I'll be back Friday. Tell Mordecai I want some of those candles they make from beeswax for Christmas presents."

By Friday, he would be gone. After the conversation he planned to have with Daed, he'd most likely be gone today. The kaffi he'd drunk earlier turned his stomach sour. "I'll tell him."

Thelma put her hand on the doorknob, the rings on all four fingers clinking against the metal, but the door opened before she could turn it. Daed stood on the other side. They exchanged greetings, and Daed held the door wide for her, then trudged in, his craggy face dour. "I took a look at the buggy Will smashed up at Mordecai's. It's nearly beyond repair."

"Will didn't smash it up. A drunk ran into it." Jesse picked up a damp rag and swiped at the fingerprints on the glass. Not that he cared much. It gave him something to do. "Besides, I've seen you do more with less."

"No need to call the boy names."

"Calling him what he is."

"What's got you in such a mood today?"

Jesse's heart did push-ups against his rib cage, making it hard to breathe. The air in the store seemed to dissipate through the cracks in the windows. His shirt stuck to his chest and arms, damp with sweat. "I wanted to have a word with you."

"What's stopping you then?"

God, help me. God, forgive me. "I took a job in town a few days ago. I start there full time on Monday."

Daed stopped mopping his face with a faded gray bandanna. "You have a job here."

"After I tell you what I'm about to tell you, I won't have a job here anymore."

The lines around Daed's mouth and eyes deepened. Furrows grew across his forehead. He stomped to the door and flipped the lock. When he turned, he looked so much like Groossdaadi, an ache blossomed in Jesse's throat.

"Best get it over with then." His icy tone told Jesse his father had switched from daed to bishop in the flick of the wrist that locked the door. "Gott willing, we'll have customers at the door anytime now."

"I took a job with Matthew Plank, working as a carpenter and gopher in his home-repair and renovation business."

All expression slid from his daed's face. He took two steps toward shelves laden with candles made from beeswax. "Matthew and Angus are shunned. You can't work with them. You shouldn't even be talking to them."

"I visited their home a few weeks ago, and earlier this week I helped them shore up some columns on an old house on Washington Street. I also learned to drive and got my driver's license."

"Why would you do this?" The anguish of a father seeped through the frigid demand of a bishop. "You know better. Your mudder and I taught you better."

"I had to have a place to go."

"I don't understand." The father again. "You have a home and a family. Baptism classes start right after the first of the year."

"I won't be there."

Daed picked up a jar of honey, wiped the lid with his bandanna as if removing dust, then straightened the rows of jars that had no need of such care. "If you're not ready now, there'll be another class this summer."

"I'm trying to tell you something."

"Doing a poor job of it, far as I can tell."

Jesse's heart hammered in a painful staccato of emotions he couldn't begin to explain or even understand himself. "I've been going to a youth group in town. We study the Bible and do outreach at the Dairy Queen. We make hospital visits and pray for folks."

Daed's Adam's apple bobbed. "You understand the Ordnung."

"I do."

"You know that once you're baptized these are not activities in which you'll partake."

"Which is why I won't be baptized in the Amish faith."

The bishop's facade cracked and Jesse got a glimpse of a father's pain. It raced like lightning through his own body, a physical pain more real than any he'd ever experienced. The sheer force of it jolted his heart. It might stop beating altogether. "Daed, I'm sorry to cause you pain. I never intended to do that. I love Gott and I've been saved by Jesus Christ. I want others to know and to be saved too."

"What have they done to you?" Daed's booming voice had been reduced to a quivering whisper. "That you would be so arrogant as to think you can guarantee your salvation or anyone else's. Do you think you're Gott? Do you know better than He what His plan is for each of His wretched children on this earth?"

"Nee. But I know what the Bible says."

"You would leave your family and your community for these people?"

"I don't want to. I could keep living at home and working in the store if you let me. I haven't been baptized." Searching for some hint that he could hope, Jesse slipped closer to his father. He stood toe-to-toe and dared to look him in the eye. "I would go into town for church and Bible study. I wouldn't share it with the others."

"You would share this *word* with strangers but contain yourself from telling your brothers and sisters and cousins and friends?" The bishop was back, along with his booming voice. "You know even as you say those words you'll never be able to keep such a promise. You've been infected with the grandiose idea that it's up to *you* to tell everyone about Jesus. It's your job; it's about you. I won't make an exception for you because you're my son. I can't and I won't."

Jesse swallowed a lump in his throat the size of the state of Texas. "I'm not trying to be proud or arrogant. I only know what I read in the Bible and what my pastor tells me."

"You've been to another church?"

"Jah."

Daed backed away, his face contorted as if he'd just seen a terrible monster. "You should leave. Now."

"Daed—"

"You've made your choice." He made a swishing motion with his arms. His voice rose. "Get out. Go on."

"I don't understand. We worship the same God. We have the same Savior."

"We don't go around proclaiming to the world that we know more than they do." Daed stomped around the counter to put a physical barrier between them. "We keep ourselves apart from the world. We shine the light of Christ by our humble, obedient example."

"It's not enough."

"You would judge me and your mudder and the rest of your

family?" The words rolled and thundered now like those of the preacher Daed was. "Your arrogance and your pride will be your downfall."

"I don't mean to—"

"Don't go back home." Daed jerked his head toward the back room that housed the district's only telephone. "Call your friends to pick you up. I'll have Mr. Carson bring you your clothes tomorrow."

The pain spiraled through Jesse, so great he clasped both hands to his chest. He might be having a heart attack. "I can't say good-bye to Mudder?"

"I'll break the news to her." Icy cold replaced rolling thunder. "Go."

"I want to tell her—"

"I won't have you poisoning the others."

"It's not poison."

"Go."

Jesse stumbled into the back room. He leaned against the wall, his legs weak, hands and arms shaking. He bent over and tried to catch breath taken by the ferocity of his father's reaction. *Gott, I didn't mean to hurt him. Gott, please forgive me. Gott, help him forgive me. Help him to see what I see.*

He slid to the floor and put his head on his knees, concentrating on breathing. *In and out. In and out.*

After a few minutes, a blessed numbness took hold. He hoisted himself to his feet and picked up the phone. His hand hovered over the buttons. In the aching silence, a hoarse sob, quickly muffled, sounded from the other side of the wall.

Swallowing his own sobs, he punched in Colton's number with fierce jabs that made his finger hurt.

His new life was about to begin.

THIRTY-THREE

Sleep at last. The baby cradled against her chest, Leila eased from the rocking chair and slipped over to the closest crib. Duncan had needed a nap because he hadn't slept earlier when the others were having their afternoon nap. His fussiness made it hard to keep the others happy. It had been that kind of day. Thankfully it was almost over. While most of her babies went down on their own, this little boy liked to be rocked to sleep. No doubt thanks to parents who now regretted his inability to sleep on his own because they rocked him when he was only a wee thing. Swaddling had helped. She laid him on his side and made sure his pacifier was secure in his mouth.

She sighed and rubbed her aching lower back. A quick drink of water and she'd begin sanitizing the diaper pails and changing tables before the parents started arriving for pickup. She snagged her water bottle and went to the window to check the weather. Lifting the red-and-white-checked curtain, she peered out. Dark and overcast. It suited her mood. Which seemed a bit selfish of her. One of the other teachers had mentioned the possibility of freezing rain, maybe even snow, in the late afternoon or evening.

All the guests for Adam and Esther's wedding would be

arriving in the next few days. Driving all the way from Missouri and Tennessee, a few from Ohio. They didn't need bad weather or treacherous road conditions. And she needed to get home to help Susan and Mudder with the baking and cleaning and flurry of activity a wedding always brought.

"Where is she?"

Startled, the water bottle slipped from her hand and bounced on the thin carpet, its contents spilling and darkening the red, blue, and green balloon patterns. She faced Dwayne. "What are you doing here? You all agreed to meet at the house this weekend to talk, with your parents."

His face dark with a five o'clock shadow and his eyes red rimmed, Dwayne stood in the doorway. He held a bedraggled bunch of daisies in one hand and a heart-shaped box of assorted Whitman's chocolates in the other. His rumpled white T-shirt was tucked in on one side of his faded blue jeans, but not the other. "I need to talk to her now."

"She's helping with the babies. She's working." Leila squatted and sopped up the water with a towel. "You might want to wait until the end of her shift to talk to her so you don't get her in trouble. Didn't she tell you to give her some time?"

"It's been a week. She isn't answering my calls or my texts. Her dad will come to pick her up and I won't get a word in edgewise." His voice rose as he moved from the doorway and stood over her. His hands fisted and unfisted. "I just want to talk to her."

"Keep your voice down. The babies are sleeping." Leila straightened and tossed the towel into an overflowing dirty-clothes basket. She eyed the door. She couldn't leave the babies. Maybe Miss Daisy would hear the commotion and come in. "She needs time. You need to give her time. Pray about it. Talk to Gott about it."

The look Dwayne gave her was a cross between blank and confused. Maybe he was like Rory, a child whose family had fallen away from faith as times got hard. "You and Rory are married. It's Gott's will for you to be together. You have to figure out how to take care of her and your babies. That will help."

"What do you know about guy-girl stuff? You ain't married. I ain't seen you with anybody but that guy who picked you up at the park."

"Jesse."

"Yeah, and he's been running around town with Tiffany and Colton and those other Jesus freaks."

"They're not freaks. They want to share Gott's love with people. That's something special."

As soon as the words were out of her mouth, Leila knew she truly felt that way.

"Then how come you don't hang out with them?"

Because she would have to give up all the same things Jesse had. "We live our lives a little differently."

"I heard Jesse's living in town now with those Planks—the ones who work on houses. They still wear the weird clothes but drive cars and all."

Jesse, living in town. The word had spread quickly through their small community when Jesse broke his news to Leroy and he'd been asked to leave. She'd thought—maybe hoped—she would run into him in town, but so far she'd seen neither hide nor hair of him. She swallowed against the ache in her throat. "I have to stay with my family, where I belong."

"You're gonna be an old maid."

If her heart continued to tell her Jesse was the one, then yes, she might very well be. She would work in the day care forever.

Or take over teaching at the school for Susan someday. She could love her scholars. "Maybe."

"I know you think I'm a bad person." Dwayne swiped at his face with the sleeve of a thin denim jacket, not much good against the kind of cold this day had brought. "She just caught me off guard, that's all. We didn't plan to have another one, at least not so soon."

They didn't plan at all. Not with Trevor. Not now.

"I don't think you're a bad person." Not all grown up, maybe, and not ready to be a father for sure. "I don't pass judgment."

"I'm going to do right by her. That's what I'm gonna tell her dad when we meet." He sounded as if he was trying to convince himself. "I promise you that. I'm gonna get a better job. No more wrestling. No more partying. Then we can get a place of our own."

"You don't have to promise me anything. It's between you and Rory."

"And Nolan. Don't forget Nolan."

He sounded so bitter. And so young. No older than Caleb. He was probably better prepared to be a husband and father, and he was only eleven.

"Leila, Leila, they're talking about the prison on the radio." Rory scurried into the room, then slammed to a halt. She panted, fear and hurt and uncertainty mingled on a face wet with tears. "What are you doing here?"

"What's going on at the prison?" Dwayne dropped the candy and flowers at her feet and caught at her hand with his. She jerked away. "Is your dad okay?"

"You killed a buggy."

"I didn't mean to. I was drunk."

"You're not even old enough to drink."

"I was drowning my sorrows. I'm sorry." He dropped to his

knees and picked up the flowers, holding them out to her. "These are for you, babe. I'm so sorry. I want you. I want our baby. I want to make a family. Please, please take me back."

"Oh baby, so am I." Rory sank to her knees and buried her face in his chest. "I'm sorry. I'm sorry. I just don't know how we're gonna make it. I feel sick all the time. I cry all the time. Trevor keeps me up at night. I'm so tired."

"I'll take care of you. I promise. I promise."

The two huddled together, arms entwined, heads bowed. They could've been praying, if Leila didn't know better. They were so lost, so very lost. What had she done to help them find their way? What kind of friend was she?

Sniffing and wiping away tears, Rory raised her head. "We have to get to the prison. I need to find out if Daddy is all right. Some prisoners got into a fight or something. Shots were fired." She burrowed closer to Dwayne. "My dad's not answering his cell phone."

As if on cue, the sound of a country-western song blared. Rory's phone. "Answer that before you wake the babies."

Rory tugged it from the pocket of her day-care smock and answered. Lines formed across her forehead. Her free hand went to her mouth. She turned her back on them and began to pace, her responses consisting mostly of "I know, I know, I heard, yeah, I know, oh no, oh no."

"What is it? What are they saying?" Dwayne followed after her like an anxious puppy who needed to go outside. "Is it your dad? Is he okay?"

"Shush, shush, will you!" Rory rubbed her forehead with her free hand. "Not you, I'm talking to my husband." She waited some more. "I will. You too. Call me if you hear anything."

The phone dropped to her chest and she gazed at Leila, her

face white and scared. "That was my friend Pam. Her dad works at the prison too. She says word has it there was an inmate uprising. Big fights. The guards had to go in and break it up."

"Is your dad all right?"

"I don't know. She says everyone is trying to call over there, but they're not getting an answer. The phones are overloaded. The injured are being taken to the hospital." She whirled and ran to the door, then stopped to look back. "We have to go to the hospital. You have to come with me, Leila, come with me, please."

Leila looked at the clock on the wall. Fifteen minutes to end of shift. Miss Daisy would have to cover her room. Rory was only an aide. Her room had a teacher. "I'll ask."

"I'll do it. Get your stuff. Hurry and get Trevor for me."

Leila did as she was told. Twenty minutes later they were at the hospital. Dwayne led the way through a crowded parking lot and swinging emergency room doors into a large room filled with padded chairs arranged in long rows so those who waited could see a big-screen TV that blared the nightly news. One hand clasped in Rory's, Dwayne threaded his way between a mother with a screaming child and a cluster of men in prison guard uniforms. Teary-eyed women and worried men and children clutching stuffed animals milled around, creating an obstacle course between them and the check-in desk.

Rory tried to stop to talk to the prison guards, but Dwayne tugged her forward. They strode toward the counter. Leila followed behind, a sleeping Trevor cuddled against her chest. A prayer bobbed in her head. *Let him be all right, Lord; let him be all right, please, Lord.*

"Nolan Beale, do you have a Nolan Beale here?"

"We're really, really busy right now." The nurse peered at them over blue-rimmed glasses perched on the end of her long, skinny nose. Her short, blonde hair spiked on her head as if she'd run her hands through it repeatedly. "We'll get to you as soon as we can."

"We're looking for my daddy, Nolan Beale." Rory's voice quavered. "Is he here?"

"Is this related to the incident at the prison?"

"Yes, he works at the prison."

"Did they call to tell you he'd been transported here?"

"No, ma'am."

"Then he's probably not here."

"Could you look, please? Please, just look."

The nurse sighed and ran her hands through her hair, creating more wild spikes. She pushed her glasses up her nose with one finger. She studied the computer screen for a few minutes. "Nope. Don't see that name."

"Are you sure?" Rory broke free from Dwayne's grip and slapped both hands on the counter as if she might hurl herself over it. "Look again."

"He hasn't been triaged, and he hasn't been admitted. I looked." The nurse turned back to a stack of files teetering dangerously near the edge of her desk. "Maybe you got lucky. Maybe he wasn't in the cell block that had the meltdown."

Rory slapped both hands to her face. Tears seeped between her fingers and ran down the backs of her hands. She bent over, her back heaving.

Leila held Trevor out to Dwayne. The look on his face told her he didn't know which was worse—corralling a crying girl or being responsible for a sleeping baby. After a few seconds' hesitation, he took Trevor. Leila turned to Rory. "It's okay. Let's sit down for a minute. He could be on his way here, or he could be getting ready to call you any second."

"Or he's unconscious or he's dead or he's being held hostage by some vicious killer inmates." Rory sank into a chair and sobbed. "All I ever do is give him grief. I make his life miserable and now I might never get to tell him I love him and I appreciate him."

"You're getting way ahead of yourself." Leila rubbed her shoulder in an awkward pattern. She tried to brush away the thought of the prisoner who had escaped the previous summer and held Phineas and Deborah hostage for a few short hours. They had escaped unscathed, but Deborah's expression when she told the story said it all. The man had been angry and desperate, a scary combination. "The prison authorities will call the families. They'll make statements as soon as they get everything under control."

Somehow that didn't seem helpful.

"We would be happy to pray for your father."

Leila closed her eyes, then opened them. No doubt about it. Jesse approached, Colton and Tiffany on his heels. He had some sort of pamphlet in his hands that he kept smoothing with his fingers. He wore gray pants and a white shirt and a jacket that looked like a hand-me-down from a bigger person. It made him look as if he'd shrunk. His gaze caught hers. For one second, he couldn't hide it. He was glad to see her. Then the spark died and a neutral look spread over his face, the kind one would give a new neighbor or a stranger passing on the street.

He squatted in front of Rory. "We've been talking to the other guards—the ones who weren't hurt. They say everything is under control at the prison. Things are still getting sorted out, but no one is in danger now."

Rory shook off Leila's hand and leaned toward the man in

front of her. "Do they know anything about my dad? Do they know if he's hurt?"

Jesse glanced back at his friends. "We'll ask around." Colton jerked his head toward two guards deep in conversation next to the admissions counter. One had his arm in a sling and a thick white bandage on his left cheek.

Jesse took Rory's hands in his and bowed his head. He began to pray in a soft, earnest voice Leila had never heard before.

She bowed her head and squeezed her eyes shut, all the while feeling as if she were being disloyal to someone or something, she couldn't be sure what or whom.

"Lord, we ask You to put Your arms around Nolan Beale. Protect him, keep him safe. Calm the prisoners and the guards at the prison. Let Your peace and grace and serenity wash over them. Bring Nolan home safely to his daughter and his son. In Jesus' name we pray. Amen."

Leila managed a whispered amen. When she opened her eyes, Jesse's gaze bored into hers. He stood and backed away. "I'll see if Tiffany or Colton found out anything."

Leila squeezed Rory's arm and stood. "I'll be right back."

She couldn't help herself. She followed him across the room. No doubt he knew she followed, but he didn't stop until he got to the double doors that led to the parking lot.

"Jesse, wait."

He glanced back. "Not here. Outside."

She followed him into the parking lot. Darkness had fallen, but the lights that bathed the lot shone brightly on the cars, reflecting on glass and chrome wheel covers. Nothing could hide the emotion on Jesse's face. Leila crossed her arms, suddenly cold. "Why are you and Tiffany and Colton here? Was someone in your group hurt?"

"We heard what happened and we came to pray for the injured. We came to pray for the guards and the prisoners. Some of our youth group members have folks who work over there. Most of Beeville does."

Leila stared at his face. She found herself memorizing the way his brown eyes devoured her, the way his dark curls hung low on his forehead, the way his full lips parted when he breathed. What would he say if he knew Will had declared his feelings for her? Would Jesse care? The awkward silence stretched. His gaze dropped to the asphalt. "I guess you heard."

"You know how the grapevine is."

"I never meant to hurt you."

"You didn't." Not much. She forced her gaze to her hands clasped in front of her, fearful he would see the truth in her eyes. "I can't believe you'll never be at church again or the singings or at the store. We won't celebrate the holidays together or see each other at . . . weddings."

"You shouldn't even be talking to me."

"You're not shunned. You weren't baptized."

"Splitting hairs."

"I know." She swallowed the lump in her throat and looked around. Several empty benches lined the sidewalk that ran along the outside of the building. "Sit with me?"

"Sure." He smiled. Leila's heart ricocheted around her rib cage in a painful *rat-a-tat-tat. No fair. Don't smile that smile.* "Anything for you."

She sank onto the cement bench. Its cold seeped through her skirt. She shivered. Jesse sat next to her, close. Leila fought the urge to lean into him and feel his warmth. "I was wondering if you could do something for me."

"Like I said, anything."

"It's Rory." She recounted the story of Rory's mother's death and the loss of her church life. "Dwayne seems so lost too. He drinks and he parties and he doesn't seem to know how to be a husband or a father."

"What do you want me to do?"

She touched the pamphlet in his hand, her fingers precariously close to his. His fingers stretched. She could almost feel the caress. "Do this thing that you do. Invite them to your youth group. They may be married and have a baby, but they're the right age for your group."

"I can do that. Pastor David works with a lot of teen parents." Enthusiasm buoyed his words. He looked happy for a few seconds, as if he'd found his place. "He teaches them that God forgives every sin. He loves their babies and wants them to be brought up knowing Him. He knew their names before they were born. He knows how many hairs they have on their heads."

Pain twisted in Leila's chest. They knew the same scriptures. Their beliefs bound them together more than they tore them apart. It was obvious to her. But not to people like Mudder.

Jesse stopped. His face reddened. "Sorry, I know you don't have to be convinced. I get carried away. Colton says all newbies do."

She did have her faith, but she'd never seen or felt the exuberance that billowed from Jesse when he talked about his. She tried to focus on the matter at hand, but a curious warmth curled itself around her heart. She wanted what Jesse had. *Focus. It's not about you.* "Trevor has never been to church."

Jesse slapped the pamphlet against his knee in a one-two-three rhythm, his expression thoughtful. "Nolan needs to go back to church too. The whole family does."

"If you get Rory and Dwayne involved, I'm thinking Nolan will follow. He has the foundation; he's just been lost since his fraa died."

Jesse's gaze skipped from her eyes to her mouth and back. She breathed, reliving for one second the moment in which he leaned down and kissed her at the movie theater. He smiled as if he could read her thoughts. He looked away. "Why are you doing this?"

"I care about what happens to them. I want Trevor to have two happy, Gott-loving parents who raise him up as Gott's child."

A wailing siren drowned his response at first. She leaned toward him. He returned the favor. His breath smelled like peppermint gum, the way it had in the theater. She imagined its warmth on her cheek. "I couldn't hear you." Her voice sounded odd in her ears, as if she'd run a long race. "What did you say?"

"And you think what I do will help them with that?"

His gaze captured her and held her, telling her how important her answer was to him. "I do."

Jesse breathed, a half sigh, then laughed so quietly she almost didn't hear it. "What about you? Can I help you?"

"I have Gott in my life."

The sirens grew closer and closer. Jesse's hand lifted and he brushed a tendril of hair from her face. Her heart stopped beating, then exploded in a rapid-fire beat that left her breathless. "I know you do, but don't you ever yearn for more?"

She broke away from his gaze, the movement so painful the soles of her feet ached, and stood. "Help them. Please."

"We'll reach out to them, but they have to come halfway." Jesse gazed up at her, his face full of conflicting emotions. "Everyone does."

"I'll push from my end. You pull from the other."

He stood, his body so close she could smell his soapy scent and see the faint dusting of freckles on his nose. "We'll make a good team."

Leila fought to breathe. A good team. A good couple. Good parents. So many things that could never be. "Only in this."

"Nee."

"You should forget the *Deutsch*. You don't need it now."

"It's part of who I am."

"Not anymore." She started toward the building, her feet stumbling over themselves. They didn't want to go. They wanted to stay with Jesse.

"Leila."

She looked back.

He chewed on his lip, his eyes wet with unshed tears. "Have you seen my mother?"

Naomi had looked old and tired when Leila last saw her. Coming to church knowing what everyone was thinking about her son must've been a hard row to hoe. No one passed judgment, but having a son not join the church made every Plain parent feel shame. "At church this past Sunday."

"Did she seem . . . well?"

"She seemed content to let Gott be in charge."

His lips contorted in a half smile. "Right. Tell Will I said hi."

"I can't."

"Tell them I miss them, all of them."

"Come home then."

"I can't."

"Is it worth it?"

He held up the stash of pamphlets. "Every life saved for Christ is one more person who doesn't have to live all of eternity in the absence of God."

"And you personally have to do this?"

"Faith is personal. Salvation is personal."

Because Jesse made it personal. He looked so sure of himself standing there, his head held high. So willing to give up everything for what he believed. What would she give up to save a friend from eternal damnation? She nodded. "Good-bye, Jesse."

His response was lost in the whoop of a siren and the roar of an engine approaching fast. An ambulance whipped through the parking lot and shimmied to a stop under the awning that led to the ER. An EMT—Tom Fletcher—jumped from the passenger side and raced around to the back. He flung the doors open as his partner, an angular woman with blonde hair tied back in a long braid, rounded the other side. Together, the two of them manhandled a gurney to the ground.

The man on the gurney sat up. "I don't need to be lying down. I'm fine. I keep telling you I'm fine."

"Nolan!" Leila dashed from the sidewalk across the parking lot, waving a hand. "Nolan, you're okay. Rory is inside. She's desperate to know if you're all right."

He didn't look all right. Dried blood stained the front of his uniform and caked his upper lip and chin. Bruises darkened both eyes. His nose appeared to have been flattened. When he talked, he revealed a black gaping hole where one of his top front teeth had been only days earlier.

"I'm fine. I keep telling them that."

"Hey, Leila." Tom jerked his head toward the woman with the braid. "Meet my partner, Sam. Mr. Beale will be fine once a doctor takes a look at him and gets some X-rays and some stitches and a few things like that. He can do the whole macho routine after we get him fixed up."

Sam was a woman. A pretty woman. A strong woman who handled the gurney with assurance. Leila didn't have time to consider all the ramifications of this discovery. Light-headed with relief for Rory, Sawyer, and Trevor, she chuckled, the sound hysterical in her ears.

Tom grinned and shoved open the door so he and his partner could wrestle the gurney into the ER. Sam nodded at her, her face full of curiosity.

Leila nodded back, then turned to Jesse. He crossed both arms over his chest and stared at the doors that settled shut behind the gurney.

"What?"

"Does Will know about your Englisch boyfriend?"

"He's not my boyfriend."

"I saw the two of you together at the café the other day. He had his hands on your shoulder."

"I choked on a cookie."

Jesse looked as if he might choke on something else. He inhaled and then shrugged. "None of my business."

"That's right."

"You can court an outsider, but not me?"

"I'm not courting him, and you left, not me."

"I didn't have a choice."

"I'm not courting anyone."

He ducked his head and studied the cement under a pair of black sneakers that looked brand new. "Not even Will?"

She hesitated. She didn't know the answer to that question. "Like you said, none of your business."

"Right."

She whirled and flounced into the ER, leaving him standing in the cold.

Where he belonged. So why was she the one shivering and bereft?

THIRTY-FOUR

Esther and Adam's wedding went off without a hitch. Leila breathed a sigh of relief as she surveyed tables filled with dirty dishes. The weather had cleared up just long enough for friends and family from out of state to make the long trip for a second time in six weeks. They had at least two more rounds of guests to feed, and then she could slip away to some corner to rub her aching feet and head. As much as she loved Esther, watching her stepsister marry Jesse's brother—who looked so much like Jesse—had been like wading barefoot through a thicket of cacti.

Determined to be happy for them, she stacked dirty plates, picked them up, and started toward the kitchen. Jesse's mother, Naomi, stood in her path. "Congratulations, mother of the groom." Leila forced a smile. She could see Jesse in the woman's dark eyes and the shape of her mouth. "You must be happy to see your oldest hitched."

Naomi nodded, but the smile on her face slipped. Leila tried to recollect if the sharp lines around the woman's mouth and eyes had been there the last time they talked. "Let me help you with those dishes."

"Nee, nee, I've got it."

Despite Leila's protestations, Naomi pulled four plates from the top of the stack with a determined air. She trotted into the kitchen ahead of Leila and deposited them in the only space left on the prep table. "I have to ask you a question." Naomi glanced around at the eight or nine women engaged in every imaginable task, from cutting cakes to pulling a golden-yellow macaroni-and-cheese casserole from the oven to slicing a ham that had been a gift from one of the Englisch families who shopped at the store. "Outside."

Leila set her plates on top of the others and wiped her hands on a dish towel as she followed the other woman out back. Two dozen or more children engaged in a game of kickball in the field that separated the house from the corral and barn. They'd dumped their coats on the ground, and their faces were red with exertion and the cold north wind that whipped their skin. They shouted and screamed with laughter. Leila longed to be so care-free. She patted her damp face with the towel and inhaled the smell of winter, decaying leaves, and damp air.

"I know it's Gott's will, but it seems so sad to me that all my kinner couldn't be here for my firstborn's wedding." Naomi's voice started out strong but tapered off in a quaver. "Adam wanted Jesse by his side for this. He was supposed to be his witness."

"I know. I'm sure Jesse would've liked to have been here."

True, but Jesse answered to a higher calling now. He believed that, and Leila had come to believe it as well. He felt it so strongly he had given up everyone and everything in his life. Including her. It had to be a calling.

"Have you seen him?" Naomi whispered despite the fact that no one stood within earshot.

Leila watched as Caleb sent the ball sailing across the yard. It bonked the boy in left field in the head. He let out a yelp and did a little dance before chasing the ball all the way to the corral fence. This was Naomi. She had a right to know. She asked in private because she didn't want to get Leila in trouble. "Jah."

"How is he?"

Leila faced the woman who had given life to Jesse Glick and then been left behind when he chose to go his own way. "He's good."

"Where is he staying? How is he living?"

The things a mother would worry about. Not like Leroy, who probably lay awake at night thinking about Jesse's sins of pride and disobedience that might earn him eternal damnation.

"He's staying with Angus Plank, I think. He works with him and Matthew now. He spends a lot of time with his Englisch friends though. Did he ever talk to you about them?"

Naomi shook her head. Her fingers plucked at the strings of her kapp. "Not a word. He never said a word. I had no idea he'd been drawn into this . . . this . . . whatever it is."

"Did Leroy tell you what Jesse wants to do?"

"He said he's fallen in with some religious group in town."

"Jesse loves the Lord and he wants to be a preacher himself."

"I don't understand how this happened."

Shouldn't a mother be proud her child was so committed to God he wanted to spend his life telling others about Him? This paradox puzzled Leila without end. She couldn't make sense of any of it. Leroy's admonition that they should obey the Ordnung and their parents in all things didn't help. She'd always done both. Never had she seen a cost in doing so as she did now.

The lost, sad look in Naomi's eyes surely matched her own.

"I'm sorry." In an impulse born in the moment, she embraced the other woman. "I'm so very sorry."

"It's not your fault, child." Naomi pulled away. Tears trickled down her thin cheeks. "We have to believe Gott has a purpose in all of this."

Leila wanted to believe that. "Jesse said to tell you he loves you and he misses you."

Naomi put a hand to her quivering lips. The tears streamed now. "I'm sorry. I don't know why I'm acting like this."

"It's okay."

The screen door opened and Mudder stuck her head out. "There you are. Esther says to tell you to get in there. She's saved a seat at the table for you."

Saved a seat. The pairing off had begun. "I'm helping in the kitchen. There's still so much serving to be done and dishes to wash."

Mudder came out onto the porch. Her smile fled as she looked from Leila to Naomi and back. "Nee, you should go. This is a celebration. You don't want to miss the fun."

The steel underlying the words told Leila her mother had assessed the situation and found it wanting. She surely knew Naomi had asked about Jesse. Mudder had been kind but firm. No contact with Jesse would be tolerated. He might not be shunned, but his choices could only lead to problems for Leila. Time to look forward and move on.

Leila wiped her hands on the towel again. "No, I don't want to miss the fun."

As she let the door shut behind her, she heard Mudder offer Naomi a cup of tea. Leave it to Mudder to find her own way to offer comfort. A way that didn't involve violating the Ordnung.

Leila smoothed the hair around her kapp and marched into the front room. The benches were full, but Esther had indeed saved a spot on the girls' side at the bench closest to the tables where Esther and Adam sat at the *eck*.

After filling a plate with roast, stuffing, sweet potatoes, and corn, she slid into the spot before perusing her companions. Directly across from her sat Will. He sopped up gravy with a bread crust and lifted it to his mouth. His gaze met hers and his hand hovered in the air. He tossed the bread on his plate. A frown spread across his face. "I was beginning to wonder if you were going to partake in the celebration. Esther said she was expecting you. That's why she left a seat open."

Leila leaned back to look around her cousin Frannie so she could shoot Esther a scowl. Esther grinned right back and jerked her head as if to say *go on*.

Everyone wanted her to go on, to get over Jesse. How she wished she could. She straightened. "I had to help in the kitchen."

"Tons of womenfolk doing that. This is where you belong . . . for now." He glanced at his companions. They were busy talking to their counterparts across the table. Tapping his fork on the table in a nervous rhythm, he leaned forward. "Can we talk later?"

"I don't know."

"I'm sorry . . . about the other day." His voice dropped to a growl. "I shouldn't have been so hard on you."

He paused as if waiting for her to jump in. Leila wanted to leap up and pound on the table. Instead she patted her lips with her napkin and counted to ten. Twice. "I'm not judging you. Or Jesse. Neither should you."

She knew which one she should choose. Her head had made that very clear. Her heart, on the other hand, disagreed. *Sorry, Will.*

He pasted on a smile, but his eyes told her he knew. He knew she longed for another. Yet he kept trying. There was something to be said for that. She needed to move on and Will sat right there in front of her, offering her a way. It made sense. It was logical. If only her heart would listen to her head.

"Let's go for a walk later, talk."

"I have to help clean up."

"Later tonight then? I'll come by in the buggy."

"Tonight I'll be too tired."

"I'll give you a few days." He wouldn't give up. He deserved something for that. Something she couldn't give him. He offered her a hesitant smile. "Have some wedding cake. I'll share mine."

He cut a huge chunk of white cake with chocolate frosting in two equal pieces, then smiled as he handed it over. His hand shook. He surely imagined that someday they would be eating their own cake seated at the eck, the single women and men nearby.

Leila accepted his offering and ate it, bite after bite, without tasting it. Will's dream most likely would never materialize unless God worked a miracle on her heart, but then her dream would die instead.

If she were a better person, she'd put Will's dream before hers.

THIRTY-FIVE

Evangelism could happen anywhere. Even during wrestling matches. Unbuttoning his overcoat as he went, Jesse squeezed past two girls, dressed in skimpy cheerleading outfits, who were screaming what he assumed was the name of one of the wrestlers on the mat. He spotted Rory on the second row of the bleachers, her red plaid coat lying in her lap, a bag of unshelled peanuts on top of it. He eased into the open seat next to her and waited for the cheering to die down. He'd never been in the high school gym before. It smelled of teenage boy sweat, dust, and rubber.

What would it have been like if he'd been born in a different family, a different faith? He might be in college, playing baseball, or in the army. Big ifs. It didn't matter. Gott had given him this path on this day. To help Leila's friend. To help Trevor and his unborn brother or sister. Jesse had told Leila he would help and he would, even if it felt as if a knife twisted in his heart every time he thought of her.

She'd asked him to do something for her that her family and her bishop would not have her do. That meant she understood how important it was. She wanted someone to step out in faith and help save a friend. That was all he wanted to do with his life. How could she not understand that? How could they not do it together?

If he did this for Rory, if he succeeded, maybe Leila would see. Maybe she would come to him willingly.

And pay a terrible price if she did. Did he really want her to suffer the loneliness and isolation he felt when he went home to his little bedroom in Angus's narrow trailer every night? He missed his mudder's apple pie. He missed his sister's goofy jokes and his brother's tall tales. He missed the sound of the frogs and the cicadas, even the smell of horse manure, silly as that sounded. He missed the clutter and junk of the Combination Store and his father's crotchety critiques of his work.

He missed his life.

He swallowed against the hollow feeling in the pit of his stomach. It was worth it. He had no doubt of that. Colton's words curled themselves around his heart, giving him warmth against the cold. Jesus called His first disciples to leave their fishing nets, their livelihood, their families, and their homes. To be fishers of men.

He'd given all that up for the very reason that he sat on this hard, uncomfortable bleacher. To help people like Rory. In the time that he had been shadowing Colton, he'd learned a few things. First, evangelism couldn't be rushed. Jumping right in made people uncomfortable and scared them off.

"Be patient. Be prepared. Have the answers to the questions they'll ask. Don't let the hecklers rattle you. You have the truth."

You have the truth.

He settled back on the bleacher and studied the match. He had a basic understanding of wrestling, but not much more. Roughhousing with friends was one thing, but the idea of rolling around in shorts with another guy in front of a screaming crowd made him cringe.

Finally Rory glanced at him, away, and then back again. "What are you doing here?"

"Checking out the wrestling match."

She giggled and tossed back her dark curls. "Thinking about going out for the team?"

"Naw, I'm too old for that stuff."

"I'm sorry Dwayne was rude to your friend Colton the other day at the park. Tell him Dwayne didn't mean it. He just doesn't know how to act sometimes."

"Don't worry about it. Nothing fazes Colton." It was the truth as far as Jesse could tell. His friend took everything to the Lord and left it there. He always walked with a spring in his step and a smile on his face. "How's your dad?"

"Right as rain. His nose is crooked and he has an appointment for a bunch of dental work. He snores when he takes a nap on the couch." She chuckled, her joy in knowing her father's problems were minor shining in her face. "The bruises are fading. He's still wearing the back brace and his ribs hurt, but he doesn't complain. He's lucky he didn't get shanked."

"Has he gone back to work?"

"Nope. Doctor won't let him. He's chomping at the bit, but he's building a play set with swings and a fort for Trevor. It's keeping him busy."

"Good for him. You're blessed to have him as a dad and granddad."

"Yep, I am."

"Is that Dwayne out there on the mat?"

She nodded, pride obvious on her face as she studied the

two grunting wrestlers, their faces red, arms locked around each other's necks. "It's Dwayne's last match. He's not going out for wrestling anymore, so Dad told me I could watch him one more time. After this, he'll be working every afternoon and Saturdays at the feed store."

"Is he winning?"

"Yep. Of course. He could be all-state if he stayed on the team, but he knows getting more hours at his job is the most important thing, with the baby coming and all." She held out her bag of peanuts. "Want some? They're the only thing staying down right now. I think it's the salt. Did you actually come here to see me?"

Jesse waved away the bag. "No, thanks, but yeah, I did."

"That's good, because I meant to find you somehow and thank you for praying for me and my dad the other day at the hospital. Nobody's done that for me in a while." She ducked her head. "It was nice."

"You're welcome. We're still praying for you and your dad. Every day."

"Why?"

"Because it seems like you need it."

She plucked at loose peanut shells on her jacket, flicking them to the gym's wooden floor. Her face had turned radish red. "How did you know I was here?"

An easier topic for her. Jesse shrugged. "I stopped by the day care and asked."

"You stopped by the day care?" She pumped her fist, causing some of the peanuts to go flying. She settled the bag on top of her coat. "Did you see Leila? I bet you did. When are you going to quit messing around and ask her out again?"

The crowd's roar halted the conversation for a few seconds.

Jesse couldn't be sure, but he thought Dwayne had made a good move. He had the other guy on the mat now. "I can't ask her out. I have to leave her alone."

"You have the guts to bail on your family so you can save the world, but you're too 'fraidy cat to ask a girl out?"

"It's not that simple."

"I know, Leila told me all about it."

"I'm not here to talk about me and Leila—"

"She told me all about it and she cried the whole time."

"She cried?" His gut roiled. Leila cried. His mother cried. His sisters cried. Even his daed had shed tears. But he never thought Leila would cry for him. "Tell her I said I'm sorry."

Rory's face colored a pretty pink. "Well, you know Leila. She hides how she feels, but she wanted to cry. I saw tears in her eyes—"

"Tell her anyway."

"You tell her."

"Look, I came here to invite you and Dwayne—"

"I know, she told me about that too. You're inviting us to the youth group."

She had promised to push if he would pull. Leila kept her promises. "We're hanging out at Tiffany's tomorrow night. There'll be pizza and after group, we're watching a movie. The girls picked the movie this time, so it'll be something you'll like. Dwayne, probably not so much. Popcorn and sodas, the works."

"Sounds cool."

"It does?"

"Dwayne won't be excited, but he promised my dad to be good to me, so what I want, he wants. He knows we only have a sliver of a chance of making this work."

"Stick with this group and you'll have a whole lot better chance."

"Talk to Leila."

"I can't."

She shot up, raised both hands in the air, and screamed. Peanuts went flying. Her coat landed somewhere below the bleachers.

Apparently Dwayne had done something good. Jesse hauled himself to his feet, watching as the referee held Dwayne's arm up and announced him as the winner of the match. The guy grinned from ear to ear, his tank top soaked, chest heaving with exertion. He looked so happy.

His last hurrah.

Rory elbowed Jesse. "People who love each other will give up a lot. There's no prom for me, no cheerleading, no volleyball, none of that kid stuff. Love is grown up."

Who was teaching whom now? "I know."

"Give Leila a chance. Maybe she's willing to give up something for you."

She hopped from the bleachers and ran out to meet Dwayne on the gym floor. She wrapped her arms around her husband, sweat and all.

Jesse stood rooted to the spot, unable to look away. He'd come to teach Rory about God's love, but Leila's friend might know more about the man-woman kind of love than he did.

She might be right. That thought sent a bolt of sheer energy through him.

It felt like hope.

THIRTY-SIX

Winter made lovely decorations on the day-care windows. Leila rubbed the glass with her sleeve. Condensation clouded her view of the play area. She breathed on the window and rubbed again. Darkness had settled in early tonight with the cloud cover. Rays from the streetlights bounced off a shiny metal tricycle left in the yard. Someone should've put it in the storage unit. The thought drifted away. Her eyes didn't deceive her. Pellets of white ice dotted the ground. They pinged against the glass in a steady barrage. "We have ice."

Talking to herself again. Not exactly. She had a roomful of babies as an audience. Unfortunately, they weren't old enough to keep up their end of the conversation. She turned with a sigh. This was the last day of work before the day care closed and gave everyone a four-day weekend for the Christmas holiday. She loved her babies, but lately she'd longed to stay in bed in the morning. Morning, noon, and night.

Rory claimed she was depressed, but Leila was fairly certain Plain girls weren't allowed to be depressed. Rory had attended her first youth group on Wednesday, and she'd felt it necessary to give Leila an update on Jesse. How he looked. How he sang. To whom he spoke. Even how much he ate. Apparently, a lot.

Leila sighed again, this time even more loudly, and picked up the diaper pail. No point in crying over spilled milk. At least that's what Mudder would say.

"No youth group tonight." As if thinking of her could make her appear, Rory stuck her head in the door. "Just got a text from Tiffany. The roads are iced over. They want everyone to stay home and be safe. Phooey. That means no Jesse sightings for you. Sorry about that."

"You know you're not helping by reminding me of him." Leila sounded as whiney as Hazel when she had to go to bed before she was ready. She tried to tame her irritation. "He's not in my life anymore. I'm happy he's moved on."

"Moved on?" Rory snorted and shook her index finger in a snooty little dance. "Moved on? He asked me twenty questions. With this hangdog expression like he's trying to hide it, but it's killing him."

"Really, hush up about it already, will you?" She shouldn't be taking this out on Rory, but her friend was the only person in the world to whom she could talk about this particular thorn in her side. "Sorry, I'm sorry."

"Don't be. I get it. You're having a bad day today." Rory's fingers were flying over her cell phone keyboard as she spoke. "Want me to buy you a donut to sweeten you up?"

"I'm not having a bad day, I'm just . . . I don't know." Simply sad. That's what she was. Sad. She missed Jesse. Which was ridiculous. She hadn't spent that much time with him. "You'd better go help Shelby. It's almost time for parents to come in."

"Uh-oh."

Leila didn't like any comments from Rory that began with *uh-oh.* "What's the matter?"

"Dad says the roads are so bad, he might not be able to get over here. He's saying a lot of parents might be late picking up their kids."

"What are we going to do? Stay all night?"

"We might have to do that." Miss Daisy bustled into the room, her brown corduroy pants making a rubbing sound as her thunderous thighs worked. Spit-up decorated her green-and-red cable-knit sweater and her bun of white hair half fell down as usual. "I'm making the rounds, letting the teachers know. You may have to stay late tonight, until parents can get here. Some of the roads are closed. You know Texas. The slightest bit of precipitation and they go hog wild, closing highways and whatnot."

Leila didn't know. Her first winter in Texas had been mild after some severe storms in the fall, including the spin-offs from a coastal hurricane. So mild she hadn't been sure it actually happened. This year, they'd had a few storms and occasional cold fronts so far, but nothing she'd call winter. "I don't mind staying at all."

She got paid by the hour and she could use the extra money, truth be told.

"Good girl. Rory, stop lollygagging about and help Shelby."

"Yes, ma'am." Rory turned to go, then turned back. "Dad's definitely not getting through. He's staying at the prison overnight. Dwayne's at the house with Sawyer so he's no good. We're stuck."

"Don't worry, I have cocoa, canned soup, and Ramen noodles in the break room." Miss Daisy made these three items sound like a feast. She headed for the door. "And lots of Girl Scout cookies in the freezer. As long as the electricity doesn't go out, we're fine."

The words were barely out of her mouth when the room went

dark. Rory shrieked and then giggled. Leila grabbed the changing table, waiting for her eyes to adjust. "What on earth would cause that? It's not like it's storming out."

"The electric lines around here don't know what to do with the extra weight of ice."

"I guess we'll make do." Leila groped on the shelf over the changing table until her hand connected with the cool metal of the large flashlight with which each room in the day care was equipped. "The babies should sleep well in the darkness. I'd better make sure they're all covered and get extra blankets. I reckon it's going to cool off in here if the electricity doesn't come back right away."

"I'll get out the lanterns. Rory, come with me. You can help me distribute them."

They left her alone in the dark with her sleeping babies. Thank Gott babies could sleep through anything. A wail from the far corner immediately followed that thought. Kaitlin. Careful to keep the flashlight aimed at the floor, Leila made her way over to the crib that held Tom's daughter. "Hey, baby girl, you're fine, you're fine." She lifted the chunky-monkey girl into her arms. "Are you wet? I reckon you're wet. A wet diaper is cold on a day like this."

She waited a few seconds for her eyes to adjust to the darkness, then moved to the changing table.

"She definitely doesn't like having a wet bottom." Tom's voice floated in the darkness. A stomping noise told her he was clearing the snow from his boots on the rug. "Sorry, I didn't mean to scare you."

"You didn't. How did you get here?" Leila made quick work of changing the diaper. She didn't want poor Kaitlin to get a chill.

Too bad they didn't have a wood-burning stove. A fire would do nicely about now. "I thought all the roads were closed."

"They are, but I'm in an ambulance made to travel in all kinds of weather on all kinds of roads."

"Are you still working?"

"Yes, but my chief said my partner and I could come check on my baby girl and take her to my sister's and then get back to the station. Everyone will stay on duty while this weather lasts."

Leila glanced past Tom, looking for his partner. Curiosity about the person he'd only referenced once or twice overcame her. *Mind your own business.* "In this weather, there's bound to be lots of accidents."

"Most folks are smart enough to stay indoors. There's always a few who think they can drive in anything. Those are the ones we have to scrape off the road."

The stark image sent a chill through Leila. That's exactly what they'd had to do with her brother-in-law, Phineas. Not because of weather, but because of a careless driver. Phineas had survived, but he would carry the marks of that accident with him for the rest of his life.

The woman who had been with Tom at the hospital trotted into the room. She wore her hair in the same long braid as that day. She wore the same blue, fleece-lined coat as Tom did, matching blue pants, and thick-soled work boots. "I saw the lights went out. Thought I'd better come in and see if I could do anything to help." She had the twang of East Texas in a voice unusually husky for a woman.

"My partner, Sam." Tom made quick work of the introductions. "Short for Samantha."

"We don't need anything in the way of help." Leila wiped her hands on her apron and hoisted Kaitlin onto her hip. "Unless you have a wood-burning stove in the back of that ambulance."

Shaking her head, Samantha held out her arms. To Leila's surprise, Kaitlin did the same. She knew Tom's partner and apparently liked her. Leila handed over the baby. Samantha cooed and hugged and kissed like a grandma who hadn't seen her baby in a month of Sundays.

"I guess you like babies."

"She's always threatening to steal Kaitlin away and keep her for a few days." Tom's tone held an undertone of surprise, as if he couldn't believe someone would want to do that. "I told her she has no idea what she's in for."

"Hey, I have nieces and nephews and three younger brothers." Sam tickled Kaitlin's neck and the baby crowed with laughter. "I know what I'm doing. Don't I, Kaitlin, don't I?"

Her chubby cheeks dimpled, the baby snuggled against the woman's chest. "See, she agrees with me."

Leila surveyed the two, laughing and chattering over Kaitlin like parents would. The thought struck her full force. Tom and Samantha could be more than partners. She studied the woman. She had similar interests to Tom or she wouldn't be an EMT. She was passable when it came to looks, not that Leila really knew what to judge her by.

Most importantly, she loved babies.

No, most importantly, did she love God? Leila picked up the flashlight and did a quick count on her babies. "Looks like Kaitlin has become attached to you, Samantha."

Tom chuckled. It was nice to hear him laugh. "What baby wouldn't? She loves to lie on the floor and watch *Sesame Street*, she does a mean patty-cake, patty-cake, and she never gets tired of peek-a-boo-I-see-you."

Someone else had gotten attached to Sam. Leila smiled to herself. Duncan stirred and stretched, his rosebud lips turning down in a frown. She pulled his favorite fuzzy blanket up around his neck. "Shhh, shhhh."

He stilled. She turned to her visitors, considering how to go about this. How would Jesse do it? Go slow, that's what he would say. "So do y'all ever do anything together besides work and watch *Sesame Street*?"

Tom stopped with the tickling that had Kaitlin wiggling all over Sam's chest. "What do you mean?"

"Do you . . . do anything for fun?"

"Sure."

"I mean . . . together."

"Your friend is matchmaking." Leila couldn't see Sam's expression in the dark, but she heard something in her voice. Some embarrassment, maybe, but also something else—possibly hope. "She's just being silly."

"You could go to church together." Leila hopped in before Tom could say anything. "That's always a good start. Kaitlin should go to church, and if you're taking her, you might as well go yourself."

"What is this? Fix Tom Day?"

Tom didn't sound mad, nor did he sound as if he would take Leila's advice. She apparently didn't have Jesse's knack for this. "No, no, I'm just saying. Christmas is right around the corner, and what better time to start going to church than on the day we celebrate the birth of Jesus."

"She's right." Sam lifted Kaitlin in the air, up and down, up and down, eliciting a stream of giggles. "Don't spit up on me, girl. I love Christmas services. You should come with me to church on Christmas Eve, Tom."

"We'll see." He scooped up Kaitlin's diaper bag and handed his partner the baby's coat. "Wrap her up good in her blanket and put her hat on. She doesn't have enough hair to keep her head from getting cold. I'll get the ambulance warmed up."

He strode from the room without saying good-bye. Changing the subject? Running away?

Samantha did as she was told, but she continued to talk to Kaitlin, promising her a visit to church for baby Jesus' birthday. She bundled the baby from head to toe, then turned to Leila. "Thanks."

"For what?"

"I don't know. Getting the ball rolling." She swung her braid over her shoulder out of reach of Kaitlin's chunky fists. "I've been trying to figure out a way for a while, but I didn't want to seem too forward. I have to work with the guy. If it doesn't work out, it'll be very uncomfortable."

"So make it work."

"Easier said than done."

"Have faith."

"I do. That's why the suggestion we start with church is a wise one. You're a wise woman." Sam wrapped her arms around Kaitlin and headed for the door. In the hallway, she turned back. "I'm sorry we can't give you a ride home. I hate to see you stuck here."

"I can't leave until all the babies are picked up anyway." She crossed the room and stood in the doorway so she could see Sam's retreat down the hall. "I'll be praying for you and Tom."

The words came out of their own volition. She'd never said such a thing in her life. *Gott, where did that come from?*

"I'll take all the prayers I can get," Sam called back. "Keep 'em coming and I'll keep you posted."

"You do that."

Leila went back to her babies. She'd done it again. With Rory and now with Tom and Samantha. She wanted people to be happy. She wanted the babies for whom she cared to grow up in God-fearing, God-loving homes. Each and every one of them. So whose job was it to make sure that happened?

It seemed God was giving her the answer to that question loud and clear.

THIRTY-SEVEN

Leila inhaled the scent of cinnamon wafting from the candle on the table. It mingled with the aroma of the star-shaped chocolate cookies baking in the oven. The kitchen smelled like Christmas. Just thinking of the children's Christmas Eve play earlier at the school made her smile. Caleb had done a fine job singing carols, a grin splitting his dimpled cheeks. He looked so much like Daed. Leila loved this time of year.

Usually.

So why did she feel so blue? Sighing, she opened the oven door and retrieved the cookie sheet. The heat bit through the ancient pot holder, singeing her thumb. She slapped the pan on the counter and sucked on her thumb. "Ouch."

"Considering what a joyous time of year this is, you sure are a sourpuss." Rebekah strolled into the kitchen, baby Timothy snuggled against her chest. The girl must like to live dangerously, as no burp rag resided between the baby and her dress. "You're supposed to use a pot holder."

"I did and I'm not a sourpuss."

"You were a million miles away during the play tonight."

Rebekah snatched a cookie from an earlier, cooled batch. "You'd better hope Mudder was too busy trying to keep Hazel from running up front to notice."

"I can't wait until Hazel is old enough to go to school. She's so ready." Leila tugged Timothy from her sister's arms. The baby cooed and sputtered, his tiny fists sparring with the air. "She was trying to read one of Caleb's bug books yesterday."

"Don't change the subject." Rebekah grabbed another cookie and plopped into a chair at the table. "You love Christmas. What's the matter?"

"Nothing."

"Leila!"

Leila eased onto a chair across the pine table. She held Timothy close to her heart, inhaling the scent of baby. She rubbed the soft silk on his head. He was like a newborn puppy, all bones in a wrinkled sack. "I do love babies."

Rebekah cocked her head and frowned. "Everyone loves babies. You'll have your own. It's only a matter of time if Will Glick has his way."

Timothy fussed. Leila forced herself to ease her grip on him. "Shush, baby, shush." She ducked her head, hoping her sister couldn't see her expression. "I know. I'm just not sure . . ."

"Not sure he's the one? What's not to like?" Rebekah began to extend her fingers on one hand as if counting off. "He's a hard worker, he's handsome, he's tall, he's smart. He likes you, and that in itself is something from where I sit."

"None of that has to do with anything when it comes to love. That's something you'll learn one day." Deborah stood in the doorway. "There he is. I was missing my boy."

Leila turned so Deborah could see Timothy's contented face.

The baby's eyes closed and his tiny body relaxed against her. "You should know. Will was interested in you first."

"At the time all the boys had an interest in all of us. We were new." Deborah headed toward the counter and the spread of four kinds of Christmas cookies, gingerbread, banana bread, and cranberry bread. She'd lost most of the baby weight already. Her apron and her kapp were clean, neat, and wrinkle free. How she did that with a newborn fascinated Leila. "They were curious. Will only wanted to get to know me to find out if there might be something there. He wasn't the least bit heartbroken when I chose another."

Maybe not, but it surely hurt his pride. The way he'd slouched on the bench the day of the wedding said as much. "Do you think it's different with me? I mean, his feelings are different?"

Deborah began to move the latest batch of cookies from the pan to a plate. "That's between him and you to figure out."

"I want cookies." Hazel trotted into the room in bare feet. It didn't matter the temperature. The girl preferred not to wear shoes. Pretty soon all of the Lantz womenfolk would be gathered in the kitchen. "And milk."

"There's no milk, but a cookie you shall have." Deborah handed it to the little girl with a flourish. "Be sure to brush your teeth before you go to bed, which you shall do very soon or you'll be too tired to open presents in the morning."

"Nee. I'm not tired." Hazel's face lit up in a grin. She was a miniature Deborah. "I made baby something special."

"No telling or it won't be a surprise." Rebekah patted her lap and Hazel crawled onto it, managing to break the cookie in three places. "Five more minutes, then it's prayers and bed."

A sense of something akin to peace washed over Leila. These three girls, her sisters, they would be fine—better than fine—no matter what happened. Startled by the thought, she straightened. Timothy fussed in his sleep. She patted his rump and rocked. Nothing would happen.

Nothing.

"What's a matter?" Rebekah peered at her. "You look like you're about to cry."

"I'm not crying."

"What's the matter?" Deborah turned from the counter to stare at her. "Are you sick?"

"I'm fine."

"She's a sourpuss." Rebekah pointed a finger at Leila. "Either that, or she has a secret she doesn't want us to know."

"Am not and no, I don't."

"Then what?"

"I love you, my schweschders."

Three mouths dropped open. Eyebrows popped up. Everyone froze for a scant second. Then Rebekah half rose from her seat, her arm around Hazel's middle. Deborah marched over to the table and slapped a hand on Leila's forehead. "You don't have a fever. What is wrong? Are you sick? Tell me now."

"Nothing." Leila shrugged away from her touch. "Nothing. I just . . . Things are changing, that's all, and I know more changes are coming. And I know we don't have any control over any of it."

"Change is gut and Gott has control." Deborah eased Timothy from Leila's arms. "Coming here was the best thing that ever happened to me, even though I didn't think so at the time. I met Phineas. I thought he was annoying and irritating and mean. Then I didn't. And now we have Timothy. Gott is gut."

No doubt about that, but change could also be hard. It could be brutal. "He is."

How could Leila tell them every bone in her body, every sinew, every muscle, spoke to her of a change coming that they wouldn't like? Not at all. It would be painful and sorrow would abound. She knew it in her heart and nothing she did could change the way she felt.

This time of year centered on hope and joy and new beginnings.

The ache in her chest said her new beginning would also be the end of nights like this, sitting in the kitchen eating warm cookies and holding baby nephews. "I'm just tired, that's all."

Deborah didn't look convinced, but she straightened and smoothed the blanket around her bundle of baby.

"It's Christmas Eve." Rebekah scooted Hazel from her lap. "Time for bed. We have presents to open tomorrow and visiting to do."

To Leila's surprise, Rebekah paused at her chair, then wrapped her arms around Leila in a quick, tight hug. "Merry Christmas, Leila."

"Merry Christmas." It took every ounce of resolve she could muster to keep the quiver from her voice. "See you in the morning."

Deborah stopped in the doorway. "Aren't you coming to bed?"

"I'll be there in a minute."

"See you in the morning."

"See you in the morning."

Everything would look different in the morning. Good or bad.

THIRTY-EIGHT

Jesse tossed pebbles at the second-story window. His pitching arm needed work. The first one missed. The second and third made contact with the glass in a *ping, ping* that he could barely hear from the ground. He peered up at Leila's bedroom window, hoping Rebekah or Hazel wouldn't be the one to wake up. And that Butch was out on some nighttime patrol. Or a nocturnal hunt. The dog didn't like him much. *Come on, Leila, come on.*

"What are you doing?"

He dropped the flashlight, even as he realized that the woman he sought stood before him. "Looking for you. I thought you were in there."

Leila pulled the door shut behind her and adjusted the shawl tight around her shoulders. She had the look of someone awakened suddenly from a deep sleep. Her blonde hair was mussed around a kapp tugged on haphazardly. She looked beautiful. "I heard the engine. I couldn't imagine who would be coming out here at this time of night."

"It's not that late. Y'all just go to bed early because there's nothing else to do." That was unfair. Until a few weeks ago, he'd done the same thing his whole life. He squatted and picked up the flashlight. "I wanted to take you somewhere."

She took a step back. "You can't."

"It's Christmas Eve, the night before we celebrate the most important event in the history of the world. The birth of our Lord Jesus Christ." His voice shook. He took a breath to calm himself. This was so important. For him. And for her. He had to make her see. "Please come with me. As a favor to me, if nothing else."

"Like you said, it's Christmas Eve. Tomorrow we'll celebrate the birth of our Lord Jesus Christ." Her voice didn't shake at all. Her cheeks reddened in the cold and her breath came in white puffs. "And then we'll visit with family. That's important to us. Family."

"Please. You won't be sorry. You won't want to miss this."

"Miss what?"

"Come with me."

Emotions warred on her face. Longing. He was sure he saw longing. And uncertainty. "Please."

She swiveled and looked behind her. "Is that a van?"

Even though he had his driver's license now, he wasn't ready to drive on his own, especially on icy roads. And Matthew didn't seem interested in risking his company van, however old and decrepit, on a newbie driver. Smart man. "Matthew's van. Angus is driving."

"You came out here in Matthew's company van driven by his brother?"

"I did. It's the only transportation I could find on such short notice." Colton wanted to spend his Christmas Eve with Tiffany. Jesse understood that. He wanted it. With Leila. "Everyone's at the Holly Jolly Christmas celebration."

"Is that what you want me to see?" She frowned, but nothing

she did made her any less pretty. "I don't care about lights and parades and Santa Claus."

"Stop arguing with me and put on your shoes."

Leila gave a most unfeminine snort and did as he directed. A few minutes later they were squeezed into the middle seat of the van. Leila wiggled and tucked her hands under her arms. "You don't want to sit up front with Angus? He's not like our driver or something."

"Nee. I want to sit next to you." He paused, trying to get control of his emotions. "I mean, the heater doesn't work very well and it'll be cold back here."

"I don't mind acting like the chauffeur. I'm good at it. I see nothing. I hear nothing." Angus shot her a wide grin in the rearview mirror. "Y'all snuggle up and keep warm."

"There will be no snuggling." As if to make her point, Leila scooted to the far end of the seat and made herself small in the corner, her head against the window. "Or anything of that nature."

Jesse heaved a sigh and tried to relax. The hard part was over. She'd agreed to come. Once she saw what she needed to see, she'd be convinced. Who wouldn't be? "How's everyone in your family?"

"Everyone's gut. My family is fine." This time her voice did quiver ever so slightly. "Esther's wedding was very nice. Everyone came. Folks asked about you."

She faltered and turned to stare out the window. The moon splashed light on the barren trees along the road and her face. She looked so sad. Jesse didn't want her to be sad. She had to see what he saw. So much joy. So much promise. A future secure. She glanced his way and their gazes held for a second. More unfettered emotion. Confusion. Hurt. Uncertainty. Longing. He was sure of it. She had missed him.

He forced his gaze back to the countryside. Tree limbs dipped and swayed in a northern wind that seeped into the cracks and crevices of the old van. Jesse shivered. He reached under the seat and pulled out an old blanket Matthew used to cover furniture at work sites. "Here, it's cold, cover up."

"Why are you doing this?" She slid closer, her voice a mere whisper. "I can't see how it's ever going to work between us."

"You'll see. It will." He shook the blanket out and covered their laps. He sneezed. "Sorry."

"A little dust doesn't hurt a person." She tucked the blanket around her legs and grasped it, her hands so tight her fingers went white. "I can't stand this. I've missed you so much. Okay, there, I said it. I missed you."

Her face reddened and she glanced toward the back of Angus's head. He leaned over and flipped on the radio with one hand, the other still on the wheel. "Jingle Bells" blared.

Jesse scooted close to her. "Me too."

"What will we do?"

"We'll figure it out."

"I don't see how. I don't know how I could bear a future without my family."

"You have to be willing to see a different future for yourself."

She lowered her head, her eyes closed. Her hand crept out and took his. Her skin was so soft. "I've prayed and prayed and prayed."

"I spent months doing the same thing before I knew what to do." He smoothed the soft hollow between her thumb and forefinger with his own calloused thumb. "I wore holes in the knees of my pants."

"And you received the answer you wanted?"

"It's not possible for us to get the answer we want." He hated to state the obvious. She tried to pull her hand away. He held on tight. "We can't live our lives the way we believe God wants us to and be together with our families."

"So you're not only asking me to choose you, you're asking me to choose a different life of faith?"

"Jah."

"You don't ask much."

The words held a certain bitterness, but also acceptance. Jesse was sure of it. He asked a great deal of her, but God asked for more. Much more. He rubbed his hands over hers, trying to create warmth. She stared at him, blue eyes luminous with tears. Jesse brought her hands to his lips and kissed her fingers one by one. She sighed, a long, ragged sigh. "Don't say anything," he whispered. "Just wait."

She nodded and leaned back against the seat as if worn out. Jesse held on to her hand for dear life.

———

Will had exhausted his supply of pebbles. Either Leila slept deeply or she simply ignored him. He studied the ground, searching for something else he could heave at the second-story window that wouldn't break the glass. *Come on, Leila, come on.*

Nothing. He set his package in the sparse brown grass that lined the house under the windows, debating whether to leave. He didn't want to embarrass Leila or her sisters. He'd waited too long and now she was asleep. His family would pass Christmas Day at his Uncle Leroy's, so it was doubtful he would see Leila tomorrow. His daed reckoned it would help take the sting out of Jesse's absence to have the rest of the family close. The first year would be the hardest. Time would ease the pain.

Sighing, he turned to go. Mordecai's dog, Butch, trotted across the yard toward him, his grizzled snoot wide in a grin. Will dropped to one knee and patted his back. "Where have you been? You should've been here, standing guard. That's your job, you know."

Butch woofed and nuzzled Will's chest. He leaned in and wrapped an arm around the animal. He smelled of wet earth and something else . . . manure possibly. The warmth of his fur felt good in the cold night air, but nothing could warm the icy feeling that had descended on Will's heart. He'd been so sure he could convince her. "What am I to do? Tell me that, Butch."

A soft whimper emanated from deep in the dog's throat.

"I know, that's how I feel too."

"Talking to a dog, are you?"

Will looked up. Rebekah stared down at him, her face one big frown. She stepped onto the porch and slid the door closed behind her with infinite care. "What are you doing here? Besides throwing rocks at the window and trying to wake up everyone in the house."

"They were pebbles." Will gave Butch a last pat, picked up the package, and straightened. "Sorry, I didn't mean to wake you. I was looking for Leila."

"It's like a bus station around here." Rebekah pulled her shawl tighter around her slim body. "Leila's okay and all, but I never imagined this tug-of-war over her."

"If you're talking about Jesse, there's no tug-of-war. That's done."

Rebekah's expression softened. "Is that package for Leila?"

He nodded, feeling even more foolish than usual.

"I'm sorry."

"For what?"

Rebekah sighed, her face full of a sad compassion that could only mean one thing. "She's not here."

"What do you mean she's not here?"

"She left about twenty minutes ago."

Someone new courted her already? Will racked his brain trying to think who among his friends would do such a thing. Nee. No one. "With who?"

"I didn't see him, but I heard an engine running so I looked out the window. I saw an old beige-colored van."

Matthew's van. "Jesse? And you let her go?"

His heart slammed against his rib cage. *Too late. Too late,* it pounded out in a painful, aching rhythm. Leila had made her choice. Not only had she chosen Jesse, but she'd chosen how she would spend the rest of her life.

Without Will in it.

All those dreams that bumped into each other and filled his mind in the wakeful moments before sleep dissipated like chimney smoke in a cold wind. No future spent with Leila turning a house into a home and filling it with kinner. No Christmases by the fireplace or having fish fries at the lake or wading in the Gulf. The future gaped, a black, empty void.

"She was already gone." The full moon cast a brilliant light on Rebekah's face, adding a glow to the tears that brightened her eyes. "Her heart's been gone a long time. The rest of her caught up tonight, I reckon." Her voice quavered. "She was acting strangely earlier, in the kitchen. I think she was saying good-bye. I don't think she's coming back. I'm sorry."

"It's not your fault." To Will's chagrin his own voice quavered, matching hers. "She made her choice. I so hoped it would be otherwise."

"You're not to blame either."

A spurt of energy shot through him. It wasn't over. He still had time. Until Leila took vows, he had time. He couldn't give in now, at the ultimate moment. "I'm going after her."

"How? In a buggy? By the time you drive into Beeville, whatever they're doing will be done."

"It doesn't matter. I'll hitch a ride. I have to try."

"Gott bless you."

Some strange impulse made him grab her hand and squeeze. "Danki."

"My mudder doesn't know yet. I don't want to be the one to tell her." She stared down at him, her face so like Leila's, etched with pain. "Bring my schweschder back. Please. So I don't have to tell her."

That was the plan.

THIRTY-NINE

Leila didn't know where to look first. Despite the hour, Main Street in Beeville swarmed with people strolling on the sidewalk. Carolers sang in the Depot Pavilion, and Santa posed for photos with little ones after hearing their wishes. Some people drank hot chocolate in front of A Box of Chocolate candy store on Washington Street. All the stores were open and business bustling. She'd never been in town during the Christmas season. The twinkling, multicolored lights decorated storefronts and trees and dangled from electric pole to electric pole, giving the entire town a festive, happy atmosphere that made her smile—almost.

She still didn't know what she was doing in Beeville at night with Jesse. The warmth she felt had nothing to do with the blanket he'd spread over their knees. It had to do with the arm he slid around her shoulder about halfway into town and the way he kept giving her these sidelong glances. She should move away, but she didn't. Because of the cold, that's what she kept telling herself. The cold.

He hadn't said much after that painful conversation at the beginning, but now he leaned forward and looked out the window. "It's really pretty, isn't it?"

"Jah, but it's not what Christmas is about."

"I know that, but they put so much into making these days special in honor of the birth of Jesus. That can't be wrong."

"I'm not saying it's wrong. I'm saying it's unnecessary. Jesus doesn't need sparkling lights and Santas."

"Ah, now who's the authority on what Jesus needs?" His grin softened the criticism. "These celebrations draw people's attention to the meaning of the season."

"Nee, they get people into stores to buy things." That acute observation came from the front seat. Angus chuckled. "It's economics, not religion."

"I know." Jesse threw off the blanket. "But that's not why I brought Leila into town."

He shouldn't talk about her as if she weren't seated right there next to him. "Then why?"

"We're here."

The van jolted to a stop. Leila peered out the window. A small, white, wood-frame church with one stained-glass window shaped like an octagon graced a corner lot. A spotlight in the yard shone on a nativity scene with a life-sized Mary and Joseph separated by a manger complete with a baby Jesus swaddled in a bright-red blanket. "You brought me to a church service?"

"Not just any church service. Come on."

She'd come this far. Leila took the hand Jesse proffered and followed him up the sidewalk to the double doors of the church. They flew open and Colton stuck his head out. "There you are. We thought you were going to miss it. Get in here."

"Miss what?"

"You'll see." Jesse hustled inside, tugging her along with him. Dozens of rows of padded chairs filled a long, rectangular room. A dark green carpet softened their footsteps and a big white screen filled the back wall. Boughs of pine needles decorated the altar, lined on each side by huge, brilliant poinsettias in red and pink. The scent of the pine needles mingled with ladies' perfume and men's aftershave in a piquant medley.

Almost all of the chairs were full on this Christmas Eve. Leila recognized some of the faces. Marie from the bakery, Miss Daisy from the day care. Samantha and Tom with Kaitlin sitting in the woman's lap. Samantha smiled as she whispered something to Tom. Her blonde hair hung loose and long down her back. She was pretty and Tom looked happy.

And there, Nolan. Rory's dad. He'd come back to church. What wonderful news. Jesse's handiwork. Did that make Samantha and Tom her handiwork? Nee. God's handiwork.

Her gaze roved back to the front and the altar. There stood Rory, wearing a red corduroy dress, which had to be a first, and black cowboy boots. Dwayne looked sharp in a blue suit and a skinny tie, his hair slicked back. They both looked so grown up. Dwayne held Trevor, who wore a suit that matched his daddy's.

"Trevor is being baptized—"

"Shush." Jesse slid into an open seat half toward the front and motioned for her to take the one next to him. He leaned close and whispered in her ear. "Not baptism. Dedication. Rory and Dwayne are just beginning to figure out what they believe and how to be parents. They still have a long way to go. This is a good first step. Trevor will decide about baptism when he is old enough to understand what it means."

Leila nodded. She couldn't keep from smiling. Rory and Dwayne might not have all the answers yet, but they understood how important it was to find them. For themselves and for Trevor.

No wonder Nolan looked so pleased. And Rory radiated happiness. Trevor crowed and she laughed. Grinning, Dwayne shushed him and smoothed his son's locks into place with long fingers.

The pastor posed the question, did they plan to raise their son in the ways of God? They answered yes.

"Will you teach him and train him in God's Word?"

"Yep."

Dwayne's resounding response brought a few chuckles and smiles from the congregation.

"Will you discipline him in godly ways and pray earnestly for him?"

Again with the hearty affirmative response. Rory brushed away tears with a bright-green hankie.

Pastor Walt picked up a brown leather-bound Bible from the podium and began to read:

*And she made a vow, saying, "*LORD *Almighty, if you will only look on your servant's misery and remember me, and not forget your servant but give her a son, then I will give him to the* LORD *for all the days of his life, and no razor will ever be used on his head."*

"When God answered Hannah's prayer by giving her a son, she remembered her vow:

"As surely as you live, I am the woman who stood here beside you praying to the LORD. *I prayed for this child, and the* LORD *has granted me what I asked of him. So now I give him to the* LORD. *For his whole life he will be given over to the* LORD." *And he worshiped the* LORD *there.*

The pastor took Trevor from Dwayne's arms. The boy went willingly, arms out, chubby cheeks dimpled in a grin. "It will be the responsibility of every person in this room to help these young parents raise this child up right. You are his church family. Take this responsibility as seriously as you've ever taken anything in your life."

Leila ducked her head and leaned closer to Jesse. "You did this?"

"God did this. I just took my cue from you and offered an invitation."

"I'm so happy for them. So happy for Trevor."

"Me too." Jesse slid his hand over hers. "You understand you played a role in this. In what's happening right now."

"I didn't do anything."

"You reached out to them. You invited them in."

"Nee."

"Jah."

Pastor Walt began to pray aloud.

Leila closed her eyes and lifted her own prayer for Trevor, Dwayne, Rory, and their unborn baby as the words of the minister rumbled over her. The prayer ended and a group of teenagers shuffled to the front of the sanctuary and picked up their guitars. Seconds later the notes of "Away in a Manger" floated in the air. The congregation stood, their voices mingling as they sang the familiar words. The notes died away. Chatter filled the air. People hugged and shrugged on coats, conversations filled with plans for celebrating and food and gifts yet to be exchanged.

It was a world different from Leila's, yet the same. She had played a small part in this evening. She'd been blessed to witness it.

"Thank you," she whispered to Jesse, "for bringing me. I'm honored to be here for this."

His face etched with trepidation, Jesse took her hand and squeezed. He leaned down until his breath warmed her cheek. He cleared his throat. "Stay with me. Love me. Marry me." His voice was hoarse and ragged. "Join me in this adventure. There are so many Rorys and Trevors out there. Walk this walk with me."

Her heart hammering against her rib cage, Leila stared at his face, so filled with longing and hope. Surely the entire room could hear her heart pound. Her world shrank until it became this room, and then this man. Only him. No other. She forced herself to break from his gaze. No one seemed to notice their little drama. They were busy congratulating Rory and Dwayne.

The happiness on Rory's face lighted the room, brilliant and all encompassing. Her baby boy crawled toward the beautiful, bright poinsettias. His chubby face scrunched up in a grin. "Ma Ma Ma Ma." Was he talking or simply babbling? "Da Da Da."

Momma and Daddy?

Dwayne strode after the child, scooped him up, and held him high in the air. Trevor giggled, a sound that made Leila want to giggle with him in the sheer happiness of it all.

"We can have that. Someday." Jesse's grip on her hand tightened. "Please. Say yes."

Her entire body trembled. Joy, like musical notes, cascaded through her. She could no more say no than she could live without breathing. When the lump in her throat eased, she locked gazes with Jesse. "Jah."

"Did you say yes?" Jesse's voice rose. He threw his arms around her so hard, the breath left her body. "You just said yes, didn't you?"

"I did. I said yes." His hug eased and she could breathe again. "Do you want me to take it back?"

"No, no, no." Jesse stuck both hands in the air, palms wide. "Woo-hoo! Hey, folks, she said yes, she said yes. We're getting married!"

Silence descended on the crowd. Colton stopped in the middle of donning his coat. Tiffany's hand, poised to knot a scarf around her neck, halted. Everyone stared. Then Rory screeched and fist bumped Dwayne. "I knew it. I knew it. Woot!"

Whoops filled the air, followed by applause that grew and expanded, the sound bouncing off the walls amid a chorus of congratulations. Folks began to file by, many people Leila had never met, to offer their best wishes. Each man shook her hand. The women hugged her. They offered help with the wedding and future evenings of child care. As if they'd known her their entire lives.

Jesse introduced the pastor to her simply as Walter. When he smiled, his craggy face lit up. "Come see me. We'll want to do some talking before you exchange your vows."

"We will." The words came out in a whisper.

"I know it must be a bit overwhelming." He squeezed her hand and nodded, his expression so kind Leila wanted to hug him. "Bless you, young lady. If you have any questions about anything, you can find me right here most days. See you soon."

Leila barely had time to offer her thanks before Colton and Tiffany were upon her. They offered high fives. "I knew the minute I laid eyes on you that you were the one for Jesse," Tiffany said, her expression smug. "I just wish Colton would hurry up and pop the question to me. He's been carrying around a ring for like two months."

How Tiffany knew this, Leila had no idea. "He'll ask when the time is right."

Tiffany waggled three fingers in the air and veered toward the door. "Reception at my house. Hot chocolate and cookies. Come on over."

Where else could she go now that she'd said yes? Yes to a new life without any thought as to where she would live until she and Jesse could properly wed. Not at home. Then where?

Rory hugged them both. "I'll be providing you with lots of marital advice, not to worry." She gave Leila an extra squeeze. "And I'll be there to step in when your family doesn't. You can always stay with me until the big day."

"Thank you. You're a good friend."

"Not as good as you are." Rory scooped up Trevor. "See you at the reception."

Leila swallowed her tears. She wouldn't think about that right now. She'd give herself a few minutes of joyful anticipation before venturing into that dark place of consequence and regret. Hand in hand, she and Jesse left the church. The streetlights cast a harsh glow on the cars that lined the curb, including the van. A figure leaned against it.

Jesse's hand tightened on hers. "Will's here."

FORTY

Leila breathed, all the earlier anticipation and relieved joy washing away in a recriminating flood of guilt tinged with sadness but no regret. Will leaned against the Planks' van, parked haphazardly at the curb in front of the church. His arms were crossed over a package held close to his chest. His head tilted down so his hat covered his face. He looked cold and lonely.

"Let me talk to him alone." Leila tugged her hand from Jesse's. "He deserves to hear it from me. Me alone."

"Leila—"

"Just give me a minute. Please."

Jesse melted back into the crowd, leaving her to go to Will on feet that wanted to run away but instead plodded forward. "What are you doing here? Did you follow me here?"

"That's your question?" He lifted his head and straightened, his features pale, his cheeks dark and hollow in the glare of the streetlights. "You're attending a church service in town on Christmas Eve and you want to know how I found you? Fine, I'll tell you. Rebekah told me you left in the Planks' van. I put two and two together."

"How did you get here?"

"I hitchhiked. It was faster than a buggy."

They never hitchhiked. A cardinal rule in a prison community. "I'm sorry. I'm truly sorry."

"I had to deliver my Christmas present." He held out the package wrapped in plain brown paper. Leila found she couldn't raise her hand to take it. He shook his head and gave an exasperated sigh. "Go on. Take it."

"You shouldn't have."

"You need this gift. You need to study it."

She forced her arms to obey her commands. The package was solid and heavy in her hands.

"Open it."

"Now? Here?"

"Open it."

The command in his voice startled her. He sounded like his Uncle Leroy. "You don't have to yell at me."

"I'm not yelling." His voice subsided. "I'm not yelling. Please open it."

She ripped the paper off with shaking fingers. The Holy Bible. In English and in German. Its heft made her arms ache. "Danki."

"Maybe you'll learn something there. Maybe it will help you figure out some things."

"Is that what you've been doing?"

"Jah." He rubbed his hands together and blew on them, his breath steaming in the cold night. "So far it hasn't helped, but I keep trying."

"We all keep trying."

"You've made your choice, then?"

"I have." She hugged his gift to her chest. Her heart ached with the pain she couldn't stop from causing him. "It almost seems as if it was made for me. A long time ago."

"You danced with me. You walked with me."

She would never forget those moments. She would treasure them, even as she treasured the memories of her childhood back in Tennessee with Deborah and Rebekah and Daed and the others. She would miss them beyond measure. "I tried so hard. I wanted it to be you."

Having Will as a husband would be easy. It would be simple. Plain. And she could have her family near her for the rest of her life. Yet here she stood, promised to another.

"I know you did." Will studied his boots. He cleared his throat. "It shouldn't be so hard, I reckon."

"That's what I'm thinking." She tugged her shawl tight around her shoulders against a brisk northern wind, but it wasn't the night air that made her tremble with cold. "I never intended for any of this to happen, but it did."

"You'll lose everything."

It would look that way to Will and to the entire community. "I'll gain everything."

"You sound like Jesse." Bitterness rasped in his voice. "You've drunk the same cup of pride and arrogance."

"Something happened tonight. Something special. I helped make it happen. I know I can make a difference in people's lives. I want that."

"Your absence from your home will make a difference in your family's life. From now until the day they die."

If he'd driven the arrow into her chest with his bare hands, it couldn't have hurt more. "I know."

He met her gaze. Tears glistened on his cheeks. She raised a hand. His head jerked back. "Your mother has been through a lot."

They all had. "I know, and it breaks my heart to hurt her this way."

"And this is more important? He's more important?"

"The two together are." She struggled with words that wouldn't wound him more. "You're a good man—"

"Don't." He held up his hand. "Don't try to make me feel better. That's not your place. I'll be fine. I forgive you."

She had no doubt he meant it. He would say the words until they were true. As would every member of her family. They would forgive, the fundamental building block of their faith. If God could forgive their every sin, how could they not forgive those who sinned against them? "Danki. That means so much to me. I never meant for any of this to happen."

"It doesn't have to happen. It's not too late. My family has already started packing. They'll be leaving right after the new year, but I'm staying. One way or another." He shoved his hat down on his forehead. "I waited here because I wanted to give you one more chance to make the right choice. To stay with your family and your community who loves you. To choose me. To be with me. If you change your mind, I'll be there if you ever need me."

"I appreciate everything you're saying. I wish I could feel about you the way you feel about me, but I love another."

"Enough to give up everything?"

"Enough to see that I have everything to gain."

"Then I'll go."

"I'll talk to Leroy tomorrow."

"Nee. You'd best stay in town from now on. I'll tell your mudder and Mordecai. And Leroy."

The cold intensified. A shiver ran through her. The skin on her hands felt brittle. Her bones might break and she would shatter into a heap on the hard ground. "I want to say good-bye to my family."

"For now, it's best you write to them. They deserve to hear

from you. Whatever happens beyond that is up to Onkel Leroy. And remember, you can always, always come home. We will always take you back. Never forget that." Will's hand came up as if he would touch her. But he didn't. "You know what Onkel Leroy would say? He would say you weren't in Gott's plan for me. Who am I to think I know better than Gott?"

She willed the lump in her throat to ease enough to assure him. "He does have a plan for you. You'll see."

His smile held no malice or bitterness. "I will. You can count on that."

Leila couldn't be sure if those words were for her or for himself. He ambled away, his stride somehow off kilter as if he was too exhausted to walk a straight line. She couldn't bear it. "Let Colton give you a ride home. Please. It's not safe to hitchhike, especially this time of night."

Will turned, lifting the collar of his jacket around his neck as he did. "Colton Wise is how this whole thing started. Better I should walk over to the Stop and Shop and use the phone. Abe Cramer stays up all night watching movies and doing crossword puzzles. He'll give me a ride."

Ignoring the first icy drops of sleet that splattered her face, she watched him walk away, his shadow bobbing in the streetlights, until he disappeared from sight, taking with him a life that had become a distant memory in a few scant moments.

A sob burbled up inside of her, but she refused to let a single tear fall. She closed her eyes. *Gott, be with him. Guide and protect him. Give him a gut fraa to love and cherish, who will bear him kinner and give him the comfort and care he deserves. Ease Mudder's pain. Ease my family's pain. Help me find a way so they aren't punished by my decision. Gott, I pray.*

Fingers squeezed her shoulder. She turned. Jesse stood behind her, his face full of worry and a caring so acute it warmed her from her frozen nose to her icy toes. She managed a watery smile. "He's gone."

Jesse took the Bible from her hands and smoothed his long fingers over the leather cover. "A parting gift. Nice. He's a good man, my cousin Will is."

Jesse had lost so much. Yet here he stood, confident of their future together. Leila breathed a silent prayer of thanksgiving. Having Jesse as her partner in this life would encompass an adventure with ups and downs and bumps along the way, but it would also mean a life filled with love. Jesse's love. God's love. "He said I can't go back home now. I don't have anywhere to stay. Tonight, I mean. Rory said I could stay with her if . . . I don't know if she meant—"

"Don't worry. You'll stay with Tiffany tonight and we'll work the rest out tomorrow. She loves having slumber parties."

A slumber party with an Englisch girl she barely knew. The shifting landscape made Leila dizzy. "This is it, then. I'm really doing this?"

"We'll figure it out together."

"I hope so, because you just told the whole world we're getting married."

"Not the whole world. Just a few good people."

Jesse slipped his arms around her waist and drew her close. The feel of his breath on her neck sent heat rushing through her. She raised her face to his. He felt so solid, an immovable object even as everything—time, the world, the questions without answers—rushed around her, threatening to crush her in an avalanche of change. She could cling to this man, knowing he himself clung to God. They had their Rock and their salvation.

His lips sought hers in a sweet, lingering kiss that reminded her of sunshine and the smell of hay and bright-yellow sunflowers. He tasted like mint and his five o'clock shadow tickled her cheeks. When she thought she would die from lack of breath, he released her. The wondering, incredulous look on his face sent her back for more. She couldn't seem to slake her thirst for him.

"Hey, you two lovebirds, you're gonna freeze to death." Pastor Walt's deep, genial voice floated from the porch where he locked the front door with an oversized key. "Go home."

Leila giggled and pulled away from Jesse. From the look on his face, he was thinking the same thing she was. They didn't have to worry about where they would spend the rest of their days. They were already home.

EPILOGUE

Ties served no purpose other than to aggravate a man. Jesse took a deep breath and exhaled. The butterflies in his stomach continued their kamikaze diving routine. His palms were sweaty and the collar of his white cotton shirt strangled him. One of the things he definitely didn't like about not being Plain anymore: the tie. From figuring out what color to buy to getting the knot right.

Another deep breath. Then another. He leaned into Leila, who peered out a narrow opening in the doorway that led to the sanctuary. Her body, heavy with child, made it hard for him to see anything. "Who's out there? Anybody?"

She giggled, the soft sound like musical notes that always managed to make him feel at peace. She'd never looked prettier than today in her soft blue dress, her hair pulled back in a neat bun, her cheeks pink from the heat, baby weight, and excitement. "Are you kidding? Rory and her family are taking up an entire row. Everybody wants to hear your first sermon."

Not everyone.

Leila put her arm around his waist and squeezed. Her sweet

scent of Dove soap wafted around him, easing the sting of that thought. "You know what I mean."

"I do." He smoothed back his unruly hair without effect. Nobody came to see what he looked like. Only to hear what he said. "It's not a sermon. I'm not preaching. I'm sharing a message."

"Whatever you call it, you'll be fine. Let God guide you and you can't go wrong."

"I guess I'd better get out there."

Leila planted a kiss on his cheek, her lips soft and warm on his skin. "I'll be right up front. Rory saved me a seat."

He grabbed her hand before she could slip through the door. "Are you sure this is what you want? You haven't changed your mind?"

"You're thinking about that right now?"

"I can't help it. This is an irrevocable step on a path I've chosen."

"Nee, this is irrevocable." She smoothed her hands over her belly. "We committed to each other and to this family, you and I. We are family. Those people out there are our family."

A bittersweet smile slipped across her face. "Do I wish our baby would know your mudder and mine, your daed and Mordecai? I do. But that's not within our control. I believe we're following the path God laid out for us. Don't you?"

"I do." The words echoed in his head, reminding him of his vows before her and God. "But I will keep praying for reconciliation."

"Me too." She smiled. "And I'll pray you don't stutter or lose your place in your sermon. I mean, your message. Now quit procrastinating and get out there!"

"My prayer companion."

"Always." She had spent the previous evening praying with him for God's will for his first message as an associate lay pastor filling in for Pastor Walter, who was taking a much-needed vacation. "They're family. Their hearts are open to your message."

Leila was a wise woman for her age. Jesse had learned that in the year since they'd married. Pastor Walt had done the honors, with Matthew and Colton serving as his best men while Rory had stood with Leila. It wasn't a Plain ceremony, but it came close. No flowers or music, just vows taken in God's house followed by a small reception at Colton's. No honeymoon trip, just unpacking their sparse belongings in a one-bedroom duplex down the street from Matthew's trailer park.

It served as one of the best days of his life. With so many more to come. Studying together every night for their high school diploma equivalency tests. Leila grilling him with questions for tests after he started classes at Coastal Bend College. Good memories with more to come.

Like the day he came home to find her waiting for him with news that fairly burst from her lips. They were having a baby. They'd begun their lives together with almost nothing to their names. Even now, with both of them working, they scraped by to pay rent and utilities and put food on the table. He'd never been happier. How they would make ends meet with a new baby, only God knew. But He did know. Jesse had faith in that.

Today was the next step. At least it would be if he could get his feet to cooperate. He forced himself to stride through the door and across the seemingly endless expanse of threadbare carpet to the front, where he stood before four dozen rows of straight-back chairs with brown padded seats, one aisle down the middle, six chairs on each side. Every chair was full. The smell of candles burning and a bouquet of floral scents born of a dozen or more ladies' perfumes filled the air. He fought the urge to sneeze. The tiny sanctuary went silent when he stepped behind the pulpit and laid his Bible on it.

"Welcome. Please rise for the singing of the first hymn." He nodded to Jack and Ricky. The two boys strummed their guitars and the sweet notes of "Blessed Be His Name" filled the room, mingling with the voices of the congregation. The singing spiraled toward the heavens in a beautiful act of worship made all the more awesome by the flat notes and occasional misspoken lyrics despite the words projected on a big screen behind Jesse.

Every note lifted him up. Every note reminded him God used him as a vessel. God filled him up and waited for the words to spill out and cover others in His grace and His glory.

The notes died away and Jesse lifted his gaze to the congregation before him, with their expectant expressions and their freshly scrubbed faces and Sunday-go-to-meeting outfits. Rory smiled up at him, her arms wrapped around her chubby baby daughter, Sophia, who slept—thankfully. The girl had some powerful lungs. Trevor wiggled in his seat and Rory elbowed him, her gaze never leaving Jesse's face.

Jesse cleared his throat. "The lesson today comes from Isaiah—"

"Oh, oh, oh no!" Leila stood, then sank back onto her chair. She bent forward, her hands rubbing her swollen belly. "I'm so sorry, I'm sorry."

She stood again. "I'm sorry, everyone, but I think I'm going to have to steal your associate pastor away."

Jesse froze, his message notes still in his hand. "Why? What's . . . ?"

"It's time."

Her meaning sank in. "It's time. It's time!"

The notes fell to the floor. He stumbled across the room

and grabbed her arm. "Sorry, folks. I'll get back to you on Isaiah. We're having a baby."

Everyone stood and clapped. Cheers echoed around him. Shouts of joy and encouragement. Their church family cheered them on as they rushed down the aisle to the double doors.

"I'll pull my van from the parking lot to the front curb," Matthew shouted as he trotted ahead of them. "We can pick up her bag later."

This body of Christ had become his family. This baby would have a church full of family.

"We're right behind you," Rory called. "I can't wait to see that new baby."

"I'll finish out the service," Colton promised. "Don't worry about a thing."

Jesse wasn't worried. God's promise. God's timing.

God's grace.

"If it's a girl, I think we should name her Grace." He helped Leila down the two steps in front of the church and guided her along the sidewalk. Panting, she paused and gasped. He wrapped his arm around her, worried she might sink to the ground. "Are you okay?"

"Fine. This baby is in a hurry to get here, that's all." She started moving again. "And if it's a boy?"

"Emmanuel."

"God is with us?" She smiled through her pain. "He is, isn't He?"

"Always."

"And I will always be with you." She stretched up and kissed him. "That's a promise."

He kissed her right back, his hands moving to her face. He cupped her cheeks and stared at her eyes, bright with tears and expectation and joy. "I love you."

"I love you too."

"No regrets."

"No regrets."

"Now let's get moving before we have this baby in Matthew Plank's company van."

Together, they hurried to meet their future.

— DISCUSSION QUESTIONS —

1. What do you think of Will's decision to honor the promise he made to Jesse not to tell his secret, even to Leila, even though he knew Leila might end up getting hurt?
2. Most Amish districts don't allow Sunday school or Bible study groups. How do you feel about their assertion that individual interpretation of the Scriptures leads to division and confusion in a church?
3. The Amish believe in keeping themselves apart from the world. Do you think Leila's decisions were affected by the time she spent at the movies, working at the day care, and in Rory's company? Had she stayed at home, do you think her ultimate decision would have been different? Why?
4. Matthew and his wife were shunned because they chose to leave the Amish church after baptism. The Amish see this as a form of tough love designed to help bring the wayward member back to their ways. How would you feel about not being able to talk to a family member or being shunned yourself? Is this practice in conflict with the Amish belief in forgiveness?

5. How do you feel about Jesse's decision to leave his family so he can answer his calling to be a minister? Have you ever been called to give up something important in your life in order to serve God?

6. Mainstream media often portrays teenagers today as self-absorbed, lazy, and not interested in service. Can you cite examples in your life of teenagers who do what Tiffany and Colton do?

7. Is it possible to mingle in society and maintain your godly principles? Do you find it hard sometimes not to fall into worldly ways even though you know it's not what God wants? How do you fight that temptation?

8. Is there room for both kinds of men—Will and Jesse—in the body of Christ? The one who shows by example and the one who is the fisher of men? Can they work together toward the same end of winning the lost and making disciples?

ACKNOWLEDGMENTS

The Bishop's Son was not an easy book to write for many reasons. I know not everyone will agree with the premise or the conclusions drawn, but I hope everyone will see the need to stand together as Christians who may live our faith a little differently but who all worship the same one, true God. It's not for us to judge, but to love our neighbors as we love ourselves. My thanks to my editor, Becky Monds, for her thoughtful insight and feedback, for her encouragement and enthusiasm. As always, I'm thankful to my agent, Mary Sue Seymour for pushing me down this road even when she had to drag me kicking and screaming. I'm deeply appreciative of Zondervan and HarperCollins Christian Publishing for taking a chance on something a little different with the Amish of Bee County series and standing by it. As always, I can't believe how blessed I am: to the love of my life, Tim Irvin, thank you for putting up with me, for taking care of me, for helping me put one foot in front of the other when that simple act seemed impossible. Love to my kids, Erin and Nicholas, and their special someones. I thank God for the blessing of grandkids who delight and remind us of innocent joy and enthusiasm for simple things—love you Carson and Brooklyn. Thank you to my Lord and Savior for making all of this possible. Let us each in our own way go about winning the lost and making disciples so that no one has to live without the glorious, redeeming light of His love.

Enjoy these Amish Novella Collections for Every Season

9781401685942-B

A CHRISTMAS VISITOR,

AN AMISH CHRISTMAS GIFT

———— ONE ————

They meant well. All of them. Frannie Mast ladled another spoonful of steaming okra gumbo into her bowl. The spicy aroma tickling her nose did nothing to calm the willies in her stomach. She couldn't help herself, her gaze wandered down the crowded table past *Aenti* Abigail and her self-satisfied smile to Joseph Glick sitting on the other side with Caleb and her cousins. A giggle burbled in her throat. *Stop it. Be kind.* Did Joseph know he had a smear of butter on his upper lip? Did he know her aunt and uncle were doing a little matchmaking? Not that they would admit it. Plain boys and girls were to find their own mates during their *rumspringas* with no interference from their elders.

Apparently her situation had been deemed an exception to the rule.

Joseph flashed Frannie a smile. A chunk of venison had found a home in a gap between his lower front teeth. She suppressed a sigh and forced a smile. None of this could be construed as his fault. She remembered Joseph from school. He had been a so-so student, but a good softball player and a hard worker. He was easy to look at, with toast-colored hair, green eyes, and tanned skin. He was also the third single man *Aenti* Abigail and *Onkel* Mordecai had invited to supper since her return to Bee County, Texas, three weeks earlier.

It seemed more like two years had passed since her arrival in her childhood community after three years in Missouri.

They meant well, but what were they thinking? Joseph was Leroy Glick's son. Leroy, the bishop. Did they think Joseph would keep an eye on her, too, and report back to his father and to Mordecai, the district's deacon? Would he keep her from going astray?

She wouldn't do that. If they'd give her half a chance, she'd show them.

A fierce burning sensation assailed Frannie's fingers. She glanced down. Gumbo dripped on her hand. The burning blush scurrying across her face had nothing to do with the soup's heat. She dropped the ladle and grabbed her napkin, attempting to wipe the hot liquid from her fingers.

"Ouch!" She stood. Her pine chair rocked on spindly legs, then tumbled back. "Sorry. I'm sorry."

"Child, you're always spilling something." *Aenti* Abigail's fierce blue eyes matched the frown lurking below her high cheekbones and long, thin nose. "Get it cleaned up."

"It's fine. No harm done." Deborah King leaned over and wiped up the soup with her own napkin. Something in her tone reminded Frannie of the way her favorite cousin talked to her two-year-old son, Timothy. "Stick it in some water."

"Rub some butter on it. It stops the sting and helps it heal." Joseph held out the saucer with the puddle of half-melted butter that remained, still unaware it seemed of the smear on his own lip. He grinned. The venison hadn't dislodged from his teeth. "That's what my *groossmammi* used to say."

"Old wives' tale." *Onkel* Mordecai shook his head. His shaggy black beard, streaked with silver, bobbed. Mordecai mostly knew everything. "Water is best since we have no ice. Go on to the kitchen then."

Relief washed over Frannie. Escape. She whirled, stumbled over a chair leg, righted herself, and rushed into the kitchen. A tub of water sat on the counter in anticipation of the dirty dishes. She shoved her hand into it, barely aware of the stinging skin on her fingers. Gumbo stained her apron. Tomato juice from the canning frolic earlier in the day provided background color. Without looking, she knew sweat stains adorned the neck of her gray dress, like jewelry she would never wear. She was a mess as usual.

Why did *Aenti* Abigail insist on having gumbo in this weather? Something about soup cooling a person off because it caused him to sweat. This had to be an *Onkel* Mordecai theory. He had tons of them, each stranger or funnier or more interesting than the last. At least life with him would not be boring. Which was good, because Frannie likely would spend the rest of her life in his house if she behaved like that in front of every man in the district. She wanted to marry and have babies like her cousins and her friends. Like every Plain woman.

Why did that seem so hard for her?

She swished both hands in the lukewarm water and stared out the window at the brown grass, wiry mesquite, live oak trees, and a huge cluster of nopals. No breeze flapped the frayed white curtains. September weather in Bee County hadn't changed, just as nothing else had. No one who grew up here minded hot weather. They embraced it. Still, Frannie would savor her memories of evenings in Missouri this time of year. The air steamed with heat and humidity, but huge elm, oak, hickory, and red mulberry trees populated the countryside. A breeze often kicked up the leaves in the evening hours, making it a perfect time to sit in the lawn chairs and watch the sun dip below the horizon.

Nee, she wouldn't think of that. Thinking of those long summer nights made her think of him.

Rocky.

She swallowed hard against tears that surprised her. Rocky was only a friend. He couldn't be any more than that. Not for a faithful Plain woman such as herself. She understood what that meant even if her parents didn't trust her to make the right choices.

Gott, *help me be good.*

"Frannie, come out here."

Clear notes of disapproval danced with surprise in *Onkel* Mordecai's gruff voice. What had she done now? Drying her hands on a dish towel, Frannie trudged from the kitchen to the front room where her family sat, scrunched together like peas in long pods at two rough-hewn pine tables shoved together. No one looked at her when she entered the room. They all sat, not moving, staring toward the door as if mesmerized by a hideous rattlesnake coiled and ready to strike a venomous blow.

She plowed to a stop.

Nee. It couldn't be.

TWO

Frannie managed to clamp her mouth shut without biting her tongue. All six foot two, two hundred pounds of muscle known as Richard "Rocky" Sanders towered in the doorway. He waved his St. Louis Cardinals ball cap at her with a hand the size of a feed bucket. Acutely aware of the gazes of a dozen pairs of eyes drilling her in the back, Frannie waved a tiny half wave. Her burned fingers complained.

Rocky cleared his throat and shuffled work boots in the size-fourteen range. "Hey, Frannie."

"Hey." Her voice came out in an unfamiliar squeak that reminded her of the stray cat out by the shed when she fed him table scraps and accidentally stepped on his tail. A drop of sweat ran down her nose and dripped onto her upper lip. She fought the urge to scratch the spot. "Rocky."

No one spoke for several long seconds. Rocky shifted his feet again. His dark brown almost black curls hung damp around his ears. His blue eyes, so like the color of Missouri sky in summer, implored her. She took another step forward.

"Introduce your guest, Frannie." *Onkel* Mordecai's disapproval had been displaced by the politeness they all were taught from childhood to show guests. "Invite him in."

"This here's Rocky Sanders from Jamesport. I . . . knew him up yonder." Frannie couldn't help herself. She glanced at Joseph. He studied his bowl as if gumbo were the most interesting food he'd ever tasted. "He used to come into the restaurant where I was a waitress."

She kept to herself the longer version, how Rocky began to make an appearance at Callie's Restaurant and Bakery two or three times a week. How he left big tips on small meals and complimented the food as if she'd cooked it herself. How he showed up at the school fund-raiser on July Fourth and spent too much on a treadle sewing machine he said his mother wanted to use as a "conversation piece" in their living room. Her throat tightened at the memories. *Breathe.*

Mordecai nodded. "We're having gumbo if you want to pull up a seat."

"No, no, I can see you're having dinner. I don't want to barge in on you." Rocky edged toward the door, but his gaze remained on Frannie. "I'm sorry to drop in without letting you know I was coming. Being you don't have a phone—not that there's anything wrong with that. No calls from those pesky salespeople at dinnertime. I was . . . in the neighborhood."

After that preposterous statement, he tugged a red bandanna from the back pocket of his faded blue jeans and swiped the sweat dampening his face. "Begging your pardon, but could I have a quick word with your niece . . . on the porch? I won't keep her long."

Frannie's breathing did that same strange disappearing act it did when she jumped into the cold water at Choke Canyon Lake.

She dared to hazard a glance at *Aenti* Abigail. Her lips were drawn down so far it was a wonder they didn't fall from her face onto the planks of the wood floor. The blue-green of *Onkel* Mordecai's eyes had turned frosty. "Go on, but make it quick. There's dishes to wash and chores to do."

Frannie whipped past Rocky, catching the familiar, inviting scent of his woodsy aftershave and Irish Spring soap—what she'd come to think of as Rocky smell—as she opened the screen door and led the way outside. To her relief he followed without another word. On the porch, she drank in the sight of him, now that they had no audience. Same tanned face, same little scar on his chin where he fell from a swing in the second grade, same little twist to his nose where he took a punch in a boxing match. "What are you doing here?"

The words sounded inhospitable. She wanted them back as soon as they fell on the early-evening air. Rocky's smile faded. His Adam's apple bobbed. He ducked his head and smoothed the cap in his hands. "Like I told you before, I have a bit of a wanderlust. You talked about this place so much, I figured I'd come see it for myself."

A wisp of disappointment curled itself around the relief that rolled over her. He simply wanted to travel. He knew her so he stopped by. Like stopping by Bee County in the far reaches of south Texas was an easy feat. Most folks couldn't find it with a map. "Are you staying long in the area—*where* are you staying?"

"I just got here." An emotion Frannie recognized—disappointment—soaked the words. "You want me to leave?"

Nee. *Not at all. Stay. Please stay.* She swallowed the words before they could spring forward and betray her. "It's just . . . surprising."

"My Uncle Richard passed."

"Oh, Rocky." With no thought for appearances, Frannie touched his hand. Richard had been the only true father Rocky had ever known. His eyes blazed with sudden emotion as his long fingers turned and wrapped around hers. His strong grip seemed to embrace her. A slow heat warmed her from head to toe. "I'm so sorry. What happened?"

"Heart attack. Sudden. He left me a small nest egg."

She itched to give this bear of a man the hug he deserved. That he needed. She kept her gaze on their entwined hands. "That was nice of him."

"He was a nice man. He was a good man." Rocky's voice had a sandpaper roughness about it she'd never heard before. "Anyway, he gave me the chance to have a fresh start if I want."

The last sentence seemed more of a question than a statement. A fresh start. Was Bee County his fresh start? Was Frannie his fresh start?

The screen door slammed. Frannie tugged her hand back, fingers burning worse than when she'd spilled the gumbo. Joseph clomped past them, a painful smile plastered across his face. "Mordecai said to tell you there's plenty of leftovers if your friend has a hankering." He tossed the words over his shoulder without looking back. "I'm headed home. Chores won't wait. I imagine those dishes won't either."

"Be safe." Now what a thing to say. Like Joseph couldn't take care of himself. Like he hadn't grown up with the javelinas, the bobcats, the rattlesnakes, and the occasional escapee from the prison outside Beeville. "Bye."

"You too." This time Joseph looked back. His gaze skittered from Frannie to Rocky. "You never know where danger lurks."

ABOUT THE AUTHOR

Kelly Irvin is the author of several Amish series including the Bliss Creek Amish series, the New Hope Amish series, and the Amish of Bee County series. She has also penned two romantic suspense novels, *A Deadly Wilderness* and *No Child of Mine*. The Kansas native is a graduate of the University of Kansas School of Journalism. She has been writing nonfiction professionally for thirty years, including ten years as a newspaper reporter, mostly in Texas-Mexico border towns. She has worked in public relations for the City of San Antonio for twenty years. Kelly has been married to photographer Tim Irvin for twenty-seven years. They have two young adult children, two cats, and a tank full of fish. In her spare time, she likes to write short stories and read books by her favorite authors.

Twitter: @Kelly_S_Irvin

Facebook: Kelly.Irvin.Author